CW00721996

Praise for Jess Michaels's
Beauty and the Earl

"This book gave me everything I want in a read, great characters, plenty of drama and excitement and of course great sex scenes."
~ *Smutty Kitty*

"...this book was awesome."
~ *Book Bliss*

"I highly recommend *Beauty and the Earl*...to anyone who loves a truly well written love story about looking past the dark to see the brightness that love and the future can hold."
~ *Unwrapping Romance*

"...very moving, very thoughtful story..."
~ *Love Saves the World*

"I thought [Liam] was the perfect anti-hero and I was not disappointed. The sizzling encounters between Liam and Violet were well, sizzling (LOL) and I love their chemistry."
~ *Eye Heart Romance*

"Take a bit of *Beauty and the Beast* and mix it with Historical Romance and you have Jess Michaels' *Beauty and the Earl*."
~ *Salacious Reads*

"If you like historical romances with high heat with just a hint of erotica added to the story, then this one is for you!"
~ *Clue Review*

Look for these titles by *Jess Michaels*

Now Available:

Mistress Matchmaker
An Introduction to Pleasure
For Desire Alone
Her Perfect Match

The Pleasure Wars
Taken by the Duke
Pleasuring the Lady
Beauty and the Earl
Beautiful Distraction

The Ladies Book of Pleasures
A Matter of Sin
A Moment of Passion
A Measure of Deceit

Beauty and the Earl

Jess Michaels

SAMHAIN
PUBLISHING

Samhain Publishing, Ltd.
11821 Mason Montgomery Road, 4B
Cincinnati, OH 45249
www.samhainpublishing.com

Beauty and the Earl
Copyright © 2014 by Jess Michaels
Print ISBN: 978-1-61922-470-4
Digital ISBN: 978-1-61921-343-2

Editing by Amy Sherwood
Cover by Kim Killion

Beauty and the Earl, ISBN 978-1-61921-343-2
First Samhain Publishing, Ltd. electronic publication: April 2014
Beautiful Distraction, ISBN 978-1-61922-174-1
First Samhain Publishing, Ltd. electronic publication: June 2014
First Samhain Publishing, Ltd. print publication: April 2015

Dedication

For Amy and everyone at Samhain. I love how you support me and my career, and I'm so happy to be a Samhain author. Also for Michael, not only for being the love of my life, but for being my best friend. The fact that you always have my back is the greatest gift of my life. Thanks for being you.

Prologue

July 1813

Liam, the Earl of Windbury, stood behind a tree across the narrow street from the house of his greatest enemy, the Duke of Rothcastle. The home rose above him, gaudy and false, like some ridiculous beacon of everything wrong with Rothcastle and his wretched family. All that man touched became soiled and destroyed.

A carriage with an ornate crest slid its way into the circular drive and Liam leaned in closer to watch as liveried servants rushed out to pull luggage from the top and open the doors for the occupants of the rig.

The first person to step out was Rothcastle himself, and Liam's stomach clenched with rage. The duke was tall with dark blond hair. Liam couldn't see them from so far away, but he could picture Rothcastle's sharp, hawkish eyes that almost glittered with cruelty and malice.

The other man hesitated and slowly turned to look across the street, almost as if he sensed someone there. Liam flattened against the tree so he wouldn't be seen, but kept his gaze firmly on the man at the carriage.

When Rothcastle moved, his limp was still apparent. Liam might have rejoiced in this proof of his enemy's pain, except for the circumstances that had caused it.

Both of them had been injured on a night over six months before when Rothcastle had chased Liam down in his carriage. The duke had been bent on stopping Liam from marrying Rothcastle's sister Matilda. Then a horrible crash. So horrible.

He sucked in a breath as pain in his chest nearly exploded at the memory. Matilda broken. Dying. Dead. His world began to spin, as it always did when he thought of that awful night, and nausea hit him in a wave.

Through his blurred vision, he looked again at Rothcastle, and he could barely contain himself. Rothcastle blamed Liam for Matilda's death, and Liam could hardly argue. But he placed just as much blame on the shoulders of her brother. If Rothcastle hadn't run them down, the accident never would have happened.

Anger boiled, a desire for revenge made him see everything in a red haze. He had a gun in his boot. He could pull that gun out, march across the street and put a bullet in Rothcastle's chest before anyone could prevent it.

There was only one thing that stopped him.

Rothcastle turned and reached up to help a passenger down from his carriage. A woman dressed in a beautiful beige gown with green highlights. She smiled as her feet touched the ground. She *smiled* up at Rothcastle, and even from this distance Liam could see there was nothing on her face but pure, unfiltered love for the man. The monster.

His stomach turned because the woman from the carriage was *his* sister, Ava. *His* sister who Rothcastle had kidnapped in a twisted revenge plot. *His* sister who had been seduced by nothing short of the Devil himself. *His* sister who had somehow convinced herself that she could love the man, no matter what that fact did to Liam. To herself.

Liam stared as Ava reached up to cup the cheek of a man he hated more than anything in this world. Her laughter could be heard on the wind, but was cut off when Rothcastle leaned down and kissed her. There was no hesitation in her reaction. His sister kissed his worst enemy back with enough passion that even the servants stepped away to give them their privacy.

After all, they were newlyweds, just returned from Gretna Green that very moment. She belonged to Rothcastle now. She shared his name.

Rothcastle broke the embrace, leaned down and whispered something to Ava. Liam's sister's smile returned, and she took her husband's arm and allowed him to lead her into his home.

Her home.

For better or for worse.

As they disappeared into the estate, Liam fought the urge to vomit into the bushes beside him. There was so much to despise in what he had just seen. Clearly Ava had been entirely taken in by a bastard. No matter what she said to try to convince Liam otherwise, he would never believe that Rothcastle didn't have some evil ulterior motive in taking Ava for a bride.

And then there was how blasted happy they appeared. In love. Planning the rest of their lives together. No matter how firmly he believed that Rothcastle didn't mean any of it, their expressions still reminded him of his time with Matilda not so very long ago. He had wanted exactly what Rothcastle had now stolen with Ava.

Matilda was dead. Liam would never touch her again. He would never be near her again. He would never love anyone ever, *ever* again.

The reality of that sunk in, deep into his bones. It made his old injuries from the accident burn with pain, it made his chest hurt, it made him feel so dull and empty that he briefly considered wandering into the Thames and letting the churning water take him, just so he wouldn't ever have to face that fact again.

Instead, he turned on his heel and walked away from Rothcastle's home. He would never return here. He would never again force himself to look upon his sister as the Duchess of Rothcastle.

Never.

Chapter One

April 1814

Violet Milford sat in her carriage outside the very large and rather intimidating London home of the Duke and Duchess of Rothcastle. She stared up at it through her narrow window and wondered, yet again, why in the world she had been summoned here.

Yes, she was without a protector at present, but she had heard all the stories about how besotted Rothcastle was with his bride of less than a year. And what kind of man would bring a courtesan like herself into his main home and flaunt her about for the neighbors and his family to see?

Not many.

The carriage door opened and she found herself looking into the grizzled, wrinkled face of her longtime driver, Gregson. He looked more like a sea captain than a driver and sounded like one too as he said, "We're 'ere, miss."

She glanced at the house again, a niggling fissure of doubt threading through her. Not dread, really, or fear, for she never ignored those intuitions, but something else.

"Miss?" Gregson repeated with a tilt of his head.

She moved toward him, taking the hand he offered so she could step down onto the crushed rock drive.

"Stay close," she said softly, lifting her hand to shade her face from the unexpectedly sunny day as she continued to look up and up at the mansion.

Gregson nodded. "You think there might be trouble?"

"Here?" she asked.

She let her gaze slip down to the front door. These kinds of places seemed so respectable and safe, but she knew full well that a great deal of misfortune could come from "proper" men in their "proper" homes.

"I have no idea," she murmured as she moved toward the door.

One way or another, her servant would come looking for her if she did not reemerge from that door in precisely one hour. He was well-trained that way.

She raised a hand to knock, but the door opened of its own accord to reveal the perfunctory stern butler that all men of a certain status seemed to employ. The man looked at her, his face carefully neutral.

"Miss Milford, I assume?" he intoned in a grave and gravelly voice.

"Yes," she responded, moving into the parlor as he indicated she should enter. He took her light wrap, hat and gloves before he began to move down the hallway as he said, "Their Graces will be made aware of your arrival immediately. Please wait for them here."

He motioned through an open door to a parlor. Violet bobbed out a nod and stepped inside. To her surprise, there was a fresh pot of tea with a few cakes waiting for her, as if she were just a normal guest. But she didn't touch them. Best not to anger a very powerful duke the moment he entered the room.

After all, she knew her place.

She settled into a seat before the fire that faced the door, despite the fact that she longed to look around the room. There were some lovely landscape paintings that she instantly recognized as works from Joseph Mallord William Turner, but she held firm in her seat and merely admired them from afar.

She didn't do so for long, though, because a couple soon walked into the room. Linked arm in arm, she knew who they were both from artistic renderings in the papers and from seeing them from afar at certain gatherings.

The Duke and Duchess of Rothcastle made a handsome couple, for both were beautiful in their own way. Lady Rothcastle had dark hair with a ruddy highlight that brightened in the firelight. Her face had an underlying sense of kindness to it, though at this moment she was not smiling or even looking directly at Violet. Not that Violet expected it, given their disparate circumstances.

Rothcastle had dark blond hair with piercing blue eyes that had been the subject of many a flighty courtesan's fantasy. He had a lean strength to him despite the fact that he had a faint limp and still carried a cane more than a year after the infamous accident that remained the topic of much gossip in her circles and in ones far above her own.

Violet rose to her feet and gave a curtsey to recognize the pair and their status.

"Good afternoon, Your Graces," she said.

Lady Rothcastle smiled, though her lips were thin. Violet sensed the other woman's hesitation instantly. But she sensed something else too. Just by the briefest of exchanged glances, the light squeeze of a hand on an elbow as they released each other, she felt the powerful, deep connection between the couple. Something very uncommon in upper class marriages.

And something that made her invitation here all the more odd.

"Good afternoon, Miss Milford," Lord Rothcastle said, motioning her back to the seat she had chosen. "Thank you for coming today."

Violet settled into her chair and arched a brow as she met his bright gaze evenly. "When the Duke of Rothcastle calls on you, you do not refuse him."

Lady Rothcastle's hands clenched as she all but collapsed on the settee near Violet's chair. Her face was pale as she speared Violet with a sharp look.

"Then you know us?" she asked, her voice as strained as her expression.

Violet fought the urge to laugh at the ludicrous nature of that question. "Forgive me, Your Grace, but *everyone* knows you."

To her surprise, the duchess blushed deeply and turned her face. "Of course. The talk never ceases, does it?"

The duke reached out to stroke a hand over his wife's shoulder briefly, and once again their connection was clear as a bell on a soundless day. As was their love for each other. It almost radiated.

It was Violet's turn to avert her gaze in the presence of such a thing.

"What I do not know," she said, her voice rough as she stared at the teapot instead of the couple, "is why you would ask me to your home and invite me into your parlor."

Lady Rothcastle pushed to her feet and paced to the window to look outside. She was silent a long moment before she turned back and looked at Violet with an even stare. Her high emotions were masked now.

"If you know us, then I can only assume you know of my brother."

Violet drew a breath as she examined the woman across the room. She was certain the duke knew exactly what Violet was, but did the duchess? Was she willingly asking this question of a courtesan?

Still, it wasn't as if Violet had intruded in their home. She had been summoned. It wasn't her place to protect the rich and titled.

"Yes, he is known in my circles," she said with a slight shrug of her shoulders and a glance toward the duke.

"*Courtesans,*" Lady Rothcastle said softly, erasing all Violet's questions with one word said with such heavy implication.

The duke crossed to his wife and took her elbow gently. "Ava," he said softly, their eyes meeting in unspoken communication.

Violet got to her feet and smoothed her dress, holding her head up high so that there would be no question of her having some kind of shame about what she was.

"Yes, my lady, your brother was known to visit women in my position, both before his accident and also after. Although, since he was injured, he has not kept any one woman for more than a short time. He and I were never...affiliated."

Not that she hadn't looked at the handsome earl long and hard on the occasions she'd seen him. Even with his disfiguring scar and brooding personality, he was a physical specimen worth swooning over.

None of that seemed to impress the duchess, though. She pressed her lips together and shot her husband a look. Rothcastle moved toward Violet and motioned her to sit. He took the seat across from hers and leaned forward, resting strong arms over equally strong thighs.

"Miss Milford, I will get right to the point. Obviously you know about the break in the relationship between my wife and her brother, as well as the long history that scars our two families. Everyone knows some version of our story, so I won't pretend as if you don't. And because of that, Lady Rothcastle and I are seeking to find out information about her brother."

Violet refused to let her surprise at this revelation be seen on her face.

"As I said, I've never had an affiliation with the man," she said, carefully measuring her tone. "I don't even know that I've ever spoken to him. So what does your desire for information have to do with me?"

"Currently, the earl is in Bath. He won't let us near him." The duke stopped and shifted uncomfortably. "But if he were to take a lover..."

He trailed off and looked at her evenly, his meaning suddenly very clear. Violet lifted both eyebrows in shock and snapped her gaze from the man across from her to his wife. Lady Rothcastle did not seem surprised by his outrageous implication, but her mouth was set in a grim, determined line.

"So you wish for me to seduce the man and report his activities and whereabouts and emotional state to you?" she asked, making their request as plain as she could since they wouldn't.

Lady Rothcastle almost sagged as the description was put so plainly. "Yes," she whispered.

Violet swallowed hard and pushed to her feet deliberately. "I'm sorry, but that isn't what I do."

She turned toward the door to leave, but she hadn't made it three steps, when Lord Rothcastle's voice echoed through the chamber.

"One thousand pounds."

Violet froze at the number he had called out and slowly turned toward the duke and duchess again. "I beg your pardon?"

"I will pay you a thousand pounds if you do this," he repeated.

All her ability to cover her reactions faded in that unexpected instant, and she stared at him, blinking rapidly as that number swirled around and around in her head.

"Why?"

Rothcastle hesitated a moment, apparently taken aback by her direct question. Then he folded his arms. "For my wife."

Lady Rothcastle sucked in her breath, looking up at him with a look of apology and love in equal measure. Her heartbreak was clear on her face, her desperation to know something, *anything*, of her brother.

And didn't Violet know that feeling well herself? She pursed her lips. A thousand pounds was a great deal of money. Almost enough money...

"Two thousand," she heard her voice say, although she didn't remember making a decision to bargain.

The duke's eyebrow arched. "There are other women we could ask."

"But you don't want to spread this request throughout the *ton*," Violet said, her hands shaking even though her voice did not. "You came to me because you know I have a reputation of discretion. You might not be able to say the same of the next woman you call here. Two thousand."

The duke let out a low rumbling sound that she wasn't certain was a growl or a sigh. It was irritated, that was all that was certain.

"Fine, two thousand."

Violet's heart lodged in her throat, but she refused to let excitement and hope keep her from continuing.

She nodded once. "I will do everything I can to obtain access to the man and uncover any information for you, but I make no promises. He may have no interest in me. But I cannot be expected to go to Bath for nothing."

The duke tilted his head, both eyebrows lifted. His wife glared at Violet, arms folded and her disdain as clear as day. Violet found herself regretting that on some level. She actually liked Lady Rothcastle, from all she had heard about her.

But that couldn't dissuade her.

"You will receive five hundred pounds up front," he said softly. "And I will cover your expenses in Bath. Does that settle this?"

"Indeed, quite amply," Violet said. "I shall depart for Bath as soon as I receive the funds in my account. Shall I send any news to this address?"

"No, I'll give you the address of a solicitor who will forward your letters to me," the duke said. "Excuse me a moment and I will fetch the particulars."

Violet watched him go, and when she turned her gaze from the door, she found Lady Rothcastle was now on her feet, watching her.

"You are surprised my husband left you alone with me," the duchess said softly.

Violet conceded that point with a slight tilt of her head. "I don't know many women of your stature who wish to interact with courtesans."

Lady Rothcastle seemed to consider that for a moment. "I wish to interact with people who I like and respect, regardless of their place in life. I don't know you, Miss Milford, though I can see from your handling of my husband that you are shrewd, and I suppose that is exactly what we need when we hire a woman meant to manipulate my brother into revealing his secrets."

Violet wasn't certain that comment was meant as a compliment, but she didn't press further. "I get the sense that perhaps there is something more you wish me to do."

The duchess gave her a long, appraising look. "I love my brother. And recent...*developments* have come to pass that make me wish very much to have him back in my life."

Violet raised her eyebrows as she stared at the other woman. *Recent developments* was a vague, yet intriguing statement.

"Do you really think I can influence him to do what you haven't been able to do in a year?" she asked, passing on her desire to inquire about those developments.

The other woman shook her head. "I don't know. And Christian..." She corrected herself swiftly. "My husband doesn't think you can, nor that it is wise for you to try. But if you could somehow convince Liam to accept us...accept me, I would make certain you received another thousand pounds as a...a bonus of sorts."

Violet nearly swayed on her feet. Three thousand pounds was a tidy little fortune and would put her far and above what she needed for her own future schemes.

"Do you have any guidelines on how to handle your brother?" she asked.

The duchess seemed surprised by the question, but her demeanor and expression softened considerably as she spoke. "He has become very hard since the accident, since the death of the woman he loved, but he was always a light soul. Quick to laugh, quick to defend those he loved. Somewhere in him, I can't help but think that he is still that man I knew what seems like a hundred years ago."

"Does he have likes or interests?" Violet pressed. The duchess's eyes went wide and Violet rushed to correct her obvious misconceptions. "I don't mean when it comes to women. I meant pursuits."

The other woman relaxed again. "As a boy, he was always very good at physical things. If it required a ball or a bat or a mallet, he was ready. In fact, he even made up his own games if there was no one else with whom to engage."

Intrigued, Violet would have asked more, but Rothcastle returned at that moment a piece of paper in his hand.

"This is the address to send your reports to. Address them to Mr. Smith and they will be forwarded to me unopened by anyone else," Rothcastle said.

"And who will read my reports?" Violet asked.

He shook his head. "I don't understand."

"Will it only be you, or will your wife also read them?" When he continued to stare, apparently not understanding what she meant, she shrugged. "There may be delicate matters and—"

"Do not hold back," Lady Rothcastle interrupted. "I know the situation may be very dire and I want the truth of it, unvarnished."

The duke didn't seem as certain as his wife that she was ready for unvarnished truth, but he didn't argue.

"Your solicitor is Mr. Green, whose office is on Cross Circle, yes?"

Now it was Violet's eyes which went wide. "Y-Yes, Your Grace. But how—"

"You are not the only one who knows and hears things," the duke said softly, his bright blue gaze holding hers. "I will direct all monies to him, under your name."

Violet hesitated, for the expression on the duke's face was unreadable, almost as if he knew something he held back. Something about her. But no one knew anything about her. Not anything she didn't choose to share.

"That is agreeable," she managed to choke out. "And now I shall go. I'll send word if I am able to—" She hesitated and shot another look to the duchess.

The other woman arched a brow. "If you are able to raise the interest of Lord Windbury, do send us word. Good day, Miss Milford."

Violet knew when she was being dismissed, so she bobbed out a curtsey and exited the home. Outside, her carriage waited, along with Gregson, whose expression was actually relieved.

"I didn't relish the idea of busting into that fortress," he grunted as he helped her up and closed the door behind her.

Violet settled into the comfortable seat and closed her eyes. A fortress. She wouldn't exactly call the beautiful home of her hosts that, but it did put certain images to mind of unwinnable battlegrounds.

She only wondered if Lord Windbury would be one of them.

"I think I might need help," she murmured.

Luckily, she knew just the person for the job.

Olivia Cranfield poured a brandy from the sidebar of the small home Violet shared with her and sighed.

"Damn, I was hoping the Rothcastles had invited you to their home to make you their secret lover!"

Violet laughed as she rolled her eyes. "Good God, Olivia, you couldn't have believed that."

Olivia smiled as she took a sip of her drink. "One could hope. Just imagine the scandal, and you in the middle of it."

Violet shook her head. Olivia did love a scandal.

"Well, it wasn't that, but I'd say hiring a courtesan in order to seduce and spy on Lord Windbury is certainly scandal enough, even though no one will know about it."

"It *is* shocking," Olivia conceded as she sat down across from Violet. "But lucrative." Her friend's face grew more serious. "You won't really run away to the country when it's over, will you?"

Violet smiled. Olivia teased, but no one knew better than her friend what was at stake for her. "I will. But you may visit me if you think you could bear the boredom."

Olivia sighed. "You deserve happiness and boredom, if that is what you choose. You *and* Peter."

Violet tried hard not to think of what images her friend's words put into her head. She was not free yet.

She waved her hand to dismiss the subject. "So, as I said, this is an important mission. But *not* an easy one. He's a hard man to reach, as a great many courtesans have discovered over the last eighteen months."

"He might not keep a woman," Olivia said with a smile. "But he does please them. I've heard very good things about his prowess, so at least you can have fun."

Violet considered that. Yes, she had heard the same whispers about Windbury...Liam. That he made absolutely no connection with any woman he took to his bed, but that he was highly passionate and talented.

"*They* are letting a place for me in Bath and covering my expenses while I'm there." Violet bit her lip. "Do you think you might come with me? I think you've heard more about the man than I have and I could use your help and advice."

Olivia's face lit up. "A few weeks in Bath! Of course I'll come. There is no downside to that offer."

Her friend continued to gush, but Violet couldn't concentrate. The fact was, she feared there were many downsides to the project she had agreed to take on.

In fact, she feared the entire thing could become a disaster of epic proportions.

Chapter Two

Liam sank up to his chin in the steaming waters, letting the supposedly healing waters of Bath seep into his injured shoulder. The warmth of the natural spring helped, but he wasn't certain he retained any miracle cures beyond the few moments of pleasure in the water.

And yet here he was, thanks in great part to the insistence of his...well, what would he call Malcolm Graham anyway? Assistant, sometime secretary, occasional estate manager...*friend*. Possibly the only one he had left, and that was likely due in large part to the fact that Mal was on his payroll.

But whatever Mal's motivation, he had dragged Liam here to "take the waters" and take the waters he would.

He measured his breaths, trying desperately to empty his head of all thoughts. It was a nearly impossible task, it seemed, for his mind was always filled with memories he didn't want to consider and guilt he refused to acknowledge.

He squeezed his eyes shut, but his thoughts continued to race, bombarding him from all sides.

"Fuck," he muttered, and then sank beneath the water entirely. Beneath the depths, there was no noise, nothing to see, and his brain began to quiet finally. Cut off from everything, even breath, he could almost pretend that his life above the surface didn't exist.

Almost.

Unfortunately, his body required air to live and so he rose reluctantly. He wiped his face off and slicked his now-wet hair back with his good hand. He opened his eyes and froze.

There, standing on the edge of the steps that led down into the large, square pool where he reclined alone, was a woman. Not just any woman, but probably one of the most beautiful women he had ever had the pleasure to look upon in his thirty years.

She was intensely exotic, with a slightly olive-toned skin and thick, sleek black hair that was drawn back loosely, though strands of it continued to bounce around her oval face. Her dark brown eyes, which were currently focused intently on his face, sparkled in the lamplight and held on him with a confidence he normally didn't see in women. Especially women wearing a white chemise that left no curve of her body to the imagination.

He licked his lips as a hot slicing shock of desire ricocheted through his body and settled in his loins. Beneath the water, his cock began to throb.

"This is a private room," he managed to croak out.

Her eyebrows lifted and a slight smiled turned up her lips. "Oh, I certainly hope that is true, considering what I have planned."

She took a step into the water and immediately that white chemise went sinfully sheer against her calves. Another step and her thighs were revealed as the water sloshed up and down against her movements.

He swallowed, his head spinning now, but not with its normally unpleasant thoughts. No, it spun with desire, confusion and a desperate need to have her come deeper into the water.

"Who are you?" he asked.

She smiled. "Violet Milford, my lord," she said, and he almost expected her to put out a hand as if they were meeting under more normal circumstances.

He sucked in a breath, and her smile broadened.

"You know my name, do you?" she asked.

He nodded. "Yes. The courtesan."

She hesitated on the third step of the pool and nodded. "And I know you, as well, Lord Windbury."

Liam settled back, resting his good arm on the edge of the pool behind him as she continued into the water. Waves covered her body, but she was waist-deep now.

"Did my man arrange for your appearance?" he asked. Sometimes Mal did that, but never without Liam's request as the impetus.

She shook her head. "That hulking beast outside? No, he has no idea I'm here."

"Then I almost hate to ask this question, but how did you get past him?"

She smiled, and something in him shifted. When her full lips tilted upward, her already beautifully exotic face became even more intoxicating. He wanted to drag her against him and kiss her until she couldn't form coherent words. He wanted to put her on his lap and grind his cock into her wet heat until she screamed. It had been a very long time since he felt such strong, animal reactions. Sex had become a necessary bodily function, not a pleasure as of late.

"I brought along a distraction," she replied, seemingly unaware of the place his wicked thoughts had taken him with just her smile. But then, her gaze dropped under the water swiftly.

He doubted she could see he was naked beneath, or hard and ready with just her unexpected appearance here, but given her vocation and knowing eyes, he would wager she had guessed both.

Perhaps she even counted on both.

"I am not looking to become someone's protector," he warned her, though he found himself offering a silent prayer that this fact wouldn't scare her away.

She moved into the water, dropping under so that it soaked her shoulders before she stood up again and revealed her chemise, utterly sheer and plastered against full breasts with dark, hard nipples. He couldn't contain a grunt of ever-increasing need.

"I'm not seeking a protector, my lord," she whispered as she reached him. She reached out and touched his face, the side without the scar, so he didn't move away from her fingers. "I'm on holiday. I'm only looking to enjoy myself."

She was so close, he could smell the light musk of some kind of perfume, and he lost all semblance of reason. He reached for her without thinking and dragged her hard against him. Her arms wound around his neck and she lifted her mouth just as he smashed his down.

The kiss was spectacular. Her lips, which looked so full, were exactly what he wanted. Soft and supple, they parted as his tongue demanded entry into her mouth. She denied him nothing, even as he fisted her wet chemise in his hand and dragged his nails against her back in the process. She merely arched against him, rotating her lips against him with suggestive and wanton response.

"Fuck," he muttered against her mouth as his blood began to boil with out of control desire.

She drew back, smiling at him. There was laughter in her voice as she nodded. "Oh yes, most definitely, for I have heard such rumors of your prowess. But first..."

She trailed off as she reached beneath the steaming water and captured his cock in her palm. When she found him rock hard, a tiny smile crossed her lips, almost triumphant. She stroked over him, and his head dropped back as a low moan escaped his throat. He hadn't been with a woman in well over three months, and now that he was being touched, he was in serious danger of humiliating himself before she did anything more.

"Why don't you sit on the edge?" she urged.

He reached back and leaned his full weight on his good arm, lifting himself up to sit on the edge of the pool. Her eyes went wide at the physical feat he had just achieved one-armed, but he didn't allow her to say anything. He grabbed her and dragged her between his legs, letting his hard cock rub against her breasts as he leaned down to kiss her again.

Her needy moan was lost in their joined mouths, swept away by tangling tongues. She pulled closer, lifting herself and sucking on his tongue at the same time. He had never been with a woman so forward, so driving in her demands, and this was just a kiss.

As if to prove that point, she pulled back, flipping strands of dark hair, ends wet from the water, away from her neck. She had a tiny, knowing expression to her face, a bright light in her eyes. It was...intoxicating. Perhaps because it felt so real, that she wanted him.

Of course, he wasn't that foolish. She was a courtesan and paid well by men to pretend desire. She was here for a reason, even if she claimed to be on holiday and simply wanted his body. But damn if he wasn't utterly willing to play along.

Slowly, she stripped her wet chemise away and tossed it on the walkway behind him, leaving her naked. He couldn't see her lower body, but her breasts were above the water, full and round, beckoning to be touched and sucked and toyed with for hours on end.

But that didn't seem to be part of whatever plan Violet had. Instead, she grabbed his cock again, but this time there was no water to separate them. She looked at it, hard and ready, thrusting against his stomach at it full length and girth, and she licked her lips.

"I want a taste, my lord," she murmured before she pressed her mouth to his chest.

Again, she chose the right side of his body to caress, rather than the left where he was scarred and damaged. But he could barely consider that because she latched her mouth around the flat disk of his nipple and sucked hard. His hips bucked of their own accord, knocking his erection through her hand and against her stomach and eliciting another needy moan from her throat.

She slid lower, tracing the muscles of his stomach with the tip of her tongue, easing herself into position, seducing and pleasing with her touch until she was finally resting directly in front of his cock at the edge of the pool, looking at him with interest and desire that, once again, seemed so genuine.

She glanced up at him, wickedness in her dark eyes, then lowered her mouth around his cock. She was hot as fire as she took him into her throat. She glided back up his shaft, swirling her tongue around and around his width until stars began to explode before his vision.

He'd had this pleasure before, of course, with other lovers, but never had a woman given it with what seemed like real pleasure and zeal. Violet made a moaning sound as she took him, her body lifting against the wall of the pool as if she were trying to find some of her own pleasure while she laved him with her hot, talented tongue.

He felt a cresting desire to shatter so quickly that he bit his tongue hard enough to nearly draw blood in able to control that explosive reaction. This strange, unexpected encounter had not been of his making, but he wasn't about to have it end so quickly and leave this woman to tell the world how he had been nothing more than pudding in her skillful hands.

No, he had other desires.

He caught her beneath her arms and drew her up. He would have lifted her from the water entirely, but his injury wouldn't allow that, a frustration that seemed especially pointed at the moment.

"Did I not please you?" she asked, not with the wide-eyed innocence of a virgin, but more with the surprise of a woman who knew exactly where her talents lay.

"Oh no, very pleased," he said, pushing from the ledge to stand back in the water with her. He wrapped his arms around her waist. "But I want more than you were giving."

In the water, she was so light that even his injured arm could do some of the work in lifting her. She wrapped her legs around his hips and slipped a hand between their bodies to position herself. He thrust, and suddenly his cock was surrounded by the white-hot embrace of her slit. He held tight as they began to move in tandem, her arching against him, him lifting his hips to fully seat himself as deeply as he could.

Her face was even with his, and she kept her gaze on his, never moving, never darting away. It was incredibly intimate, something he would normally shy away from, but he was so taken in by this stranger's utter acceptance, utter surrender, that he couldn't manage to break away from the prison of her stare. He was rewarded when her cries increased, and she slammed against him as orgasm hit her.

He cupped her backside and thrust harder, harder. His body was on fire, alive, and the pleasure built with such pressure that when the dam broke, he only had a moment to pull out before his seed was spilled in the warm, swirling waters.

His breath was short, as was hers as they stood that way, her arms around him, the water bobbing around them. It was only then that he broke their gaze and extracted himself from her embrace.

"I apologize, Miss Milford," he said, turning away to gather some vestige of his composure. "I assure you I do not normally unleash my animal lusts on a woman I've never even been properly introduced to."

She laughed, and he spun to look at her because the light tone of it was almost like music in the echoing room.

"Great God, you act as though I'm some virgin daughter of a duke you just tumbled." She shook her head and dunked herself under the water to backstroke toward the stairs where she had entered the private bath. "I wanted this, my lord. And I am vastly pleased to have had it."

She didn't wait for a response, but walked up the marble stairs, giving him a view of her rounded hips and perfectly shaped backside before she took a robe from a chair beside the door and wrapped herself away from his gaze.

She glanced at him with another smile. "Perhaps we'll do this again...*after* we're properly introduced, of course. Good afternoon."

He stared in stunned silence as she padded through the door and out of the bathing area, leaving him staring after her.

Before Violet had the chance to touch the knob, Olivia threw open the door to the home Lord Rothcastle had let for them. Her friend's face was pink and her eyes bright as she ushered Violet inside.

"And?" Olivia asked without preamble.

"And?" Violet repeated as she stepped into the parlor to pour herself a cup of tea. Her hair was still wet and she smiled as she pushed a lock away.

Olivia huffed out her breath. "I have been waiting here for you forever. How did it go with Windbury?"

Violet sank into the closest chair and took a long sip of tea, stalling for time to think about that question. Her plan was advancing perfectly...but she wouldn't say it had gone "well". Not when she felt such a discomfort about the entire arrangement.

Although none about the physical encounter, which still made her body hum with pleasure.

"Violet?" Olivia said with a laugh. "You are making me mad! Tell me."

"Well," Violet said slowly. "He is—"

When she broke herself off, Olivia stepped closer. "A beast?"

Violet flinched. "No. Well, yes, but no."

Her friend shook her head. "You are terrible at this. I want to know details."

She thought of the man, with his too-long dark hair and his bright green eyes that seemed to seer into her. Not to mention his body, molded into hard muscle. It was like wrapping herself around the body of an Adonis. Only he was all too real.

"He is scarred, of course," Violet said, working on patience as best she could. "But it is anything but unattractive on him."

In fact, she had been very drawn to that scar that slashed across the left side of his face. It added a rugged realness to what was otherwise almost too perfect beauty. The scars on his shoulder and the arm that had been damaged by the accident did the same.

But she hadn't touched them. She could well imagine women, especially women of a certain type, cooed over his injuries. He would not allow someone in who did such a thing.

"And were you able to enact your plan?" Olivia pressed.

Violet nodded. "Yes. As soon as you distracted his friend...thank you, by the way."

Olivia's smile was a little too wide. "It was entirely my pleasure."

Violet's brow furrowed. "How far did *you* go?"

"Not as far as I would have liked. That man is..." Olivia shivered. "He is very attractive."

Violet laughed. Bringing Olivia had been for support, but she was already proving to be helpful in other ways. If Liam's hulking bodyguard could be swayed by Olivia's attention...well, all the better for her plan.

"Well, once you distracted him, I was able to enter the private bathing room and..."

She found herself almost blushing as she recalled the searing encounter that had followed. She hadn't quite intended to go so far, but the moment she touched him, she had felt a wild, unexpected desire to have him. All of him.

"Your seduction is underway," Olivia finished when she wouldn't. "So what is your next step?"

Violet bit her lip. "I have captured his attention by giving him pleasure, then walking away. He was taken aback, I know that from his face and demeanor. He will be thinking of me, I'm certain, but if I pursue him, his desire may fade. When we next meet, I must make him believe it is an accident."

"Reel him in," her friend said with a knowing nod.

Violet hesitated. Why did the truth have to sound so damn cold and unfeeling? And why did it make a pit form in her stomach that she would never reveal to Olivia?

"I suppose that is one way to say it," she admitted with a sigh. "But for now my next move will be to write to Lord and Lady Rothcastle and tell them I have encountered Lord Windbury. I'm sure they are awaiting my report."

Olivia arched a brow. "And will you give them details of that 'encounter', as you so appropriately put it?"

Violet shook her head swiftly. "Of course not. They know what methods I shall employ to gain his trust, but I would never be so crass as to elaborate on them. There are some things better left unsaid."

Unsaid like that she had felt something...*odd*...when she kissed the Earl of Windbury. Something...special. She would never confess such foolishness to Olivia or anyone else, because that would be utterly stupid. And untrue. It was definitely untrue.

Chapter Three

Liam paced the length of his office before he stopped at the floor-to-ceiling window and stared out onto the rolling hills of his small estate just outside of Bath. He had things to do at present, a great many things.

But he was doing none of them. He was staring out a window thinking about a woman. A woman whose body, touch and kiss had been haunting his mind for two days, since their wicked encounter at the bathhouse.

Violet Milford.

"Are you still mooning about that woman?"

Liam jumped and turned to face the door. He found Malcolm there, leaning on the doorjamb. His friend looked utterly unimpressed that a sexual encounter with a courtesan could leave Liam so nonplussed.

"Are you talking about *that woman* you let into my private bath?" he asked with a raised eyebrow.

Mal's stern expression softened as he laughed. "She had a pretty friend, Windbury—what was I to do?"

Liam shook his head. They were a pair, that was for certain. "It's good to know your loyalty is so connected to your cock."

"Ah, well, you didn't seem to have such a bad time, at any rate. Even if she hadn't distracted me with perfumed hair and soft lips, I probably would have let her in." Mal shrugged.

Liam flashed to Violet's lips closing over his cock. To her body squeezing around him in wet, heated urgency. He could hardly breathe. "No, I didn't have a bad time."

Mal lifted his gaze from the papers he was staring at in distraction. "She could still be in Bath, if you have an interest in seeing her again."

That was certainly a benign way to put the desire currently coursing through his veins. It was strange. He hadn't had an interest in a woman beyond a night of pleasure for a very long time. But he was so damn drawn to the exotic beauty who had so unexpectedly intruded upon his privacy.

"Do a little research," he said, hoping his tone was even. "If she is still here in Bath..."

He trailed off, and Mal nodded. "I'm certain you'll make the best decision should that prove to be true."

Liam chuckled. He wasn't entirely sure of that, but he nodded anyway. "Yes."

Mal shot him a side glance. "Will you go out today?"

Liam's good humor faded, as did thoughts of Violet. He hated that manner Mal took when he asked the question. Like he was tiptoeing around a person who was dying. Like he was making some grand, important inquiry.

Just because Liam locked himself away didn't mean a damn thing. But if he said no, if he told Mal that he intended to stay on the estate again, his friend would grunt and make pained faces and try to encourage him to get out.

Liam was too exhausted to go through it all. So he shrugged.

"A book I ordered upon our arrival has likely come in. I suppose I could go into town to pick it up."

"Good," Mal said, his voice suddenly light. "I shall have the carriage readied immediately."

Liam nodded as his friend left the room, but the moment he was alone, he sighed deeply. He loved Mal almost as a brother and he appreciated his friend's companionship and aid, but Malcolm wanted to save him. Just like everyone wanted to save him.

What none of them seemed to grasp was that there was little worth saving anymore.

"Perhaps there never was," he murmured before he left the room to ready himself for the ride into town.

Liam's order had not yet come in, but he didn't feel any disappointment now that he was here. There were few pleasures he allowed himself anymore, but a bookshop was most definitely one of them. He breathed in the dusty smell of the pages as he strolled through the aisles.

At one time he had indulged more in physical escapes, letting his body be his strongest asset. But since the accident, sometimes the only thing that kept him sane was a book to read during a sleepless night. Stories could carry him away, dragging him from reality when he needed it most.

He turned a corner to the next shelf and stopped dead. There, standing at a shelf, perusing the titles, was Violet Milford.

He couldn't breathe as he stared at her. Unlike their last meeting, she was wearing a fine gown, but the fabric hugged her curves and left little doubt that the fantasies he had been having about her were not exaggerations when it came to her body. Nor her beauty. Her thick, dark hair was coiled about her head in a complicated style and her lightly olive skin was clear and fresh.

She must have sensed his stare, for she turned from her study of the shelf and faced him. Her eyes widened slightly with what seemed to be surprise, though not unpleasantly so.

"Good Lord, Miss Milford," he forced himself to say as he took a step toward her at last. "I didn't expect to find you here."

She smiled, the surprise she had initially shown wiped away in an instant. "Lord Windbury, what an unexpected treat."

The way she said treat and looked at him with such a long stare made him shift with increasing discomfort thanks to the rush of blood to his cock. Was he really about to have an erection in the middle of a bookstore? Had he suddenly become a green boy facing his first sexual encounter? It was truly ridiculous.

"I thought you might have left Bath," she continued, seemingly unaware of her effect on him.

"Why?" he asked, moving closer again. He almost couldn't stop himself.

She drew back. "Well, I have not seen you since..." She smiled. "Since we last bumped into each other, and that has been two days. It isn't such a large place that I would expect to have you disappear entirely."

"I have a small estate just outside the city," he explained. "So I don't come into town every day."

"Ah." She nodded. "That would make perfect sense. But books brought you here today."

He looked around them. "Books, yes."

She tilted her head and continued to stare at him. There was no mistaking the challenge in her eyes. She knew he wanted her, no matter what his body did to protect or betray him, no matter his careful politeness in public. She knew, and she was daring him to say something, do something about it, with just an arch of one finely shaped eyebrow.

The boldness aroused him beyond measure, just as it had done during their first encounter.

"Will you join me for supper at my home?" he asked, and winced. It was an abrupt question.

She smiled slowly. "Do you count this as our proper introduction?"

He found himself smiling in return at her cheeky reference to her parting volley the last time they were together.

"Indeed, I do. And I would like to share a meal with you tonight."

She drew in a deep breath as she considered the question. "I do not believe I have any prior engagements tonight, my lord," she finally said after what seemed like an interminable amount of time.

"Then I will send a carriage for you around seven?" he asked. "And we can eat at eight?"

"Yes," she said softly. "I look forward to it. Now I must go. A friend is waiting for me at another shop."

He nodded as she gave him one final smile and exited the bookshop. For the first time in almost as long as he could remember, he looked forward to a night too.

Violet leaned forward and peered out the window in wonder as Liam's home came into view through a copse of trees that lined his long, curving drive. He called this a *small* estate? It seemed massive to her, with a large main house rising up in the darkness and a few outbuildings visible by lamps that lined the pathways.

But then, she was accustomed to a very different kind of man than the Earl of Windbury. She took men as lovers and protectors who had the money and status to keep her comfortable and add to her accounts, but she had always avoided men of title. There were too many trappings that came along with a name and five estates and possibly a family who would be crushed by the truth of what he did in the dark.

The carriage pulled to a stop, and she shook her head to clear her suddenly spinning mind. Lord Windbury was not going to be her protector. She wasn't even really here for him, but for his secrets. Her body was just a way to access those.

Her body which betrayed her with shocking pleasure the moment he touched her.

"You are a foolish girl," she snapped at herself, loud enough that when the carriage door opened, Liam's servant gave her a funny look.

She ignored it and allowed him to help her down, then moved toward the door. It opened before she could knock and to her surprise, it was Liam himself who waited on the other side.

She looked at him with a barely suppressed growl of pleasure. He truly was a beautiful man. His face was all hard angles, giving him a lean, hungry look that was only accentuated by the bright, harsh line of the scar that ran along the left side of his face. His hair was dark and too long for the current fashion of close-cropped Grecian-inspired silliness.

He was wearing a buttoned white shirt but no jacket, and he had removed any cravat he might have worn at some point. With the shirt open at the collar, she saw a glimpse of warm skin, touched by the sun and lean and muscled.

But even though he was a draw in many physical ways, in the end it was his eyes that captured her most. Dark green, almost emerald, they focused entirely too closely on her as she moved toward him, hand outstretched as if they were two people meeting in a normal exchange, rather than lovers who had already shockingly surrendered to pleasures more powerful than she had felt in a long time.

It would take a good deal of control to maintain her normally casual and rather dismissive façade in the light of the fact that something about this man intrigued her.

"Miss Milford," he said, taking her outstretched hand and tugging her gently through the doorway into his foyer.

She smiled despite her complicated thoughts. "Are we to be so formal, my lord? Even now?"

He began to stroke his thumb back and forth across the place where her thumb met her hand. He held her gaze.

"Should I call you Violet, then?" he asked, his tone softer.

She caught her breath at how intimate things had suddenly become between them. And how out of control his touch made her feel. Wasn't she to be seducing him, not the other way around?

"Yes," she said, hating how breathless she sounded. Good Lord, she had never played the wide-eyed, panting innocent with men, and yet she couldn't seem to stop now. "But what shall I call you?"

"Liam," he responded without hesitation. "For I truly despise being called Windbury."

She drew back slightly at that unexpected confession. "And why is that?" she asked softly.

Now he released her hand and stepped away. "Forgive me, it was a foolish thing to say. I will not bore you with 'heavy is the head that wears the crown' complaints." He motioned down the hallway. "Will you instead join me for a drink before we dine?"

Violet's lips parted, but she swallowed back any desire she might have had to push the subject further. She had plenty of time to get to know this man's secrets. If she overplayed her hand now, she might not obtain what she desired, and then all this, and all her confusing turmoil about what she was doing here, would be for nothing.

"Of course," she said, surprised when he held out an elbow for her to take.

"It is a beautiful home," she said, admiring the place honestly as they entered a parlor. There were fine lines to the place, though little decoration. "Did you let it for your holiday?"

He shook his head as he released her and crossed to the sidebar where he held up a decanter. "Sherry?"

She nodded, and he poured one for each of them.

"It isn't let," he explained, handing over her glass. "This is actually a family home. One of many pretty little places my father kept so he could flit about the country being very important."

"Did he drag you and your sister along on those very important missions?" she asked, walking away from him so that the question seemed less important than she knew it was. She held her breath, wondering how he would react to this first mention of Ava, her first acknowledgment that she knew some part of his story.

He hesitated, and she glanced at him. His expression was pained, tension around his lips and eyes that made him look suddenly very stern and unbendable.

"Yes," he finally said with a shrug. "Occasionally he brought his family for company. I always liked this place best of all. It is the least ostentatious."

She pivoted to look at him fully. "Our definitions of that word are clearly not the same. I think this is one of the finest homes I've ever been in. But I've moved in slightly different company."

He studied her. "You have always been around my circles."

"Yes, but not fully in them," she said. "I have not taken a titled lover before."

He seemed surprised by that revelation. "Ever?"

"Not until I snuck into your private bath," she corrected herself, moving toward him.

He cleared his throat and set his drink down on the sidebar with a clink that echoed in the suddenly quiet room. "And was it worth the wait?"

She met his gaze. There was hot, burning desire in his stare that made a low ache begin between her legs. One that had very little to do with her real purpose here, even though it would further that purpose.

"Are you fishing for a compliment, my lord?" she asked softly.

He took a long step toward her. "Do you have one?"

She bit her lip. "Was I not clear when we made love last time? Did I not properly express my pleasure?" He didn't respond, so she walked toward him, only stopping when he was within arm's length. "Should I tell you how I have thought of you as I touched myself in the days since? Or that I have awoken from dreams of your body inside of mine? Will that be clear enough?"

He made a low sound in his throat and grasped her wrist in an iron grip with his good hand.

She smiled. "I *very* much enjoyed every moment of our encounter in the baths, Liam. And I have thought of little else since we parted."

"Then allow me to return the compliment," he said, his voice rough with desire he didn't seem willing or able to control. "Since you intruded upon my privacy and utterly shocked me with your seduction, I have thought of you every moment. I do not keep women, Violet. I will not keep you. Nor did I bring you here in order to share my supper. I want to take you upstairs to my bed and strip you naked. I want to have you until I cannot move, until I cannot think, until I can feel nothing but the slick remnants of fucking you all night."

He pulled her closer. "*If* that is agreeable to you."

Violet could hardly breathe. She was in the business of passion, but so often she had chosen men who wanted her to generate it. She avoided men like this, men who dominated a room just by entering it. Men who could make a woman weak. She knew the consequences.

And yet she didn't pull away. She couldn't. Because she wanted him.

"Take me upstairs," she whispered. "Now, Liam."

Chapter Four

Violet entered Liam's bedroom feeling a little like a virginal bride, thanks to her nervousness. It was a ridiculous reaction. After all, she had been with many men—she had even been with Liam.

But invading his private, personal space felt...more complicated.

Not to mention the fact that as he pushed the door shut behind them and leaned against it, she felt a powerful urge to wrap herself around him and never let go.

"You are an enigma," he said as he placed a big hand on her hip and cupped the curve possessively.

"How so?" she said, trying not to wither beneath the heat of his desire.

"I cannot read your facial expressions," he said.

She held her gaze on him. "You are one to make such a claim, when you do not allow any emotions on your own face."

"I suppose we will have to show what we feel and what we want in different ways," he murmured.

She looked up at him, nodding. She might have said something more, but he crushed his mouth to hers and silenced her in the most delicious way possible: with his lips, with his tongue, with his hard, heavy hands dragging her hard against his wicked, ready body.

She could hardly find air as she wrapped her arms around his shoulders. Her nails raked against the fabric of his shirt as he spun them so her back was against the door instead of his and leaned into her. There was no mistaking the rock-hard erection that pressed to her belly, even through his trousers and her gown.

She wanted that erection without the barrier of clothing. She wanted long, languid lovemaking until she couldn't move. She wanted him, tonight, all night.

So she lifted her trembling fingers to his shirt and began to undress him. She focused on each button, hearing her breath echo around her as she slipped them free and revealed his chest, bit by bit. She moved to push the shirt away, and he stiffened.

She jerked her face up to him at his sharp intake of breath.

"Did I hurt you?" she asked.

He eased his injured arm into a different position and shook his head.

"There is occasional pain," he admitted, heat flooding his cheeks. "But the pleasure of your touch makes up for it."

She shook her head. "Don't be silly, Liam. I have no desire to hurt you. I want anything we do together to be nothing but pleasure."

He arched a brow. "That may not be possible."

She slipped his shirt down, more careful now. "Anything is possible."

He didn't respond to that statement, but his expression changed. It became more guarded, filled with a hint of disbelief that cut Violet to her core, especially when she thought of the pain she had seen on his sister's face at their estrangement.

This man was utterly alone, even when surrounded by people.

And she wanted to fill him for a few hours. To make whole what had been broken, even temporarily.

Those feelings were terrifying, and she shoved them away, removing them from her mind by lifting on her tiptoes and kissing him.

He returned the kiss passionately, pinning her to the door as his mouth claimed her. His hands cupped her backside, lifting her with his good arm as he rocked himself against her just as he would once they were naked. Her body reacted instantly. She felt hot, her nipples hard and her body growing wet and slick for him.

He pulled away, searching her face for a moment too long before he stepped back and motioned for the big bed that was the centerpiece of the room.

"We'll be more comfortable here," he suggested.

She didn't argue. Partly because she could see the weakness his body betrayed in him was not something he wished to discuss, partly because she truly wanted to climb into that big bed and lose herself in pleasure.

She moved forward and stopped when she reached the edge of the mattress. Turning, she smiled at him.

"Will you undress?" she asked. "Although I did have the massive pleasure of seeing your body at the baths the other day, I would greatly like to take my time observing you now."

"Do you always so fully take control?"

Her lips parted in surprise at the question. "I-I suppose I do. It is my profession, in part, but also the kind of men I have been affiliated with."

"Ones who wanted their mistress to take charge in bed?" he pressed.

She shrugged. "Sometimes men who are in control all day like the idea of surrendering it."

He shook his head. "I am not one of those men." He moved closer and spun her around, opening her dress in rapid time. "You don't need to tell me what to do, Violet. I know exactly what I want."

He leaned down and bit gently where her neck met her shoulder. She gasped, but as the shock of the act faded Violet arched her back with a shuddering sigh that didn't fully express her pleasure.

He pushed her gown forward, trapping her arms in the folds of fabric as he bent her over the bed, lifting her partially exposed backside to grind against her in hard, insistent circles. When she shuddered, he slipped a hand inside the gaping opening in her gown and slid two fingers down the parting of her bottom, then around to stroke her aching slit.

She shivered as those exploring digits found her tingling clitoris amidst the folds of her sex. He circled it swiftly, teasing and stroking. To her shock, the expert touch caused an almost instant reaction. The orgasm hit her, and she buckled, just catching herself on the edge of the bed as she cried out and slammed her hips against him, looking for more, looking for release, looking for something she couldn't quite name.

Finally, he slowed his working fingers, and she collapsed on her stomach against the bed, panting as the final tremors of pleasure echoed through her shaking body.

"As you can see, I am more than capable," he whispered before he leaned down to press a hot kiss against her neck.

She peeked over her shoulder at him. Rising above her with the firelight behind him, he looked like a dark god of pleasure and sin. And he was unlike any lover she had taken in a long time. He would dominate their encounters, he would demand control.

She shouldn't have liked that idea, but oh, how she did.

But if she gave herself over to him, would she be able to obtain his secrets? More importantly, would she be able to fully extract herself from his power when this affair was over?

She straightened up and faced him.

"You are most definitely capable, Liam," she said, her knees still shaking even though she tried hard not to show him that weakness. "No one could doubt that."

The corner of his lip turned up in a smile, and her heart stuttered. Great God, but he was stunning. She looked at him, staring at her with possessive, powerful control, and she almost forgot everything else.

Including her real reasons for coming to him.

"You hesitate," he all but purred. "You *fear* the fact that I could steal your control in a moment."

It was meant as a challenge, and it took everything in her not to rise to the bait.

Instead, she pushed her dress off fully and stood before him naked, flushed from orgasm, aching for more. "Do I look afraid of you?"

He swore under his breath, so low she couldn't fully make out the word, and then he moved on her. But he didn't slam her backward onto the mattress, as she thought he might. He cupped one breast with his right hand, stroking a thumb over the already distended nipple. She bit back a sound of pleasure and squeezed her eyes shut.

Her body wasn't normally so pliable. She found pleasure, yes, with every lover, but not like this. Not like a wildfire that needed to be extinguished before it destroyed everything in its path.

The power of it *did* frighten her, even if she denied it.

"You are beautiful," he breathed, lifting his gaze to look at her like he was seeing her for the first time. "And I want to be inside of you, to take some of that beauty for a short time."

She drew back at that unexpected sentiment. She examined his face, all the hard lines and angles, the dark green eyes dilated with pleasure. It would be easy to only see control, passion, lust there...but deeper, in a place she doubted he wanted anyone to see, she saw desperation. Sadness.

"Take what you need," she whispered as she reached for the waistband of his trousers. "Take everything."

He kept his stare on her for a moment, then brushed her hands aside and all but tore his buttons open. His pants dropped around his ankles, and she sucked in a breath.

The lean, muscular body she so admired was something to behold in a fully nude and fully ready state. His cock nearly touched his navel, proud and heavy with lust.

She reached around to cup his firm backside as she drew him closer, kissing him, tasting his tongue and letting the ache of desire he had satisfied with his fingers just a moment before build again, this time to greater, more frantic heights.

"Lay down," he ordered, his voice rough and low as he pulled away from her kiss.

She slid onto the bed and rested back against the pillows, enjoying every moment as he crawled up to join her. He covered her body with his, settling himself between her legs and letting the tip of his cock nudge at the opening of her body. She wiggled, trying to get closer as he delved into her with a deep kiss that stole everything that kept her grounded.

She clutched at his shoulders, massaging his hard, warm flesh as he dragged his hand between them and guided his cock to the right place.

He thrust, and she was utterly lost. She lifted to meet him, kissing him deeper. He was heavy over her, but she reveled in his weight, reveled in the rhythmic thrusts between her legs. His pelvis hit her clitoris every time he dove deeper into her body, and it didn't take long before her second orgasm of the night began to build deep within her.

She tilted her head back against the pillow, biting her lip as pleasure mounted, mounted and finally burst like a dam holding back water for far too long.

"Scream for me," he ordered, staring down as she did just that, losing herself in release so powerful that the world spun before her eyes as she rocked through it.

His movements came faster now as she continued to come, squeezing his cock with her body while the tremors spiraled faster and harder. She could see he was on the edge, the tendons in his neck straining, his mouth tightening. He barked out a massive shout of relief and then pulled from her to spill between them in a hot burst of satisfaction.

Then he collapsed over her, his mouth against her neck where he showered light kisses and his body shaking with the same powerful pleasure that still made her tremble too. She put her arms around him, holding him as their breath merged into one. And as she stared at him, she wondered yet again if she was truly prepared for what she had agreed to in London that seemed like so long ago.

Liam shut the chamber door and walked back to the bed with the heaping tray of food balanced precariously on his good arm. As he set it down on the rumpled coverlet, Violet let out a sound of excited pleasure that made his stomach clench and his cock ache.

Damn, but the woman did entice. Especially when she was wrapped in nothing more than his thick white sheets, which seemed to accentuate the olive tones of her soft skin.

"Oh, this looks divine," she breathed as he sat down beside her.

He looked at the tray, which was laden with food easily eaten in just such circumstances. He was certain his cook wasn't pleased to have been asked to alter her supper menu, but the olives, cheeses, chicken and breads did look tempting.

"Eat," he ordered as he shed his robe and slid into the bed beside her.

She popped an olive between her full lips and almost rocked with pleasure. "Mmm, so famished. I'm so glad you didn't decide not to feed me."

He looked at her in surprise for a moment, then laughed. She was like no woman he had ever known. Certainly not like any of the women he had bedded since the accident. She didn't coo or play or pout. In fact, he never knew what she *would* do or say.

"How long are you in Bath for holiday?" he asked.

She buttered a slice of thick-cut bread before she answered. "A few weeks, and you?"

He felt his smile fall at the question, but kept his tone even. "I had not made specific plans."

"Hmmm," she replied, her eyes still on the plate of food. He thought he saw her cast a side glance in his direction, but her gaze flitted away too swiftly for him to be certain if there was any meaning to the look.

"Violet, why don't you forget your place in Bath? Stay here with me instead."

The moment he said it, he shook his head. He hadn't intended to invite this woman to stay with him. And yet here he had done it and somehow he did not regret it. He should have been finished with her, but he wasn't.

She tilted her head with a slight smile. "You mean as your houseguest?"

He shifted slightly. She was teasing him, but she was also forcing him to ask for what he wanted directly. Another move in what was turning out to be a battle for control between them. He found it rather...invigorating, actually. Too often everyone just gave him what he wanted, either out of deference to his title or pity for his past.

"No," he said. "Stay with me as my lover."

She didn't respond for a long moment, nor did she look at him. "I told you, my lord, I am not in the market for a protector at present."

"And I told you, I'm not in the market to become one," he replied, his voice a little sharp.

She jerked her face up at the statement, and her eyes narrowed. "You are saying you want me to come here as your lover simply because I choose to be? No ulterior motives, no exchanges of promises."

He looked at her evenly. He understood why a woman in her position might not accept such a bargain. He'd never judged courtesans for trading in their bodies for survival. And although he hadn't spent time with Violet over the years, he had seen her enough and heard about her enough to know she was very good at the bargains she made. Men liked her, wanted her, and they were willing to pay for the privilege of her company, both in and out of bed.

But he couldn't go down that road. Keeping a mistress was not in his mind, and he wouldn't insult her by implying she was a lightskirt who would accept trade for a night. Nor would he lie just to keep her. It wasn't fair to her.

"So far we have had no promises or ulterior motives, have we?" he asked.

Her gazes flitted away for a moment, and he stiffened. Despite her claims at the baths that she had come to him simply for pleasure, *had* she approached him with the idea that he would keep her? He couldn't blame her if she had, but he wouldn't have his mind changed.

"You do intrigue me," she admitted as she rested back on the pillows and stared at him through a hooded gaze. "Let me think about your offer."

He pushed the tray aside and reached up to the edge of the sheet. Slowly, he pulled it down, uncovering her breasts inch by inch. She gasped at the fabric dragging across her skin.

"Let me give you something to think about," he whispered as he leaned up and braced his arm beside her head. She opened her legs and he took the unspoken invitation, driving hard into her body with a groan of pleasure that spiraled him away from reality, away from everything but the tight grip of her pussy around him.

As he pounded into her, her body jerking beneath his as her pleasure built, he realized how much he wanted to be lost in what she offered. For a few weeks, he needed what she provided.

After that? Well, he had his own plans. And they were ones which no one in his life could alter. Even the woman whose legs were wrapped around his hips, whose mouth dragged across his, whose folds clung to his cock as he fucked himself into blissful, pleasurable oblivion.

Chapter Five

The sun was already high in the sky when Violet slipped back into the home Lord and Lady Rothcastle had let for her. She smiled at the servant who greeted her.

"Thank you, Simms. Could you tell Rachel to begin preparations for a bath?"

The butler sniffed dismissively, but nodded regardless of his obvious judgment of her. "Yes, miss. Right away."

Violet held back a sigh as she walked up the stairs toward her chamber. She had grown so accustomed to her own home in London, with her tolerant servants, that she found herself stung by the new man's disregard. Though she recognized some of that sting was multiplied by her own hesitation about what she was doing.

She sighed as she turned the knob at her chamber door. She hadn't fully opened it when the chamber across the hall opened and revealed a bleary-eyed Olivia, still in her dressing gown.

Violet forgot the snotty butler and laughed. "You were still abed?"

"I am not a morning person."

"Lucky for you it is afternoon," Violet teased.

Olivia stuck out her tongue as she crossed the hall and gave her friend a squeeze before she followed her into her chamber. Violet sat down to toe off her slippers.

"Considering you are just returning home, I assume things went well with the earl?" Olivia asked, motioning Violet to turn around so she could unbutton her, since Rachel was likely arranging water for the tub that was set in the corner of Violet's chamber, behind a screen.

To Violet's surprise, her cheeks flamed with sudden heat at her friend's observation. She lifted her hands to cover them and shook her head. She hadn't blushed in years! She prayed the pinkness would fade before she was forced to look at Olivia again, for her friend would surely notice and crow endlessly.

"He wants me to stay with him," she said.

Behind her, Olivia unfastened the last button and then grabbed her by the elbow to swing her around to face her. Her friend's eyes were wide. "Really?"

Violet shoved out of her gown and caught up the robe that was draped over the chair beside her fire. Before she could respond, Rachel opened the chamber door and smiled.

"Good afternoon, miss. They're bringing the water now."

Violet nodded, stepping back as footmen entered the room with steaming buckets of clean, hot water. She could feel Olivia bouncing with impatience as they filled her tub and Rachel fussed with scented oils to add to the water.

For her part, Violet was just as happy not to have to respond to Olivia's surprise right away. Although she had come here with the express purpose of getting closer to Liam, his invitation had surprised her. Especially when he kept repeating his mantra that he would not, could not keep her.

She brushed aside any unwanted feelings his declaration might have foolishly caused in her and turned to Rachel as the other servants left her room.

"Thank you," she said to the girl. "Will you oversee the laundering of the gown?"

She motioned to the discarded outfit, and the girl swept it up. "Of course, miss. Will you need anything else?"

"I'll help her," Olivia volunteered.

Rachel bobbed out a nod and once again Violet was grateful for a servant she knew well. Rachel had been with her long enough to be accustomed to the fact that she and Olivia often spent long hours gossiping and chatting, sometimes while requesting privacy. Rachel didn't even find it odd anymore, nor did she intrude.

And right now, Violet did not want intrusion.

"Very good," the girl said. "I will come back in an hour to help you dress and do your hair."

She slipped from the room without another word, shutting the door behind her.

The moment they were alone, Olivia faced her. "You are trying to drive me mad! What did you say when Windbury asked you to stay with him?"

Violet shrugged from her robe and stepped into the tub. Before she answered, she sunk under the scented waters with a sigh of pleasure. She ached from the sexual acrobatics of the previous night, though she would not take back a moment of pleasure.

"Violet!" her friend said with a laugh as she dragged a chair up next to the tub.

"I told him I would consider the request," she finally replied.

Olivia leaned back, eyes wide. "Consider it? I thought *that* was your whole purpose in coming here."

Violet grabbed the soap and scrubbed a thick lather onto her hands as she pondered the point. "It is," she admitted. "But I need him to *want* me, to pursue me."

Her friend laughed. "Ah, I see. A merry chase, even if it is only pretended on your part. You are cold."

Olivia only meant it as a teasing statement, but Violet stiffened. Yes, she was manipulating Liam, but *was* she truly cold? She didn't do anything to hurt him, after all.

Though she couldn't imagine he would be happy if he knew the truth of why she had come to Bath and who had sent her.

"Does he want to be your protector?" Olivia asked, interrupting her thoughts.

Violet shook her head. "No. It is as has always been rumored about him. He doesn't want a woman to keep."

"And yet he asks you to stay with him throughout the duration of your stay here." Olivia arched a brow. "I have always heard a woman could only expect a night or two in his company."

Violet shrugged. "I suppose, as you say, I have manipulated him into wanting more."

That was certainly the only explanation she had for his desire for a longer affiliation.

She looked at her friend. "I was going to tell him that I am in town with a friend and ask if you could join us at his estate."

Olivia's eyebrows lifted. "Me?"

"You can keep his guard or friend or whatever that man is busy."

"Malcolm?" Olivia asked, her tone very even, though Violet thought she saw something in her friend's eyes.

She leaned closer, but it was gone, so she nodded. "Malcolm. I didn't see him last night or this morning, but I think if I stay there, he might take an interest in my intentions. That could prove difficult for me."

Once again, she was hit hard by the ulterior motives of her seduction, but she ignored the guilt that threatened to undermine her plans. There was a reason she was doing this. A reason far more important than Liam.

It would all be worth it in the end.

"Malcolm," Olivia said with a dreamy smile, interrupting Violet's thoughts. "He was awfully handsome. And quite a good kisser. I wouldn't mind distracting him."

Violet silently thanked her friend for her teasing as she laughed and the mood lightened.

"Then I shall write Lord Windbury this afternoon and tell him I will accept his offer, as long as you may accompany me. I'm certain he will say yes, since I will make it clear you won't be any interference to our...*connection.*"

"Excellent," Olivia said, rising with a clap of her hands. "Then I will have my maid begin packing me right away. And so it begins!"

Olivia squeezed her shoulder before she left. Once she was gone, Violet sank deeper beneath the water and stared up at the ceiling. So it began, indeed.

She only wished there wasn't anxiety...and utter excitement...gripping her heart at that prospect. She could afford neither.

By the time two days had passed, the arrangements had all been made and Violet had arrived at the estate in Liam's carriage, her things being moved in another, she had convinced herself that she felt nothing about the entire arrangement. This charade was something she had agreed to do—it was a duty, a job. If it brought Liam back to his family, it would not hurt him. Certainly it would go no deeper than that, on either side.

And once it was over? Well, she would walk away from Bath, from Liam, and forget it, free to finally live the future she had always dreamed of.

It was with those firm, clear thoughts that she stepped from the carriage onto Liam's drive. Olivia followed her down and stared up at the estate with a low whistle.

"Lor'," she murmured, reverting back to a Cockney drawl she had worked years to overcome. It only came out when she was excited, or in this case, impressed.

"Yes," Violet whispered with a laugh. "And Liam behaves as if this is a snug little cottage."

Olivia rolled her eyes. "Men with money are so often utterly ridiculous."

Of course, Liam wasn't ridiculous. Violet might have said as much, but before she could answer, a tall, broad-shouldered man came around the house from the direction of the stables. Violet recognized him from the afternoon in the bathhouse. He was Liam's right-hand man, Malcolm Graham.

There was no doubt why Olivia was attracted to him. He was a head taller than the average man, with close-cropped dark hair and eyes that were almost black. He was thickly muscled from head to toe and walked with the air of a man who knew how to get things done. He wasn't titled, but he had just as much confidence as someone who had been born to rule an empire. Probably more, in some cases.

He was just Olivia's type, when she actually got to choose a man for looks and not assets. But Violet scarcely looked at him except to acknowledge his presence. She rather preferred Liam's lean strength.

Besides, she found herself a little intimidated by Malcolm. He hadn't even noticed her thanks to Olivia's flirtation at the bathhouse, but now he stared at her. She saw his questions and hesitations about her seduction in the bathhouse and her further intrusion in Liam's life since.

Malcolm could be a problem if Olivia couldn't rein him in with her talents. Violet would definitely be relying on her best friend more than ever, it seemed.

"Miss Milford," he said, extending a hand as he reached the carriage. "I apologize, I would have been here to greet you the moment you arrived, but I was called to deal with an estate issue."

Violet smiled. He had a very firm handshake, and his appraising glance hadn't changed even with welcoming words. He was judging her.

But she'd been judged before. It was the nature of her profession. She refused to be unnerved by it...or at least she tried not to be. Sometimes it was impossible not to feel the sting.

"You were here not a moment after our arrival," she said with a wave of dismissal for his apology. "You must be Mr. Graham."

"I am." He nodded and released her hand. "Your items follow behind, do they? You had no trouble with the move?"

"No trouble at all," she reassured him. "Thank you for arranging for the multiple vehicles to ferry both us and our items."

His lips thinned ever so slightly. "I was following Windbury's directives."

So he didn't approve, if his tone was any indication. Well, she would have to be careful. And use all the methods she had in her disposal to keep Malcolm off the scent of her deception.

To that end, she turned and motioned toward Olivia. "I believe you have met my friend, Olivia Cranfield?"

It was exactly the right thing to say, for Malcolm's attention moved from her to Olivia, and his gaze, which had been so appraising, changed immediately to one of interest and unmistakable desire.

"Mal," her friend purred as she sidled up to him and took his hand.

Violet drew back in surprise as the hulk of a suspicious man kissed her friend's hand with as much delicacy as the biggest dandy in London might have exhibited.

"Miss Olivia Cranfield. It's been too long."

"It's been less than a week," Olivia laughed, swatting him playfully. "But I do agree."

The two of them began to talk, and Violet moved away a step, both to offer them privacy and also because she was distracted by the house that rose above her. She would stay here as Liam's lover for as long as he would have her. She would lie. She would manipulate. She would betray any trust she managed to wheedle out of him.

She had her reasons...but suddenly her firm belief that she was in the right in doing so faded.

The front door to the house opened and she turned her attention to the entrance. Liam stepped from the darkness of the interior and out onto the front step.

All her thoughts faded, for good or for bad, and she stared at him. Unlike two nights before, when he had greeted her with an unbuttoned shirt and casually tousled hair, today he was pulled together as an earl should be, perfectly coifed and pressed by a valet.

How she longed to strip him of all the trappings of his rank and unleash the animal desire she knew bubbled just beneath his currently proper surface.

She shifted with surprising desire as Liam came down the stairs to join their party in the drive.

"Good afternoon," he said, reaching for her hand.

Unlike Malcolm had with Olivia, he didn't kiss the top, but only squeezed it gently and then released her. Still, there was a friendly comfort in that gesture that made her doubt herself even more.

She shoved those thoughts aside and instead turned to her companion.

"Liam, may I present to you my dearest friend, Miss Olivia Cranfield. Olivia, the Earl of Windbury."

Olivia managed to extract her attention from Malcolm long enough to step forward, offering Liam a hand. "Good afternoon, my lord. I'm so pleased to meet you. Thank you so much for including me in your invitation to Violet. I would have been gutted had we not been able to spend our planned holiday together."

Violet fought the urge to roll her eyes. Olivia was laying it on a bit thick, but she smiled so sweetly that it was hardly noticeable to anyone else.

"We are happy to have you join us," Liam said, casting a quick glance at Malcolm, who still stared at Olivia. "Some of us more than others."

As Olivia laughed and Malcolm scowled, Liam turned back to Violet. He looked straight at her and there was no doubt that he had missed seeing her in the two days they'd been apart as much as she had missed seeing him. He wanted her, which was exactly what she wanted and had planned for.

What she hadn't expected was how deeply and sincerely she wanted him in return. Her need to touch him and to be touched by him was a deep ache low in her belly. It was far harsher than any desire she had ever felt for any man who had shared her bed.

"Mal, why don't you have Miss Cranfield shown to her chamber?" Liam asked, his voice rough as he kept his gaze on Violet's face.

"With great pleasure," Mal said behind her, but Violet didn't turn. In fact, she hardly noticed as Olivia and Mal brushed past her to go up the stairs into the house together.

She stood with Liam, sunshine against her back, hearing the carriage being taken away, the servants dispersing.

"And what will *we* do?" she asked when they were alone, moving toward him without meaning to do so. She fell into his arms to stare up into his angular face.

He didn't answer, but let his lips take hers. The kiss was deep, probing, filled with heady passion, but not desperate passion. After all, she was his, at least until he tired of the game or decided to leave Bath. There was no rush anymore. No worry about being separated at dawn.

"*I* am going to take you to my bed," he murmured in response to her earlier question.

She shivered at the low possessiveness of his tone. Reaching out, she took his hand and let him lead her into the house and up the stairs.

"There is nowhere I would rather be," she whispered.

And to her utter terror, she realized how true a statement that was.

Chapter Six

This time when they entered Liam's chamber, Violet took a moment to look around her. He stepped back to shut the door and watched as she took in her surroundings.

"I noticed when I came here before that you don't have any art in the room," she said, turning to face him. "Or really any niceties. Just the barest of furnishings, despite the fact that it is a pretty room."

He shrugged, trying not to be put off by what was no more than a truthful observation.

"I hardly stay here," he said as explanation, though that wasn't the real reason why the room was so sparse. Not that he had any intentions of defending himself on that score.

She looked at him, and he saw her reading his face, dissecting him. If she came up with a decision about what he said or what it meant, she didn't say anything. Instead, she moved toward him and smiled.

"I'm happy you invited me," she whispered.

He stared at her. Her dark eyes were soft with emotion, with desire and as she leaned into him, her warmth seemed to surround and fill him as he hadn't felt for a long time.

"I am too," he replied.

He cupped her cheek with his good hand, rubbing his rough fingers against her satin skin. She leaned into his palm, her eyes fluttering shut on a sigh that hit him in the gut and made his cock ache with the need to bury himself in her.

And now he could, as long as he wanted to do so. And though he had avoided any long-term entanglements for years, he found himself looking forward to the days and nights ahead.

He leaned down and kissed her, reveling in the sweetness of her tongue as it swirled around his with wild abandon. She was an indulgence he didn't care to give up, at least for now.

He drew her back toward his bed, never stopping their kisses or breaking to look where they were going. But when his backside hit the mattress and he moved to turn her, she stepped away and shook her head.

"Not this time, my lord," she said, the corners of her mouth quirking into a wicked smile. "This time, I want to pleasure you."

He sucked in a breath, taken in by this battle of wits in which they kept engaging. Clearly, Violet had as dominant a personality as he did. And he wanted to break her and have her bending to his every pleasurable whim.

"We talked about this," he began.

She shook her head. "I want to pleasure you, my lord. And you can tell me how, if that helps you. I will do whatever you wish."

His eyes widened. She would give, but he would dictate? His already hard cock twitched at the thought.

He sat down on the bed and stared up at her.

"Remove your clothes, Violet. Slowly."

She swallowed hard, and the strain of obeying was clear on her face. She was so accustomed to men who wanted her to take the lead that she bristled under command.

And yet, she surrendered despite her hesitation, lifting her hands to the buttons along the front of her gown and loosening them one by one. Slowly, she peeled the fabric open and revealed a pretty pink chemise beneath the silky fabric of her day dress. A pretty pink chemise he wished to rend in two, perhaps with his teeth.

But he remained seated instead, watching as she shimmied her dress down her body. She kept her dark stare on him the entire time, reading his reactions, metering her movements to torture and best please him.

Finally she shoved her gown to her waist and let it hang there. She lifted her hands to her breasts and massaged them until the nipples became hard against the flimsy fabric of the chemise. He shifted.

"Take it off," he repeated, his voice low. "Take it all off."

She gave a husky laugh. "Your wish is my command, my lord," she murmured, then slid her fingers beneath the chemise and shoved both gown and underthings down the length of her body.

She toed off her slippers, then lifted one leg and slowly, so slowly, rolled her stocking down to remove it. She let her hands drag across her stomach with a hissing moan before she repeated that action on the other leg.

She kicked all the clothing away and stood before him deliciously naked. His heart stuttered as he stared at her in the glowing firelight and dimming lamplight. Her curves were almost unreal. From her full breasts to her rounded hips, it was a body men would have painted in the Renaissance. A body men had worshipped since the dawn of time.

"Are you only going to stare?" she asked, arching her back to give him a better view of the breasts he wished to suckle until she screamed in pleasure.

"For now, yes," he managed to choke out. "Touch yourself, make yourself ready for me."

She laughed, and the sound was intoxicating. "If you don't already think I'm dripping and ready, you underestimate your allure, my lord."

Plenty of women had said something similar to him over the years. Women who then flinched when they looked at his scars. But the scars didn't seem to bother Violet. She hardly seemed to notice them. He could almost believe her.

"Touch yourself. Now," he repeated. "Or I shall punish you."

Her eyebrows lifted. "How?" she asked, but she was breathless and her nipples got even harder.

He stood up but didn't approach her. "I will hold you down on my bed while I lick your pussy until you are writhing and begging for release. And I won't give it to you. I will hold you on the edge of pleasure until you weep and scream my name. Is that plain enough?"

Her hand slipped between her legs, and she shuddered as she touched herself. "I'm not certain that would be a punishment. It sounds like heaven."

"Breaking you sounds like heaven?" he asked. Her eyes widened, and he chuckled. "Actually, I tend to agree."

"You can't break me," she replied, but her hand worked in earnest and, judging from the flush that had begun to work across her chest and up her neck, Violet was enjoying the idea he presented.

"Don't tempt me," he said. "Now stop touching yourself. I don't want you to come until I give you the orgasm you will so richly deserve."

She hesitated but pulled her hand from between her legs. He could see the shining evidence of her utter arousal on her fingertips. Without warning, he reached out to catch her wrist and dragged her closer. He lifted her hand to his mouth and sucked her fingers, licking her earthy, sweet essence from the tips.

She shivered, and he thought she might come there and then.

"You said you want to please me," he continued, releasing her hand reluctantly and reaching for a pillow, which he dropped at her feet.

She looked down and smiled. "Please you, *my lord?*" she repeated.

He nodded slowly. "Yes."

She unfastened his trousers as she slithered down his body to kneel on the pillow he had provided. They hit the floor as she did, and he stepped out of them and kicked them away, just as she had done with her gown a few moments before. She pushed his shirt up and away from his waist and he went to work on removing it, even as he watched her, her face a breath away from his hard cock.

She cupped him gently, looking at him like he was a treat she had been offered after a long fast. She licked her lips, and he nearly spent right there and then.

And when she darted her tongue out and swirled it slowly around the head of his cock, his knees buckled and he had to reach back and balance himself on the bed before he finished stripping his shirt away. She sucked his cock into her mouth and at the same time slid a hand up his hip to stroke her hand over the hard muscles of his stomach.

He clenched at the bed with a groan. God damn, she was good at this. She took him deep into her throat and back again, using her tongue to lave him even as she popped him away from her lips. She looked up, and the wickedness of her stare was a challenge and a promise he could hardly ignore.

Slowly, she took him again, gripping the base of his cock in one firm hand, licking and stroking, dragging him toward release. He stared at her, eyes closed, humming pleasure deep in her throat, and he realized *this* was how she maintained control. Distance. She pleasured and knew that with most men they didn't care about anything else.

He shouldn't have, but he did care. He wanted more than her mind-blowing mouth. He wanted her purring beneath him, above him. He wanted her begging. He just wanted her.

"Stand up," he ordered.

She froze, looking up his body slowly. She sucked just a fraction before she popped him from her lips. "You don't want this?"

"I want *you*," he said, sitting down on the bed and pulling her to stand before him. He put a hand behind her knee and dragged it onto the bed next to his hip.

She smiled and straddled him, lifting straight on her knees so that she was slightly above him. She didn't lower her body onto his cock yet, but instead reached up into her hair and pulled a few pins loose to clatter on the floor. The mass of thick, dark, perfumed locks came down around her shoulders, her breasts, his face.

Violet's gaze stayed on his, unwavering, unflinching as she lowered herself onto his waiting erection. As he entered her, they both shuddered, her hands coming to grip his shoulders. Normally pain would burn from his injury at such a touch, but for now he was too focused on her welcoming slit to care.

Once she was fully seated, he reached out and tugged her legs out from under her, forcing her to lock them around his back. They were face-to-face, nose-to-nose as he thrust up and growled out a noise of possessive pleasure.

Her head tilted back as she ground her hips against him, panting and mewling with every thrust. He cupped her backside, pulling her closer, guiding her movements, pounding and reaching to go deeper, to pull more from their joined bodies.

He could tell when she was close to orgasm. Her back arched and her gaze became clouded and distant. Her pulse throbbed as she slammed her hips to his. Finally, with a cry of his name, she buried her face in his neck and sobbed as her pussy clenched his in an erratic, wild rhythm. She pulled at him, milking him, and his balls tightened as his own orgasm loomed. He held back, trying to work her through pleasure as long as he could.

But when he could take it no more, he stood up, turning to place her on the bed, and pulled out to spill his seed with a growling cry of utter satisfaction. He collapsed over her, showering kisses along her neck and chest, cupping her breasts, stroking his hands over her hips, her legs, as if he could memorize her lines to savor in his mind later.

She held him close, dragging her fingernails along his spine as her breath slowed. She sighed, content as he rolled for a better position on the bed. Stretching like a cat, she moved to rest her head on his chest and smiled up at him.

"I might like being told what to do after all."

She teased but those words did so much to him. Too much.

He looked down at her in all her exotic beauty. "How did a woman like you become a courtesan?" he asked.

She stiffened for a brief moment, and he knew he had hit a nerve. He expected her to pull away, but instead she began to stroke her fingers over his chest in a small circle.

"I was offered a marriage with a man I didn't want," she explained softly. "Or perhaps *offered* is too gentle a word. My father...well, he is a man of means, of power. He never publicly acknowledged me, but when I came of age, he decided to 'help' me."

Liam nodded. "Help you how?" he urged.

She was quiet for a long moment, and he didn't fill the silence, but allowed her to collect herself. "He demanded I marry a man I loathed. But the man had a son, who..."

She stopped abruptly and was silent, as if she were considering the prudence of revealing something personal to a man she hardly knew. He recognized the look on her face. One of regret, sadness, the remnants of fear. He shouldn't have wanted to know more, but he did.

So he waited, without offering her an easy escape from her tale.

"To prevent a dilution of his father's inheritance, his son did something that made certain that his father wouldn't want to marry me." She shook her head. "That *anyone* would want to marry me."

Liam's eyes narrowed. "What did he do?"

She looked up at him, dark gaze hooded and her expression one of silent, long-fought acceptance of a painful past. "He tricked me into getting very drunk. I was young and didn't understand what he was doing. And then he...well, he did what some men do with girls who cannot say no."

Liam swallowed hard. "So he raped you."

"My father didn't call it that." She shrugged, but there was nothing dismissive in her low tone. Acceptance or not, the story still hurt her to her core. "He demanded that if I had ruined the good match he had lowered himself to arrange for me, that I now marry the man who had taken advantage."

Liam sucked in a breath through his teeth. He might have complicated issues with his sister, but he couldn't imagine demanding she do such a thing. He couldn't imagine anything but murdering a man who harmed someone he cared for.

"I refused and walked away. Cut off from what little protection he once offered and without my virginity to bargain, I had little choice but to turn to alternate methods of protecting and supporting myself." Her lips were thin, they were pressed so tightly together. "I met Olivia not long after I left my father's protection, and she helped me."

Liam nodded. "Do you regret your choices?"

She pondered that a moment. "No. No, I believe the path I am on is the one I was meant to travel. I came to enjoy sex, to appreciate the men I choose as my protectors. My body is my only commodity and I think I have used it well, without being harmed or abused."

She smiled and Liam could hardly stand how beautiful she looked in that moment. Her strength ran deep and made her all the more alluring.

"I'm sorry you endured so much," he said, stroking a hand along her arm.

She smiled. "We all endure, Liam. I think you know that better than anyone. Once we are dealt our cards, what else can we do but play them?"

He stared at her, so certain in her life and her response. How she had "played her cards", as she put it, was very different from his way.

She sat up, tossing long locks of hair from her shoulder.

"What time is supper?" she asked.

He yawned, just as happy for the change of subject. "Eight o'clock."

She glanced at the small clock beside his bed and stretched. "Then I have just enough time to ready myself beforehand. Where is my chamber?"

Liam hesitated. He had prepared a chamber for her, even though he hoped she would spend her nights with him. But sharing space with her things was far too intimate.

"Normally I would put you in the guest wing with your friend," he explained. "But that is too far for my taste. I've put you across the hall."

She smiled as she slipped from his bed and gathered her discarded gown and other things. When they were piled neatly in her arms, she blew him a kiss and turned to pad naked out his door and across the hall, with only the barest glance back at him.

Liam stared, then flopped back on his bed with a laugh. He had never known a woman like Violet Milford before. And he had a feeling he would never experience a force like her again.

So he had best enjoy it while he had it.

Chapter Seven

An hour later, Violet was sitting at the dressing table in the chamber Liam had provided, staring at her reflection as she replayed everything that had transpired between them. She had revealed something of herself, as was her plan...but the knowledge that she had become so vulnerable made her hands shake as she pressed them against her hot cheeks.

There was a knock behind her, and she called out, "Come in."

In the reflection from the mirror, she saw Olivia come into the room. Her friend's hair was still down, but she was dressed for dinner.

"Did they perhaps put my small bag in your room by mistake?" Olivia asked as she stepped inside.

Violet motioned to the stack of trunks and luggage that had been deposited in her corner by the time she claimed the room. Rachel had wanted to unpack her, but Violet had refused, insisting on time alone after she had been dressed and her hair fixed.

"Look there, it's possible. Who knew we had so many things? It's a little embarrassing."

"We are women, we *must* have many things. I feel no embarrassment whatsoever." Olivia laughed as she went to the pile and began moving things around. She glanced up as she went about her work. "Your face is a little grave—did things not go well with the handsome earl?"

Violet strummed her fingers along the top of the dressing table and shook her head. "No, everything went just to plan."

"Ah ha!" Olivia emerged from the pile with a small bag, and Violet couldn't help but laugh even though her nerves persisted.

Olivia didn't excuse herself immediately, but sat down at the end of Violet's bed and looked at her.

"If everything went 'just to plan', as you say, why do you seem so nervous and anxious? It isn't like you to be so affected by a man."

Violet wrung her hands. "I-I told him just a little about John Salsworth."

Olivia stared at her as the bag she had been clutching in her hand slipped away to clatter on the ground.

"Why?" Olivia asked, her voice rising. "What would make you be so forthcoming?"

Violet swallowed hard. Her friend's reaction was making her question the prudence of an action she already doubted.

"Have you ever heard of Scheherazade?" she asked.

Her friend shook her head. "You know I'm no scholar. What is a Scheherazade?"

Violet pushed to her feet. "She is the main character of a story written very long ago in a country very far away. I read a translation in French when I was a girl. Essentially it is the story of a king who executes his wives after spending just one night with them, for fear of them cuckolding him."

"A vast overreaction," Olivia said with a shake of her head.

Violet shrugged. "That is another discussion entirely. In the story, Scheherazade is given to the king as another in his string of brides. She doesn't want to die, so on the first night, she tells him a story. Well, part of a story. He's so interested that he doesn't kill her and encourages her to tell him more. Every night for a thousand and one nights, she continues to tell him a piece of her tale. By the end, he is in love with her and does not murder her, but keeps her as his bride and queen."

"Well, I hope you don't think the earl intends to kill you," Olivia said.

"No, of course not. But I do think that I, like Scheherazade, must lure him in. Capture his interest." She sighed. "I give him my trust in the belief that he will return it in time and tell me more about himself so that I might complete my mission for Lord and Lady Rothcastle."

"How much do you intend to tell him?" Olivia asked.

From her expression, Violet saw that her friend was as torn about this idea as she was. As courtesans, they dealt in mystery, not this kind of intimacy.

"I don't really know," she admitted. "I know there are things I shall never reveal."

"You mean about—"

Violet nodded to interrupt her. "Yes. About him. But as for everything else, I'll have to see how far I need to go to open Liam's heart and get past his defenses."

Olivia pursed her lips.

"What is that expression?" Violet asked, folding her arms.

"I worry, Violet," her friend admitted, utterly serious, which was unusual. "You say you are trying to open this man's heart, but I fear you will be opening your own as well. What if you come to care for him, even love him, because you shared so much of yourself?"

Violet straightened up, her heart clenching with her friend's pointed question.

"I had to consider that, of course," she admitted. "But I know what we are, Olivia. Courtesans cannot love—we cannot afford it."

Olivia's gaze dropped from hers and her cheeks paled. "I-I suppose you are correct about that."

Violet shrugged, as if to dismiss the topic. "And this man has made it clear he will not want to keep me. If he uncovers my deception, he *certainly* won't want to keep me. So I do this with no illusion that it is anything more than deception on my part."

Olivia nodded. "Be careful," she advised, then stood up. "Now I should finish readying myself before supper."

Violet smiled at her friend as Olivia slipped from the room. Olivia worried about her, which she appreciated. But she could handle this. She had to.

With a sigh, she moved from the chamber and walked downstairs. Since there was time before supper, she had the perfect opportunity to do a little looking around. She knew full well one could tell a great deal about a person from examining his surroundings.

She looked around the wide hallway at the bottom of the stairs. There were many doors and many rooms to explore, so she chose the first one on her right to start with. It was a parlor, though not the one she had been guided to upon her first visit. Like Liam's bedroom, the room was rather sparse, with minimal decoration and plain furniture. Strange, since his sister had a sense of style. And yet Liam went as minimal as he could in his home.

She walked from the room to the next in the hallway and caught her breath. This was an office, likely Liam's office, judging from the paperwork stacked on the desk, waiting to be addressed. A parlor couldn't tell her much, but this room most definitely could.

She moved inside and walked the perimeter of the room slowly. Again, there was little to see and only the work indicated someone bothered to live here at all. There was no art, plain paint colors, the furniture seemed comfortable, but there was nothing with personality to be seen here. It was as if he had come into this house and stripped everything of value and joy out.

Her breath hitched at the thought. It seemed like the man *wanted* to be wrapped in the pain his past had created. As if he shunned anything that might help him move forward in his life.

Once again, Violet thought of his sister and the fear in her eyes when she spoke of him. Lady Rothcastle feared for his future. At the time, Violet had simply filed the information away, but now she wondered...

Was Liam even thinking about a future? Did he believe he would be around for one? Or was his cutting off of everything good around him a symptom of something far more sinister and fearful?

She shivered and pushed those thoughts aside, though she knew she would be watching him far more closely from now on. She stepped up to his desk and looked at the papers there. They were estate business, mostly. A few pieces of correspondence that looked like they had gone unanswered for a while. She was about to turn away when she saw something else.

There was a small framed portrait on the corner of the desk. She reached out, taking it from its stand and turning it toward her.

It was a woman whose picture was in the frame. The artist had rendered her in a seated position, half turned toward him. She was beautiful, with blonde hair and blue eyes. She had a half-smile on her face that was just a touch mischievous.

It was evident who she was, even if Violet hadn't just met her brother less than a week ago. This was Lady Matilda. The woman who was the center of—and a casualty of—a war.

Violet stared at her, so lifelike in this portrait. No wonder she had been so loved. There was just something about her.

"Put it back."

She jumped at the voice behind her and spun around to find Liam standing in the doorway. His face was red and his good hand clenched at his side, while he held the injured one in front of him, as if he could guard his heart with the broken, scarred extremity.

Slowly, she set the picture down as she had been told.

"I'm sorry," she said, moving away from the desk. "I didn't mean to intrude."

"But you did," he hissed out on a short breath.

She hesitated, drawn in by the rich, profound emotion on his face. He was angry with her, but also with himself, and she also saw a brief glimpse of a deep well of sadness within him. Her throat seized, and she longed to reach out, but it was evident he would not allow it. He was still too closed off.

She thought again of Scheherazade and wondered what that fictional queen would do in this tense moment.

"You know, I am shocked you haven't questioned me more about why I came here," she said, moving away from Matilda's picture step by step, hoping to create distance between the past and the present.

His brow wrinkled, and confusion replaced the other emotions on his face. Not that she could blame him. Most people would have pressed him on what had just happened. But she couldn't. Not yet.

"I thought you were just on holiday," he said after a long pause where he seemed to gather himself.

She smiled, passing him to exit his office and go instead to a parlor across the hall. He followed her, his expression still wary and tense.

"I *was* on holiday," she admitted. Lied. "But when I found out you were in Bath, I pursued you, didn't I?"

He nodded. "You did indeed. You think I am not curious about that fact?"

She laughed. "If you are, you have hidden it well."

He shook his head. "Very well, Miss Milford, tell me. Why did you pursue me?"

She bit her lip. "I had heard you were a prolific lover, which is true. But I also heard other things. The loggerheads you and I have been at in your bed about control, the challenge you have presented me with to surrender to your will...your rumored dominance intrigued me. As I told you, my other lovers have always deferred to me."

She watched him shift and change with this new, safer topic. The way he watched her was so possessive, like she was already his but hadn't yet realized it.

It wasn't true, but it was oh-so-alluring regardless.

"You want the surrender I demand?" he asked, his tone very rough.

She turned on him and met his gaze evenly. "I am intrigued by it, yes. But I'm afraid you would have to teach me how, for my nature is to seduce and claim and take, just as yours is. But the idea of bending and giving and even breaking is—"

She might have finished that thought, but behind them a servant appeared, clearing his throat. "My lord, Miss Milford, supper is served."

Violet smiled. She could not have planned the timing better. An interruption at the height of seduction would drive Liam mad all through supper until they could be alone again and she could further delve into the dangerous topic that truly did intrigue her.

And she could only imagine what he would do once they were alone after hours of pondering her utter surrender to his every whim.

A servant placed a plate before him, but Liam hardly noticed the steaming, fragrant delicacies prepared for his liking and the liking of his guests. Just as he had done during the previous courses of the meal, all he could do was stare down the table at Violet and think of the scandalous things she had said just an hour before.

Had she brought up his dominance and her interest in such topics simply to make him forget he had found her in his office, holding a portrait of Matilda?

And even if she had...did he care? He was still wrapped up in the idea of taming Violet. Of bringing her to heel and making her give over control in every way.

She was such a bold woman that he realized how much of a sacrifice surrender would be, yet she seemed to welcome his dominance.

But he only had a few weeks with Violet at best. What they discussed would take far longer. It would involve earning her trust on a deep, physical and emotional level. And that wasn't something he ever intended to do.

Frustration bloomed in his chest, and he swept up his fork with a grumble of discontent and took a bite of food.

Oblivious to his thoughts, Violet's friend Olivia hummed with pleasure as she did the same.

"You do have a splendid cook, my lord," she said. "I envy you these delicious meals every single day and night."

Liam looked up to answer, but it didn't appear as if his answer was required. Mal was speaking for him, leaning closer to Olivia and making his interest in the pretty, petite blonde very clear.

"Wait until you taste dessert, pet," he murmured.

Liam jolted. It was entirely inappropriate for his man to be so familiar with a woman at his table. More than that, it was entirely unexpected. Mal never took an interest in women beyond a fulfillment of his physical needs. He was too wrapped up in his duties.

But right now Mal didn't seem capable of breaking his gaze from Olivia's.

"How long have you worked for Liam?" Violet asked, arching a brow at her friend as if to encourage her to tone down the physical expression of her attraction.

Mal jolted and straightened up. "Windbury and I have been friends since..." He shook his head and cast a quick glance toward Liam. "School, I suppose. We've been friends for years and I began managing his estates when—"

He cut himself off, and Liam shifted. Mal had taken over some of his estate business when the accident happened. When he had been too injured and emotionally gutted to do anything but drown in laudanum and anger.

Mal had seen him through the worst and Liam appreciated it. He *didn't* appreciate the fact Mal had very nearly revealed that truth to strangers. Although Violet didn't feel much like a stranger to him anymore.

Olivia continued to ignore the tension in the room and reached out to squeeze Malcolm's arm.

"Violet and I have also been friends for an age, haven't we?"

Violet cleared her throat, her gaze held firmly on Liam's face, trying to read him. Irritation sluiced through him. *This* was why he didn't keep company, this constant appraisal and talking and dancing around topics.

"We have," she said. "I think it is lucky that both I, and Lord Windbury, have had such good friends."

"Foolish as they may be," Liam grumbled.

His short dismissal made Mal look at him sharply.

"And now we've all met thanks to those friendships," Olivia continued, her attention still on Mal. "We're lucky indeed."

His friend seemed torn now, looking back and forth between the man he'd called brother for years and the woman he clearly wanted to fuck. To Liam's surprise, it was the girl who won in the turmoil, and Mal's lips turned up in a smile as he leaned closer.

"Very lucky."

Liam pushed his chair back with a screech and every person in the room swiveled their heads to look at him. He clenched his napkin in his hand and stared at the group at his table. This all felt like a game to him.

And he was no longer capable of playing it.

He opened his mouth, but nothing would come out. So he threw his napkin across his plate and left the room without so much as a glance behind him.

Chapter Eight

Violet flinched as the room sat in stunned silence for a moment after Liam's departure. His sudden anger and inability to control that reaction worried her. What troubled her more was the idea that *she* had caused it by her intrusion on his office earlier that day.

Liam was on the edge. She had now seen him balancing there. Once that happened, she couldn't see anything else or do anything but fear the consequences for him in the future.

Olivia leaned back in her chair. "His ill-humor is impressive. I didn't mean to bother him with my silly chatter."

Mal shook his head, staring at the door where his friend had departed. Violet explored his face carefully. He was worried about Liam—the lines of concern were deep in his handsome face. It made her own trepidations all the sharper and more in focus.

"I apologize, ladies," Malcolm finally managed. "My friend has been a little...*rough* since his accident. And he doesn't keep company often, probably because his emotions can overtake him when he isn't expecting it. I think the reality of being around others remains troublesome to him."

"He was hard on you," Olivia pressed, reaching out a hand to cover Mal's.

Now she wasn't flirtatious, but comforting. Violet couldn't help but be surprised at that shift. Normally Olivia was all about fun. Her expression of other emotions, especially with men, was vastly limited, and purposefully so.

He shrugged. "Sometimes he lashes out. I can ignore it most times, though we do occasionally have words if he takes things too far. I have been through the worst with him and seen him when I thought he might—"

Malcolm cut himself off and his face twisted with pain and worry and deep sadness. He took a breath before he continued, "I understand Windbury's motives for lashing out. Though I admit, he can be harsh."

Violet tilted her head. "And yet you stay with him."

Mal looked at her, his face clear of any judgment of his friend. Any anger. "He needs me."

She flinched. Need. Yes, Liam had needs, that was crystal clear. And *she* was exploiting them for the bargain she had made with his sister and brother-in-law. Even now, questioning his friend was as much an exercise to wheedle more information about the enigmatic man she pursued as it was because of her own interest.

What a person she was to do such a thing, whatever her ultimate motives might be.

She pushed her plate away and folded her hands on the table before her. "I would like to follow him, talk to him," she said, looking at Mal.

He drew back. "I warn you, he will likely be inhospitable."

She swallowed. "Yes. But if his anger comes from pain, then he may need company, even if he refuses to acknowledge that fact to any of us. He may desire a friend, if you don't mind my offering myself in that position instead of you."

"Is that what you want to be to him? A friend?" Mal asked, tone carefully neutral.

There was an immediate reaction inside of Violet. A screaming voice that said *yes* to that question so loudly that it shook her. But she pushed it away, pushed it far down. She couldn't afford it—she had other people to think about.

"If he would allow it," she whispered, hating the catch to her voice.

Mal looked her up and down. Yes, he still maintained a detachment from her, his questions about her purpose lingered in his dark eyes. But he lifted his eyebrows in acquiescence nonetheless.

"Actually, Miss Milford, I think what you offer may be what he needs more than anything I can provide. If you want to follow him, I would assume his office is where he will lick his wounds. It generally is."

She frowned as she got to her feet. Their encounter there before supper now felt even more like an intrusion.

"Good evening, you two. If I don't see you again, I hope you enjoy your dessert."

Olivia caught her hand and looked at her with concern as she passed her friend.

"Are you certain?" she asked softly.

Violet hesitated. She was not certain. But this was her course. She could not vary it when so much was at stake.

"Of course," she said with a smile far brighter than she felt. "Good night."

She left the room, her hands shaking as she made her way back to the office where she had encountered Liam earlier. The door was closed, a clear, ominous message that he wished to be left alone. She stared at the barrier that now separated them. She could turn and walk away. She could continue her plan without going inside.

She could do all those things, but she lifted her hand and knocked anyway.

Silence greeted her, another message to leave him alone. Another message she ignored as she opened the door and stepped inside.

The fire had burned down, dimming the lights in the room, and Liam hadn't lit a lamp, so it took her a moment to find him in the big room. He wasn't at his desk or the chair by his fire.

He stood in front of the massive picture window across the room, standing and staring into the inky black nothingness outside. He had removed his jacket, tossing it across a chair before the fire.

"I didn't give you leave to enter," he said. "Can't you leave well enough alone, Mal?"

"It's not Mal," she said softly.

He pivoted and stared at her in surprise. The scar slashed across his lean, angular face was bright in the firelight, but that wasn't what she noticed. She more saw how his face was filled with emotions: anger, sadness, regret. They were written across every line and every curve. And she wanted, so desperately, to erase them in that moment. To find a way to make him whole again.

That realization nearly had her turning on her heel and running, not just from the room, but from his house, her bargain be damned. She didn't *want* to take care of this man. She didn't want to get close to him or think of him or wonder what made him who he was.

"Why did you come?" he asked, his voice rough and barely carrying.

She blinked. "I-I don't know," she admitted, the truth spilling from her lips before she could fashion an adequate lie. "I was worried about you."

Again, the truth rather than a manipulation. Her heart pounded and her hands shook as she forced herself to step into the room and shut the door behind her. She had gone too far to run now. She had to calm down and put herself back on track.

A rather humorless smile turned his lips up slightly. "Ah yes, *everyone* worries about me, don't they? It is almost a household pastime."

"You give them reason to do so," she said quietly. She moved forward and stopped at his desk. She couldn't help but notice that the portrait of Matilda had been removed from view. As if her touching it had spoiled it somehow and forced him to hide it.

Why that stung, she didn't want to consider.

"I suppose I do," he said, shaking his head as he turned back toward the window. "I would like to ask you a question, Violet."

She swallowed hard before she said, "Go ahead. I have nothing to hide."

"I rather doubt that," he murmured, just loud enough for her to hear. She tensed further but was not allowed to reply, for he continued speaking. "Why don't you comment on my sister or my troubled past or my accident? Hell, you don't even coo over my scar. Women always do that during their 'seductions'. They stroke and mewl and pity me."

She stepped closer. "And you feel their expressions of concern aren't true."

He glanced over his shoulder and pursed his lips. "No."

When he turned away, she gasped in a breath. Guilt swelled in her, so powerful that it nearly took her off her feet, but she forced that reaction away. If she did her duty, she would not only help herself but very likely help him as well.

At least that was what she kept telling herself.

"I know full well about your past," she began, somehow managing to wrestle free of her emotions and refocus on matters at hand. "Your accident, your family's feud with the family of your sister's husband and your eventual break with her after she married your greatest enemy...all of that is the stuff of legend, even in my lowly circles."

He didn't face her, but his shoulders stiffened in reaction.

"But I'm sorry, my lord, I do not preen or pity, even under dire circumstances. If you want a woman to do that, you have not found her." He faced her in surprise, and she shrugged. "Everyone has their heartaches, Liam. Yours are *very* tragic, yes, I would never deny that or pretend otherwise. But ultimately, they are no more tragic than a hundred or a thousand others I have met or seen."

He didn't move or say a word for a very long moment. As the firelight hit his face, she caught his breath, both at how handsome he was and how unreadable he had become.

"Do you count yourself amongst those with tragedies to contend with?" he asked.

She met his gaze. She might have to reveal something of herself to get what she wanted, but she refused to do it with a bent head. What she had endured had made her who she was, she felt no shame about her past.

"You know some of my story. I suppose it is tragic enough."

"Some of your story, yes," he said, and now he was the one to step toward *her*. His green gaze never wavered from her face and she found heat filling her cheeks under his close regard.

"But your father's attempt at a forced marriage and the bastard who tried to subvert it in the most disgusting way possible isn't the whole story, is it?"

She shook her head. "No, of course not."

"Then tell me more."

She forced herself not to fold her arms across her chest in an expression of self-protection. She drew in a long, deep breath and began the next part of her tale.

"Obviously, you can see I am not the usual woman who walks the streets of London. My mother was Spanish and came here to work as a servant when she was a young woman."

He examined her face and she waited. Some men flinched away if her heritage was revealed. One of her protectors had once broken with her when he found out, though he had praised her for her "dark, exotic looks" before that moment.

"Spanish," he repeated with a nod. "That was my first guess."

She drew back slightly. Most men didn't even try to guess her background.

"And did you wax poetic in your mind about how exotic it made me?" she asked, bitterness tingeing her tone.

He tilted his head in surprise. "I think your heritage gives you a unique look, yes. I suppose some might call it exotic, though I think that might reflect their lack of worldly awareness. Judging from your reaction, though, I suppose that is how you have been labeled all your life."

"Not all my life," she said, trying hard not to sound resentful after she had just given him such a speech about everyone having troubles. It was very difficult when she was revealing one of the most painful aspects of her life.

"What else were you called?" he asked.

She sighed. "As a girl, children were cruel. I was, after all, the bastard child of a former servant and the titled man who made her believe he would love her. I was tortured for it and for the olive complexion and dark hair that has never been the rage."

"Your mother must have been a comfort," he suggested.

She flinched. "She was, until she died when I was just eight. Then my father, who couldn't claim me as his own, of course, not with a wife and children and a title to be protected, arranged for me to be taken in by a middle-class family who owed him a debt. They did so, but I was never accepted or loved. They weren't abusive, they didn't physically harm me...but I knew I wasn't wanted."

His lips thinned. "For that, I am truly sorry."

"Are you petting and cooing and pitying, my lord?" she whispered.

He shook his head slowly. "Not in the slightest. You seem too strong and confident a woman to desire such false foolishness. I only think it unfair that you were treated with such little regard, both by your father and by the people who took you in. No child deserves that."

She smiled sadly. "And yet many receive so much worse, don't they? Especially in these modern times. I'm sure their tales would make us both weep."

He tilted his head in acquiescence. "Probably true."

"You see, Liam, we all have stories. We all have pasts." She leaned closer to him, touching his lips with just her fingertips. His eyes fluttered shut. "I am more interested in this moment."

He let his eyes open and smiled. "Suddenly, so am I."

"Should we go upstairs?" she asked.

But to her surprise, he shook his head and motioned to the settee in front of the fire. "Why not right here?"

She hesitated. "You wouldn't feel as if that was an intrusion?"

His lips thinned for a brief moment, but then he caught her hand and guided her to the couch. He urged her to sit and sank to his knees before her, wedging himself between her legs.

"Have I not made myself clear?" he asked.

She smiled. "Clearer by the moment, my lord. But I suppose you can never have enough clarity when it comes to these sorts of things."

For a moment, all his seriousness faded and he smiled. It was a very real expression and made him look a decade younger. She stared in stunned amazement and her heart swelled unexpectedly.

How she wished she could make him smile like that every day. Every night.

He began to shove at her skirts, tangling them around her calves, her thighs, and finally he lifted her hips and tucked her gown around her stomach so that he could look at her. And look he did.

She very rarely wore drawers and her chemises were quite short and flimsy affairs, which meant she was almost entirely naked except for a pair of dark stockings and her hand-stitched slippers with a little heel.

"Should I remove the rest?" she asked.

He stroked a hand over her stocking-clad calf. "Are these silk?" She nodded, and he grinned again. "Leave them on, though some time I will tie you to my bed with these."

She jolted at the image that created. She had never been restrained by a lover and until that moment, she wouldn't have thought she would want that. But now, the idea of being naked, tied to his bed, at his utter mercy...well, it was intoxicating.

She groaned, and his smile fell, replaced by something more heated and possessive.

"Open your legs a little further," he ordered.

She met his gaze and held it there as she slid down a fraction and opened her legs so that her pussy was revealed in the firelight.

"Better?" she asked with an innocent flutter of her eyelashes.

He groaned. "So much better. Now hold still. If you move, if you make a sound, I will stop what I'm doing."

"What *are* you doing?" she asked, made breathless by his forceful tone and the idea that he would stop the pleasure if she disobeyed.

He looked at her with an arched brow. "Don't make me stop before I start. Hush."

He lifted his weaker arm to cover her lips with a finger as he used his good hand to spread her lower lips and reveal her sex fully. She shivered at the touch of his hands on her flesh, already hot and tender from their shared glances and his unexpected control.

"I don't think I've ever seen such a delectable pussy," he growled, opening her wider and stroking a thumb across the sleek entrance he found hidden there. "So pink and wet. It looks good enough to eat."

She squirmed and couldn't help the moan that burst from her lips. No one had licked her in so long and she loved nothing more. From Liam's full lips and talent with kissing, she knew his mouth on her sex would be better than anything else.

He froze as she made the sound in her throat and looked up her body to shake his head. "So disobedient. Now I must punish you."

She didn't have time to question. He lightly brought his hand down against her open sex for a slap. She jolted as the tingle of pain met the wet heat of pleasure, and her body's reaction was utterly unexpected.

She almost came.

Her eyes went wide as she stared at him in disbelief. He was watching her very closely as he returned his hand to her sex, but this time to lightly cup and stroke the slit, brushing his fingers at her entrance with gentleness.

"You are very responsive," he murmured, almost more to himself than to her. "And so open to—"

He cut himself off with a shake of his head and dropped down so his face was very close to her sex. He brushed his rough cheek on her thigh and she jolted, but bit her lip so she wouldn't make a sound. He smiled and looked up at her.

"That's a girl. You can learn." He laughed. "Though I think you rather liked my punishment."

She bit her lip and closed her eyes, heat filling her cheeks. It was amazing how often this man made her blush. She, who had been in the business of pleasure for years. And yet with a few simple touches, with a few heated words, Liam could make her feel almost like a virgin again, untested and shy, uncertain and thrilling with anticipation of what he would do next.

He didn't disappoint. With a little moan of his own, he gently licked the smooth folds of her sex, spreading her open before he burrowed deeper and began to stroke his tongue along her slit in earnest.

She arched beneath him, clutching at the settee pillows as he sucked and licked her most tender flesh. Waves of pleasure began to rock over her and controlling her cries was increasingly difficult. But she didn't want him to stop. Even if the house burned down around them.

She'd had lovers, of course. Most assumed she was there as an instrument of *their* pleasure. If she reached release, then bully for her, but they weren't about to go out of their way to ensure she would come, let alone do something like this, which was only for her.

And yet Liam enthusiastically stroked his tongue along her, rolling it around and around her swollen, tingling clitoris until she thought her lip would bleed from biting it to control her moans and cries. He fingered her folds, pressing one to her opening and sliding it deep inside as he continued to pleasure her with his mouth.

He looked up at her as he tormented her, his green eyes holding her prisoner and increasing all the pleasure tenfold.

"Do you want to come?" he asked between licks.

She nodded, afraid to say yes for fear he would stop when she was on the edge and aching for release.

He smiled a little against her flesh. "Then come. Let me hear what you've held back."

She cried out a needy sound that echoed in the room around them and probably pierced the hall and other chambers, but she didn't care. Let the house know that he was giving her such pleasure. She doubted it would be a surprise to them.

She lifted her hips, reaching for more as he sucked her clitoris, laving it with his tongue as he gripped her backside with both hands and held her up for the feast.

Finally the pleasure was too much, the dam broke and she screamed his name on a broken breath. The tremors began, deep and harsh waves that broke over her and overwhelmed her. He licked her through them, keeping her coming and coming, keeping her pleasure at its peak as long as he could. And just when she didn't think she could bear it anymore, just when the ripples of her orgasm had her weak on the couch, unable to do anything but moan and whimper, he stripped off his trousers in a smooth motion, lifted her weak legs around his shoulders and speared her with his cock.

The pleasure, which had finally begun to ease its vise-like grip at her loins, immediately returned, and she lifted her hips to meet his hard thrusts. He pushed her back on the settee, his hands under her, lifting her, holding her steady as he swirled his hips, stroking deep inside her. Almost immediately, she saw the strain on his face, the need to spill his seed, to release the tension that had built between them for hours.

She reached between them and found her swollen clitoris. He met her gaze in surprise as she rubbed her hand over herself, bringing back impossible pleasure with only a few certain strokes. As she cried out again, he pulled himself from her body with a guttural, animal roar and spent.

He collapsed onto her, gathering her close, and she held him to her, stroking his thick hair, murmuring soft sounds of satisfaction and surrender.

Surrender. She knew what it meant now more than ever. And more than ever, she feared that she might do just that—surrender everything to this man. And when she left, she wouldn't be able to take back all she had given.

Chapter Nine

Liam drew a deep breath before he knocked on Violet's chamber door and pushed it open. She was seated at her dressing table, writing a letter. As he came in, she covered the page up with a blank sheet and turned to face him with a smile.

"Good afternoon," she said, rising.

He nodded, but he couldn't help but look toward what she had hidden. What was she writing that she didn't want him to see?

He pushed the thought away. She could have her secrets. He wasn't going to keep her anyway.

That was a reminder he kept giving to himself, especially in the few days since Violet's surrender in his office. Since that heated night, they had made love a dozen times and each time she gave him a little more control over her body. She was a quick study and allowed him things he had forgotten he wanted over the months of desolation and isolation since Matilda's death.

"Did you come here with a purpose?" She laughed, and the sound touched him far more deeply than he wished it would. "Or just to stare at me?"

He smiled despite his discomfort with how she continued to move him. "Staring at you is always a very good purpose in my mind, but that isn't why I'm here this afternoon."

She pretended disappointment with a playful pout, and he longed to suck her distended lip between his and bite down. He knew exactly how that action would end.

He shook his head. Somehow he had to find focus and put away this sexual animal which had been unleashed in him since her arrival.

"Malcolm and Olivia are taking a walk around the estate," he said. "I thought we might go with them. You could see something beyond the gardens."

She pushed to her feet and brought her hands together with a bright smile.

"That would be wonderful," she said. "I've been wanting to see more of this beautiful place. Although I'm not complaining about how my hours have been kept." She gave him a saucy wink that went straight to his cock and then added, "Let me just fetch a wrap and I'll be ready."

She moved to her wardrobe and took a thin wrap from within. He watched in fascination as she tied it around her shoulders. He was captivated by the way she moved, by the way she was so easy in her own body. If she ever worried about what or who she was, he didn't see it. Despite what was obviously a painful past, she didn't seem to be affected permanently by what she had been through.

He envied her that, though he had hesitated to ask her more about it. They were going so deep already...

"I'm ready now," she said, motioning for him to lead them.

She followed him from the room and down to where Mal and Olivia were standing in the foyer, heads close together in discussion. Liam frowned. He found his friend that way more and more in the last few days.

"Mal tells me there is a pretty picnic spot by a lake," Olivia said with a wide smile for the pair as they reached the foyer.

Liam nodded. "Yes. The servants will arrange a late snack there for us, if that is agreeable to you both."

The women exchanged a glance, and Violet smiled. "I never turn down a snack."

"Especially if it is from your kitchen, my lord," Olivia added as Mal opened the door and motioned them out.

They began to walk down a long path that led them away from the house and the drive and through the rolling hills of the small estate. As they walked, Violet looked around, her eyes wide and her smile very real.

"It is gorgeous," she said after they'd gone a quarter of a mile. "Truly, Liam."

"Thank you," he said with a sigh. "My father had many estates, but I must say this is one of my favorites."

She glanced at him from the corner of her eye. "Because of its proximity to Bath's healing waters?"

He looked at her. Was she finally asking him about his injuries? She had so avoided all that for so long, he was almost more willing to share what he normally withheld.

"I don't find the waters to be very helpful," he admitted. "You must have noticed I haven't returned to the baths since you found me there over a week ago."

She gave him a small, mischievous smile. "I thought you might have found yourself too busy to do so. I feel I have monopolized your time."

He laughed at her teasing. "Your company seemed to give me greater relief at any rate, so if you are monopolizing my time, it has its benefits beyond the obvious."

She looked at him more fully. "I'm glad, Liam. If I help at all, then I am very glad for that."

He shifted with discomfort at her focused words and stare. What did one say to it? What she offered was so temporary, it could change nothing. Even if it sometimes felt like it changed everything. That was an illusion brought on by physical pleasure.

He returned his gaze to the path and frowned. Mal and Olivia were several paces ahead of them. Olivia had wound her hand with Mal's and she rested her head on his shoulder as they walked.

It was more than evident that their two friends had begun their own intensely physical relationship. Liam hadn't thought much about it, really. It kept Mal and Olivia busy while he drowned himself in Violet. And his friend deserved his own pleasure, especially after putting up with Liam for so long.

But as he watched Olivia and Malcolm stroll up the path, for the first time he realized just how deep their relationship had gone. His friend wasn't one to show affection for a woman in such ways, not something sexual, but something that spoke of a deeper connection.

He found himself glancing again at Violet. Violet who did not hold his arm, let alone his hand. Violet who was staring straight ahead, obviously seeing exactly the same thing he was but not saying a word about it. Violet who kept their relationship as surface and physical as he did, a few dark confessions aside.

He scowled, though he couldn't think of a way to explain why he was suddenly annoyed at both the couple before him and the woman at his side. He didn't *want* to keep her.

And yet the fact that she didn't want to be kept burned him down deep, in places he thought had died after his accident. But they weren't dead after all. They were very much alive. And that was so terrifying he could hardly take it as he forced himself to remain calm and keep his feelings from his face.

Now if only it was so easy to keep whatever feelings these were from troubling his already troubled heart.

An hour later, Liam found himself increasingly irritated and, from Violet's side glances, she recognized that he was angry but couldn't understand why. And damn, neither could he. He just felt...out of sorts. And since he had spent years avoiding exactly these feelings, he wanted to lash out at everything and everyone around him.

Instead, he was sitting on a picnic blanket, watching Olivia, Malcolm and Violet chat like nothing in the world was wrong. Not that he was listening to a word they said, only stewing in his own thoughts.

A fact made very clear when Olivia took a sip of wine and said, "Will you ever return to London, my lord?"

He blinked, looking at her. "You are asking me?"

She drew back slightly. "Yes, Lord Windbury. We were talking about our return to the city in a fortnight or so. And I wondered if we might expect to see you and Malcolm there at some point in the future?"

She looked so damned hopeful, her eyes wide as she purposefully didn't look at his friend. But there were dreams in the brightness of her face. Worse, Mal didn't seem to be discouraging those dreams.

"I don't know," Liam forced himself to respond. "I haven't put much thought into where I will go after our time in Bath is finished. But I don't care for London. I swore to myself I wouldn't return there again."

He flinched as he thought of the circumstances under which he had made that vow. His words again revealed too much.

Olivia tilted her head, her gaze holding his. But unlike when Violet looked at him so closely, Liam felt the intrusion of Olivia's stare.

"I suppose I can appreciate that vow," Olivia continued. "After all, I understand there is little to bring you back to London. You have cut ties with your sister since her marriage, haven't you?"

Liam heard Violet suck in her breath in surprise, and Mal jerked his gaze toward Liam. But he couldn't do anything but stare at Olivia, feel her question sink into his skin.

"I do not speak about such things," he managed to choke out.

Olivia hesitated, but only for a moment. "Of course, after what you went through—"

Liam pushed to his feet and turned away from his friends, from Violet. He stood there, on the edge of the blanket, hands clenched at his sides as he tried to measure his breathing, tried to find a way to control himself when what he wanted to do was snap at Olivia in a way he knew would bring Malcolm to her rescue.

He felt a touch on his elbow and looked to find Violet at his side. She looked up at him, dark eyes tinged with concern, but also with interest. So the topic of his past wasn't as disinteresting to her as she pretended.

"Why don't we walk around the lake?" she asked, her voice soothing like she was talking to an injured animal or frightened child. "I think we could both use the exercise."

He looked at her, both wanting her at his side, and driven to push her away in order to protect himself, to protect her. Instead, he let her take his arm and led him away from Mal and Olivia.

In silence, they began a slow circle around the large lake. After a few moments they moved into a copse of trees that would put them out of the sightline of the other two and suddenly Liam felt as though he could breathe again. As he sucked in air, Violet shook her head.

"I'm sorry about Olivia," she said softly.

"She only says the same thing everyone else does," he said with a shake of his head.

"But it isn't her place to do so. And she knows it." Violet sighed with frustration. "Sometimes she just doesn't think."

Liam pursed his lips, his displeasure still bitter on his tongue after this very long and unsatisfying day.

"And what about you?" he bit out, his tone sharp.

She stopped in the path, released his arm and turned to look at him. "What do you mean?"

"You're playing a game with me."

All the color left her face in such a swift moment that he nearly reached out to steady her in case she would faint.

"A game," she repeated, her tone flat and drained of all emotion. "I don't understand you."

He shook his head. "You found me and seduced me, but you pretend you don't want to know anything about me. You never ask me about those things your friend addressed with me today."

"Is that what you want?" she asked, folding her arms. "Because I'm confused by your sudden anger at me. After all, you tell me how women stroke you and pretend to care, how they try to force confessions out of you about a painful past and you don't like it. But if I don't do the same, then I'm wrong?"

He folded his arms. When she put it that way, it made him sound like an ogre. But he couldn't help his frustration, even if he couldn't explain it in the slightest.

"I don't know," he admitted through clenched teeth.

Her expression softened a fraction and she reached out. He watched as she took his hand, quite like Olivia had done with Malcolm earlier in the day. She wore no gloves and her fingers were soft and warm in his hand.

"I have been open with you," she said softly. "More open than I have ever been with a man. And if I don't ask you about the past, Liam, it isn't because what has happened to you isn't of interest to me. If you want to tell me something, I'm here. I'm listening."

He turned his face, hearing his breath loud in the quiet around them. God damn, but he wanted to tell her everything. Everything he remembered and felt. He even wanted to tell her about his despair. About his emptiness. He wanted to pour himself over her and let her take, even for just a moment, the burden he had carried for years.

But to give her that burden meant to give her himself. If he did that, it couldn't be taken back. It couldn't be changed. And the future it implied wasn't one he was destined to have. He had made that decision long ago.

He shook his head.

"We should go back," he said softly, refusing to meet her gaze.

She was still and silent for a moment, then she released his hand. "Very well."

She turned her face, but he saw a flicker of hurt in her normally unreadable dark eyes. He found himself opening his mouth, moving to comfort her or to make those confessions once more, if only to please her.

Instead, he motioned for them to turn around. "If we walk around the lake it will take us half an hour at best. Why don't we return the way we came?"

She nodded. "Of course, whatever you'd like, Liam."

Though she said the right words and didn't seem to be pouting, Liam still watched her as they walked back to the lake and their blanket. He had hurt her, a fact that shocked him.

"Violet," he began, but she stopped, staring, and his attention was drawn away to whatever had caused the shocked look on her face.

He drew back as he saw it. There, on the blanket, the food pushed out of the way, were Mal and Olivia. Naked and making love with an abandon that was as enviable as it was utterly shocking.

Chapter Ten

Violet stared in astonishment as Mal moved into a seated position, dragging Olivia with him so that she wrapped her legs around his back. He lifted his hips, the two of them groaning in time with every thrust.

Violet sucked in a breath. She and Olivia had never involved each other in their sexual escapades, though more than one lover had asked them to do so. But seeing her friend be so thoroughly pleasured was a surprisingly arousing thing.

Beside her, Liam seemed as transfixed, and they stared together as Olivia threw back her head with a cry that signaled her release. Mal laid her on her back on the blanket and she cupped his firm, muscular backside as he began to drive into her in earnest. He exploded without withdrawing from her body and they cried out together before he cupped her face and kissed her deeply, passionately.

Seeing them fuck was one thing, but watching them kiss with such passion, with such intense and connected emotion, was what made Violet turn her face in embarrassment.

Liam took her hand and motioned for the path. She hurried after him, casting a few glances behind her as Olivia and Mal continued kissing like they couldn't get enough. Like they would never part if they had their choice.

And through her shock, through her titillation, she felt something else—jealousy.

But she couldn't feel that. That would mean she wanted that kind of intense connection with...with *someone*. She cast a glance at Liam, who was dragging her along with a grim expression.

"I'm sorry," she said. "I don't know what she was—"

She didn't get to say anything else. Liam interrupted her by grasping her by her shoulders and spinning her around until he pinned her on a large tree by the side of the path. His mouth came down, hungry and hot on hers, and she melted against him.

He wasn't angry, he wasn't shocked by what he saw...he, like her, was utterly aroused. She felt it in the desperation of his kiss. She felt it in the hard swell of his cock that nudged her stomach through their clothes.

"I want you," he growled, pulling away just enough to loosen his trouser fly and free his erection.

She gasped and reached for him, stroking her hand over him as he cupped her hips and lifted her, positioning her better to be taken. His mouth caught hers and he kissed her, rough and demanding, sucking her tongue and biting her lip. It was harsh and dark, and she clung to him as he lifted her skirts and shoved them aside to find her sex.

When he touched her, she shuddered, for she was already wet, already ready for what he would do. She rocked her hips toward him, demanding his taking, his claiming.

He obeyed her silent demands by pressing her sex open and lifting her into position to spear her in one, slick movement. She groaned as he filled her, stretching her and making her feel complete like no other man had ever done before. She dropped her face into the crook of his neck as he began to thrust, smelling his scent, feeling his pulse pound. She was lost.

She had been lost for a long time, but now she didn't fear it. She welcomed it, she welcomed him.

He rotated his hips, cupping her close, and the slow burn of pleasure between her legs began to increase. He hit her so perfectly, rubbing her clitoris with his pelvis even as his cock stroked her inside until she was panting with the sensation. She drew back to look into his eyes and he smiled at her, so slow and so sensual.

She exploded, digging her nails into the rough fabric of his jacket as her orgasm ripped through her, took her over, stole everything except her awareness of him. He was everything, *they* were everything, and she cried out his name over and over as her entire body went limp with satisfaction.

He groaned as his own release followed shortly after and lowered her to the ground as he pulled out to spend away from her. She watched him tuck himself back into place and frowned.

Olivia and Mal had taken no such care. They could have created a child that day. It was a consequence she was certain Olivia was aware of. But she and Liam...well, they would never look into the eyes of a baby who shared his smile and her dark hair.

She blinked as she smoothed her gown and brushed loose pieces of bark from the back of her dress.

Liam offered her his arm. "You have a strange expression on your face, Violet. I didn't hurt you, did I?" he asked as they continued on their way to the main house.

She flinched. "No, I was just having...it was an odd day and my thoughts are equally odd."

He laughed. "I don't know how you *couldn't* have odd thoughts. What we just did doesn't happen every day."

She smiled because she liked his lightness after an afternoon of watching him fight with darker emotions. But inside, she felt no joy at what he said. After all, he was correct that what they had done didn't happen every day.

And soon it wouldn't happen ever again. And that reality troubled her far more than it should have.

Violet sat in the library, her legs tucked beneath her, leaning over a side table as she stared at the letter she had been writing to Lady Rothcastle. This was not her first letter to the duchess since her arrival in Bath, but it was the most difficult so far, mostly because she didn't know how to explain what she had been doing. She didn't know how to explain *Liam* to a sister who feared for his well-being.

"I don't know anything anymore," she admitted out loud to herself as she rested her head on her hand with a long sigh.

She was about to give up trying to write the note when Olivia stepped into the library. With a frown, Violet folded the sheet of paper and tucked it away. She didn't stand, but merely stared at her friend evenly. It had been over an hour since she and Liam had discovered Olivia and Malcolm making love by the lake.

Olivia shook her head. "Where did you and Liam go? Why didn't you return?"

Violet pursed her lips, her frustration with her oldest and dearest friend growing.

"Before we discuss that, I want to talk about something else. Why did you try to talk to Liam about his sister? His past?"

Olivia stared at her without even a fraction of guilt or remorse over her intrusions. "Isn't that what you're here for? To wheedle the facts about those things out of him and report back?"

Violet shot to her feet and rushed around her friend to close the library door. "Mind your tone, Olivia, you could ruin everything!"

Her friend folded her arms. "What *everything*, Violet? We've been in Bath for over a week and as far as I can tell you've only confessed your own secrets to the man. Have you even tried to pry any out of him?"

"Not exactly. I told you, it's part of my plan," Violet retorted, but she turned her back so Olivia couldn't see her expression.

Olivia huffed out a breath. "Yes, I do recall the plan, but it only works if you begin to obtain information from your target."

Violet spun and shook her head. "He isn't my target—you make it sound as though I'm attacking him."

"No, you aren't. Though you should be." Olivia sighed. "I'm sorry you feel I interfered by asking Windbury a few questions, but I was trying to help you. Though I judge by your frustration with me that you didn't attempt to walk through the door I created by bringing up tender subjects."

Violet sat back down hard in the chair she had vacated. She rubbed a hand over her face.

"No," she admitted softly. "I didn't. I suppose I could have—I think he might have told me something had I pushed. But...I couldn't."

Now Olivia's expression softened considerably as she took a seat beside Violet and examined her closely. "Why?"

"Because I have been increasingly questioning what I'm doing here, Olivia. This man has been through so much and though his sister means well, what she and her husband have asked of me is a terrible violation. The guilt of that..." She cut herself off with a gasp of breath. "It eats at me."

Her friend nodded. "You are a good person, Violet. You always have been, much better than I. But you cannot forget your goals, my dear. You have more to think of than just yourself."

Violet dipped her head. "I know. I *know* that and I know that what I'm working for, *who* I'm working for, it's worth this. But I can't focus on the future too hard, Olivia. I don't want to be disappointed if it doesn't work out."

She was shocked when a single tear rolled down her cheek. She hadn't even realized she was crying, but there was such an ache in her chest. Such a familiar ache of regret and longing. But now she felt a similar ache when it came to Liam and what would ultimately be her betrayal of him.

"It will," Olivia said, squeezing her hand. "If you do this."

She nodded as she swiped the tear away with the back of her hand. "I know you're right."

Olivia smiled gently. "Now where *did* you and Liam go today?"

Violet lifted her eyebrows, happy for the change of subject. "Oh, you have questions about that? I'm surprised considering what you and Malcolm were doing while Liam and I took our walk."

Her friend's eyes grew wide and redness flooded her cheeks. "I—we—you—"

"Oh yes, we came back earlier than perhaps you thought we would, and we saw you," Violet confirmed with a shake of her head and a half-smile. "We saw *all* of you, actually."

Olivia was shocked silent for a moment, but then she shrugged with a nervous laugh. "We may have gotten a wee bit carried away. I was truly sorry I upset Liam and Mal decided to...comfort me."

"You did seem *comforted*," Violet teased. "If comforted is a euphemism for something else."

Olivia covered her face, but she was smiling beneath her hands. "I am embarrassed. I'm sure Lord Windbury dislikes me more than ever."

Violet flushed herself as she thought of Liam's passionate and utterly pleasurable reaction to that wicked scene.

"I wouldn't say that," she croaked. She shook off the memory. "But tell me about you and Malcolm."

Her friend lowered her hands and to Violet's surprise, Olivia's face was glowing with such happiness that Violet could hardly look at her.

"He's—he is—I—" Olivia stammered, trying to express herself as she clasped her hands before her heart.

Violet drew back, her eyes widening as the truth became so very clear, as clear as it had been when she saw them kiss after they made love.

"You care for him?"

Olivia swallowed and then she nodded slowly. "I do, Violet. I truly do."

Violet could hardly respond. Her friend, who had always dealt with men by keeping a level of playful detachment, was now admitting she had come to care about someone. And it could be nothing less than true, judging from her bright, joy-filled face.

"I can see that," Violet whispered. "Does he feel something for you in return?"

"It is hard to say, for men are so difficult to read when it comes to matters of the heart." Olivia paused. "But I have reason to hope he does care for me."

Violet's brow wrinkled. "What about the future? Will he become your protector?"

Olivia dropped her chin. "Perhaps that is all I should expect, considering my past."

"But you want more." Violet said it as a statement, not a question, for there was no doubt in her mind that it was true.

"I do." Olivia's voice was no more than a faint whisper.

Violet reached for her friend, patting her hand gently. "Then I wish for nothing less than you deserve, happiness and joy...and love."

Olivia lifted her face with a smile, and Violet returned it before she stepped away so that Olivia wouldn't see her true feelings. Yes, she did hope for everything good for her best friend. But just like when she'd seen the powerful physical and emotional connection between them outside earlier, she felt something else as well.

Jealousy.

And the reaction made her feel ugly and cruel in its wake. But worse, it forced her to realize that she too, longed for the same joy that she now saw on Olivia's face. The same joy she caught a brief glimpse of whenever she touched Liam.

But she wouldn't ever have it.

When Malcolm came into his office, Liam was still reeling from the day's events. But Malcolm seemed to have no patience for that as he slammed the door behind him and folded his arms.

"Do you know that you made Olivia cry?"

Liam closed the ledger he had been half-heartedly examining and glared at his friend. "How did I do that?"

"Getting up and stomping off like a child does that sometimes," his friend sneered. "And you have been cold to her since her arrival."

"She attempted to intrude upon—" he began.

To his surprise, Malcolm slammed a hand down on his desk. "She attempted to connect with you, as people sometimes do. You *do* remember how human beings treat each other, don't you?"

Liam pressed his lips together, fighting to control emotions that bubbled up within him and threatened to overflow. Anger, no rage, coursed through him. Malcolm was his friend, but he was also his employee and now Liam wanted to put him in his place more than anything.

Consequences be damned.

"Bollocks," Liam snapped. "She wasn't worrying over me as a friend and you know it. She was poking at a wound, hoping to see if it would bleed."

"She isn't like that," Mal snarled, his face reddening.

Liam recognized he should have stopped, but now that this had begun, he had to finish it. He wanted to yell at someone, to purge some of this emotion in the hopes he could keep it at bay for a while.

"How would you know? You've been fucking her for a week—you know nothing but her body."

Mal was purple now and he grasped Liam's collar and shook him. "Shut up, Windbury, you're talking about the woman I love."

Liam wrestled free and stumbled back, staring at his friend in utter disbelief. Mal didn't look much less shocked that he would say such a thing. But he also didn't look sorry.

"Love her?" Liam drew back in surprise. "What the hell are you talking about?"

Malcolm hesitated, as if he was letting the concept roll around in his head. Then he nodded. "I love her," he repeated and there was no hesitation. "And I want to marry her."

Liam froze. Mal was so certain and it put him to mind of himself, just two years before, when he had asked Matilda to marry him. He had been just as certain, just as filled with nervous joy and anticipation.

And it had ended with blood and pain and death.

"You idiot," he muttered, uncertain if he was directing the comment to himself or Mal, or perhaps both of them.

Mal's eyes narrowed. "You would prefer that I follow you around my whole life, trying to keep you from walking over a cliff or putting a bullet through your ear?"

Liam's eyes widened, but Mal didn't allow him to reply.

"Oh yes, I know your dark thoughts. I've seen them on your face when no one else was looking. And I have watched you, guarded you from yourself because I care for you, you pompous ass. Because I know you will allow no one else to intervene on your behalf. I don't regret any sacrifices I've made to be your friend and your confidante. But I do not agree to live in your misery forever, Liam."

"My *misery*," Liam repeated and his anger began to mount again. "I never asked you to."

"No, but you tend to drag everyone else into it with you. I have done my best to help you, to carry you through your suffering, but there comes a point when you must stand up and decide to live again. But you won't. You utterly refuse to do anything except stand with one foot in the grave, waiting to die alone. Well, that is your choice, my friend. But I think you are a god-awful fool to let the past destroy your future. And for what?"

Liam clenched his fists. "Have a care, Malcolm."

His friend ignored him and pressed on. "For what? Guilt? Or is it fear that stops you from moving on? I have no idea, but I do know that you dishonor Matilda's memory every time you lock away those who would love you. With every time you think of taking your own life, you murder her all over again."

Liam swung without thinking, and his fist hit Malcolm's face at full force. Mal staggered backward, hitting a chair so hard that the wood splintered and flew in all directions as he hit the floor.

Slowly, his friend got up, checking his jaw.

"Feel better?" he asked, eyes narrow but fists firmly at his sides.

Liam, on the other hand, still had his raised. "You won't fight?" he barked, spoiling to throw another punch even though guilt had begun to wind its way through him as he looked at Malcolm's already swelling eye.

"You haven't fought for two years—why should I?" his friend sneered. "Not fought for anything worthwhile, anyway. I just hope you remember how before you lose everything and anything of value in your life."

Malcolm turned, seemingly oblivious to the fact that Liam was still in a fighter's stance. That he could attack him and have Mal on the ground even with his weaknesses.

But he didn't. He simply watched as his friend left the room with his final words ringing around him, a better placed shot than any punch could have been.

Chapter Eleven

Violet paced her room, her mind racing. She hadn't seen Liam since they parted ways after the afternoon outing. He hadn't shown up at supper, he hadn't made himself known at all.

What she *had* seen was the dark bruise under Malcolm's eye. She had seen his hollow gaze as he said he didn't want to talk about how he got it. He and Olivia had skipped dessert and drinks and gone straight to what she assumed was Malcolm's room and whatever comfort Olivia could offer to the man she obviously loved.

There was a knock at her door and she turned, expecting Rachel to come in to offer assistance in readying herself for bed. But when the door opened, it was Liam standing on the other side.

He had often been disheveled, though always rakishly, handsomely so, but now his appearance was all the more wild. His hair stuck up at odd angles, tangled by fingers running through it in frustration. He hadn't shaved and dark whiskers slashed across his face and around the bright white of his scar. His clothing was wrinkled, crisp white shirt half-untucked and lacking cravat or jacket. He wasn't even wearing shoes.

He was gloriously, beautifully undone, and she nearly lost her breath when she looked at him in this state.

"Liam?" she breathed.

He stepped into the room and shut the door behind him wordlessly. When he lifted his good hand, she saw his knuckles were bruised and had a little dried blood on them. She rushed forward with a gasp and took his battered hand.

"What did you do?" she asked, urging him to sit down as she took a clean cloth from her dressing table and dipped it in the small basin of water there. She moved to kneel before him and gently washed his hand off as he stared at her.

"I hit Malcolm," he admitted, his face twisted with emotions he normally hid. Anger, heartbroken despair, regret...

She focused her attention on his hand so she wouldn't break down in tears at the look of him.

"I saw that," she whispered.

"Is he all right?" Liam asked, his tone broken.

She jerked her gaze to him. Malcolm Graham was this man's best friend, and sometimes his only anchor to reality and sanity. And from his broken expression, Liam knew he had jeopardized everything by doing something so foolish as swinging on him. Whatever they had fought over must have been desperate, indeed, to inspire such a reaction.

"Malcolm is fine," she reassured him. "A little bit of a black eye that will fade in a few days."

He was silent, the facts seeming to bring him no comfort at all. She continued to gently wash his hand and then pressed the cold cloth there to sooth whatever ache his bruised knuckles felt.

"But that couldn't have bruised you so deeply or cut your knuckles," she said, lifting her eyes to him.

He shook his head. "It didn't. I punched a wall as well," he admitted.

She sucked in a breath. "Why?"

He stared at his hand wordlessly for a long time before he spoke. "I was fighting a war with myself and Mal is the unfortunate casualty. As is our friendship, if I cannot repair it when next I see him."

She drew back. "A war over what?"

"You," he whispered. "Because I was trying to determine if I should come to you, Violet."

She rose to her feet slowly and stepped back. "Me? Why should I cause you pain or frustration or confusion?"

"Because you are you," he whispered, standing and moving to position himself a breath away from her. He tossed the cloth in his hand away and cupped her cheek gently. "And you make me want to say things I have kept to myself for years."

She shook her head, uncertain she understood what he meant.

"Do you know that I became involved with Matilda because of my sister?"

Violet's lips parted in surprise. He was going to tell her about the love of his life. He was going to tell her what she'd come here to hear. And despite the fact that this was part of her plan, she didn't think about the Rothcastles or about triumph. She wanted to know his heart. She wanted to know his pain.

And her desire for that knowledge had nothing to do with a bargain she had struck or an assignment she had taken.

"No," she said, "I didn't know."

He gave a nervous bark of laughter and sank into the chair again. She took the other and sat silently, waiting for whatever he would give.

"She doesn't know it either, I would wager. When our father died, she begged me to let go of our hatred of their family. She was so passionate about it, so filled with sadness and need that I determined I would try. I knew I could never overcome how much I hated Christian, but I thought perhaps I could come to some kind of understanding with Matilda that might make things...*better* somehow."

His face twisted as he relived memories she could only imagine were both beautiful and painful. "For almost two years, I became her...her friend."

Violet drew back. "I hadn't realized you were in contact with her for so long."

He nodded. "No one does—they all assume it was some kind of instant thing. But I truly came to know that girl, to see how good and decent she was, despite her family of origin. She had a marvelous sense of...fun. And I couldn't help but be drawn to it."

"How did you end up deciding to marry her?" Violet asked.

"One day I realized I loved her," he admitted. "That I couldn't live without her. It was as immediate as that. Like I had turned a corner and run straight into the truth. So I asked her to run away with me. She told me we could talk to her brother, that he had a reasonable side I refused to see. She begged me, but I wouldn't listen and said we would run away or nothing. She loved me, so she agreed."

Violet squeezed her eyes shut. "But Rothcastle discovered the plan."

"He had known I was involving myself with Matilda, which only fed his rage toward me. I believe he had spies watching us, so yes, he ran us down and then..." He stopped, his breath heavy. "Then the accident," he finished.

"Oh Liam," she whispered, taking both his hands.

"I still remember the way she looked when she took her last breath. She *smiled* at me. Somehow, even in death, she found light. And she told me and her brother to make amends. But I couldn't. Her loss was too profound to inspire anything in me but hate. Hate for him, hate for myself. I wanted us both dead."

Violet jerked at the loudness of his tone when he said the last sentence. Both of them dead. Meaning he would kill Rothcastle...but he wouldn't care if he died doing it. That he would, in fact, ensure that would happen.

Her heart began to pound. Did he still feel that way? Was this knowledge of his reckless disregard for his life what caused his sister so much fear for Liam and his cloudy future?

"What stopped you?" she asked, trying to maintain calm in the face of mounting terror in her soul.

"My injuries at first," he said. "I could hardly move after the accident."

She found herself looking at the scar on his face, thinking of the weakness on his side. How horrible those foggy days must have been.

"And then he took my sister," Liam continued, his voice breaking. "Took her away and took her from me by tricking her into loving him. I couldn't kill him. I could see by the way she looked at him that it would kill her too."

She stared at him, all his pain exposed like an open wound, his vulnerability a gift he gave without knowing what she would ultimately do with it. In that moment, she both hated herself and cared for him even more deeply.

"That's why you left London," she whispered.

He met her gaze and nodded. "I vowed I would never return. I did once, but it gave me no pleasure and only deepened the lacerations on my soul. Since then, I have kept that promise." He sighed. "*That* is the story I don't share, Violet. That is the truth of my past. Now that I have given it to you, I fully expect your pity."

He smiled, but she could see he meant those words.

"You could not be further from the truth. I do feel for you, for your loss and for your heartbreak," she said. "But my empathy is not pity, for I do not think you are pitiable. I do cherish your trust. I do think I could not possibly deserve it."

She shook her head, knowing full well she did *not*.

Liam caught her hand and pulled her to her feet to stand in front of him. Once again, he rose and caught her in his arms.

"You deserve much better, much more," he whispered. "I lose myself in you, somehow I forget...I forget all that the moment you look at me, kiss me. No one has been able to do that. No one but you. And I can only thank you like this."

He lowered his mouth to hers, kissing her gently. She wound her arms around his neck and tilted her head to grant him better access.

Liam had kissed her more times than she could count in the time they had spent as lovers. He had surprised her, captivated her and controlled her with that simple act of lips joining. But now, in this moment, when he tasted her with tenderness and gentleness, she felt something different.

She felt loved.

Oh, she knew it was an illusion. That he would not, could not give her his heart. More to the point, she couldn't give him hers. But that didn't matter. This was still an act of love, and she clung to it and to the promises that it made in the quiet of her bedroom.

She backed up until they reached her bed, unbuttoning his already loosened shirt. She did the same with her gown, both of them breathing hard as they did away with the clothing which separated them.

He stepped back as he pushed her gown and chemise away, leaving her naked before him. He said nothing, but just looked, a small smile tilting his lips. Then he unfastened his trousers.

Even though they had come together so many times, he had seen her and touched her before, now it felt different. New. She almost wanted to cover herself, to stop this feeling of being vulnerable, revealed.

If he recognized that feeling in her, he didn't allow her to pull away. He wrapped his arms around her and lowered her to the bed as he returned his mouth to hers. He lay on her, making no movement to breach her as he kissed her again and again, deeper and deeper. She was lost in it, in him and clung to him as waves of pleasure and surrender took her away from her hesitations and fears.

Took her to a place where only this moment mattered. Only he mattered. Only this mattered. For the moment, she could push everything else away.

He cupped her face, stroking his thumb against her cheek, smoothing her skin, and she shivered. How could he be so arousing and so comforting all at once?

She slid her hand over his chest, caressing lightly as she glided down his flat stomach, over his hip and finally she caught the hardness of his cock. He was already ready for her, despite how gently they came together.

And the feel of him, hard and big against her hand, her belly, made her body weep and open for him.

She spread her legs and he settled between them, offering no resistance when she positioned him at her entrance. He glided forward, slowly, reverently. They both sighed as each inch of him disappeared inside of her.

When he was fully seated, he stopped kissing her and looked down. They were eye-to-eye, close enough that she felt the gentle stirring of his breath against her cheek.

"Look at me," he whispered, gliding his hands into her hair.

She forced herself to do so and gasped as he began to move, slow and steady, circling his hips as he kept his gaze on her. She arched beneath him, but any time she tried to look away, too overcome by the intensity of their joining, he held her in place with a whispered reminder, "Don't look away, Violet. Don't look away."

"I can't," she moaned. "It's too much."

He shook his head. "It's not. Just hold on to me."

She forced herself to stay eye-to-eye with him as her orgasm built fast and heady. When she exploded, she clung to him, crying out his name as he kept moving, kept holding her, kept watching her so closely that she felt utterly and perhaps permanently joined.

Even when he withdrew, crying out as he poured out his seed in release, she knew they were bound in a way they never had been before. They had made love. That term was overused and false most of the time, but this was it.

And as he gathered her to him and she slipped into a warm and contented sleep, she wondered how in the world she could ever separate herself from him again.

For the first time in nearly two years, Liam felt free. He looked down at Violet, sleeping in his arms as she had been for nearly an hour, and he felt utterly and completely whole. He hadn't moved because he was both terrified and filled with joy and even... *hope* at this feeling.

When Matilda had breathed her last, he had been torn apart inside, and he had assumed he would never be right again. He had accepted that, but now...

Now things were different. Somehow things had changed and all with the arrival of an unexpected woman who seemed to understand him.

He shook his head as he slipped his arm from beneath her shoulders and sat up. She made a soft sound in her sleep but curled up without waking.

He watched her, relaxed in slumber. She seemed younger now, without her knowing smiles and come-hither stares that had tempted him so much since her first intrusion in his bath. He saw the vulnerability he had come to know she experienced, he saw the woman who had been abandoned and mistreated by people who were supposed to take care of her.

He got out of the bed. He was all wrapped up in these thoughts because the physical connection between them was so intense. Anything else he felt couldn't be real.

He pulled his trousers on swiftly and looked around the room. In the time she'd been here, she had taken over the space. Her robe lay draped across a chair, her toiletries were set along the dressing table. The air smelled of her perfume. Would he ever come in here and not think of her?

"Stop," he muttered to himself.

On the end table on the side of the bed there was a stack of blank sheets and a pen and ink. There was also a burning candle, which he moved to blow out before he left the room and hopefully left these thoughts behind him. But as he leaned down to douse the flame, he noticed that some of the sheets stacked there weren't blank. There was one with the beginnings of a letter that had been shoved amongst the other sheets to hide it.

Just as she had hidden whatever other missive she was writing the other day.

It was none of his business who she wrote to. To look at the paper would be a violation of her privacy. And yet he found himself reaching for the paper anyway and pulling it away from the others. He held it up to the light, first looking at her neat, feminine handwriting before he swallowed hard and read what she had written. It was only two lines, but he staggered slightly as he read them:

My Dearest Peter,

I am writing to tell you how much I miss you, but we'll be together soon.

She had obviously been interrupted, probably by him, before she could write more. But what he saw was more than enough.

There was another man in Violet's life. One she cared for.

The jealousy hit him hard, and he forced the paper beneath the others and walked out of the room and back across the hallway to his own chamber, leaving behind the rest of his clothes.

He shut his door and leaned against it, his heart pounding and his hands shaking as the line she had written bobbed in his head incessantly.

Peter.

She had never spoken that name to him, even in all of her confessions of secrets and pains which had bound them together. Who was he, this man who inspired Violet to yearn for him? Was he another lover? A past protector? Was what she said a manipulation for the sake of self-preservation, or did she mean what she had written?

The questions tore at him, and he strode across the room and poured a glass of water from a pitcher. He downed the entire thing before he sank down in a chair before the fire.

The strangest part of how he felt was that he wasn't angry with Violet. They had made no promises; in fact, Liam had been careful to tell her again and again that he would not, could not keep her in his life. Being with him offered her pleasure, but no security.

So how could he hate her for having another man in her life?

And yet he despised that man, that mysterious *Peter*, for the fact that Violet wanted him. He wondered how long she had known him, how they had met, what the circumstances had been in their apparent parting.

He wondered if she loved the other man, and he burned when he considered that possibility...because *he* cared for her.

He jolted as the thought entered his mind, but as much as he tried to deny it to himself, he couldn't. It was true. He did care for Violet.

That was far further than he had gone with a woman since Matilda. But feeling it now didn't seem odd or out of place. It simply...*was*.

But it wasn't love. No, he couldn't love Violet. That would go too far and be a betrayal of Matilda's memory.

Caring for Violet seemed less so. He didn't want her to go to this other man. He didn't want her to want to be with anyone but him.

And yet if he offered her no future, how could he expect her to do anything except leave his side in a few days and go to another man? This Peter person or someone else.

"Could I keep her?" he asked himself out loud, jolting at the sound of the question, even in his own voice.

Keep Violet. When he heard it, it didn't sound as mad as he thought it would. He could offer to be her lover, her protector. She would have security then, she would have a reason to stay with him. He knew she cared for him—their connection could not be pretended. And if she thought Liam would be there for her, perhaps she would push away this other man and whatever he offered her.

They could come to an arrangement. It could work. It had to work, otherwise he would see her leave his side and know she would go straight to someone else.

And suddenly that thought was unbearable.

Chapter Twelve

Malcolm had a small office in the servant area of the house where he completed his duties as estate manager for Liam. That was where Liam was waiting the next morning, pacing the room as he considered everything he had come here to say.

When the door opened, he pivoted and faced his friend. He flinched at the shadow of a bruise beneath Malcolm's left eye and at the way his friend's mouth turned down in an angry scowl when he saw him.

"What do you want?" Mal growled.

Liam stiffened, but refused to take on the "lord of the manor" attitude that would only make this situation worse. Mal deserved his outrage after yesterday; Liam didn't.

"I came here to tell you I'm sorry for my reaction to our conversation yesterday."

Mal's eyes were still narrowed. "Are you now?"

Liam pursed his lips. "Yes. I am. More than you will ever know. I'm especially sorry I punched you, which was entirely uncalled for."

His friend's arms were still folded. A bad sign. "It was," he agreed.

Liam swallowed. It seemed he would have to go further than a mere apology to make this up to Malcolm.

"You are my best friend," he said softly. "In truth, my only friend. I recognize the value of that, even though I rarely show it and probably less often express it. And I owed you a great deal more than I offered when we last met. I hope you'll accept my apology."

For a moment, Mal's face remained unreadable and Liam nearly went weak at the thought that he had irrevocably damaged his friendship, but then the other man smiled slightly.

"I would only just call it a punch," Mal said. "It hardly hurt."

Liam found himself grinning, part in relief and part in true humor. "I blackened your eye, didn't I?"

Mal shrugged as he motioned for Liam to sit across from him at the desk. "Ladies always like a man with battle scars."

"Olivia tended to you, then?" Liam teased as he took a seat.

Mal's smile grew, but there was something behind it that Liam couldn't quite place. "Indeed she did."

"So perhaps you should thank me."

Mal shrugged. "I'll keep that in mind, though I certainly hope we don't go around coming to blows regularly just to impress the women into comforting us."

Liam shook his head. "Amen to that."

"How are you, other than suffering from wracking guilt that obviously brought you down to my lair this early in the day?" Mal asked as he turned his attention to papers on his desk.

Despite the fact that his friend didn't look at him, Liam could feel Malcolm's regard fully focused on him. He shifted slightly. Now to move to the other topic he needed to discuss.

"I'm well, especially now that we have resolved our differences," he said. "But I do need to talk to you about something."

"Yes?" Mal continued to focus on his desk.

He swallowed hard before he said out loud what until now was only a wild notion in his own mind. "I-I am going to offer to become Violet's protector."

Slowly, Mal lifted his gaze to Liam's face. His eyebrows were raised and his eyes were wide, though he seemed to be able to contain his shock from the rest of his neutral expression.

"Her protector," he repeated, his tone noncommittal.

"Yes."

Liam nodded. Mal's shock was to be expected. After all, he had spent a long time expressing how he would never allow any woman near him for more than a night. This was a turn around, for certain.

But Malcolm didn't say any of those things. Instead, he asked a question that hit Liam in the gut harder than the punch he had aimed at Malcolm the night before.

"Will it be enough?"

Liam pushed up from the seat and paced across the room. That was the very question he had been avoiding thinking about, though he had been less than successful at the avoidance. It was the question that had continued to force itself into his mind and his dreams since last night.

"It is all I can give her," he said softly. "I have nothing else—the rest was buried with Matilda."

He turned to find Mal with an incredulous expression, but his friend didn't argue. "I know you well enough that I doubt this confession doesn't have a motive. What do you need me to do?"

"I haven't had a mistress in years," Liam admitted. "And even though I trust Violet, I still have things I want to know, to be certain of…"

He trailed off as that blasted letter invaded his mind again. He wasn't going to mention *Peter* to Mal. He didn't even want to speak the other man's name.

"Would you like a cursory investigation, some basic background?" his friend asked, saving him from expanding and perhaps revealing more than he wished to say.

"Exactly." Liam shifted despite his swift response. Investigating Violet behind her back seemed a bit like a betrayal, but it needed to be done. "How soon could you complete something like that, being in Bath?" he asked.

"If I send a missive to the solicitor this moment, I could have it reach London by tonight," Mal said, glancing at the clock. "With a day or two for investigation and a return message, I would say it would be no more than three to four days before you'd have the answers you'd like."

Liam tensed. Suddenly that seemed like a very long time to have to wait to forge a longer bond with Violet.

"Windbury?" Mal asked, tilting his head.

Liam blinked. "Yes, that is perfect. I can wait."

"Then I'll compose something and send it immediately." His friend drew a sheet of paper from his drawer and began scribbling.

"Excellent," Liam said, backing toward the door. "I'll see you at breakfast."

Mal nodded as he wrote, and Liam left him to his business, but as he walked away there was anxiety heavy in his chest that told him to forget the investigation. To take Violet, claim her and run before something happened that would change everything between them.

Violet stepped into the breakfast room, and her breath caught as she saw Liam already at the head of the table, a paper open beside him. He lifted his gaze from his reading and smiled.

"Good morning."

She moved in, almost without meaning to, and pressed a kiss to his cheek before she sat down at his left-hand side.

"I was surprised to wake and not find you with me," she said, hoping her voice would be calm and not reflect her true feelings at waking alone.

It had felt a bit like abandonment, though she pushed those silly thoughts away. She was here for a purpose. Connection wasn't that purpose.

His smile faltered slightly, but he recovered it swiftly.

"I apologize," he said. "Sometimes I have trouble sleeping and I didn't wish to wake you with my pacing, so I returned to my own chamber."

Violet nodded. It was a reasonable explanation and yet she felt somehow unsatisfied by it.

"Does your injury trouble you?" she asked, smiling as a servant poured her tea and motioned silently to the sideboard with its selection of breakfast items.

He hesitated. "Occasionally, yes, my shoulder does hurt at night. Or during the day. Or when I think too hard about playing cards..."

He smiled, and she supposed he meant for her to laugh at his last flippant statement, but she couldn't when she knew he remained in pain.

"Perhaps I could apply a poultice of some kind," she suggested. "Or we could experiment with warmed oils."

He locked eyes with her. "I certainly like the idea of experimenting with warmed oils with you."

Now she couldn't help but smile, nor could she seem to control how her body clenched with what could only be described as immediate, powerful desire. This man did this to her, he did so much more. And those reactions had nothing to do with any agreement she had made to come here and wheedle information from him.

They had gone far beyond that now. So far that her feelings scared her sometimes and she had to distance herself from them.

This time she did it with a sultry glance that made the sexual connection between them rise and any other connection fade.

"And what would you do with oils, my lord?"

He held her stare evenly, then leaned forward, covering her hands with his. His voice dropped.

"We would rub them on each other until our bodies were slick, until our skin slid against each other with no resistance. Then I would stroke you until your pussy was wet with excitement. Can you imagine being fucked while covered with oil, when there was nothing to stop the slide of your flesh against mine?"

She shifted in her chair, trying to find a position where her tingling pussy was more comfortable, but moving only made her arousal worse.

"That doesn't sound very therapeutic," she gasped.

He grinned. "You would be surprised. It sounds exactly like the kind of thing that would make a man forget his injuries and worries."

The door to the dining room opened behind them and Violet jolted as she was dragged back to reality by the entrance of Olivia and Malcolm. Violet had never been so sorry to see friends in her life, but she gently extracted her hands from Liam's and leaned back in her chair, hoping her flushed face and shaking body didn't reveal too much.

"Good morning," Olivia said, chipper as always as she took a place at the table. Her friend shot Violet a look that told her Olivia could sense her discomfort.

Violet fought to keep her arousal from her voice as she croaked out, "Olivia, Mal."

She did not look at Liam as the others got their food and servants appeared with more tea. She was so focused on her plate she almost didn't hear Olivia when she said, "And since Mal and Liam have a little business in town, I thought you and I could go to a few shops."

Violet blinked and looked up. "I'm sorry?"

Her friend tilted her head. "You and your woolgathering. You didn't hear anything?"

"I'm sorry, I was..." She smiled at Liam. "I was distracted by a topic Lord Windbury and I were discussing before you two entered. What is happening?"

Liam sat back, smug satisfaction on his handsome face as he said, "Mal and I do have a few things to do in Bath. And rather than abandoning you two here for the day, Olivia suggested we all go into town together and you two can see the shops."

Violet fought a strong urge to pout. She'd begun to picture her day with Liam very differently thanks to his wicked suggestions. Now she had to adjust.

"I wouldn't mind stopping at a few places," she agreed.

Olivia laughed. "Don't let your enthusiasm take you over! Great Lord, Violet, I've never known you to be so reluctant to shop."

Violet shook her head, her cheeks flushed as she felt Liam grinning at her. The man knew exactly why she hesitated and she could have slapped him...or more likely kissed him...for it.

Olivia popped her last bite of scone in her mouth and moaned with delight. Violet couldn't help but notice how Mal stiffened with the sound. So it seemed their friends were playing games too.

"I need to get my wrap and my reticule," Olivia said with a laugh. "Then I'm ready when you gentlemen are."

Violet nodded. "I'll need to take a few things as well."

The men pushed back from the table as the ladies stood.

"We'll meet in the foyer in twenty minutes?" Mal suggested.

Violet sent Liam one last look. "Certainly."

She and Olivia went upstairs, parting at the top to go to separate wings of the house. She opened her chamber door and looked around. The servants hadn't yet had time to tidy up since she left and so Liam's clothes were still scattered around the room, her bed remained rumpled, taunting her with memories.

She shivered and moved into the adjoining room to find her wrap. When she returned, Liam was standing against her now-shut bedroom door. She dropped the wrap and stared at him.

"What are you doing here?" she asked.

He crooked a finger and beckoned her toward him. "Come and find out."

She didn't hesitate, but flew to him, lifting her mouth to his. He spun her around as he kissed her and thrust her against the door as he began to lift her skirts.

She found the buttons of his trousers even with her eyes closed and loosened them, letting his pants slip down just enough to free his erection. He lifted her with his good arm and she wrapped her legs around him as he slid deep within her shaking, ready body.

She cried out as he began to thrust hard and fast. He hit that place deep inside of her that made her body shake, and after a few moments the well of pleasure began to overflow. She rotated her hips against him and cried out as her orgasm ricocheted through her. He didn't slow his tempo as he drove into her, just pressed her to the door harder as his breath came short. Finally, with a guttural cry, he set her aside and spent as he leaned on the door with his arm and panted.

Eventually he straightened up and looked at her with a grin that made her heart leap and her body clench.

"We should have breakfast together more often," he said, then kissed her on the mouth, pulled up his trousers and left her to stare after him as he exited the room.

And as she smoothed her skirt down over herself, her body still twitching from release, she couldn't help but laugh.

Even though she knew breakfasts together, sex against walls and the connection they had formed were all things that couldn't last.

Chapter Thirteen

Violet strolled through the streets of Bath, her arm linked with Olivia's as they peeked into shop windows. Normally her mind would have been on the pretty hat there or the hint of a discount there, but not today.

Today she could hardly enjoy the late spring air and the pleasurable company because her mind spun far too fast and hard about Liam.

"You are terrible," Olivia said, giving Violet's arm a light, playful slap.

Violet shook her thoughts away and turned toward her friend. "What have I done now?"

Olivia arched a brow. "I have asked you three questions in the past few minutes. Would you care to tell me what they were?"

Violet swallowed. "I—um—well—"

Olivia rolled her eyes. "First I asked you if you thought that fabric might be pretty for a gown. You said three."

Violet bit her lip. "Oh dear."

"Then I asked you if you had recently been to France. You said Tuesday."

"I'm sorry," Violet said with another shake of her head.

"And finally," her friend declared with a laugh, "I asked you if you would like sugar with your fish and you declared you liked nothing more."

Violet motioned toward a little garden that was in the square where they strolled. "There is a bench there. Perhaps we should sit and I will gather myself."

Olivia led her to the place she indicated and the two women sat together. Her friend folded her arms.

"When you made this arrangement of yours and invited me to come here with you, I thought certain you would have gathered your information within a week and be finished. But the longer we stay here, the more I see you with Lord Windbury, the more concerned I become. Violet, you are not yourself."

Violet sighed. Perhaps what Olivia said was true, but she had never felt more like herself than when she was with Liam. There were times she forgot all her manipulations, her important goals, her seductive wiles and lost herself in the man and all he offered.

In fact, that happened more often than not.

"Are you woolgathering again?" Olivia asked with a put-upon sigh.

"No, no," Violet reassured her. "I am simply pondering what you have said."

"And what is your response?" her friend asked.

Violet dipped her head. "I don't know. The fact is that I thought Liam would be one thing and he is entirely another. When I am with him, there is nothing pretended about it. And I haven't felt that way with a lover for years. So many years that I cannot even recall it."

Olivia's cheeks grew pink.

"I can understand that," she whispered. Then she cleared her throat. "But what have you *learned*? Surely Windbury must have told you something worth writing to the Rothcastles about."

Violet hesitated. At any other time, with any other man, she would have told her friend everything. But with Liam, that seemed so very wrong.

"I-I have written letters to Lady Rothcastle. In fact, I have written her a letter every other day, reporting to her what he is doing, how he is. And I have reported what I've learned."

Though she had hesitated greatly and even left a few facts out when she felt they were too raw and personal, even for a beloved sister.

Olivia took her hand, her face gentle with understanding. "Then if you have completed your task, why do you stay?"

Violet shifted. Perhaps Olivia was correct and she had done enough to make the Rothcastles happy. And perhaps it was time to abandon her part of the deal. And yet she couldn't walk away.

"You wish me to make some kind of confession," she whispered, refusing to meet Olivia's eyes.

"No, I simply wish to understand," Olivia said. "Though I think there must be a confession to be made judging from your demeanor."

"There is none, I assure you," she said, perhaps too quickly and strenuously. But she had to make Olivia stop prying, if only to keep her own thoughts from roaming.

Olivia touched her cheek. "If you don't want to tell me anything, I won't force a confidence. I only see you struggling and I hate to see that. Especially when this will all be over soon."

Violet stiffened. "Why do you say that? Did Malcolm tell you something?"

"No," Olivia responded slowly. "But it is a foregone conclusion. After all, Windbury will leave Bath in a short time, and then the affair will be over. Unless you have made some other arrangement."

Violet shook her head. "No."

"Would you if he asked?"

Her body clenched. She already knew that answer, even though it stung.

"I have made promises," she whispered. "I must keep them. So even though I doubt Liam has any thought of keeping me, if he wished to, I would have no choice but to refuse him."

Olivia nodded, but there was a knowing expression in her eyes that made Violet flinch.

"Well, then it is better it is almost over." Her friend straightened up. "And there are Mal and Windbury now."

Violet stared in the direction her friend indicated and sure enough the two men stood together, Liam lean, Mal muscular. Liam lifted a hand to wave and Olivia returned the gesture.

But Violet didn't. Because suddenly the wave felt like it would be one of goodbye. And her heart broke when she considered that.

Even though it had always been a certainty.

Liam watched Violet from across the carriage as they made their way back to his estate after a day in town. There was something different about her at present. A distance in her eyes as she stared out the carriage window into the gathering darkness outside.

Malcolm and Olivia seemed immune to her change in mood. They continued to talk and laugh with each other as Olivia showed his friend a hat she had bought earlier in the day.

But Liam couldn't contribute to their gaiety. Not until he understood what was troubling Violet. Now that he knew he would possibly become her protector, her comfort and ease was more important to him than ever.

The carriage came to a stop at the house, and Malcolm stepped down and helped Olivia from the rig. Violet glanced toward the door and Liam repeated Malcolm's action. Once they were standing on the drive, he leaned over to his friend.

"Violet and I are going to go upstairs. I'm sure you and Olivia can find an amusement for yourselves."

Mal arched a brow in Olivia's direction. "I'm sure."

Violet looked at him in surprise, but she didn't resist when he placed her hand in the crook of his good arm and led her into the house and up the stairs. He took her into his room, then stepped out to speak to a servant in the hallway.

"I would like the tub in my adjoining room filled," he said, softly enough that Violet wouldn't be able to hear.

The footman bowed. "Of course. Right away."

The other man scurried off and Liam rejoined Violet, shutting the door behind him.

"Have I done something to displease you?" she asked, shuffling with discomfort.

He shook his head. "Not at all. Why would you think you had?"

She shrugged. "Your expression is very grave."

"As was yours in the carriage." He moved toward her and touched her arm. Her olive skin was soft, irresistible. "Violet, I'm actually worried about you."

Her brow furrowed. "About me?"

The way she said it made his heart drop. Of course she didn't expect anyone to worry about her.

"Your whole life it seems you have been tasked to give to others." He leaned down to press a gentle kiss against her smooth forehead. "And now you do not know what to expect when someone wants to tend to your needs."

116

She swallowed. "You tend to my needs just fine, my lord," she whispered, twitching her hips in an attempt at seduction.

His body reacted, but he refused to surrender to the call. She was trying to push him away through sex. Why hadn't he ever recognized that before?

Aside from the obvious reasons, of course.

"I'm not talking about the needs of your flesh," he said, moving away to pour her a glass of wine from the side bar by the fire. "I'm talking about your *needs*."

Her discomfort only seemed to increase as she took the wine he held out toward her. She downed half of it in one sip but refused to meet his eyes as she released a nervous laugh.

"Oh Liam, you misunderstand. I don't have any needs unfulfilled or—"

"You have trusted me with part of your story," he interrupted and tilted his head to try to find the stare she so skillfully withheld. "Can you not trust me with something more?"

She didn't speak for what seemed like forever.

"I don't know," she finally whispered, and he realized that was the most honest statement she had ever made to him.

He saw the fear in her stare, the longing, and a desperation that made him both sad and nervous.

He drew her closer, holding her free hand between his.

"What troubled you today in Bath?" he asked. "I left you a happy, laughing woman chattering about shopping with her friend. I returned and you were withdrawn."

He thought of the letter he had seen, the one to Peter. Could *he* be the cause of her concerns? But he didn't ask. He feared the answer too deeply.

"Liam," she whispered, covering his hand with hers. "You really needn't worry yourself."

He pressed his lips together. "Do you not wish to share the truth or just not share the truth with me?"

Her eyes widened. "I have confided more in you than I have in any other person," she said. "I promise it isn't a lack of faith in you that keeps me silent. I had a great deal on my mind today. I have concerns about Olivia and Mal and the relationship they are developing, I have been thinking about London and I sometimes reflect upon what I've told you and wonder if I've gone too far."

"I wouldn't betray you," he promised swiftly.

Her cheeks paled, and she pulled away slowly. "Yes. I'm certain you wouldn't."

Liam frowned. "And this is truly all that troubles you?"

She hesitated, but when she turned back, she nodded. "Yes."

He had his doubts, but he shoved them aside, determined not to withhold his faith after all she had revealed since she came to Bath.

"I wish I could ease your troubles," he said, smoothing a lock of hair away from her face with the back of his hand. Her eyes fluttered shut at the touch and she sighed almost imperceptibly.

"You do," she vowed. "Liam, you do. You make me—well, you make me forget everything else when I'm with you. Even though I shouldn't."

"Why?" he pressed.

"Because if I don't take care of myself, no one else will," she burst out. The moment she said the words, her eyes widened. "I didn't mean that."

He let his fingers caress her face. "It has always been that way for you, I know. You had to be strong when your mother died, when your father passed you off to people who resented your presence and didn't care for you. Even when he came back into your life and pretended to do something for you, it was another way to help himself. I cannot imagine what you felt after you were assaulted and he insisted you marry your attacker, nor how you have guarded your heart since becoming a mistress. But I am not any of the people who have mistreated you, Violet."

She blinked, tears welling in her eyes. "I know that. I wish you were."

He tilted his head at that surprising statement. "Why?"

"Then this would be easier," she gasped.

He spread his fingers open on her cheek and gently kissed her. It wasn't a kiss meant to inspire passion, but to bring her close. To comfort her. To give the tenderness that had been withheld from her for so long. He couldn't yet offer his protection to her with words, but he hoped to offer that and more with his kiss.

She sighed as they parted, and he drew her toward the connecting chamber where the bath he had ordered was likely waiting for them.

As he opened the door and drew her inside, he said, "I want to make this easier."

She stared at the steaming tub, the candles that flickered all around it in a romantic scene. Slowly she turned toward him.

"This is...this is for me?"

He nodded. "It's all for you. Not as a seduction, though I wouldn't doubt we'll end the night making love. But I do this because you need it. You need me. And I want to be there for you. Now."

She bent her head, and her face was all surrender. Almost against her will surrender. She nodded.

"I need you, Liam. More than you will ever understand."

Then she stripped the front of her gown open and undressed for the bath they would share. And for the first time, Liam was more concerned with how to best tend to her heart than her body. He would do this tonight. And he would not regret it.

Violet stroked her hand across Liam's bare chest as the steaming water sloshed around them. They had been in the bath together a quarter of an hour and he hadn't made any move to seduce her.

She had no idea how to respond to that. To men, she had spent her life as nothing more than a body to own, to barter with, to take. She had adjusted to accept that fact and eventually even use it to her advantage.

But now she felt lost. And more than lost, she felt exposed. She had made a confession to him in his bedroom that went far further than any other. She had made it without a thought to quid pro quo.

She had talked to him because of his kindness and his gentleness and his promise to protect her that she longed to believe even though it couldn't be true. It *wouldn't* be true when and if the facts about why she was here were exposed.

And yet here she still lay, his arms wrapped around her, cradling her as they shared the intimacy of silence.

Her mind turned again and again back to Olivia's earlier statement that all this would be over soon. It was true, and it left her with anxiety and concerns.

She knew things about Liam, she knew thoughts that troubled her. Could she walk away without doing everything she could to address that?

She rolled over in the water so that she lay on his chest facing him. He smiled at her and shook his head as she straddled his hips. She felt his cock stir at the movement.

"You do test a man," he chuckled.

She smiled in return, despite her troubling thoughts. "Oh come, Liam, you are strong."

His eyebrows lifted. "No man would be strong enough to resist you."

She laughed but found herself looking first at the scar that slashed down the length of his face and the one on his weaker shoulder. Slowly, she reached out to caress his arm. Despite the injury, she still felt muscle there beneath the skin. Her hand touched his other arm, though, and it was obviously much more powerful.

"You compensated for your injury well," she said, gliding a fingertip down his scar lightly.

In the past, her intrusion on this subject had seemed to make him uncomfortable, but now he merely watched her touch him with an unreadable expression.

"Since the accident, I have learned that the human body is an amazing thing. It does adjust itself."

"And you helped it," she pressed.

He nodded slowly. "I admit, once I was well enough to move freely, all I wanted to do was forget everything and anything. Part of that was working with my body. Soon I found myself capable of lifting something heavy with one arm rather than two. Now it is a habit."

"You can certainly lift me without any trouble," she mused softly, thinking of how many times he had done just that while they were making love. "But do you think you will build up your injured arm at some point?"

He hesitated. "I will work past the pain someday, I'm sure."

His voice was soft and she realized they were no longer talking about simple physical pain. The loss of the use of his left arm was tied to the loss of Matilda for him. And that led her very easily to her next point of inquiry.

"I know the pain caused by your accident was great," she said, treading carefully. "And I have been thinking a great deal about what you told me in regards to your reaction to that pain."

His expression was unreadable as he nodded. "Mmmm."

She swallowed. "Thinking about your statement about wanting to...to hurt yourself after Matilda's death."

Once again, he was unreadable, though his gaze slid away from hers. "Yes."

She touched his chin, drawing him back to focus on her, and asked the question that terrified her more than any other she had ever asked.

"Liam, you don't still have those terrible thoughts, do you?"

Chapter Fourteen

Silence stretched between them, and Violet fought hard against tears that welled in her eyes the longer it took for Liam to respond. She watched his face, and the neutral expression was gone. He was struggling with memory and loss, sorrow and pain. All things Violet wished to strike from his heart and mind forever.

"Liam?" she whispered, her voice breaking. "Please."

He reached up to touch her cheek, stroking a wet thumb along her jawline and her lip.

"I don't know," he finally admitted.

Her body clenched at that answer, which wasn't the worst one he could have given, but was far from the best.

"What does that mean?" she asked, voice trembling.

He bent his head. "Violet, I haven't thought about or been able to picture a future for so long. The one I had in mind was snatched from me when Matilda died." He stopped talking for a moment, as if to gather himself. "But I can tell you that right now... Right now I don't wish for death. I don't court it or plan it."

She supposed that was as much comfort as she might expect, but it wasn't enough. It wasn't nearly enough. She cupped his face and forced him to look at her.

"Promise me you won't ever desire such an end again."

He didn't respond, but leaned forward and pressed his lips to hers. She allowed the caress, but her heart broke and she couldn't stop the tears that began to stream down her face.

She broke the kiss and said, "Liam, promise me!"

He swiped at her tears with his hand and sighed. "I can tell you that you make those thoughts go away. You make all the ugliness in my life go away. If that has given me meaning back to what had become a meaningless life, than I suppose you could say you have saved me. And you can walk away if you like and know that you gave me that."

She stared at him, taken aback by this powerful confession. And taken aback by something else, as well.

As she stared at him, moved by his words, touched by the way he looked at her...she realized she was in love with this man.

She stilled, still straddling him, her hands cradling his handsome face, and his eyes locked with hers. She loved him. With everything good and hopeful left in her, with all the naivety she had been able to save even through years where life had stolen everything and anything that mattered. She hadn't realized it, but some part of her hopes and dreams had remained, slumbering until the right man came along to wake them.

A part of her had been waiting for Liam all her life.

She had been lucky enough to find him, and her heart soared in that moment, filling with enough love that she felt like she could fly.

But just as quickly, the air left her lungs and despair replaced joy.

She couldn't be with him. Not only were their circumstances vastly desperate, not only had he vowed he would not make a deeper connection with her...but she was a liar of the worst kind. When—not if, but *when*—he discovered all she had done, he would despise her to his very core, and rightly so.

More to the point, she had somewhere else to be when this was over. She had another life to lead and it couldn't include Liam.

So her love, so joyful and warm and true, was destined to break her heart. And yet she didn't regret it, even as she hovered between laughter and tears. She had never expected to love someone, and she cherished it now, despite the fleeting nature of their relationship. And she would cherish it always, even long after Liam had come to regret her, or had even forgotten her entirely.

"You have suddenly become very intense in your expression," Liam said, laughing low.

She smiled, hoping the gentler look would cover some of the intensity of her newfound feelings.

"I suppose I am just beginning to want something a bit more than a chaste sharing of this tub," she teased, shifting over him.

He held her gaze for a moment, exploring her face with focus to his expression. It felt like he was reading her, analyzing her and for a terrifying moment she feared he would see the feelings she now held in her heart.

But finally his arms came around her, he cupped her backside and drew her firmly against what was most definitely a growing erection.

"Whatever the lady desires," he murmured before he slipped a hand into her hair and dragged her mouth to his for a deep, penetrating kiss.

She melted against him, lost in how powerful their physical connection was. Now merged with the far deeper feelings she could finally acknowledge, the kiss meant so much more and her body reacted accordingly. There was a fire that began where their lips met, and slowly it took her over, spreading down through her chest, her stomach, settling in her loins. She had never wanted him more. She had never wanted any man more.

It was almost as if she had gone back in time, before she had ever been touched, before she had become jaded to passion. It was all new again, exciting and heated and powerful.

And she was going to enjoy every moment, even if she knew it would end sooner than later.

She shifted as they continued to kiss, rising up slightly to position her weeping, aching body over his. She shivered as she slowly took him inside and he broke the kiss with a grunting moan.

"We fit so perfectly," he murmured, resting his face against her neck so that his words were muffled as he kissed the slope of her skin.

She squeezed her eyes shut so he wouldn't see how deeply moved she was by his statement. When he lifted his hips to thrust deeper inside of her, she was transported away from her emotions and down into a spiraling freefall of pleasure.

She met him thrust for thrust, crying out, not holding back, giving with her body what she could never reveal with her voice. She poured her love into him as she kissed him, stroked over him, rode him toward mutual orgasm. Her pleasure built and she reveled in it, reveled in how easily his touch could make her weak and trembling. Reveled in how passionate their lovemaking was.

She fought to keep her release at bay for as long as she could, but pleasure mobbed her, washed over her, and she was lost to it. As she arched against him, her body quivering and cries of pure desire pouring from her parted lips, she saw him lose control. The veins in his neck pulsed, his face flushed and he cried out her name.

She waited for him to gently set her aside to spend his seed, but he didn't. Instead, he thrust up hard within her, and she felt him spend deep inside of her body.

For a moment, panic overtook her. If she became pregnant...

He gathered her close to him, keeping their bodies connected as he pressed soft kisses to her cheek and hair.

Calm washed over her in that moment. What he had done was something intimate, something that bound them. The chances of her bearing a child at this point in her current cycle were slim. And now she had more memories to tuck away and keep when her time with Liam was over.

And as she wrapped her arms around him, she realized how important those memories would soon be. She would have to make as many as she could as swiftly as she could.

Liam looked across the table and smiled as he watched Violet read the paper while she slowly lifted a piece of toasted bread to her lips. After their night of making love in the tub, a night where he had finally allowed himself to feel bound to her in a way he had avoided for years, they had spent two blissful days together. Not just making love, but spending time together. They had laughed, they had shared parts of themselves.

This breakfast now felt so utterly...normal. And once he offered to be her protector, he would have this time with her every day for as long as they both desired it.

That future suddenly felt very comfortable and happy after so many years of darkness.

"Where is Mal this morning?" Violet asked without lifting her eyes from her reading.

A tiny twinge of guilt filled him at the question. "He—he is in town. He is finishing an errand for me."

He didn't elaborate, for he didn't know how to tell her that the errand involved collecting final information about her. Somehow he doubted she would appreciate that.

"And what about Olivia?" he asked as a way to change the subject.

She barked out a laugh and pushed the paper aside to smile at him. "Olivia? Up before noon? She wouldn't dream of it."

He laughed with her. "Perhaps she has the right idea of it. We could still be abed, you know."

He leaned closer and kissed her, lingering on the sweetness of her tea-flavored lips. When they parted, she actually blushed, and he grinned at the sight of such an innocent and unpracticed reaction.

She returned to her reading for a moment, but he could tell she no longer concentrated. She glanced up at him a second time.

"You know, I have been thinking about our talks over the past few days."

He arched a brow. "If what you recall most from our time together are our conversations, I must not be as irresistible as you have led me to believe."

She reached out to lightly slap his arm and laughed. "You idiot! You know you are irresistible. I think my utter surrender—multiple times!—and screaming pleasure must prove that to you."

He caught her hand as she pulled it away and drew it to his lips. "The feeling is mutual."

She bit her lip and her voice shook as she continued, "All that aside, I only meant that some of our recent conversations have come back to me. I wanted to ask you a question, but I'm not certain it is one you will want to answer."

He released her hand and looked at his plate for a moment. Considering their recent deep conversations had included talk of his thoughts of suicide and ponderings on loss, he wasn't certain he would want to answer either.

He cleared his throat. "I have been more open with you than perhaps anyone else in my life," he said. "You may ask me what you wish, though I can't promise that I will enjoy the question."

"I've talked to you about my thoughts of returning to London," she began, her tone halting. "Will you ever go back there yourself?"

He froze at the question, which was certainly unexpected. When he didn't immediately answer, she continued.

"I know you told me that you wouldn't, but I wonder if your mind might have changed given recent...events."

He squeezed his eyes shut, measuring his breathing as he tried to find an answer in the muddled emotions of his mind.

"There are memories there, Violet. But it is more than that which keeps me from London. There are unresolved issues."

She hesitated. "You mean between you and your sister. Because of her marriage?"

Liam scrubbed a hand over his face as images bombarded his mind. Images of Ava with Rothcastle.

"Yes," he admitted in a breaking voice. "Seeing her with that man—"

He broke off because he wasn't certain he could properly express the emotions that plagued him when he considered that tender subject.

"It is difficult," she finished for him. "Because of your hate. Your anger."

He looked at her finally, her gaze even and nonjudgmental.

"It isn't even anger anymore," he choked out, realizing the truth of his words even as he said them. "It is sadness. I feel sadness for Ava...for the love we once shared and have now lost forever."

Violet's brow wrinkled. "Forever? Must it be forever lost? Your sister lives, and I would wager she would want to repair your relationship. Couldn't you bridge the gap?"

He pushed to his feet and paced away from her to stare out the window over the rolling green hills. "You don't know what you are asking me."

She was silent for a long while, though he wasn't certain if that was because of her own discomfort with the topic or because she was allowing him to gather his thoughts. Perhaps a bit of both.

Only when he heard her chair scrape across the floor did he turn to look at her again. Her hands were folded before her, but her expression was anything but comfortable. It seemed she struggled with this discussion as deeply as he did.

"Liam, I will go back there, probably soon," she whispered. "I ask you not to cause you pain, but I wonder if I might see you again in the city."

He stared at her. She had no idea of his plans for their future and yet she reached out to him, bearing her soul by asking him if they would remain connected. Judging by her expression, it was a difficult question to ask.

Malcolm would be back, probably within the hour, with all the information he would need to have about her past, but in that moment, looking at her lovely face, Liam didn't care about any secrets his friend might have uncovered. They could overcome them all, couldn't they?

"Violet," he said, moving toward her to take both her hands in his. Hers were shaking as she stared up at him, expression unreadable. "I want to talk to you about that very subject. I've been waiting, but I can't wait anymore. I've already taken too long. I want to act. I need to act."

Her brow wrinkled. "Liam?"

"Violet, I don't want us to hope for some kind of chance encounter in London. In fact, I don't want you to go back there at all. At least, not alone."

She shook her head, her eyes going wide. "I—what do you mean?"

He lifted her hands, drawing her closer as he pressed them to his heart. "Violet, I want you to stay with me. To go where I go, to sleep with me and wake with me and continue to heal me with every smile, with every laugh, with every touch. I want to be your protector."

She swallowed and slowly withdrew her hands from his.

"You want to be my protector," she repeated.

He had been waiting to say that very thing for days, but now that he had, the words felt...empty somehow, especially when they were repeated back to him.

"Yes," he said, trying to find a better way to put the offer so that it felt right. "I want you to come with me to my estates. I want you to be with me wherever I go. Violet, will you be my mistress?"

She stared at him, eyes wide, cheeks pale. Then, to his shock, she slowly shook her head in the negative.

"No, Liam. I-I can't."

Chapter Fifteen

For one horribly and beautifully unguarded moment, Violet saw the depth of Liam's pain at her refusal of his proposition. There was no pleasure in causing him that pain, but seeing it made her question everything.

Couldn't she take his offer?

Couldn't she throw all else to the wind, everything she had done and was meant to do, and simply give herself to him until he tired of her?

If she loved him, couldn't she accept and take the consequences of that action when they came to visit her in a week or a month or a year?

She let herself ask that question, but then the answer came clear.

She could not.

"You don't want to be my mistress?" he asked, lifting his chin with all the arrogance of the highest lord of the realm.

"Want has nothing to do with it," she whispered, reaching out to take his hand. She was pleased when he allowed it. Even more pleased when he let her lead him back to the settee. They sat together. "Allow me to explain."

He nodded, a jerking motion he made only once.

She drew in a breath. All her honesty up until last night had been part of a manipulation, a seduction. But what she was about to say, to do...it was everything to her.

"I haven't told you the whole story of when my father arranged my marriage," she whispered, forcing herself to look Liam straight in the face even when she wanted to turn away.

"You said he arranged a marriage, that the son of your would-be fiancé feared a young bride would cause a dilution of his inheritance so he...assaulted you. That your father demanded you marry the bastard."

She nodded, trying not to flinch at the recitation of the most painful time of her life.

"He wanted me to marry the son of my fiancé because my virginity was compromised," she whispered. "But it was more than that. There were other...*consequences* to what happened."

He sat perfectly still for a moment and the color drained from his cheeks. "A child?"

She nodded slowly. "Yes," she gasped out. "I became pregnant. And when I refused to marry my attacker, my father cast me into the street, completing the abandonment that had begun years before. I was lost, utterly bereft, and that was when I met Olivia. She took me in, explained her trade to me. Took care of me until my child was born."

Liam shook his head. "A boy or a girl?"

She stared at him. Here was her deepest secret, and Liam wanted to know more about her child. No wonder she had come to love him, for he was unlike any man she had ever met in her life.

"A boy," she whispered, thinking of that boy in ways she rarely allowed herself to do. "I named him Peter."

Liam straightened. "Peter? *Peter* is your son?"

She nodded slowly. "Yes. Why?"

He stared at her, his eyes wide, and then shook his head even as a wide grin broke over his face.

"Nothing. No reason. Please, tell me more. What happened to him?"

"I had nothing except the kindness of my friend with which to support my baby," she explained. "But I was beginning to see how Olivia could use her assets to make a life for herself. I made the most difficult decision of my life. Together we found a kind family in the North in Romwell who took my child and raised him. They are good people, I made sure of that. They love him and do not judge me. He knows me, we write letters, and I visit him whenever I have the means to do so."

She realized she was weeping only when Liam produced a handkerchief and held it out to her. She took it and wiped away the tears that had begun to fall down her cheeks.

"You love him," Liam said softly.

She nodded. "With everything that is worthy and good in me."

"Does his presence not remind you of the circumstances of his conception?" he asked, and she heard the hesitation in the way he asked the delicate question.

She shook her head. "I cannot judge him by his father no more than I hope others judge me by my own. Peter has no control over that and knows nothing of the man who sired him."

"And so you became a mistress and used your earnings to take care of him," Liam said.

"Yes." She sighed. "For years I have taken any penny I could scrape away and saved it, in the hopes that one day I could leave London and go to him, to live with him there by the sea. And now I've nearly saved enough that I could fulfill that dream. That is why I can't be with you as your mistress, Liam. In the next few weeks, I will settle my business in London and I will finally go to my son."

He stared at her, and there was regret as well as relief in his eyes. "Violet," he whispered, holding her hand tightly in his. "You are the most remarkable woman. Thank you for telling me this."

She nodded. "I wanted you to know. Although you are the first person I've ever confessed this secret to, outside of Olivia, of course."

He drew back. "Never a lover, never a friend?"

"No." She shivered. "It had to be someone I trusted. Someone who...who understood me."

His fingers came up to stroke her jawline. "And that is me."

She nodded, her love swelling inside of her even as she kept it to herself, letting it crash against the barrier that would always stand between them.

He smiled. "I am happy that you came to Bath," he said. "Although I'm surprised you didn't spend your holiday with your son."

She tensed. She had never considered that hole that had been created in her story by the revelation of the truth. She *never* took a holiday, unless it was to visit Peter. And yet she had told Liam that she was here to kick up her heels and forget her troubles.

"I—well, Olivia insisted," she said weakly, hating the falsehoods that seemed to pile upon each other.

Liam's expression was beginning to change. He was thinking through her story.

"You say you will soon leave London and be with your son," he pressed. "What has given you that freedom?"

She shifted and pulled her hands away. "A—a windfall," she whispered, and that wasn't exactly a lie. It was simply an ugly truth.

"A windfall," he repeated, stressing the word as if he were testing its veracity. "From a former lover?"

"Why all the questions, Liam?" she asked as she stood a second time and moved away from him. "You are interrogating me about something very private and personal."

He stood as well. "I'm sorry. I'm not trying to interrogate you, but you tell me that this desire to be with your child is why you cannot be with me, be my lover. I'm simply trying to understand why and how this moment has come now, just as we have met, have come together."

She hesitated, for she had no answer, or at least no answer she could share.

He didn't seem to expect one. "I have always dealt in reason and I'm sure there is something here I'm missing. Is there more to this decision?"

"What do you mean?" she croaked.

He pursed his lips in what seemed to be frustration over her avoidance.

"I mean why is *now* the time that you must leave London? To go to your son?" His brow wrinkled further. "And if you are leaving London, why did you say we would meet again there if I returned?"

Violet's head had begun to spin. Her carefully laid deceits and manipulations were beginning to unravel and she had no idea how to maintain them. Liam was treading close to the truth, and she knew him well enough to believe his dogged interest would only increase, not fade, the more he considered her past, her stories, her future which she denied him.

"Violet," he said, his tone sharp in the face of her continued shocked silence. "What are you keeping from me?"

She covered her face. How she longed to tell him everything, to explain what she had come here for, but how coming here had changed her so much. She wanted to tell him, but she had no idea how.

"Liam," she began, her voice shaking.

But before she could say anything else, the door to the parlor opened and Malcolm strode through, his face dark and angry as he looked at her.

Terror sliced through her at that look because it only meant one thing.

"I overheard you in the hallway, asking the young woman what she was keeping from you," Malcolm said, his voice vibrating with anger. "I believe I can answer that since she will not, or at least not with honesty, since that is not in her nature."

Liam turned on his friend, his cheeks dark with color and his eyes snapping with anger. "What do you mean?"

Violet stepped forward, wishing this wasn't happening. Wishing it were all a dream.

Only it wasn't a dream. It was a nightmare and it was real as Malcolm said, "Your lovely paramour came here on the behest of Ava and Rothcastle. *You* have been sleeping with a spy."

What Liam would remember most about the moment later was two things. One was the horribly broken expression that all but collapsed Violet's beautiful face. The second was that she never denied what Mal said. She only turned away with a sob that seemed to echo through him and stab him in the heart.

"What are you talking about?" Liam asked his friend. At least it was his voice that asked the question, he didn't recall using the mind power to do it.

Mal looked at him, his expression softening with regret...pity. Liam had seem that look before. He hated it just as much now as he had then.

"I'm sorry, Liam," his friend said softly. "The report from London was very clear."

"Report?" Violet asked, looking first at him, then Mal, as pink flooded her cheeks. "You had someone looking into me?"

Mal glared at her. "And for good fucking reason, don't you think?" He pivoted toward Liam. "She was hired by your sister and Rothcastle a few weeks ago. They paid for the place she was letting in Bath before she was moved to your estate. In fact, they are still letting it for her— she never gave the place up at all."

Violet sucked in a breath that sounded painful, but before she could respond to Mal's charge, Olivia entered the parlor, smiling broadly before she took in the tense, charged scene before her.

"Violet?" she murmured, looking between the three of them. "What—"

Mal spun on her, his face dark and angry. All the light Liam had seen in his friend since Olivia's arrival, all the joy, was gone.

Liam felt for him, understood the betrayal in Mal's voice as he hissed, "Did you know? Did you know why she was here?"

Olivia turned her gaze to Violet and for a moment the women held stares. Then Violet jerked out a single nod.

And Liam's world collapsed around him. Mal wasn't mistaken. Violet couldn't explain this away.

Everything his friend said was true.

He remained silent, but Mal didn't. "Of course you knew. You two are so bonded together, you would probably stab me through the heart if she told you it would help. So you were the distraction not just the first time we met, but all along. How hard did you laugh, Olivia?"

"Malcolm," Olivia sobbed, reaching for him even as he jerked away and exited the room without a backward glance or another word. Olivia sank onto the settee, staring toward where his friend had sat.

Violet, on the other hand, seemed to gather herself. "Liam," she whispered. "Please let me explain."

She moved toward him, but he backed away a step. "Were you hired by my sister to come here? To spy? *Have* you been reporting back to her and that bastard she married?"

She caught her breath, and he knew the answer before she said it out loud.

"Yes," she admitted, her voice cracking. "But Liam, I swear to you that everything I ever shared with you, everything I ever said...it was all true. I came here with one agenda, but the moment I met you, there was more to it than that."

He stared at her, her eyes brimmed with tears, her hands shaking. Her expressions of remorse, of emotion were very real...but then that was what she had been trained to be. To appear real when everything she did was a lie.

And he had been taken in by it. And given her, and Rothcastle, everything they needed.

"Please leave," he said, his tone flat and emotionless even though inside he felt like someone had ripped his heart from his chest and crushed it.

"Liam," she gasped.

"Just go," he repeated, spinning away before he lost all control and said and did things he couldn't take back.

She was silent for so long that he looked back at her. She stood, staring at him, pain lining every part of her face. Pain and regret, heartbreak and sorrow. And he wanted to believe it all, even though he refused to allow himself to be so foolish.

"Did I not make myself clear?" he asked, fighting to keep the break from his voice that would fully reveal his weakness to her.

She shook her head. "No, my lord. You are very clear. I'm sorry. I'm so very sorry."

She turned and moved toward the door. Only at the settee did she hesitate. Slowly, she caught Olivia's elbow and drew her to her feet.

As she wrapped an arm around her friend's waist, Liam heard her whisper, "Come, Olivia. Come away."

The other woman seemed too much in shock to resist and together they left his parlor. Left him alone.

He moved to the front window and looked out as a carriage was brought along for them. They climbed in and the vehicle pulled away, its horses prancing like there was some kind of joy left in the world.

But as Liam drew the curtain and enshrouded himself in darkness, he knew the truth.

There was no joy left. There would be no joy again.

Chapter Sixteen

It was early evening when the lady's maids arrived at the house back in Bath with all of Olivia and Violet's things hastily packed. Once the footmen had unloaded the items into each woman's room, Violet looked at Rachel.

"How bad was it?" she asked softly.

Her maid shrugged, but her tense face said more than her words would ever express.

"Belle and I were watched every moment while we packed for you, miss," she admitted.

"By his lordship?" Violet asked, her heart aching as she tried not to think of Liam and failed, just as she had been failing since her departure from his home earlier in the day.

"Oh no, miss," Rachel said with a blush. "His lordship locked himself in his chamber after you left."

Violet squeezed her eyes shut. *She* had done that to him. His renewed isolation was her fault.

"I could hear him crashing around and breaking things from across the hall," Rachel continued, unaware of how deeply her words cut into Violet's very soul. "Should I unpack for you, miss?"

Violet covered her chest with both hands, willing herself to breathe, to remain stoic when all she wished to do was collapse.

"No, Rachel. We will return to London in the morning, so there is no need to unpack anything." She squeezed the maid's hand. "I'm certain it has been a trying day. Why don't you rest for a while? Have your supper. I'll call for you later and we can make our arrangements."

Her maid bobbed out a nod and slipped to the door. But there, she stopped. "I-I'm sorry, miss."

Violet looked up at her. She knew what Rachel meant. "So am I."

The maid left the room quietly and Violet stared at the open door. Across the hall was Olivia's chamber, and her friend had been locked in alone since their return to this house.

It appeared Olivia hadn't even let her own maid in, for her trunks were stacked beside the door.

With a sigh, Violet moved across the way and knocked on her friend's door. There was no answer.

"Olivia, darling, it's me. Let me in, won't you?" she said though the barrier.

There was a moment's silence, then she heard Olivia come across the room and the key turned. Violet let herself in and watched as Olivia silently walked across the room to a chair beside the window. She sat there and stared outside, her face blank and nothing like the normally vivacious and bright expression she normally kept.

Violet flinched in guilt. After all, this was her fault as well.

"Olivia, have you been sitting there all this time?" she asked as she dragged a chair of her own to the same spot and sat across from her friend.

Olivia nodded but didn't make eye contact. "I have."

"It was an ugly scene," Violet said softly, trying not to allow images from that awful morning to bombard her. She failed miserably. All she could see in her mind was Liam's face, the betrayal he so keenly felt.

"Very," Olivia agreed, and one tear escaped to roll down her cheek.

Violet gasped at the sight of it. She had not yet allowed herself tears, but seeing her friend's made her denial all the harder. She just had to get through the next week or so and then she could cry all she liked.

She swallowed past the lump in her throat and caught Olivia's hand.

"We knew it could happen," she said, half hoping to reassure herself as much as she tried to reassure Olivia.

Olivia looked at her evenly. "I *never* knew any of this would happen."

Violet looked out the window to the small garden below. She had no idea how to respond in the face of her friend's despair, not when she was trying so hard to keep her own heartbreak and disappointment in check. But there was nothing to be done about it. She knew that. She had accepted it.

Mostly.

She pushed to her feet and smoothed her hands over her skirts.

"Tomorrow we'll go back to London," she said. "I will collect my ill-gotten gains and then that will be all. I'm sure eventually we will forget this...we'll forget."

Of course that wasn't true, but she said it anyway. Perhaps one day she might believe it if she said it enough.

Olivia glanced up at her. "I'm not going back to London."

Violet's thoughts fled and she jerked her gaze toward Olivia. "I—what do you mean? Of course you'll come back to London with me!"

Olivia shook her head. "No."

Violet dropped down to her knees in front of her friend and caught both her hands. "Oh, Olivia, please don't be angry. I'm so sorry I involved you in this, I didn't mean to bring you grief. You are my best friend and my sister. Please don't hate me, I couldn't bear it if you hated me too."

Olivia touched her face. "Dearest, my reasons for not going to London have nothing to do with you. I'm not angry with you in the slightest."

Relief rushed through Violet, along with confusion. "Then...then why won't you return with me?"

"Because of my feelings for *him*," her friend whispered, eyes welling with tears again, which she blinked away.

Violet stood slowly. "For Malcolm."

Olivia nodded. "I am in love with him, Violet."

Violet felt no surprise at this admission. She had seen it happening in front of her, even if she wasn't fully focused on anyone but herself. "Of course you are."

"And *because* I love him, I have no choice but to stay and try to fix this wedge between us." Olivia sighed heavily. "Even if it takes a great deal of time, I must try."

Violet paced away, praying her friend wouldn't see her wince. Olivia loved Malcolm and she was free to pursue that love for him. And if anyone could convince a man to forgive her, it was Olivia. It only put the finality of Violet's own situation into stark focus.

"If you love the man, you should fight for him," she said without looking at Olivia.

Her friend got to her feet. "And what about *you*?"

"What about me?"

"I think it is evident you care deeply for Liam. I wager you may love him too." Olivia tried to meet her eyes, but Violet refused to do it.

Just as she refused to confess her heart, even to her best friend. Knowing it in her mind was painful enough, allowing the words to be spoken…that could very well break her in two.

"You are mistaken," she said, pressing a hand to the cool glass and staring outside.

"Am I?" Olivia's tone was gentle.

Slowly, Violet turned and looked at her friend. There was no doubt Olivia saw through her.

"Even if I did harbor some kind of tender feelings for him, he despises me now. And with good reason." Her voice broke and she sucked in a harsh breath.

"Oh, Violet." Olivia moved to comfort her, but Violet stepped away. She was like glass now. If someone touched her, she feared she would shatter and never be put together again.

"It doesn't matter. I did what I did in order to be with my son. And as soon as I can finish this dreadful business with the Rothcastles, I can go to him. It will be worth it. It has to be worth it."

Olivia nodded, but it was a jerky motion. Neither one of them was certain of that and they had both lost so much.

"You go back tomorrow?"

"As early as I can depart in the morning," Violet said, shaking her head in the hopes she could clear thoughts of Liam away. "I've already sent a missive ahead to Lord and Lady Rothcastle. It will likely arrive just ahead of me, but at least they will anticipate my coming. And hopefully we can deal with our business swiftly, I have no desire to linger on it."

"And then you'll move on?"

There was doubt in Olivia's voice. In truth, there was a great deal of doubt in Violet's heart. But she couldn't falter.

"Yes," she whispered.

Olivia took her hand. "It will work out."

Violet flinched. "I hope so."

But even as she said it, it didn't feel like it was true. And she wasn't certain it ever would.

Morning had broken after a long and sleepless night, but Liam could not celebrate its beauty, despite staring out at a perfect day from the breakfast room window. The fact that the weather was magnificent and the birds were chirping actually felt like an affront. Why could it not rain when he was torn into pieces?

The door behind him opened and when it slammed shut behind him, he knew who had entered without even turning.

"Malcolm," he said, and he did turn to look at his disheveled, red-faced friend.

While Liam had withdrawn into himself and brooded over Violet, only expressing his anger and upset in the privacy of his now-slightly destroyed chamber, Mal had taken a different tact.

His friend had stormed, he had slammed, he had bitten the head off of nearly every servant in Liam's employ. Now Liam wasn't surprised to see the same dark and dangerous expression on Mal's face that had been there for almost twenty-four terrible hours.

"She left," his friend snapped as he slammed a plate onto the sideboard and shoveled food onto the dish without even looking at it.

"She?" Liam said without clarifying what his friend meant. There was only one *she* now. "Not they?"

Mal snorted and Liam shook his head. Perhaps his friend didn't mean what Liam thought he did.

"Which she?" he asked, his heart throbbing.

Mal slowed his violent dishing and glanced up at him. "*Violet*. Gone early this morning back to London. Olivia remains in the home that was let by Rothcastle."

Liam turned toward the window again as emotions he did not want seemed to bombard him mercilessly. Violet's departure only solidified what he already knew—everything they'd shared had been a lie. Despite all appearances to the contrary, she had never given a damn about him.

That her betrayal was deep and dark.

And yet, he still cared for her. Stupidly, foolishly and desperately.

"Why do you track their movements?" he asked. "I don't want to know."

Which was a lie, but he said it regardless.

"I want to fucking know," Mal said.

Liam turned as his friend sat down at the table and shoved his plate as far from him as he could. Mal sprawled back in a dining chair, and for the first time Liam saw how rough his friend looked. His eyes were rimmed with red from lack of sleep and his face was drawn and desperate.

His expression was in every way a reflection of how Liam felt.

"Why?" Liam asked.

Mal looked at him and beyond the anger, Liam saw something else. Pain. Heartbroken, razor-sharp pain, the kind that destroyed a man.

He knew it well.

"I told you I loved Olivia a few days ago," Mal said. "In the heat of an angry moment."

Liam raised his brows. He had never considered his friend's confession that day to be anything but truth and had been so wrapped up in himself that he hadn't realized Mal was struggling with his feelings.

"Was that a lie?" he asked softly.

"It was never a lie. It was just utterly stupid. I do love her."

The words were rather shocking considering all the two men knew now about their lovers' deception, but somehow Liam wasn't shocked. Over the time they had been together, there was no denying how swiftly and powerfully Malcolm and Olivia had come together. He had seen their bond grow, he had seen his friend happier than he had ever been.

"And how is that utterly stupid?" Liam asked.

Mal shook his head. "Come, Liam, she was as part of this deception as Violet was. She came here to keep me from developing suspicions about her friend. I was just a pawn in their game."

Liam stared at him. He felt the same way about what Violet had done, but somehow he could forgive Olivia.

"Let me ask you a question," he said.

Mal shrugged and fiddled with a loose string on the tablecloth without answering.

"Would you lie for me?"

Mal jerked his gaze up. "What?"

"If I asked you to lie, would you?"

His friend swallowed hard. "Yes."

"In fact, you have lied for me in the past, haven't you?"

"Yes, but that is different."

Liam sighed. "Probably not to those you lied to." He shook his head. "If Violet ever told me the truth, and I think there were times when she did, then the bond she and Olivia share is powerful, *very* powerful."

"And so that means I should forgive?" Mal asked, but Liam could see his friend was thinking about what he said even if he tried to fight it.

"What you do is up to you," Liam said. "But the fact that Olivia didn't go back to London with Violet says a great deal to me about where she stands."

Mal bit out a bitter laugh. "Perhaps she thinks she can get something from me."

Liam shook his head. "Weren't you the one who told me if I wanted to die miserable and alone, that was my prerogative, but that you didn't approve? Seems you might wish to follow your own advice."

Mal rolled his eyes. "Says the man who has been in hiding for years."

"Well, do as I say not as I do." Liam smiled even though he felt no joy in this conversation. "At least go talk to the girl, Mal. At least let her explain. Unlike Violet, she didn't orchestrate this mess. And she *stayed*. As I said, that has to mean something."

"I'll consider it." Mal shrugged as if it didn't matter, but there was something in his eyes that told Liam he had hit his mark.

Liam knew what that meant. Mal would do it. Mal would do it, and he and Olivia would probably work it out. Which made him happy for his friend.

But it left him more alone than ever.

"What will you do?" Mal asked. "Leave?"

"You mean run?" Liam said.

Mal didn't respond to the question, but said, "Your sister might come."

Liam folded his arms. He had been so wrapped up in Violet's part of this betrayal that he had hardly thought of Ava. How desperate she must have been to set this wicked plan into motion. Or was it her husband who had arranged it, laughing all the while?

"My sister went to all this trouble," he said. "Perhaps it's time to settle what is between us once and for all. So let her come."

Chapter Seventeen

Violet pushed the curtain away from the window as the carriage wound its way through London's streets. Home again. Except this place wasn't home. At least, after her appointment it wouldn't be.

The vehicle turned down the drive toward the Rothcastles' beautiful estate. Unlike the first time she came here, Violet wasn't impressed by its beauty or fascinated by its inhabitants.

She was, however, nervous about the meeting she was about to take. She had no idea how the duke and duchess would receive her.

The driver helped her from the carriage and she moved to the door. Once again, the Rothcastles' servant greeted her, but this time there was no chilliness to his demeanor. The man actually smiled as he said, "Good afternoon, Miss Milford. We have been expecting you. Allow me to take your wrap and your gloves and then you may follow me to the parlor."

She blinked, uncertain why the previously stern butler was now so warm toward her. But she handed over the items he requested nonetheless and followed him to the same parlor where she had met with Lord and Lady Rothcastle what seemed like a lifetime ago. She flinched as she entered, recalling every moment of the arrangement she had made.

The arrangement that had changed her life in ways she never could have imagined.

"Help yourself to tea and biscuits if you'd like," the butler urged. "Her Grace will be along shortly."

Violet nodded as the man left the room and pulled the door shut behind him. As soon as she was alone, she braced herself on the back of a nearby chair. Suddenly being here felt so very wrong. It only highlighted the pain she felt. It made her keenly aware of the loss of Liam, as well as the love she still carried in her heart.

A love he had never known, wouldn't believe and likely wouldn't even want if she confessed it.

"God," she whispered, covering her eyes. "What have I done?"

The door behind her opened, and Violet spun to face Lady Rothcastle with what she hoped was a blank expression. One she could not maintain when she saw the duchess.

The last time the two women had met, Lady Rothcastle had been all cold reserve and hesitation. Now the lady had a broad smile on her face that made her even more beautiful than she had been. She rushed forward.

"Oh, Miss Milford," the duchess gushed. "How happy I am to see you."

The duchess stopped before her and for a moment Violet thought the lady might actually *embrace* her, as wild and inappropriate of a thought as that was. Of course, she didn't, and the duchess's cheeks darkened pink as she motioned to the settee instead.

"I'm afraid my husband won't be able to join us this afternoon. But please, won't you sit with me and share tea?"

Violet shifted with discomfort. She had hoped to come here, make the briefest report she could manage and flee. But now that did not seem possible.

"Of course," she said, taking the place Lady Rothcastle had indicated beside her.

As the other woman poured tea and pointed toward cream and sugar, flavoring Violet's tea as she liked it, Violet sat in discomforted quiet. What in the world could she say when all she could do was look at this woman and see hints of Liam in certain ways she moved? Being with her was like a heated blade shoved into her heart again and again.

Torture that would not end.

"Miss Milford," Lady Rothcastle said once Violet had set her tea aside without tasting it. "Violet. May I call you Violet?"

Violet drew back. It was a highly unusual request, but then a lady of the duchess's rank rarely shared a room with a woman of her type, let alone tea.

"Of—of course, Your Grace."

"Ava," Lady Rothcastle corrected as she met Violet's gaze and held there.

"Oh, I couldn't," Violet said with a shake of her head. Even she would not be so bold.

But Ava didn't blink or withdraw. "I'm afraid I insist." Without allowing Violet to argue further, Ava continued, "Violet, I cannot tell you how much your letters over the past weeks have meant to me. After so much time knowing nothing about my brother and his life...then to receive so much information, written with such detail and care...that meant everything to me."

Violet felt a shocking urge to break down into tears, but somehow managed to maintain her composure. Ava had no idea what her praise did. How it reminded Violet of her betrayal of a man she loved. And what she had sacrificed to bring Ava that information she coveted.

"Thank you," Violet choked out. "I am so pleased the information was helpful to you."

Ava took Violet's hands unexpectedly and squeezed them. "When we first met, I realize I was uncertain, perhaps even cold toward you, but you must understand how painful this estrangement from my brother has been for me."

Violet drew in a shaky breath and managed to extract her fingers from Ava's.

"I can understand that perfectly," she whispered. After all, she would suffer an estrangement from Liam now too. Permanent and unalterable.

The pain she had been trying to pretend away since the previous morning now hit her in waves, threatening to overtake her and make her an even bigger fool than she already was. She could hardly sit still as her mind turned, again and again, to Liam.

"My lady," she whispered. "*Ava*, I appreciate your warmth, probably more than you know, but I would like to conclude our business. The past few days have been trying and I must return home to make some arrangements, as I intend to leave London as soon as I am able. There is much to be attended to and planned before I can do so."

Ava drew back a little, and for a moment Violet feared she had offended the duchess. But as she looked closer, she could see that wasn't the case. Instead, the woman was watching her closely, reading her. Sizing her up.

"Of course," Ava finally said softly, without revealing any conclusions she had come to in her analysis. "Your missive, which arrived early this morning, alluded to developments in the situation with my brother. Your swift arrival now, which I assume means you hardly stopped along the road to London, makes me believe something dire has happened. Perhaps you would like to share that information with me?"

Violet nodded. She had been practicing how she would reveal her final hours with Liam during the carriage ride from Bath. It was important not to reveal her heart to this woman above all others.

"Do you know your brother's man, Malcolm Graham?"

Ava nodded. "Yes. He has been a loyal friend to my brother since Matilda's death. Perhaps the only one he has remaining."

Violet nodded slowly. "He is a good man. But he is also a smart one and driven to protect Liam—*Lord Windbury's* interests in every way. I tried to introduce certain distractions during my stay, but eventually Malcolm uncovered the connection between my arrival in Bath...and you."

Ava's face paled two shades and her fingers dug into the settee arm at that revelation. "I see."

Violet swallowed, ignoring her memories of that horrible moment by sheer act of will. She forced herself to continue, "Yes. Of course Malcolm reported it all to your brother."

Ava shook her head slowly. "Great God. Liam must have been furious."

Violet blinked wildly as the sting of tears made it difficult to see. There was Liam's face again, staring at her with that horrible look of betrayal and disgust. She would never forget it as long as she drew breath.

"Yes, he was very angry," she whispered. "He put me out of his home immediately, which is why I returned to London as soon as I could."

Ava didn't respond for a moment, but looked closely at Violet. She felt the duchess's gaze burning into her, peeling away her layers of protection.

Finally Ava said, "If I know my brother at all, it must have been quite a scene."

Violet couldn't bear to speak, but merely nodded.

"You were with him for some time," Ava said, leaning closer. "What were your thoughts, your impressions beyond anything you already wrote to me?"

Violet pushed to her feet and walked away from the duchess toward the bright fire across the room. It was rude to do so, but she needed the space to gather her thoughts, to determine what secrets were safe to tell, both for herself and also so her betrayal of Liam wouldn't become even worse than it already was.

"I don't think it's a surprise to you that your brother is troubled," she whispered. "At least, that is the impression he first gives when one meets him. But the more time I spent with him, the more I saw of his true character."

She faced Ava to find the lady perched on the edge of the settee, hands clasped.

"He is getting better, Your Grace," Violet admitted. "I have seen the depth of his kindness toward others. He laughs, though not excessively. But he doubts others and puts up walls."

Ava's shoulders rolled forward. "Something I'm certain will not be helped by discovering your connection to me."

Violet flinched. "I'm certain he will lift those walls even higher when it comes to anyone who comes into his life and asks him to be more than the shell he presents to the world."

"Is that what you did?" Ava asked and again her gaze was appraising.

Violet ignored her question. "I must tell you that he had...he once had very troubling thoughts after Matilda's death."

Ava's eyes went wide and her face paled. "Suicide?" she whispered.

Violet couldn't speak as her heart ached for Liam. She nodded slowly.

Ava covered her mouth with a gasp. "I knew it was probably true, but to hear it." She shook her head. "But now?"

Violet swallowed. Liam's words echoed in her head, telling her that he had put all those thoughts aside...because of her. It was the most powerful thing he had ever said to her, that she had given him back thoughts of a future. It gave her a value no other man had ever placed on her.

Her reward to him for that value had been bitter, indeed.

"Violet?" Ava whispered. "Please tell me my brother does not still plan to harm himself."

"He told me he wouldn't." Violet turned away again.

Ava's breathing was rough. "Do you believe him?"

"I don't know. I hope so. He is different now than he was even when I first met him." Violet stared out the window with unseeing eyes.

She heard Ava stand and looked at her. The duchess was pale and her eyes were bright with tears.

"I'm going to tell you something, Violet. Something only a handful of people know."

Violet drew back a step. Once again, she was struck by how odd this situation was. A duchess and a mistress, sharing tea and apparently secrets.

"I'm having a child." Ava's hand came down to cradle her stomach, and as her dress went taut, Violet *could* see the hint of roundness that Ava's fashionably high-waisted gown hid.

"Congratulations," Violet stammered. "When will your child be born?"

"They believe in four to five months," Ava said. She smiled, but the worry hadn't left her eyes. "But you must see now why I went to such lengths to gain information about my brother. I *need* him in my life, Violet. Now more than ever. But I have no idea how to bring him home."

Violet blinked as Ava tilted her head in what appeared to be expectation.

"Are you asking me to tell you?"

"It seems you developed something very special with my brother," Ava said. "You are the closest thing to an advisor from his inner circle that I have."

Violet leaned back against the window, letting the cool glass permeate and sooth her overheated body. "I am not in your brother's inner circle. I'm certain he must despise me, and as you know, he does not forgive easily, nor does he have the incentive to do so with me that he has with you."

"So you will not tell me anything?" Ava asked, her voice cracking.

Violet sighed. If Ava wanted her advice, than perhaps she had a final chance to do something for Liam, after all.

"I think you and your brother have danced around your estrangement long enough. You have hurt each other, just as all families do. But sending spies and refusing to talk to each other isn't going to fix this. I think you should go to Bath, march up to his door and confront him. End this once and for all, it has torn apart too many lives as it is."

Ava nodded slowly. "Perhaps you are correct that it is time to face this issue head on. But do you think he will allow that? Might he be packing up and leaving Bath this very moment?"

"I don't know, but it seems foolish to remain here in London, locked in uncertainty and pain, just because he *might* be leaving Bath." Violet shrugged. "If he has, then follow him to the next place. You know where his properties are, go there."

Ava tilted her head. "You are a breath of fresh air, Violet Milford."

Violet felt heat flood her cheeks. "I'm sure I don't know what you mean."

"My brother and I are, I'm afraid, not exactly direct, at least when it comes to each other. Having you sweep in with your perfect self-assuredness and frank advice...well, I can see how it likely meant as much to him as it has to me." Ava shifted. "In fact, could I convince you to perhaps join my husband and I if we made the trip to Bath in the next day or two?"

Violet's heart lurched until she swore she could feel it beating in her suddenly thick throat. "Return to Bath?"

"I realize you just came from there, but the trip isn't hard and I would like to have your counsel," Ava said.

Violet sidestepped away, shaking her head. "I couldn't. As I said, I have a great deal to do since I intend to leave London. Too many things to arrange to think of—"

"Do you mean your home?" Ava asked, moving on Violet even as she continued to try to escape. "I admit, my husband has done a little checking up on you. I realize you own a modest home here in the city. If you are leaving permanently, as your demeanor seems to indicate, you must want to sell the place to obtain extra funds."

Violet's lips parted. "Y-Yes. But that is complicated by the fact that my friend lives in the home with me and I-I do not currently know of her circumstances. She didn't return to London with me."

"We would buy the place from you," Ava said without hesitation. "For twice its current value. And I will personally assure you that we would allow your friend to continue to live there if she decides to do so. We won't even charge her rent if she hasn't been paying you up until this point."

Violet hesitated. That was a great deal of money. Money that would give her and Peter additional comfort. And yet the terms of the bargain were very hard. Return to Bath? Probably see Liam again? Feel his disdain and see his disgust?

"I can't," she whispered.

"We will manage the house as I have described," Ava offered. "And I will give you...a thousand pounds for your travel with us." When Violet continued to shake her head, Ava said, "Three thousand pounds? Five?"

Violet spun away.

"Please!" she cried out, her shoulders shaking as she supported herself on the wall.

Ava stopped calling out sums of money and after a moment's silence, she said, "I-I can't believe I didn't fully realize it before. How could I have been so blind? You are in love with my brother, aren't you, Violet?"

Chapter Eighteen

Violet rested her head on the cool, smooth surface of the wall, trying to catch her breath, trying to stop her head from spinning wildly. It was a losing battle, for her emotions were too out of control now to hope to rein them in even the slightest.

Ava spoke again when she did not. "I don't judge you," she said softly.

Turning, Violet stared at the duchess in her fine clothing with her perfect hair. "How could you not? A woman like me with a man like your brother?"

"Who is a woman like you?" Ava asked. "A woman who has made the best of what I imagine are bad circumstances? A woman who holds her head high and does what she must, and yet maintains enough kindness in her heart to give me hope when I was hopeless?"

Violet moved to the nearest chair and sank into it because she feared her legs would no longer support her. "I meant a whore, my lady."

To her surprise, Ava didn't flinch at the vulgar term. In fact, she smiled. "I have known 'ladies' who have done far worse than anything you have. 'Ladies' I wouldn't fraternize with for the world because their indecency goes to their rotten cores, even as they present perfection to the world."

"How do you know mine doesn't do the same?" Violet asked softly.

Ava tilted her head. "Because I know. I just know. I will ask you, am I right, do you love my brother?"

Violet shivered, despite the comfortable temperature of the room. Once she said those words out loud, there would be no escaping them ever again. Speaking them made them real.

And yet she refused to deny them.

"Yes," she whispered, breaking eye contact with Ava to stare at her lap. "I am in love with Liam. With all of my heart, with all that I am."

She gasped as she said it, reaching for air as everything around her seemed to fade. This was the last step, speaking those words. Now she couldn't go back. She would have to live with what she felt, what she had sacrificed, for the rest of her days.

Ava leaned forward and held out a handkerchief. Violet took it, and only then did she realize tears were streaming down her cheeks. She swiped at them with a shake of her head.

"I'm sorry," she whispered.

Ava's lips parted. "Why should you be sorry? I, of all people, understand what it is like to love someone the world believes you should never have."

Violet stared at her. "I suppose you do."

Ava smiled. "You see, I am far more infamous than you could ever be. I fell in love with my family's greatest enemy. And it tore everything in my world apart. But I will tell you it was worth it."

"Yes," Violet murmured. "You and the duke seem very happy together."

"We are," Ava said with a faraway look of contentment on her face. "But you change the subject. I want you to know that I view you as a friend, nothing more."

"A-a *friend*, Your Grace?" Violet repeated, utterly shocked.

"You and I are friends, Violet Milford, whether you want to accept it or not. We are friends because I like you, I respect you...and more importantly, because we have something in common that will bond us for life. We both love my brother."

Violet stared at her. There was no manipulation on Ava's face. She seemed to be utterly truthful in her words, her desire to connect with Violet as more than a woman of rank and a woman who could help her.

"Thank you for that," Violet said softly. "I would never turn down a friendship."

"Good." Ava tilted her head. "Then may I ask you again to come with us to Bath. As a friend, both to me and to my brother? You may leave directly from there to wherever you would like to go, and my husband and I will take care of any business you may have in London. I swear to you, it will be done."

Violet swallowed. There seemed to be no way to refuse this woman. More to the point, in some deep part of herself, she didn't want to refuse. This final act to help Liam would be her last act of love for him. If she knew he had repaired his relationship with Ava, she could leave him and begin her new life with some happiness.

Even if there would always be something missing.

"Yes," she whispered. "I'll go with you."

Ava clapped her hands together, but Violet held up a hand. "But I can't see him, Ava."

The duchess's face fell slightly. "No?"

"It will be too painful," Violet whispered, her voice catching. "It is too much to ask."

"Then I won't," Ava said, reaching out across the space between them to take her hand. "Now why don't you go back to your home and rest? Prepare whatever you must. I'll send word to you tomorrow morning about when we will depart. I hope within a day or two."

Violet squeezed Ava's hand and stood. "Very good. I'll look for your message."

She turned toward the door, but before she could leave, Ava stepped toward her and suddenly she was being embraced by the duchess. She froze for a moment, torn apart by uncertainty and numb from the pain of the past few days.

But then, slowly, she returned the embrace, clinging to the woman who was now the last line she had to Liam. When she stepped back, she fought for breath.

"Thank you," Ava whispered.

Violet nodded and fled the house. It was only when she was in the safety of her carriage that she laid across the seat and allowed herself to weep in a way she hadn't been able for the past few days.

"Your sister has arrived in Bath," Malcolm said without preamble as he entered Liam's office.

Liam jolted at the news, but refused to cease his work. He kept his eyes on the ledger before him and carefully placed an x in one of the columns which required marking before he said, "It has been nearly three days since Violet left. I'm surprised it took Ava this long. I assume she will knock on my door before the afternoon is over."

"Violet is with her," Malcolm said, and Liam saw the slight shift in his friend's expression, the careful gaze that said Liam's reaction was being cautiously gauged.

He saw this, and yet it was a reaction he couldn't control. He froze in his place, hand hovering over the ink container. All the emotion he had been trying to suppress for days rushed over him. Anger, betrayal, heartache crushed him from all sides. But one feeling was strongest.

Joy.

Deep within him, the idea that Violet was so close, that she had returned to Bath, to *him*, filled him with a joy so powerful that it stole his breath even though he knew he was a fool for feeling this way.

He pushed all the reactions away and set his quill down deliberately before he spoke again.

"Why?" he asked.

Malcolm shrugged, still standing in the doorway. "My spies do not go so far, Windbury."

Liam arched a brow. "No? Not even Olivia Cranfield?"

Malcolm's jaw tensed and the reaction verified any guesses Liam had harbored over the last few nights.

"Yes, I had speculated you've been seeing her, sneaking out at night to meet with her."

Malcolm fully entered the room now and slowly took a place at the desk across from Liam. He folded his arms.

"Do you judge that as a betrayal?" he asked softly.

Liam pondered the question. In truth, he had been so wrapped up in his tangled emotions regarding Violet that he had hardly considered any reaction to Malcolm and Olivia's continuing passion for one another. Now his feelings on that subject became quite clear, especially when he considered the desperation that flickered faintly in Mal's eyes.

"I told you myself to go to her, to hear her," Liam said and watched relief soften Mal's features in an instant. "I believe my misery has extended to everyone else in my life, especially you, for far too long, my friend. If you care for her, if you love her as you told me you did…then love her. Be with her. You have my blessing if you require it."

Mal smiled. "I don't, actually, but I appreciate it nonetheless, as well as your graciousness regarding the situation."

"I suppose I'm making up for lost time in the grace department," Liam said with a humorless chuckle. "Olivia must have explanations that soothe you, for you were so very angry with her just a few days ago for her part in Violet's deception."

Mal nodded. "I was. But I also understand the sacrifices one makes for a friend one loves like a sibling."

The two men met gazes and Liam nodded, taking his friend's meaning completely. "You probably understand that better than most, I would wager."

"But what about you?" Mal pressed.

Liam tilted his head in surprise. "Me?"

"There is still much for me to worry about," Mal said. "I assume you have guessed that Ava has also brought Rothcastle with her to Bath."

Liam tensed. "Yes, I assumed so. He cannot let her out of his sight, you know."

Mal arched a brow. "Or they are so in love that they are inseparable and your sister desires his support for fear you will refuse her when she comes here."

Liam stared down at the ledger, though he did not see it. "Yes," he whispered. "I suppose that is also possible."

Mal drew back. "The fact you would allow for the chance speaks volumes."

Liam cleared his throat. "I know she loves him."

The words tasted bitter, no matter how true they were.

Mal looked ready to respond, but before he could Liam's butler stepped into the doorway and cleared his throat softly to indicate his presence.

"Yes, Pruett?" Liam asked.

"Your sister has arrived, my lord." Though the servant spoke calmly, his eyes reflected the tension that simple statement created in the room.

Liam sighed. "That is earlier than I expected, but I've never known Ava to waste time. Is she alone?"

"No," the butler said.

Liam's breath caught as thoughts of Violet immediately leapt to his mind. The idea that she could be in his parlor at this very moment, so beautiful, so kind, so—

"The duchess has her husband with her," Pruett said.

His heart sank and Liam felt his shoulders roll forward with disappointment. It was funny, for so many years, his first thoughts would have been of the intrusion of Rothcastle, the hatred that had driven Liam almost his entire life.

Now they were of Violet and how desperately he wished to see her.

He cleared his throat, as the servant remained, waiting for him to formulate some kind of response to the news of his guests.

"Put Rothcastle in the parlor. You may serve him tea, I suppose, since that is the polite response to a duke in one's home," he said, waving a hand as if Christian's presence here was unimportant. "And bring my sister to me."

If the butler was surprised at this unorthodox handling of guests, he made no indication. He bowed and left the room without another word.

Once he was gone, Mal pushed to his feet. "Would you like me to stay?"

Liam shook his head. "No. I've hidden from this long enough. And you should go to Olivia, shouldn't you?"

Mal grinned, and the love and hope in his eyes made Liam's heart ache all the more. He was happy for his friend, but how jealous he was of his certainty in his feelings, his future.

"Try not to murder anyone," his friend said as he exited the room.

Liam smiled, though he knew, probably as well as Mal did, that not that long ago that might have been a possibility in this situation. But he had changed.

Violet had changed him.

In the hall, he heard the muffled voices of Mal and his sister as they exchanged a polite greeting. He stiffened, rising as he waited for her to enter the room. It took what seemed like an eternity, until the seconds on the clock all but rung in his ears like a gong.

And then she came into view, passing through his door and coming to a halt as she stared at him. He couldn't help but stare back, for she was changed from the last time he saw her.

His sister had always been pretty, but now she was stunning. Her dark brown locks were swept up in a delicate fashion that framed her oval face and accentuated her clear, porcelain skin. Her blue-gray eyes were bright and there was no doubt they were also filled with happiness.

It was that emotion, written all over her appearance, the way she held herself, the way she moved...that was what made her even more beautiful than she had ever been.

And he could not begrudge her that, no matter the source of the change.

"Ava," he said softly.

"Liam," she whispered in return.

Then she all but ran to him, wrapping her arms around him and squeezing so tightly that she almost dragged the air from his lungs. He felt her tremble, her breath broken with emotion before she pulled away. She searched his face, her fingers coming up to brush the line of the scar down his cheek before she pulled it back and stepped away.

"I-I'm sorry," she said with a shake of her head.

He smiled and to his surprise, the expression was very real. Having his sister in the room with him was far sweeter than he'd ever thought it would be.

"It's all right," he reassured her as he came around the desk and motioned to the chairs before his fire. "It's been a long time. Why don't you sit? Clearly, we have a great deal to discuss."

She nodded and slowly sank into a chair beside the fire. When she did so, he saw her shift, slight discomfort on her face.

"Are you well?" he asked.

She nodded. "Of course. But the more important question is how are you?"

His lips pursed at her dismissal of his inquiry, but then that was Ava. She had always been too worried about others, often at the expense of herself. That drive to repair broken people had led her to Rothcastle. A bargain made to save Liam. One that had changed them all irrevocably and altered the course of all their futures.

He winced at the memory of finding his sister with that man after she had been kidnapped, compromised and utterly ruined. He had never been closer to homicide than in that moment, never been closer to utter destruction.

He shoved the thoughts away and forced himself to speak.

"I am as well as can be expected when I have only recently discovered how far you would go to uncover any facts about me." Somehow he kept his voice even, calm and his eyes on her face.

The color drained from her cheeks and her hand clenched into a fist on the arm of the chair.

"You mean, I suppose, my sending Violet here," she said.

He nodded slowly. "Yes. I mean your sending Violet here," he repeated, accentuating every word. "So tell me, Ava, why did you send a beautiful spy into my midst to seduce and betray me? And why did you have to choose Violet Milford?"

Chapter Nineteen

Liam hated the tremble in his voice as he spoke the question. He hated the fact that his expression likely revealed far more than he would have his sister see. But Ava didn't shy away from the raw emotion on his face. She didn't react to it at all, except to lean forward and take his hand in hers.

"My dearest brother, I realize I betrayed you, perhaps far more than I ever intended to do," she said softly. "But you must understand the depth of my desperation. We have been estranged for so long. I have reached out to you over and over again, but none of my attempts met with any success. I *had* to get to you somehow. I had to ensure you were well by any means."

He tightened his jaw. When she put her feelings that way, he could see why she would reach for such desperate measures. He could also see the role he'd played to place her in that utter torment.

"I realize I've hurt you by my actions. I never wanted that. But seeing you is so very difficult," he admitted. "Because of *him*."

"*Him*," she repeated, her eyes going softer and filling with both trepidation and love. "You mean my husband. You mean Christian."

He nodded once, unable to say more on the subject. That would have to change soon enough, he knew, but he was still adjusting to that reality for now.

She sighed. "For nearly two years *he* has done nothing but love and protect me, Liam."

"Was sending Violet here his idea or yours?" he asked.

She arched a brow and her mouth grew tight. "Mine, actually. He didn't approve for a very long time, but when he saw I wouldn't be dissuaded, he did as I asked and looked for the right woman for the job. He determined that would be Violet. He vetted her. He introduced us."

Liam squeezed his eyes shut. "Great God."

She didn't respond, and when he looked at her again, there was a deep sadness on her face. "You cannot blame him for this, Liam," she whispered, releasing his hand abruptly. "He is not the villain in this play."

It was hard to agree to that, for Christian had been the villain of every play for so long. And yet she was right. Damn her, but she was utterly right.

"Why now?" Liam asked in order to avoid the subject of Rothcastle as much as find out the answer.

She blinked. "What do you mean?"

"As you said, we have been estranged for such a long time. What drove you to suddenly seek such drastic remedies to that problem?"

Ava sighed and in answer, rose to her feet. Slowly, she smoothed her high-waisted gown down flat across her body and revealed the burgeoning swell of a child growing within her.

His breath caught and he slowly rose to his feet and stared at her. She nodded at the unspoken question in the air.

"I'm having a baby," she whispered. "And you are my brother and I love you. I want you to be an uncle to this child. I want him or her to know you."

Liam swallowed hard as emotion rushed over him. He was shocked by the news of her pregnancy, but further shocked by his own reaction to it. Immediately and without warning he felt protective toward the baby inside of her. More to the point, he felt love for his future niece or nephew, regardless of the child's father.

"Do you understand now?" she asked, searching his face.

"I understand more," he said, retaking his seat with a thud. She did the same, though she sat on the edge, watching his every move. "But having Violet seduce me, pretend to care about me...that goes very far, Ava."

She shook her head. "You judge Violet too harshly, Liam. She didn't pretend anything—it is evident she cares for you. Even if she wishes she didn't."

Liam turned his face. Could that be true or was his shrewd sister perpetrating another lie in the hopes it would soften him?

"And yet she betrayed me," he said, his voice rough.

"On my orders," Ava pointed out softly.

Liam looked at her, brow arched. "Are you trying to make me angry with you too?"

She smiled slightly. "No. I already know what your anger can do. What I want you to do is forgive both Violet and I for our parts in the past few weeks."

Liam squeezed his eyes shut. How he wanted to do just that. To forget everything. But unlike his sister, he wasn't certain of Violet's feelings. And unlike Malcolm, he still had a great many barriers that separated him from the woman he...

Well, how he felt about her wasn't something he wished to analyze too deeply.

"Forgiveness isn't easy for me," he finally said.

She nodded. "I realize that. I understand it even. Our father didn't preach forgiveness, only hate."

Liam flinched. "Indeed, that is true."

He thought of their father. A hard man, a man driven by his inexplicable feud with the Rothcastle family. A man who railed at his son until Liam had the same prejudices. Even long dead, Liam could still hear the old earl's voice close to his ear.

Never forgive them. Stop being weak.

He shook the sound from his head and sighed. "He gave no quarter to anyone," he said softly.

She nodded, deep sadness in her eyes. "But he isn't here anymore, Liam. He isn't here, and I am. I'm asking you to be bigger than he was. To be better than he was. To learn from the mistakes all those generations of bitter men made, from the damage you and Christian did. Please."

He looked at her for a long moment. There was such hope in her stare, but even more than that there was faith. Faith that he could do this impossible task she asked of him. Faith that there could be peace.

Faith he found himself wishing he could share. Wondering if he could share in it...

"I want to speak to your husband."

He heard his voice say it and realized it was true.

Ava's hands gripped the arms of her chair, and she shivered from head to toe.

"Liam—" she began, fear lighting in her eyes and trembling in her voice.

He shook his head. "You want this to end, you want me to be part of your life again, you want me to learn this forgiveness you claim is possible...but I'm afraid all those wishes are tied to Rothcastle. We must speak at some point in order to grant you those things you desire."

Ava considered that a moment. "May I stay?"

He drew a deep breath. Having Ava in the room would complicate things between he and Rothcastle. Sisters had always tended to do that.

"Let me see him alone," he insisted.

She squeezed her eyes shut. "Fine. I will stay away, but only on your promise that you won't hurt him, Liam."

He stared at her, quivering with worry, hands clenching at her sides reflexively, bright eyes sharp with emotion.

"The time for that has long passed, Ava," he said with a sigh. "I wouldn't do that to you, to your child. I swear it on my life."

And for the first time, he found he meant it.

"I'll fetch him," Ava said, moving toward the door.

"Good," Liam murmured as she stepped away and down the hall to her husband. To a man he had called an enemy his entire life.

Only now he didn't know what to call him. And he could only hope he might figure it out before they came face to face in a showdown that had been coming from the moment each man had been placed in a cradle.

Violet sat in the window seat at the home she had left only a few days before. It felt like a lifetime, but somehow it wasn't. She stared toward the long road that led from Bath and toward Liam's estate, just a short ride away.

So close. So far.

A servant came in quietly and Violet glanced over. She had been without Rachel almost since her arrival in London. The Duke of Rothcastle had helped her find a place in Romwell, a pretty cottage judging by the sketches. She had offered on the place and Rachel had been sent ahead to prepare it for her and for her son.

That was how quickly the duke could arrange things. All done to convince her to come here, to come back to Bath and be near a man she loved. A man who hated her.

"Would you like tea, miss?" the young woman asked with a smile.

Violet shook her head. "No, thank you."

When the girl left, Violet looked at the clock. It had been over an hour since the Rothcastles had departed for Liam's estate. They would long be there by now. Had Ava been able to see her brother? Would Liam look past his anger to accept her into his life again?

Violet hoped so.

"He needs them," she whispered.

Of course, people needed people every day and couldn't or wouldn't see it. She knew that keenly enough.

The door to her chamber opened a second time, and now Violet had to force her smile at the intrusion. "No tea," she reiterated.

"Yes, miss," the same little maid said, with flaring cheeks. "But you have a visitor. Miss Olivia Cranfield."

"Olivia!" Violet said, jumping to her feet and moving for the door.

At the same moment, the servant stepped aside and Olivia burst into the room and rushed to embrace Violet. She heard the door close to give them their privacy but hardly registered it. Not when her best friend was here.

She drew back and Olivia urged her to the window seat where they perched together.

"Why didn't you tell me you were coming back?" her friend asked.

Violet shook her head. "I didn't know where you were. When we arrived and we were told you'd left this residence, I didn't have a thought of where to write. And I didn't dare send a message to Liam's home in case you were there."

Olivia's expression wavered slightly. "No, I'm not there. I let a smaller place almost as soon as you departed. I didn't want Malcolm to see me staying here, in case he thought I was still under the direction of the Rothcastles. Of you."

"Of course," Violet said with a shake of her head. "And has he decided that is true? Will he see you?"

Olivia nodded. "Yes. He comes to me every night."

"Excellent!" Violet clapped her hands together. "Then my actions didn't permanently damage his regard for you. I feared I had destroyed your chance for happiness."

Olivia cleared her throat. "He comes to me, but he is changed. I feel him holding back. And when I try to explain myself, when I try to tell him my heart, he only distracts me in the most pleasurable ways. And then leaves me before the night is over."

Violet lowered her hands at Olivia's brokenhearted expression. "He wouldn't come if he didn't feel something for you. He is conflicted."

"Yes, I'm certain that is true," Olivia said. "But what side of the conflict he will come out on is another story entirely."

Violet caught her hand. "I never meant to catch you up in my difficulties. Not after the true friend you've been to me."

"I was happy to be caught up," Olivia said with a smile. "If I hadn't, I wouldn't have even met Malcolm. And I cannot live with that idea, even if he never comes back to me again."

It was funny. Her friend had just expressed the same feelings Violet had. Despite the ending, she was happy she had come to Bath. Happy she had met and made love to Liam. Loving him was worth the fall. It was even worth the pain.

"I doubt he'll never come back," Violet reassured her friend.

Olivia smiled. "Yes, I intend to simply break him down. Wear him out until he can do nothing *but* love me back."

Violet laughed at her friend's teasing, but she couldn't deny the pain of it.

"Does he tell you anything of Liam?" she asked softly.

Olivia shook her head slowly. "No. That subject is off limits between us, I'm afraid. But the fact that they have remained in Bath rather than departing to avoid Lord and Lady Rothcastle's arrival certainly says something, doesn't it?"

Violet pressed her lips together. "You are right," she finally said. "Before Liam would have done anything to escape the confrontation Ava has brought down upon him."

"So you see," Olivia said, squeezing her hand. "You saved him."

"I wouldn't go that far." Violet got to her feet and smoothed her dress, still watching out the window toward that long, lonely road. "And even if I did, he will hate me for it for the rest of his days. The disdain on his face a few days ago told me that better than any words he could ever speak."

"I'm sorry," Olivia whispered. "You have been hurt, and I wish I could repair your heart."

"You can't." Violet smiled even though she felt no joy. "That is the way of broken hearts. They only heal with time and distance."

In that moment, she realized what she had to do.

"I'm leaving," she whispered.

Olivia jolted. "Leaving?"

"Yes. I believe there is a stage leaving for Hertford in a short time. I could make arrangements there for transport to Romwell."

Olivia shook her head. "But what of the duke and duchess? Did they not make some arrangement with you?"

She nodded. "They did. But I will break it. They will understand, I think. And it isn't as if I had much to do here at any rate."

"Don't you want to see Liam again?" her friend asked, her expression softening.

She stiffened at the inquiry. "Of course I do," she said softly. "I want to see him so much that I ache whenever I think of it. But he doesn't want to see me. And if I forced that issue, I would only find ruin and deeper heartache. It is time for me to forget this folly. To go to my son and live the simple life I was meant to have."

"And there is nothing I can say to dissuade you?" her friend asked, searching her face.

Violet laughed a hollow laugh. Unless Olivia could tell her that Liam loved her, that he would forgive her and welcome her and her son into his life...well, there was nothing else to say.

"No," she answered softly. "I never should have returned to Bath in the first place. I let my heart lead me when it was time to put my head in charge. I must remedy that now."

Olivia looked as though she might say something more, but at that moment a flash of movement caught Violet's eye from the road outside her window. There was a man, riding hard up the road toward the house.

"Malcolm," Olivia gasped, pressing her hand to the glass.

"Has he ever come to you in the middle of the afternoon?" Violet asked softly as they watched him turn toward whatever place Olivia had been staying at before Violet's arrival.

Olivia's breath was short. "N-No. Not since the first day."

"Then it seems you might have worn him down far faster than you thought."

Olivia's stare jerked to her and Violet smiled. "Go to him. Write to me in Romwell in a few days and let me know all the news."

Olivia briefly embraced her. "I wish you would stay."

"I can't," Violet insisted as she turned her friend and pushed her toward the door with laughter. "Now go!"

Olivia didn't have to be asked again. She hustled from the room, her eyes bright with excitement and love that wouldn't be stopped by anything in the world.

Violet turned and looked around her. She hadn't unpacked, so it would be easy enough to slip away to the coach and make her escape. And now that she knew Olivia would be happy there was no other reason to stay.

"No other reason at all," she said, gathering up her reticule and ringing for the little maid to make arrangements for her departure.

Chapter Twenty

Christian came to the entryway to Liam's office and stopped there, his bright blue eyes flicking over the room and analyzing all he saw in an instant. Liam felt him stare at the scar across his face, the way he held his arm. They were the remnants of the accident that had stolen Matilda's life that horrible winter night.

Liam's first reaction was to clench his fist, hating how he was being judged by a man who had no room to do so. After all, Christian bore his own scars. He still leaned on a cane from his injuries, though perhaps not as heavily as he had before Ava came into his life.

Liam pushed the anger in his reaction back, trying to remember why he was doing this.

Slowly, he nodded to the other man.

"Rothcastle," he said.

Christian met his stare with an even one of his own. "Windbury."

That was all that was said for what seemed like an eternity, until Liam pushed cleared his throat.

"Come in, won't you? This is getting ridiculous."

To his surprise, the corner of Rothcastle's lip tilted slightly in a smile.

"Some would say our entire feud has been ridiculous," he said as he did as Liam asked and stepped into the room, shutting the door behind him.

"A lot of people with opinions who don't understand," Liam said with a shake of his head. "My sister, for one."

"And mine." Now Christian's smile was gone, replaced with pain. But to Liam's surprise, no anger any more.

His own pain returned at the thought of Matilda. And yet it had faded a little with time, with Violet's entry into his life. He had never thought that would happen.

"Yes, neither of them wanted to be party to what was between us," Liam whispered.

"And we made them party to a battle we didn't even understand," Christian said, his tone heavy with regret.

Liam stiffened. "What do you mean we didn't understand? I understand exactly how I feel about you."

Christian's mouth went tight and Liam could see he was fighting to control his emotions. After a moment, he spoke again, his voice frustratingly calm.

"Obviously over the years, you and I developed our own reasons to hate each other," he said. "But I only mean that our fathers and grandfathers instilled that hate in us from birth. And no one knew the cause of it. Why did our families despise each other?"

Liam paused. Had his father ever shared that information with him? All he could remember were the admonishments to despise, to battle, to never trust.

"I have no idea," he finally admitted with a shrug. It felt like he was giving over the upper hand to Rothcastle and he didn't like it. Old habits, it seemed, died hard.

"I do now." Christian reached into the inside pocket of his jacket and withdrew two packets of letters.

He moved forward and set the letters on the edge of the desk near where Liam stood, then took a long step back away from him. Liam stared at them, but made no move toward them.

"You can read them for yourself," Christian said. "Keep them if you'd like. But I would be happy to give you the annotated version for the sake of time."

Liam arched a brow. "With your own slant?"

"You think I would lie and then leave these with you to uncover the truth anyway?" Christian asked with a tilt of his head. "You may despise me, but I hope you give me more credit for intelligence than that."

Liam let out a long sigh. "Why don't we start before all that? What made you seek out these answers you claim you've found?"

"Ah," Christian said and his gaze slipped to the sidebar across the office. "May I have a drink?"

"Of course," Liam said.

Christian crossed to the bar and quickly poured himself a scotch. He held up the bottle and Liam nodded, so he poured a second one. As he returned to Liam, he held out the glass.

"I was like you, Windbury. I never cared why our families hated each other, I did as I was told to do and as I learned to do. And when Matilda died, well, I lost any sense of reason at all."

"As evidenced by your actions toward Ava," Liam said softly. He motioned to the chairs by the fire and they took them.

Christian stared at the fire. "Yes. I did something horrible when I took your sister in revenge. But since it ended with our marriage, with the fact that I love that woman more than I have ever loved another person or thing...I won't apologize for that."

Liam flinched. Hearing this man profess his love for Ava still stung. And yet, as he looked at Rothcastle, he could see for the first time that the duke truly felt what he declared. There really was a deep and abiding love for Ava in this man.

"Are you saying that your marriage to my sister made you wonder about the origins of our family feud?" Liam said, avoiding the tender subject of love.

Christian nodded. "The more I loved her, the closer we grew, the more I felt I needed to know what had taken things to such a desperate level between our families. And so I began to seek out the answers. I searched family homes, I looked into vaults, I asked questions. And finally, I found the first pack of letters sitting untouched in a secret compartment in my father's old desk."

Liam glanced at them. "All right, Rothcastle, I'll ask. What do these letters magically reveal?"

"Your great-grandmother, Eleanor—do you know much about her?"

Liam wrinkled his brow in confusion at what seemed like a change of subject. "No, she was long dead, as was my great-grandfather, by the time I was born."

"Well, Eleanor was quite the diamond of the first water the year she came out in Society," Christian explained. "She caught the eye of my great-grandfather, Bennett. They even got engaged, and I suppose the world would have been a very different place until she met a dashing young man named Edward."

Liam shook his head. "My great-grandfather."

"Yes." Christian sighed. "My letters were ones she wrote to my great-grandfather. The other letters are ones I managed to collect from one of your family estates when I convinced Ava to take me there a few months ago. They are to *your* great-grandfather, as well as a few other things she wrote or received about the situation."

Liam got up and paced to the packets. He lifted them, yellow with age, the handwriting old fashioned.

"Are you saying she sported with them?" he said, jaw clenching. "Blaming my family for it all, are you?"

To his surprise, Christian said, "No. Actually, I don't think she liked the situation. She was engaged to one man and fell passionately in love with another. But she cared for my great-grandfather—it's evident in her letters to him. Still, she didn't handle it well, but she was young. And a hatred began to fester."

Liam swallowed, trying to think about what he knew of his great-grandparents. Little, for he had never delved with much interest into family history.

"How was it resolved?"

"She ran off to Gretna Green with your great-grandfather," Christian said. "It would have created a huge scandal, but it was all hushed up somehow by their fathers and monies were exchanged. But the two men despised each other and they spent the rest of their lives engaged in a war with one another. A war which they passed to their sons, their sons' sons and so on until it landed in our laps."

"She died young," Liam mused, fingering the yellowing sheets. "Eleanor, I mean. I recall that from our family history."

"Yes, very young." Christian frowned. "She bore a son, your grandfather, and within two years, she was dead from some kind of wasting disease. But I wonder, was she like our sisters? Was she torn apart by the war between the two men? Was she simply not strong enough, like they were, to weather it?"

Liam pinched his lips together. "So it was all over a woman."

Christian nodded. "It appears so. We have battled and hated and destroyed for four generations...all over a woman who died nearly a hundred years ago."

"Does Ava know?" Liam whispered.

Christian shook his head. "You and I have carried this on. I thought you should know first. And Ava had a great deal on her mind, I didn't want to trouble her with the particulars of my investigation until I could be certain it would bear fruit."

Liam paced the room, the horrible truth of this sinking deep into his soul.

"God," he murmured.

"I know." Christian nodded. "I felt the same way. It is the horror that binds us, Liam."

Liam flinched at the other man's use of his given name. He'd never used it before. It sounded foreign coming from his lips.

"We have hurt those we loved," Christian continued, rising to move toward him. "We've broken everything around us in order to hurt each other. Over *this*. Over something that seems so foolish now."

Liam nodded. His stomach turned at that thought.

"I love your sister," Christian said. "Perhaps you don't believe that, but I do."

Liam looked at him. "Actually, I do believe that. I see it in your eyes when you talk about her."

Christian nodded. "Then you must also know how much I love the child which grows within her too. I cannot allow that baby to endure this foolish battle, Liam. I cannot allow him or her to grow up as we did."

"No," Liam said. "Nor can I."

Christian hesitated and then he stepped forward, hand outstretched. Liam stared at the offering. If he took Rothcastle's hand, he would be turning his back on the hatred. He would be offering forgiveness and receiving it. It was something he had never thought to do. It was something he wouldn't have been able to do.

Before Violet.

He took Christian's hand and they shook. In that moment, something utterly strange happened. All the hatred, all the pain, all the ugly feelings he had held seemed to melt away. He actually staggered as they left him, and he stared at Christian. The other man had a similar expression to the one he knew was on his own face. Relief and shock, mixed together.

Liam pulled back first, rubbing his hand as if the emotions had bled out through it. He looked at Christian.

"So what will we be now? Not enemies, but...what?"

Christian smiled slightly. "We could start with brothers-in-law. Leave it at that for a while. Though I'm certain Ava will be pressing us to be friends three minutes after she realizes we are attempting to make peace."

Liam shook his head with a small laugh. "Yes, that would be our Ava."

"Our Ava," Christian repeated, and he smiled. "This will make her very happy."

"Yes, I'm sure it will," Liam agreed. "But before we speak to her, I have something to discuss with you. She tells me you were the one who found Violet."

Christian stiffened slightly. "Yes, I did. But if you believe I took pleasure in sending her here, I did not. I didn't agree with Ava's methods, though I went along with them because she insisted."

"Yes, she told me that as well," Liam said. "And I believe her, though it is more natural to me to make you the villain who rubbed his hands together and planned my ultimate heartache."

"Those habits will die hard for both of us, I'm certain," Christian said with a shrug. Then he looked at Liam closer. "But are you saying that Violet's presence here and her leaving have caused you heartache?"

Liam drew back. He hadn't meant to share that much of his heart with this man he was just agreeing to stop hating. They weren't friends, after all. He had no idea that they ever would be.

"To say you experience heartache to me means you have feelings for the woman," Christian said after Liam didn't answer for a moment. When he continued his silence, Christian shrugged. "I know from experience that love rarely comes along. If you've been lucky enough to find it again after the loss of my sister...well, I don't think you should deny it."

Liam stared at him. Was Rothcastle actually encouraging him to seek out happiness? The world was truly spinning off its axis today.

"I'll consider that." He motioned for the door. "Shall we go see my sister? I'm certain she is wearing a path in my parlor rug as she waits for us to either kill each other or come to an agreement."

Christian laughed. "*That* is certainly our Ava."

Liam led the way and they walked down the hall, silent and slightly uncomfortable with this newfound peace between them. Liam was certain at some point it would become natural, he just had no idea when.

But when he opened the parlor door and they stepped in together, Ava turned. Her face dismissed any misgivings he might have about burying the feud with Christian. She lit up as she saw them standing together and tears immediately began to flow down her face as she rushed to them.

She stopped in front of them. "You are both alive, that is more than I would have hoped for not so very long ago."

Liam smiled and would have spoken, but Christian did so first. He touched Ava's shoulders turning her to face him.

"This war is over," he said, his voice soft and yet trembling with emotion. "I swear to you that your brother and I will never, ever bring you pain or fear or worry again. At least not when it comes to each other."

She blinked up at him, her lip quivering. "Truly?" she whispered.

"Truly," Liam said for Christian.

Ava turned toward him slightly, reaching out to take his hand. With the other hand, she grasped Christian's fingers, standing between them as the bridge she had fought to become. The bridge she was and that she and her children would be from now on.

And Liam would have felt utter and complete peace if it weren't for one thing.

Violet.

He squeezed his sister's fingers gently before he released them and paced away as thoughts of the other woman pounded through his aching head.

He felt Ava's eyes on him as he moved restlessly through the room, as well as Christian's. He flinched at revealing so much to them, but he couldn't help it. The resolution of long held hatreds could only take him so far when his mind was tangled up with thoughts of a woman who had set him on his head and heels for three weeks.

"Why did you bring Violet with you?" he asked, refusing to look at his sister and brother-in-law.

He heard Ava catch her breath. "I won't lie to you."

He faced her. "Please don't."

She nodded. "I wasn't certain that you would see me. I have come to view her as a friend to me and I wanted to have her here in case I needed her counsel."

His lips thinned at the answer. "So she was to use what she knew against me if you couldn't get what you wanted?"

Ava stepped forward. "Are you so determined to think the worst of this woman? I practically bribed her into doing it, Liam. She was terrified to return to Bath and risk your wrath, risk your disdain."

He arched a brow. "What did you bribe her with?"

Christian cleared his throat. "She needed a residence in Romwell and I assisted her with finding an arrangement as well as bought her home in London so that she could move as soon as possible."

Liam squeezed his eyes shut. Of course she would want to go to her son immediately. She would go to the life she had desired for so many years. Though he doubted she had told his sister and Christian that. It was a private pain, even if he had spent the past few days refusing to allow her even that quarter.

"She'll leave for the north as soon as our business here is concluded," his sister added softly. "Which I suppose will be today now that you have seen me, now that we have made our peace and can finally move forward with our lives."

Liam didn't respond. Move forward with his life? He had spent so much time avoiding just that and now he was going to be forced to do it without Violet. Without the woman he...

He broke the thought off. There was no way he could feel what his mind was screaming at him that he felt. Love was something he had been lucky enough to find once. There was no way he could feel it again for a woman who had come to him under false pretenses. Who had lied to him. Who had used him.

Who had tenderly cared for him. Who had offered him solace and painful secrets. Who had given herself over to him and asked him to do the same.

A woman who meant everything to him.

He shook his head as the emotions he had been fighting washed over him fully. He loved Violet Milford.

"Liam, come back with us to the home we've let here," Ava urged, moving toward him to touch his arm. "Come back and talk to Violet."

He shook his head. The very idea was terrifying. "I can't do that."

"You can," Ava whispered. "Please, Liam. Come back with us and see her."

He felt the ice he'd kept around himself melting. He *wanted* to see Violet. It felt like an eternity since he'd smelled her, touched her, held her. He needed it like she was water in the desert, food in a famine, and perhaps that was exactly what she had been to him. Rescue after years of being lost and alone.

"I will," he whispered with a shaky nod. "I'll come. I'll see her."

When they entered the house in Bath less than an hour later, Liam's hands were shaking. He stood in the parlor, a servant taking his coat and hat, saying words he didn't understand as he stared up toward the chambers on the second floor.

Somewhere up there, Violet was waiting.

"What do you mean she left?"

His sister's voice pierced through his fog and he jerked his face toward the servant, truly seeing the man for the first time. "Left?"

The butler cleared his throat and shot a quick glance toward Christian. "Y-Yes sir. Miss Milford departed about an hour after Lord and Lady Rothcastle left to visit your estate, my lord."

Liam staggered back. "Could she have simply gone shopping?" His eyes went wide. "Or perhaps to visit a friend she has here in town, Olivia Cranfield?"

The way the servant's eyes went down, but not before Liam saw the pity in his glance answered the question, but the man spoke anyway. "Miss Milford took all her belongings, my lord. And she said that Lord and Lady Rothcastle would find a note of explanation in her room."

Liam clenched his fist at his side, exchanged a brief glance with his sister, whose cheeks were pale and eyes wide. Then he turned on his heel and started up the stairs.

"Where was she staying?" he demanded.

He glanced back to find the butler looking at Christian for permission to answer this question from a man he had never even met. Christian bobbed out a quick nod that made Liam happy they had set their differences aside.

"Up the stairs and to your right, my lord," the servant explained as he motioned upward. "The third chamber on the left was Miss Milford's. I haven't yet had it cleaned since I wasn't sure what their Graces would have me do."

"You did the right thing, Simms," Ava reassured him softly. "Will you leave us for a moment?"

The servant seemed just as pleased to depart as Liam was to see him go. Liam turned on his heel and moved up the stairs. His breath came short, not with exertion, but with emotion as he turned toward the room the man had indicated. He hesitated before the chamber and slowly reached out to touch the door handle, as if it would shock him.

As he stepped inside, his knees very nearly buckled. Indeed, the room was empty and there was no indication anyone was returning to it. But even though she had only been there a few hours, he could smell Violet's perfume in the air. He could feel her presence, and it cut him down to the bone because she wasn't there.

She had gone without even trying to see him.

He rested a hand on the back of a chair and leaned heavily, staring at the bed she had never slept in, thinking of her in his bed.

"Liam?"

He turned to find only his sister standing at the door. Although he and Christian had made peace, the man seemed to respect and understand that they had not yet reached the point where Liam wished to share this darkest moment of his soul with a man who had been his greatest enemy up until just hours ago.

"Please," he whispered as he turned away. "A moment."

He heard her sharp intake of breath, but she didn't leave. Instead, she stepped inside the room, briefly squeezed his arm as she passed him and then moved toward the bedside table he had been too distracted to fully notice. There was a note there, folded, with Ava's name written across it in Violet's flowing, expressive script.

"Shall I read it?" his sister asked. "Or would you like to do it?"

He stared at her, stared at the letter not meant for him. It was torment to hear Violet's words read to him, but not knowing what she said was worse.

"The letter is yours—you may do as you wish," he forced himself to say.

Ava's lips pursed, and she slowly unfolded the note and began to skim the words.

"She apologizes for breaking our bargain for her to stay here until all was resolved with you and offers to pay Christian back for certain expenses she feels he might have incurred."

Liam flinched. "How very businesslike of her."

Ava looked at him before continuing. "Not really. Let me read you this: 'You guessed my heart in London, Ava, so you must understand how utterly painful returning to Bath is to me. I have spent my time since my return haunted by memories and battered by regrets. If I stay, this will only grow worse, I fear, as I know your brother's feelings toward me will not change, even if his connection to you can be reformed. I pray it will be, for I know he needs you.'"

Liam stiffened even as Ava smiled at him. "You see, she is not businesslike at all and thinks of you often and with great depth."

"Yes," he said. "Is there anything else?"

"Yes, a bit," Ava said. "'If you do manage to soften your brother's ear enough to hear you, I hope you will convey to him how deeply I am sorry that he was hurt or betrayed by my actions. I never should have gone so far, nor allowed myself to become so involved. Because of this, I must now live with the great and permanent consequences of my actions. I appreciate all the kindness you have shown to me and I remain...'" Ava stopped reading. "And it goes on et cetera, et cetera before she signs it with what appears to be a very shaky hand."

Ava held the letter out, but Liam shook his head. "I cannot look at it."

She frowned but did not insist, and merely placed the pages back where Violet had left them such a short time ago. She folded her arms.

"You know where she is going don't you?" Ava didn't wait for him to respond. "Even if you don't, I do."

He bent his head. "I know where she is going. I know why as well."

"Then what will you do, Liam?" Ava moved toward him a step.

He thought of that question, but didn't answer it. "In her letter, she mentions that you guessed her heart in London. What did she mean?"

Ava bit her lip and seemed to be considering that question. "You shouldn't hear this from me."

"Please," he said. "Consider it an act of good faith to repair the damage done by your meddling."

Ava nodded slowly. "Very well," she said, voice low and a little broken. "When she came to London, I confronted her with the fact that she loves you."

Liam reeled once again as his stare came to Ava's face. He knew he had no color remaining in his cheeks and his eyes were likely wide as saucers. He could no more control those reactions than he could have forced himself to never take breath again by sheer act of will.

"Love me?"

His sister nodded. "Yes, Liam. Violet loves you. And I believe you love her. So I ask you again—what you will do with that knowledge?"

He pondered the question and finally walked away to the window.

"Violet Milford has spent a lifetime being controlled and forced and hurt. She may love me, but there is no doubt from her words that the feelings bring her nothing but pain and heartache. So I believe that it might be best to simply let her to her new life. Let her go to the life she has dreamed of for years. She deserves peace. She deserves that more than anything."

He turned to find his sister staring at him, a hand covering her mouth in shock. Slowly, she lowered it and her face was filled with disbelief.

"You would turn away from love, Liam?" she asked.

He nodded, though he felt no pleasure or happiness or even peace in that agreement to her statement.

"Yes," he choked out. "After seeing all the damage that emotion can do, I think it is my only choice. No matter how deeply that wounds me."

"Liam," she began, her arguments clear in her eyes.

He held up a hand and smiled at her kindly. "Please, Ava. Let this go. I have done nothing to deserve Violet. And my decision is not one that will change. But I do not wish to discuss it further."

He turned and moved to the door. "Now I must return to the estate, for I have much to plan."

"Plan?" his sister said with tears in her eyes. "What do you mean?"

"If I am to return to London, there is much to be readied."

He saw her smile even though her face was still pale, and he walked away with that as his last vision of her. There was nothing else to be said or decided anymore.

It was over, and he had to accept that.

Chapter Twenty-One

Violet smiled as she watched Peter wade into the cool water at the mouth of the cove and splash about madly, his shrieking laughter cutting through the air to where she sat on the sand. It had been a month since her arrival in Romwell and they were still growing accustomed to one another.

Mrs. Wilcox, who had been taking care of him since his birth, had ensured he knew about her and read her letters to him religiously. But he still ran to the other woman when he skinned a knee or needed a snuggle. That stung, but Violet was ready to accept it. These things took time. And Peter was a sweet child, full of love that he gave to her freely. She had no doubt he would one day accept her fully and come to *feel* she was his mother, not just say it.

She wished that was not the only thing she thought time would fix. Her heart was another matter.

It wasn't that she wasn't happy. She loved the cottage she had purchased, she loved waking up in the same house as her son, she loved having her freedom.

But she dreamed of Liam every night, she thought of him every day.

"Because you are a foolish girl," she muttered to herself, rising as Peter came running out of the water, shaking his wet hair as he headed toward her and her towel.

"Mummy, look!" he said, holding out a shell. "An oyster. Do you think there's a pearl inside?"

She wrapped the big towel around his slender frame and pulled him into her lap. He tucked into her arms perfectly and continued to hold the oyster toward her.

"We would have to get it open to see," she said, looking at the little shell like it was the most fascinating thing in the world. "How do you suppose we could do that?"

"I have a pocket knife," came a man's voice behind them.

Violet's heart lurched into her throat, and she turned to look at the man who matched the voice she knew so well. There was Liam, up on a horse, staring down at her with intensity.

This was a dream. It had to be a dream. He couldn't really be here, standing with her, staring at her with an expression that was so gentle and kind, yet so possessive and charged with desire that her whole body reacted without any leave from her mind.

Slowly, she pushed to her feet, lifting Peter with her, and stared at him.

"Liam," she breathed, incapable of saying anything else.

He nodded, seemingly calm, as if they were meeting by chance and there was nothing in the world odd about it.

"Violet." Then he smiled. "And this must be young master Peter."

Violet shook as she set Peter on his feet on the sand. He leaned into her slightly, seeking comfort as he gazed up at the handsome stranger on the horse.

"Who is this, Mummy?" he whispered, but loudly enough that Liam couldn't help but hear. He laughed in response.

She smiled as she took Peter's hand, offering the reassurance she couldn't give to herself as she fought to breathe while she looked at Liam.

"This is...this is a friend of mine, love. Lord Windbury."

Liam swung down from the horse and stepped forward, holding out a hand. Peter watched him warily, his gaze holding on Liam's face.

"You have a scar," he pointed out with the perfect clarity and lack of self-awareness that only a child under a certain age could get away with.

Violet stiffened, watching Liam for his reaction. She knew what emotions that scar carried for him. But to his surprise, Liam took one knee before her son and smiled.

"I do indeed, my friend. Quite a sight, isn't it?"

Liam being at his level seemed to make Peter more comfortable and, to Violet's surprise, he reached out and rubbed a wet, sandy thumb over Liam's cheek, feeling the raised surface with wonderment.

"Are you a pirate?" he asked.

Liam grinned, and Violet's stomach flipped at the sight. He seemed so...*light* with her son. There was an easiness to him she had never seen before. And she liked it so very much, despite how fleeting it had to be. His coming here could bode for nothing good, considering how things had been left between them.

"Ask your mother," Liam said.

Peter looked up at her. "Is he?"

She smiled and shot a quick glance toward Liam. "He is a rogue, but not a pirate. Though the two could very well be related."

Peter twisted his mouth a little. "No, I think he's a pirate."

"Then a pirate I shall be," Liam said with a shrug. "Do you think you might sign on to be my first mate? I need someone to swab decks and manage the affairs of the crew."

Peter seemed to consider that. "Maybe when I'm six."

He arched a brow. "When will you be six?"

"November," he said with a wide grin.

"I will look forward to your application at that time, then," Liam said with a smart salute.

Violet's heart ached as she watched them interact. Peter was smiling so widely and Liam treated him with respect and care that many men of his class would not have done with a whore's bastard son.

But then, Liam wasn't like anyone she'd ever known before. It was why she loved him, even though it was an impossibility.

"Peter, Mrs. Wilcox is coming right now," she said, looking down the little path out of the cove. The woman was hustling up, watching Liam with a wariness that spoke so very highly of her. "Would you like to go with her and get dressed?"

Peter wrinkled his brow. "Will you come?"

"I will walk you to her, but I must speak to Lord Windbury," she said, meeting Liam's eyes. "He has come a long way to talk to me. But I will return in just a little while and we can have our tea."

The boy seemed to ponder that and then he nodded. "All right."

"I'll be back in a moment," she said softly to Liam.

Liam nodded. "I'll wait."

"Goodbye, sir," Peter said as he tossed the towel from his shoulders, released Violet's hand and began to sprint toward Mrs. Wilcox.

Violet shook her head, smiling despite herself and picked up the towel before she followed him. When she reached the older woman, Peter was already chattering to Mrs. Wilcox.

"—and he's a pirate," he concluded.

"Is he?" Mrs. Wilcox said with a meaningful look toward Violet.

Violet shrugged. "A man from before," she said.

Mrs. Wilcox nodded. "When Tom Higgins told me he'd sent a stranger who was looking for you down to the cove, I raced here to make sure he wasn't giving you no bother."

"He isn't," Violet said with a quick glance over her shoulder.

In the distance, Liam was shaking out the sandy blanket. His movements were graceful and fit the long, lean form that made her want him so very badly.

"Handsome devil," Mrs. Wilcox said with a whistle.

Violet ignored that. "I need to speak with him. Will you take Peter back and help him get dressed? I could be an hour or more."

Mrs. Wilcox nodded and Peter easily slid his hand into hers. "See you later, Mummy!"

She bent to kiss his forehead. "I'll be up soon, love." As they began to turn, she mouthed *thank you* to Mrs. Wilcox and then drew a deep breath before she faced Liam again.

To her surprise, he had plunked himself down on the blanket a hundred yards away and now leaned back on his elbows, watching her as she walked toward him.

This was as good a place to talk to him as any, despite being out in the open. The cove was almost entirely private, for few knew of its existence at all. There were rumors that the servants in the area came down here to bathe nude at night, it was so secluded.

Now swimming nude with Liam was all she could think about as she crossed the final few feet to him and dropped to her knees on the blanket.

"Liam," she whispered.

He didn't allow her to say more. He sat up, cupped the back of her head and drew her against him for a deep, probing kiss that made everything she might have said to him melt away in an instant.

It had been little more than a month since she last touched him, but it felt like an eternity had passed. She was starved for him. No matter how she tried, she couldn't stop herself from wrapping her arms around him and molding her body to his as he lowered her back on the blanket and continued to kiss her with such tender passion.

His hand slid down, cupping her breast gently as she arched up into the touch without shame. God, how she had missed this. And even though she knew she should stop him, she didn't. She couldn't. Her need was too desperate to do anything but fully surrender to it.

He began to unbutton her gown, and she gasped as his fingers slipped into the space he had created. Even through her chemise his hand was hot, heavy against her. She moaned as he found his way beneath the flimsy fabric and stroked a thumb over her distended nipple.

"God, I missed you," he muttered against her neck as he sucked there, continuing to pluck her nipples until she thought she might go mad. "I missed this."

"Please," she urged, cupping his backside with her hands and drawing him closer. "I need you."

He stared down at her, face filled with wonder. Then he nodded and the expression changed to one of more desperate drive. He slid her beneath him and hiked her skirts up around her waist. She opened her legs without hesitation and he slid his hand between them, finding the parting of her drawers so that he could slide a finger across the slick opening of her sex.

"God, you are ready," he grunted.

She cupped his face gently and pressed a kiss to his lips. "I have been ready for you for weeks."

He said nothing else, but fumbled at his trouser waist. Finally, he opened the buttons and his cock popped free. He positioned himself at her entrance and stared down at her, holding her gaze as he slipped inside, inch by inch, filling her to the hilt of his cock.

Once he was fully seated inside of her, he cupped her face, pressing light kisses against her lips. He was so gentle, so tender that tears filled her eyes and she clung to him.

He began to move, gently thrusting deep inside of her. It was evident he was trying to draw out the pleasure, but it had been so long since he touched her that her body had no patience. She felt the wall of her orgasm building at massively rapid speeds. She couldn't control her body and rocked against him, crying out in broken gasps that were lost to the sound of the waves breaking on the sand behind them.

She dug her nails into his shoulders as the pleasure washed over her. Her hips thrust wildly against him, and she whispered his name into his neck as her sex fluttered with release.

He drove faster, his neck straining, and as her orgasm began to slowly fade, he grunted out his own pleasure and she felt the splash of his seed deep inside her. She drew him down, reveling in his weight, reveling in this one last happy memory that would wash away the less pleasant thoughts from their last encounter in Bath. And that would be enough.

It had to be enough. For she knew he could offer no more. She wouldn't even ask him to do so. But she would take this.

Liam couldn't have said how long they lay together, bodies still joined as the waves rolled in behind them in a soothing melody that matched their shared breath. Finally, though, he moved away from her, tucking himself back into his trousers as she smoothed her gown over her body.

There was no shyness as she looked at him. There wasn't even regret, which was a fact he was pleased about. Violet had always been pragmatic about their physical union. She never minced or pretended.

But that was Violet. Real and true, beautiful and sometimes broken.

But he so longed to fix that.

"Why did you come here?" she asked, propping herself up on her hand.

He shook his head. "I couldn't stay away," he admitted and felt no hesitation at the words. "I wanted to, I tried to, I forced myself to... but I kept hearing your voice in my head, seeing you in my dreams. With every hour and every day that passed, it grew louder until you were all I could think about. And I needed to see you more than I needed breath."

Despite his confession, her expression was unreadable as she traced a small pattern of circles in the sand beside her. "Your sister told you where I was?"

He nodded. "I'd guessed Romwell because of your son, but yes, my sister and Christian gave me the full particulars so I didn't need to roam the town, asking at every door."

Her face jerked up. "Does that mean—?"

"Yes," he whispered. "We have made our peace. Thanks to you."

She bent her head but he could see relief written on her face. "I'm so happy for you, Liam. And proud that you've come to such a difficult reconciliation. Although I'm not certain I had anything to do with it."

"Aren't you?" He laughed softly. "You appeared in my life almost like magic. You flipped my world on its head. And you reminded me about the good and the beauty in this life."

She bit her lip and refused to look at him. "And lied to you. And manipulated you."

He slipped a finger beneath her chin and forced her to meet his eyes. "No one is perfect," he teased, hoping to lessen the tension between them.

She didn't smile and turned away from his touch. "Liam," she murmured. "I know you were angry with me when you realized your sister hired me. You can pretend you weren't, but—"

"I *was* angry," he agreed without hesitation. "I was furious. But I've come to realize that perhaps I needed manipulation, since reason wasn't working."

She looked at him, and there was no masking the surprise on her face at those words. "Then you don't blame me for what transpired between us."

He shook his head. "You told me in Bath that you had been truthful with me when it came to our connection. Is that correct?"

She nodded swiftly enough that Liam's heart soared.

"When I began, I used sharing information as a way to obtain your trust," she admitted. "But Liam, I ended up telling you things that no one else in this world knows. And the more I shared, the more I came to know you, the more bound to you I became. That was all real, no matter my motives at the start. In fact..."

She shifted, swallowing hard and Liam leaned closer. "Yes?"

"Not being able to talk to you has left me bereft," she admitted softly. "It was like a part of me has gone missing this past month. Until you rode up, I couldn't find it."

He stared at her, taken in by her beauty, swept away by her honesty, loving every part of her and hoping, with everything in him, for a future.

"It is funny you say that, for I have missed talking to you, as well. Especially since Malcolm left."

Her eyebrows lifted. "Left?"

He nodded. "Yes, run off to Gretna Green with Olivia."

She lifted her hands to her cheeks, and there was no mistaking the joy on her face at the news. "That is why she hasn't written to me! I hoped but wasn't certain."

"Oh yes. I imagine they will sweep in from some fantastic, private escape any day now." He smiled, just as happy for their friends as she was. "But you can see how that absence would affect me."

She nodded. "Yes, you two are so close."

"It's more than that." He reached out to brush the back of a hand down her cheek, reveling in the softness of her skin and the way she leaned into him.

"How so?" she asked.

He could see how much she needed to hear him declare himself. A good thing since he intended to do just that.

"When Malcolm left, I lost not only a man at arms, but a friend and confidante. And yet, as I lay awake in my bed at night, I realized the person I wanted to see most, to confide in most, whose voice I wanted to hear...was yours."

She caught her breath, but didn't interrupt. He was just as happy, for saying those words out loud made him want to say so much more.

"Violet, may I tell you all my troubles?" he asked.

She drew back, clearly confused by his question. "Y-Yes."

"You see, I love a woman," he said, his hands nearly shaking as he said those words he never thought he'd say again, let alone have his heart so light with the feeling. "I love a beautiful, wonderful, unexpected woman. And I do not know if she could ever love me in return."

A tear trailed down her cheek, and he reached out to catch it on his finger. "Could she love me, Violet?" he whispered. "Could you love me?"

Chapter Twenty-Two

Violet stared at Liam, hardly able to breathe, to think, let alone speak as he cupped her chin and stared into her eyes with the focused expression of a man bent on possession.

"You love me," she murmured when she could find words.

He grinned, his face lighting up as bright as the blazing sun above them. "Was I not clear? I'm sorry, let me say it again. I *love* you, Violet. I adore you. I want to spend every day of the rest of my life worshipping you."

She gasped in her breath, reaching out to grip his lower arms as she was filled up by his love. And yet, she couldn't surrender to him.

"You don't know what your words mean," she said. "But Liam, I cannot go back to the world of a mistress. Even yours. I would love you, but I couldn't bring my son into the madness that would create. And now that I have had a month with him, I could never, ever find the strength to leave him again."

"I don't want you to leave him," Liam said, drawing back as if she was speaking nonsense. "Truly, I must make myself plainer. What I have come to realize, through sleepless nights and troubled dreams and analyzing every moment with you, is that I want to *marry* you, Violet Milford."

Now her world screeched to a halt and she flinched back, staring at him with what she knew were wild eyes. Wild eyes that reflected a wild heart at his declaration.

"Marry you," she said, scrambling to her feet and backing away. "But that would make me a countess, Liam."

He got up, watching her like he feared she would bolt. "Yes, the last time I checked the lines of titles, that would be correct. And that is a problem because...?"

She stared at him. "Please do not sport with my intelligence, Liam. Or forget your own. I am no woman of rank, no matter who my father was. And I have made my living for the past five years as a mistress. The men of your stature will know that and many would gleefully share it with the women in their lives. We would be whispered and talked about for months, years. We might never find acceptance."

Liam's eyebrows lifted, but he showed no hesitation about what she said. "So it is the scandal you worry about?"

She lifted her hands in frustration. "Amongst other things, yes!"

"Well, let me deal with those worries one by one then. First, your scandal," he said, folding his arms. "I don't know why you think a scandal would trouble me, considering the feud I have engaged in with my brother-in-law for decades. Not to mention the accident that we were both involved in that people talk about to this day. Oh, and the fact that he kidnapped my sister, ruined her and married her. If you think marrying someone outside of rank or who was a mistress will lead the pack in our family scandals, you are really very conceited."

Violet's jaw dropped open in shock. Not only because she wanted to laugh at the playful way he dismissed her concern, but because he dismissed it at all.

"You may close your mouth, my love," he drawled. "I have been whispered about before. I will survive it. Are you weaker than I?"

She swallowed hard. "No. No, I have experienced scandal before as well. But—"

He waved her off. "Then it is settled. Neither of us is so delicate a flower that we cannot bear a few whispers. What is your next concern?"

She blinked. "You are most disconcerting."

"No, I am a man in love and I will find a way to slay these dragons," he said with a smile. "Next concern please, Miss Milford. I would very much like to conclude this apparent negotiation and get on with the celebrating."

She shook her head, filled with wonder at this new attitude. One she rather liked, actually.

"You are so certain of yourself?"

He nodded. "Since meeting you? Yes, I would say you have reminded me of the confidence I once had. Another reason to love you, by the way. Now, next concern."

She fumbled for her thoughts, which were jumbled by his unexpected reaction.

"My son," she said softly. "He is of great concern."

Now the playfulness left Liam's face and voice. "Of course he is. You would not be a woman I could love if you didn't adore your child and didn't think of him in every decision you make. What specifically is your worry?"

"If I agreed to marry you," she said and shook her head when his face lit up. "*If*, would you accept my son?"

"I would treat him as my own," Liam said without hesitation. "I would include him in my life and yours and never let any children we might have of our own believe that I felt anything for him other than the love of a father. I would also include him in my financial arrangements after my death. I cannot leave a son not of my blood my title, but I will leave him a hefty inheritance and a property if he desired that."

"How do you know you could feel love for him?" she whispered. "When his own grandfather looks at him and sees him as bastard trash?"

His jaw set. "Is that what he said to you at some point?"

She nodded, trying not to recall that moment when she could have ripped her own father's eyes out. It had been their last encounter. It would forever be their last, as she would never set foot in a room with the man again.

"Your father is an idiot," he said softly. "I looked at that boy today, all sweetness and brightness, and I can't imagine anyone not loving him. I will be there."

"And what if he doesn't accept you?" she asked, taking in a sobbing breath. "To be honest, he's not yet fully accepted me. It would be so much for him to bear, so much change in such a short time."

He tilted his head and seemed to ponder that. Finally, he spoke again, low and sweet.

"I would like to marry you today if I could, Violet. But we must consider Peter, I know that. If you would agree to be my wife, I would buy a home near yours here in Romwell so we could be near each other. And I would wait until he was ready to accept you, until he was able to accept me."

She tilted her head. "And if that took a month? Six months? A year or even more?"

He shrugged as if those timelines meant nothing to him. "It seems I've been waiting for you for a long enough time as it is, Violet. I wouldn't be so foolish not to practice some patience if it meant having you in my life forever. I would wait. Although I would require conjugal visits in my prison down the lane."

"Would it be a prison?" she asked on a broken laugh.

He smiled. "Without you? Definitely."

She reached out to touch his face, tracing the line of his scar that spoke of his strength, his fortitude, his stubbornness. He leaned into her hand and smiled.

"You make it hard to say no," she whispered.

"Then say yes," he urged, catching her fingers and drawing them to his lips where he kissed the tips. "Say yes and save me. Say yes and let me save you. Please say yes."

She leaned into him, staring up into his eyes and seeing a future she had never dared dream about.

"Y-Yes," she stammered and squeezed her eyes shut as she laughed. "Yes."

He drew back a fraction. "Truly?"

"Yes!" She shouted it now, letting it echo off the walls of the protective cove. "I will marry you, Liam. Assuming approval of my son, I will marry you."

He caught her in his arms, lifting her to spin her in the sand as he showered kisses against her lips. When he drew back, his smile was wide and bright and as beautiful as he had been to her from the first moment she saw him rise up from the water in the baths.

"I love you," she whispered. "I love you so very much."

He didn't say anything, but bent his head to kiss her one more time.

Epilogue

One year later

It was quiet in the sunroom, light streaming in the floor to ceiling windows, but Violet couldn't help but grin as she looked out over the garden below. It wouldn't be quiet for long.

They were coming.

She turned quickly reorganized the biscuits on her tea tray and then turned to face the door. It flew open and in came a group of babbling, laughing people.

Her family.

First came Ava and Christian. Christian had their eight-month old son Julian in his arm and hardly leaned on his cane at all anymore. Ava always beamed and said love had cured him, though Violet was fully aware that the duke still suffered from pain from that long-ago accident that had changed all their lives so much.

They were followed by Malcolm and Olivia, married for a year with their own newborn baby tucked into her mother's shoulder, sleeping despite the ruckus.

Just after them entered Lord and Lady Weatherfield. They were new friends to her, but Portia was quite possibly the kindest woman she had ever met. Despite her misgivings and anxieties, Portia and Miles had welcomed Violet into their fold as if there was nothing abnormal about a former mistress marrying an earl.

Of course that earl followed them all, swinging Peter with his good arm as her boy belly-laughed. Her fears of her son's acceptance of Liam had been utterly unfounded. In fact, he had been closer to her husband than to her for many months.

"Do the other, do the other! So you can get strong," Peter cackled.

Liam laughed along with him. "My own physician," he said to the group at large. "We will practice lifting you with my bad arm a little later, Peter. I promise you."

Her son groaned but let Liam go. Her husband moved straight to her, his single-intentioned movements making her heart race even after nearly nine months of marriage.

"Hello, darling," he said, pressing a kiss to her lips despite all the company. His hand slipped down to cover the swell of her belly. "And how is Agatha today?"

"You don't know that this baby is a girl," Violet said, laughing even as she covered his hand and they both felt the baby move inside of her. "And I never agreed to Agatha."

"Hmmmm," he murmured, his fingers spreading slightly. "But I have ways to convince you." The last was said in a whisper that made her cheeks darken with a blush.

He smiled and backed away, turning his attention toward the group. Everyone was gathering around, Ava pouring tea, Portia rallying the children and handing out sweets when she thought no one was looking, but as Liam stepped away, what made Violet happiest of all was how the three men flocked together.

Christian and Liam talked for a moment and Liam actually laughed at something their brother-in-law said. Violet exchanged a quick smile with Ava. It was a slow process, but it felt like finally the men were coming to some kind of comfort with each other.

Perhaps one day they might even be friends.

Violet sighed as she settled herself into a comfortable chair and took the tea her sister-in-law offered her with a smile. After a lifetime of loneliness and knowing she didn't belong with her family, with anyone...now she had everything she'd ever wanted.

She had more.

Beautiful
Distraction

Dedication

For those who have supported me, thank you for the encouragement in times of struggle, especially Michael, who has to live with my often chaotic and creative mind. For any detractors, thanks for lighting fires under me. Amazing what a woman can do when she's told she can't or shouldn't.

Chapter One

April 1814

Malcolm Graham squeezed his eyes shut as a tremendous crash echoed from the adjacent chamber. He strummed his fingers along the ledger before him and waited. When a moment had gone by in silence, he returned his attention to the line of numbers before him. But he had no sooner regained his concentration than another explosive smashing sound came from the other room.

Malcolm sighed, shut the ledger and got to his feet, just as the butler, Simms, stepped into the room. The other man's face was long and stern, and he met Malcolm's eyes with disapproval.

"Mr. Graham," he began, his tone steeped in long-suffering agitation.

"Yes, yes," Malcolm said as he picked up the jacket he had discarded earlier in the day and slung it over his shoulders. He smoothed it into place before he spoke again. "I have ears, Simms. I'm perfectly aware and I shall take care of it."

The butler's eyebrow arched. "So you say, but we had another maid resign this morning. One cannot run a household in this fashion, Graham."

"Try running a life," Mal muttered.

The butler folded his arms. "I beg your pardon?"

Mal stretched his fingers slowly and counted to ten in his head. There was already one unreasonable party in this household—he could not be the second.

Slowly, he faced the butler. "I do understand your concerns, Simms. But as I said, I am taking care of it. And you and your staff are compensated for your trouble, I would say at a much higher rate than any other household. So if you do not think what you endure is worth it—"

The butler held up his hands. "Of course not."

Mal nodded once as he moved past the servant and stood at the door next to the room he had just left. He and Simms played this game regularly, but he certainly hoped the butler wouldn't one day call his bluff. It would be near impossible to find another servant who would last a week under the conditions Simms regularly complained about. And Mal could scarcely stand the idea of the search. He was already worn to near his limit and he was tired.

Straightening his shoulders, he pushed the parlor door open and stepped inside. Although it was a perfectly beautiful and bright afternoon, all the shades inside had been drawn.

"Great God, man, light a lamp," he muttered as he shut the door behind himself and leaned against it, allowing his eyes to adjust to the darkness.

"I don't want a lamp," came the sour, angry mutter from somewhere across the room. Probably in a chair beside the cold fire, judging from the sound of it.

"So you have something against the light," Mal said as he slowly made his way across the room. "What do you have against the dishes?"

As he asked the question, he caught the edge of the curtains and drew them back in one swift motion that flooded the chamber with sunshine. He turned in time to see his best friend and employer, Liam, Earl of Windbury, recoil from the sudden brightness.

Liam did not look well. His hair was too long, his whiskers unshaved for at least three days, which made the bright-white line of the scar that sliced from his forehead to his chin all the more noticeable. His skin was pale and there were circles beneath his eyes that marked how little he was currently sleeping.

Perhaps under other circumstances Mal would have been concerned about this. But he had been through this with Liam for over eighteen months now. He had grown accustomed to his friend's mercurial shifts in mood. Some days it was rage, some days sorrow and sometimes, just for a moment, Mal caught a glimpse of the man Liam had once been.

He lived for those moments. They kept him going when Liam was petulant, as he was now.

"Damn it, Mal, what did I say?" Liam asked, casually tossing a china cup in his direction.

Mal sidestepped it without much thought and it shattered against the wall beside him. He brushed a rogue piece of china from his shoulder and rolled his eyes.

"You know that every time you allow yourself to descend into foolishness that you lose at least three servants."

Liam glanced up at him and for a moment his eyes lost their glassy emptiness. "I do?"

Mal snorted out a humorless laugh. "Most people don't have the constitution I do for your moods, my friend. They don't like the monster of the manse, crashing around, yelling and breaking things. It makes it very difficult for Simms and for me."

Liam dipped his chin. "I apologize."

Mal tilted his head to look more closely at his friend. *There* was the Liam he'd known since childhood, the one not entirely steeped in his own pain. The Liam who actually gave a damn about other people. Mal celebrated those brief glimpses of his true friend, for that person would be gone soon enough.

"I wish I could control my feelings," Liam continued, fisting his hands at his sides. "But there are times when they take over so fully."

Mal swallowed. "It is a great loss that you suffered when Matilda died, my friend. No one begrudges you that pain, nor the physical pain which lingers from the accident. But I think, if you try, you *can* control your feelings more."

Liam jerked his gaze to Mal, his eyes narrow. "Do you?" he asked, his tone a dangerous warning.

Mal ignored it. "I do. We have come to Bath on your request, Liam. So instead of locking yourself away in a dark chamber, throwing crockery, why don't you think of availing yourself of the waters, or seeing the town, or looking at the property, or anything else except act a fool in the sitting room?"

Liam's face went hard, as it always did when his reactions were questioned. Slowly his friend pushed to his feet. He glared at Mal before he started for the parlor door.

"It must be nice for everything to be so easy," Liam said as a parting shot before he stormed up the stairs. A few moments later, Mal heard the shuddering slam of Liam's chamber door.

Mal sighed as he walked over to the fire where Liam had been seated. Broken dishes were scattered around the floor for some poor maid to clean up. Lucky her. She only had to clean up broken dishes. Mal had been cleaning up the rest of Liam's messes for years.

Serving as his friend's man of affairs for almost five years, Mal had been the only one of their circle to stay after the accident that had killed the love of Liam's life and made him the shell of a man he now was.

Mal had given up a great deal to help Liam. Most of the time, he didn't regret it. Sometimes he wondered what exactly he had lost in doing so.

He was about to turn away when he noticed that one plate in the pile on the floor was almost entirely intact. He picked it up gingerly, shaking off the broken china that littered its top. With a frown, he tossed it against the fireplace and watched it shatter fully.

"Hmm, it does help," he muttered. "But Liam is a fool if he thinks any of this is easy."

Then he turned to ring for Simms and whatever maids were left who could clean up the mess Liam had made.

Olivia Cranfield paced the small parlor of the home she shared with her friend and fellow courtesan, Violet Milford. It had been a remarkably trying day. Despite the fact it was only just after noon, Olivia currently wished she could just go back to bed and forget any of it had happened.

She had lived the life of a mistress for seven years, but she had never kept a protector for very long. The protector she had parted ways with that very morning was not much different. After six months, she had felt the familiar itch of anxiety that he knew her well enough to see through her act, her disguise.

Despite being a "gentleman", David had not behaved very gentlemanly in their parting. His cruel words still rolled around in her mind.

Stupid, low bitch.

The *bitch* part she could ignore. It was a slur that didn't trouble her. But *stupid* and *low* hit very close to home, and she couldn't help but go over and over in her mind if there was any way she had revealed herself to him. Had she slipped and let her real accent through? Had she said something that would make him see what she truly was?

Violet couldn't understand Olivia's fears. But then, Violet didn't come from the same background. She would never understand the hesitation and terror that came with being unmasked as an uneducated Cockney chit no highborn man would want as his mistress. She could be ruined.

Her thoughts were interrupted as the front door was opened and shut in the foyer. She heard Violet speaking to their servant, Rodgers, but she couldn't tell from her friend's tone if her unexpected meeting with a duke and duchess had been a positive experience or a negative one.

How she envied Violet's ability to hide so much about herself without accompanying fear or grief.

Olivia moved to the door of the parlor and met Violet's eyes as Rodgers took her wrap away. Swiftly, she masked her insecurities and reactions from the morning and put on the guise of a light and knowing courtesan.

"Do you need tea or brandy?" she asked with a half smile.

Violet laughed. "Brandy, I think, to start, despite the early hour."

As Violet entered the parlor and sank into the settee with a sigh, Olivia watched her. "So it didn't go well? Do they accuse you of something?"

"No, not anything like that," her friend reassured her. "They want to hire me to seduce and spy on the duchess's brother, the Earl of Windbury."

Olivia's eyes went wide and she couldn't help but let her mouth drop open. "You are in jest."

"Not at all," Violet said, toeing off her slippers as she rubbed her eyes. "Won't you get that brandy, dearest?"

"Of course," Olivia said, rushing to the sidebar to pour two drinks. As she gave one to her friend, she tried to lighten the mood with her next statement. "Damn, I was hoping the Rothcastles had invited you to their home to make you their secret lover!"

Violet laughed, but she rolled her eyes. "Good God, Olivia, you couldn't have believed that."

Olivia smiled before she took a sip of her drink. "One could hope. Just imagine the scandal, and you in the middle of it."

Violet shook her head, but Olivia knew that a scandal could make a courtesan. Violet was the perfect one to be in the middle of such a storm. She was always so certain of herself.

"Well, it wasn't that, but I'd say hiring a courtesan in order to seduce and spy on Lord Windbury is certainly scandal enough, even though no one will ever know about it."

"It *is* shocking," Olivia conceded as she sat down across from Violet. "But lucrative."

She looked at Violet carefully. Yes, such a scheme would be something that would make Violet a tidy sum. And she knew full well what Violet was squirreling money away for. The very thought made Olivia's hands shake. She almost didn't want to ask the next question in her mind.

"You—you won't really run away to the country when it's over, will you?"

She held her breath, hoping she had sounded light when she asked the question, not stricken. Violet had her reasons to leave London; there was no cause to make her friend feel guilty, with an expression of her true feelings on the matter.

"I will." Violet smiled and there was a flash of joy, of *relief*, on her face. "But you may visit me if you think you could bear the boredom."

"You deserve happiness and boredom, if that is what you choose. You *and* Peter."

Olivia sighed. They always joked about retiring to the tedium of a country life, but sometimes it sounded heavenly. But she didn't have the reason, a child, nor the means that Violet did to depart London. Violet had always been the more successful courtesan. She had far surpassed Olivia's training years ago.

Violet waved her hand to dismiss the subject of the child she adored and missed so deeply that she never spoke of him for fear of breaking down. "So, as I said, this is an important mission. But *not* an easy one. He's a hard man to reach, as a great many courtesans have discovered over the last eighteen months."

Olivia refocused. Violet wished to strategize and that was the best she could do for her friend at present.

"Lord Windbury might not keep a woman," Olivia conceded, "but he does please them. I've heard very good things about his prowess, so at least you can have fun."

Violet seemed to consider that point, though her expression did not become less troubled.

"They are letting a place for me in Bath and covering my expenses while I'm there." Violet bit her lip. "Do you think you might come with me? I think you've heard more about the man than I have and I could use your help and advice."

Olivia couldn't help but smile at the offer. "A few weeks in Bath! Of course I'll come. There is no downside to that offer." Violet nodded, absentmindedly, so Olivia continued after a brief pause. "And I have no protector at present..."

Violet friend snapped her attention back to Olivia. "So you *did* end things with David this morning?" A slow nod was all Olivia could manage, and Violet's face fell. "Was he very cruel?"

"He was not entirely kind," Olivia said softly. "He was angry."

"He was an ass from the beginning. I do not know why you choose such wretched men to cater to," Violet said, wringing her hands in frustration.

Olivia shrugged, continuing to maintain the façade of flippancy. "Because they have money?"

Violet frowned. "You are so much more than that, Olivia. I am truly asking you the question."

Olivia bent her head. Being honest was difficult, even with her best friend in the world. "Because it makes it far easier to keep myself distant and remember every day that when I'm with them I'm not the real me. And when it's over, I don't miss them or think of them again."

Violet was quiet for a long moment, then reached over to take her hand. "You deserve to be *you*, to be happy."

"Impossible," Olivia protested with a weak smile. "And I *am* happy."

Violet looked at her closely, but then she nodded. "Well, all the more reason to escape stuffy London and go to Bath together. A change of scenery will do us both good."

Olivia laughed with relief that her friend had not further pursued the subject. It was better not to think of it, of any of it, too much. "Yes,

I think Bath sounds divine. No distractions, and I can be of help to you. It sounds exactly like the holiday I need."

Chapter Two

Malcolm leaned against the cold stone wall next to the little door that led into the exclusive, private bathhouse and shook his head. Liam was utterly predictable in so many ways. He would growl and sputter and allow his emotions to overtake him. When Mal pointed it out to him, he blustered. But within a few days, he was all apologies and attempts to make amends.

It hadn't always been like that. There had been months, especially just after the accident, when he had feared Liam would take his own life. Nightmares of the times he had thwarted the earl in his designs to do just that still haunted him.

Mal squeezed his eyes shut to block out the thoughts. He drew a few deep breaths before he opened them again. To his surprise, he was no longer alone in the narrow alleyway that hid the secret entrance to the baths. A lady stood in the entrance to the side street, watching him.

An extremely beautiful lady.

She did not wear a hat and her blonde hair was spun up in an elaborate style. Little tendrils fell down to perfectly frame a heart-shaped face. She had full lips, finely boned cheeks and dark-brown eyes that were currently focused on him. She wore a silk gown in a fetching shade of green that highlighted the warmth of her creamy skin. She was obviously a lady of breeding and money, though that made her appearance in the dingy alleyway all the more confusing.

"Good afternoon," he said, not moving from his leaning position against the wall.

"A very good afternoon to you as well," she replied, the corner of her lip tilting into a seductive half smile. "Mr. Graham, isn't it?"

Now he straightened up, stepping toward her. "It is indeed, though I don't know how you know it."

She laughed, a low, husky sound that hit him in the gut and wound its way into his loins. Already his body stirred with a reaction that he fought to tamp down.

"A woman of my kind has means, Mr. Graham," she responded.

A woman of her kind. He looked at her more closely. She was staring at him boldly, brazenly, with the knowing heat of a woman who recognized sex as a tool in her arsenal. So not a lady after all.

She slid toward the street, and he found himself following behind, lured by her presence.

"You leave me at a disadvantage," he said, coming around the corner to find her waiting for him. The street was quiet, a mere means to the back entrance to the private baths.

"Because you don't know my name?" she asked, arching a brow.

"That is one reason," he conceded.

She laughed again. "I cannot imagine there are others. You do not appear to be a man who is often at a disadvantage to anyone else."

He shrugged. "Not often. I find it interesting, I admit. So, what *is* your name?"

"Olivia Cranfield," she said, extending a hand in greeting.

He took it. Just as her head was bare, she also wore no gloves, and her skin was exquisitely soft against his. He lifted her hand and without thinking, flipped it over to press a most inappropriate kiss to her palm.

She shivered almost imperceptibly and her pupils dilated, showing him the reaction he craved. She wanted him. That was real, even though he knew she had an ulterior motive in approaching him, namely the woman who was now creeping past him into the alley toward the entrance to the bath where Liam was taking the waters.

He should have stopped that mystery woman, but he didn't. Liam could use a woman's touch to calm him down. In truth, he could himself. Mal was realizing now just how long it had been since he'd felt soft skin on his, smelled honeysuckle and mint on a woman's hair and breath, felt wide eyes watching him with desirous intent.

Too long.

"And what is your friend's name?" he asked.

Her gaze, which had been heavy and hooded, suddenly widened. "My friend?"

208

"The one who just scurried down the alley in order to seduce Lord Windbury?" he pressed, drawing Olivia closer, close enough that he could feel her body heat in the cool spring-afternoon air.

She tensed, and there was a flash of fear that briefly crossed her face before she erased it with the effortless pretending of a woman of a certain profession.

"Do you intend to have her arrested?" she asked, her tone even and still flirtatious despite the question.

He grinned. "For what, exactly? I assume she has no intentions of hurting him."

"None whatsoever," Olivia reassured him swiftly. "Nor do I have any intentions of hurting you, Mr. Graham. Quite the opposite, in fact."

She leaned in and he felt the gentle stir of her breath on his cheek. His blood was pumping hard now, making it nearly impossible to think of anything except her—taking her, seeing her naked beneath him.

But he somehow managed to control all those instincts.

"I assume you were sent here as my distraction?" he whispered, touching her cheek with the back of his hand.

"Something like that," she verified, breathless.

"Because *she* asked you to?" he pressed as he jerked his head toward the alley.

Her gaze locked with his. "Yes," she admitted calmly. "But that doesn't mean I find the task to be an unpleasant one."

He held her stare for what seemed like an eternity as thoughts invaded every corner of his mind. She was willing to seduce a stranger for her friend. The fact that she now found him attractive didn't change the fact that she had probably taken that duty before she knew anything about him. Which meant she would do anything for that friend.

Something he knew a great deal about. And yet he wasn't entirely pleased at being on the receiving end of such a "sacrifice".

"You must care for her a great deal," he mused out loud.

Her brow wrinkled, not that he blamed her. They were a hair's breadth apart and yet he was talking about some other woman instead of taking Olivia's offer of distraction.

"I do care for her," Olivia admitted softly.

"And you are willing to do what she asks," he continued.

She withdrew a fraction. "Yes."

"But do you do anything for yourself, Olivia?" he pressed, tilting his head to explore her pretty face closer. "Or are you so wrapped up in her welfare that you forget your own, forget what you want and need?"

He realized as he said it that it was a question he also asked himself. A question he had avoided for a very long time. But now that he had said it out loud, even ostensibly aimed toward another person, he felt the question sink into his skin, his body, his soul.

"You think I only martyr myself for someone else?" Olivia asked, interrupting his troubled thoughts.

Her eyes flashed as if she was angry and her face flushed with pink color that made him wonder if she blushed the same way when at the heights of pleasure.

"I don't know," he said. "I've only just met you."

She scowled at him for a moment, then to his shock, she stepped up to him, cupped his cheeks and drew him down to press her lips to his.

He was stunned by the unexpected kiss, but only for a moment. Then he sank into it, his arms coming around her waist, drawing her against the length of his body as he angled his head for better access to her mouth. Her lips parted, an invitation to further pleasure, and he dove in, driving his tongue to duel with hers as he spun her around and pressed her against the cool stone wall of the building behind them.

She offered no resistance as his kiss grew more demanding; in fact, she parried his attack with a passionate offense of her own. Her arms came up to wind around his neck and she moaned softly as she lifted herself, ever so slightly, into his embrace.

Everything was rapidly spinning out of control. What had started as her response to his jab was now a kiss so erotic that he found himself gliding his hand down her side, feeling her shudder as he settled his fingers against her hips. He wanted to pull her skirts up and have her, right here in the street, in the broad daylight. He wanted to feel her body ripple around his in release and watch her face when she found that pleasure.

He had to stop this before all that became reality and they were arrested. After all, this wasn't exactly the kind of neighborhood where such acts of public obscenity would be ignored.

He tangled his tongue with hers one last time, memorizing her taste, the feel of her kiss, and then he gently set her away and stepped back, panting with desire as he stared at her.

"Go home, Olivia," he managed between ragged breaths.

Her desire-glazed expression faded and there was no mistaking the confusion and hurt that replaced it.

"I beg your pardon," she said, edging away from him and folding her arms as a shield in front of her breasts. "Are you dismissing me?"

He nodded even as he reached out to run a finger along the angle of her jaw. "Only with great difficulty," he said softly. "The next time you see me, Olivia Cranfield, offer yourself to me again. But this time, I want you to do it only for your own pleasure. And mine."

He leaned forward to steal one last kiss and then took all his wavering self-control to turn away from her.

"And where are you going?" she called out from behind him.

"To get a very stiff drink in the hopes it will make other things less stiff," he said without looking back. "I have a feeling my friend will be a while before he finishes his fun."

"You could have had your own fun, you know," she called out.

He paused and turned back toward her. He wanted to rush back and take her somewhere quiet and have that fun. Just not on these terms.

"I hope I'll have another opportunity, Olivia," he said. "Until I do, trust that I will think of you often and in most uncomfortable ways."

With that, he saluted her and then forced himself to continue walking away as he questioned if he had lost his mind entirely.

Over an hour had passed since her encounter with Malcolm Graham, but Olivia couldn't stop thinking of him as she paced the small parlor in the pretty little house they were letting in Bath. Being asked to seduce Lord Windbury's friend to help Violet hadn't exactly been the escape Olivia had been thinking about when she accompanied her friend here, but once she saw the man...

Well, the seduction had ceased to be a duty almost immediately.

He was *beautiful*. That was the only accurate description of him. He was a head taller than the average man, with close-cropped black hair and dark eyes that were almost obsidian when they focused on something. Or someone. Her. She had been captured by that stare, held captive until he chose to release her.

And his body. Great God, it had been too long since she'd touched such a specimen. He was thickly muscled from head to toe—she had felt that beneath his coat when he'd spun her against the wall and pinned her there with passionate kisses. His physical strength was impressive, almost as impressive as the confidence with which he wielded it.

This was not a man who ever doubted himself. She found herself a little jealous of that fact. And irritated by his dismissal of her.

If there was one thing she had learned in the past seven years it was that she knew how to control a man with her body and the promise of pleasure. But this man had not surrendered so readily. Oh yes, he'd kissed her...my, how he had kissed her. She didn't think she had ever been so thoroughly kissed. Even now, her lips tingled at the memory and her body reacted with as much desire.

But then he had withdrawn, talking to her about *choice*.

"Choice," she muttered to herself as she slid her finger around the edge of a long-ago abandoned teacup. "It is easy for a man to say when he has nothing but choices in his life. I've never had a choice. Pretending is my only way of survival."

She turned and looked at herself in the mirror above the fireplace. She saw the fraud she hid from the world, but had Malcolm sensed it? Was that the true reason he had denied her advances? She racked her mind for any slip of her accent, for any way she might have shown her true self and put him off.

Her thoughts were interrupted by the sound of voices in the foyer down the hall. Violet had come home, and Olivia took a long breath. Even with her friend, she sometimes pretended. Today would be no different. She would have to hide her own experiences with Malcolm and focus instead on Violet. She smoothed her gown, then moved to the door and threw it open with a wide smile that she hoped masked her confusion with what had transpired with Malcolm.

"And?" Olivia asked without preamble. She was curious, that was not invented. Had Violet had better luck with the earl?

"And?" Violet repeated as she stepped into the parlor to pour herself a cup of tea.

Olivia couldn't help but notice that the ends of her friend's hair were wet.

"I have been waiting here for you forever. How did it go with Windbury?"

Violet sank into the closest chair and took a long sip of tea.

"Violet?" Olivia said with a laugh when her friend had stalled for far too long. "You are making me mad! Tell me."

"Well," Violet said slowly, "he is—"

When she broke off, Olivia stepped closer. "A beast?"

Violet flinched. "No. Well, yes, but no."

Olivia shook her head. "You are terrible at this. I want to know details."

"He is scarred, of course," Violet said. "But it is anything but unattractive on him."

Olivia blinked as her mind brought her unbidden images of Malcolm's face. She shook them away swiftly.

"And were you able to enact your plan?" Olivia pressed.

Violet nodded. "Yes. As soon as you distracted his friend…thank you, by the way."

Olivia forced a wide smile, but she didn't lie when she said, "It was entirely my pleasure."

Violet's brow furrowed. "How far did *you* go?"

Olivia hesitated. She was not about to admit the humiliating truth to her friend. That Malcolm had refused her was something she would keep to herself.

"Not as far as I would have liked," she said carefully. "That man is very attractive."

Violet laughed and Olivia sighed in relief. Her words and demeanor had worked and now there would be little prying from her friend.

"Well, once you distracted him I was able to enter the private bathing room and…" Violet trailed off with a smile that left no doubts as to what had happened.

"Your seduction is underway," Olivia finished and was shocked at the spiraling attack of jealousy that mobbed her in that moment. She clenched her fists at her sides and ground out, "So what is your next step?"

Violet bit her lip. "I have captured his attention by giving him pleasure, then walking away."

Olivia blinked. That certainly sounded familiar, though she had been on the receiving end today.

"He was taken aback," Violet continued, oblivious to Olivia's thoughts. "I know that from his demeanor. He will be thinking of me, I'm certain, but if I pursue him, his desire may fade. When we next meet, I must make him believe it is an accident."

"Reel him in," Olivia whispered. That was the way it normally worked, wasn't it? Just not today.

"I suppose that is one way to say it." Violet sighed. "But for now my next move will be to write to Lord and Lady Rothcastle and tell them I have encountered Lord Windbury. I'm sure they are awaiting my report."

Olivia arched a brow. "And will you give them details of that 'encounter', as you so appropriately put it?"

Violet shook her head swiftly. "Of course not. They know what methods I shall employ to gain his trust, but I would never be so crass as to elaborate on them. There are some things better left unsaid."

Olivia pressed her lips together. That was a most certainly true statement. She lived her life leaving things unsaid. She had found it was the only way to protect herself. And despite the confusion of the day's events, she had to *keep* protecting herself. Even if she did meet again with the alluring Mr. Graham.

Chapter Three

There was no doubt that Liam had been utterly distracted by his encounter with Violet Milford. And Malcolm could not have been happier at the change. Instead of brooding over the past, his friend was caught up in the woman who had invaded his bath.

Mal couldn't say he didn't understand the obsession. Since his meeting with Olivia just two days ago, he had found himself thinking of the beautiful blonde almost constantly. And scolding himself for not taking what she'd offered, regardless of the reason behind it.

"Are you here?"

Mal jolted at the question and looked across the carriage toward Liam. His friend was staring at him, a mixture of amusement and annoyance on his face.

"Here?" Mal sputtered. "Of course I'm here."

"Really? I've said your name three times since the carriage stopped and you haven't moved a muscle."

Mal blinked and looked toward the carriage window. They had indeed stopped. His cheeks filled with heat as he tried to play off his distraction.

"Woolgathering," he muttered. "Estate business."

Liam's brow wrinkled. "Is that all?"

"What else could it be?" Mal asked as he unlatched the door and threw it open to step into the street.

Liam followed him, his gaze still fixed on Mal. "If you say so, my friend. I have that book to check on. Will you be at Mathers?"

"I will," Mal said. "I'll see you there shortly."

The carriage pulled away as Liam headed up the stairs toward the bookstore they had parked in front of. As the vehicle pulled away and Mal was about to cross the street, he stopped. There, standing on the opposite side in front of a shop, was Olivia Cranfield.

She had her head bent, examining something in the window, so he had a moment to observe her without her knowledge. Over the past forty-eight hours, he had relived every brief moment they'd spent together, but now that he looked at her, he realized she was even more beautiful than the image of her he had created in his mind. Every move she made was graceful, every selection—from the way she wore her hair to the cut and color of her gown—accentuated all her finest physical qualities. Of which there were too many to count.

He found himself moving across the street toward her, not paying attention to the traffic on the lane, hardly noticing anything else but her. He just needed to get to her.

She still hadn't noticed his presence as he sidled up to her softly. He could smell her honeysuckle hair, and it roused his cock to partial attention as he thought again of pinning her against the wall just two days before.

"Olivia," he said softly, close to her.

She jumped and spun toward him, eyes wide and expression startled. Her look quickly turned to one of pleasure as she realized who it was that had crept into her personal space.

"Mr. Graham," she said, raising a hand to cover her heart, which only served to draw his attention to the smooth curve of her breast.

"Mal," he said, voice rough as he forced himself to stop looking at that breast, to stop picturing what it would look like naked or taste like between his lips.

She blinked. "Mal?"

"I insist you call me Mal," he clarified, "since I intend to be improper and call you Olivia."

A slight smile turned up her lips. "Very well, *Mal*. What in the world brings you here?"

"Into town?" he asked.

"In front of a hat shop," she said, motioning to the window where dozens of fancy bonnets were on display for wandering female eyes on the street.

He laughed. "I do not think they are my type."

"The blue one there is your color," she teased as she tapped the glass with a fingernail.

He laughed before he gestured toward the bookstore across the street. "Windbury wished to come to town to check on a book he ordered."

Olivia nodded slowly. "Ah, well, he will likely encounter Violet. She also wished to look at the books."

"And yet *you* are here," Mal said, drinking in her every move.

She looked at him, wickedness in her dark stare. "Indeed I am. And so are you. In fact, *you* approached me. Was that the order of your employer? Are *you* sent on the errand this time, Mal?"

"As your distraction?" he said with a smile.

She nodded.

"Do I distract you?" he purred, moving closer even though he couldn't exactly mold himself to her, not on the busy street.

She swallowed hard at his ever-increasing proximity. "I would be lying if I said you did not. Is it by design?"

"I'm happy to hear I affect you as much as you do me," he said. "But it is not something I was sent to do by anyone."

A flutter of a smile turned up her lips before she spoke again. "Then if you were not sent to keep me busy, that means you are here for yourself. As am I."

"This time it appears that is true," he whispered, though he knew that wasn't entirely true. He hadn't been wholly for his own desires in so long he couldn't recall it.

"What will we do, then?" she asked, her gaze locked with his, unblinking, unwavering. She did not simper or pretend or hide her desire. It was written on her face and in her intense gaze.

He shrugged. "My friend desires your friend," he said. "If I know him, he will encounter her in the bookstore and I would wager he'll invite her to supper tonight because he cannot get her out of his mind. Which means *I* will come to you tonight, here in town."

Her eyes widened. "Will you now? Without my leave?"

He laughed, enjoying their sparring more than he had enjoyed anything as of late. "Do I not have your leave, Olivia?"

She hesitated and then nodded. "If you came to my home, I would not turn you away. Are you always so bold?"

He pondered the question and then answered her honestly, despite what she might think of it. "Not recently. But you apparently bring it out in me. I will be there tonight at eight."

He longed to kiss her, but instead he merely took her hand, lifted it to his lips and then moved to leave.

"Wait, you don't even know where we are staying," she called after him.

He laughed as he turned back toward her. "Oh, my dear, of course I do. I found that bit of information out the very same day I met you. I will see you later."

He left her gaping after him and felt her eyes on his back long after he had moved down the street, his step lighter and his mind filled with images of what he would do once he had her alone.

Olivia glanced at the clock on the mantel and sighed.

"Why are *you* pacing around so?" Violet asked as she paused to glance at herself in the mirror. She looked beautiful, of course.

Olivia shifted beneath the question. She hadn't told Violet about Mal's intentions to come to her tonight. She couldn't place why she'd hesitated. Normally she confessed nearly everything to her friend, at least when it came to sex. But she didn't want to tell Violet about him. Perhaps because then whatever was happening between her and Mal would become even more entangled in Violet's seduction and deception of the Earl of Windbury. Olivia wanted her attraction to Mal, his flirtation and, she hoped, his dalliance with her to be hers and hers alone.

Even though she knew it wouldn't be possible. The further Violet went with the earl, the more she'd want Olivia to be a diversion for Mal. But tonight wasn't about that.

"Olivia?" Violet said as she faced her.

Olivia shook her head. "My, you are beautiful," she said as a means to avoid the answer her friend sought. "The earl won't be able to resist you."

Violet frowned. "I fear I won't be able to resist him either."

"He is that attractive to you?" Olivia asked in surprise. Violet always seemed so in control, but now she nibbled her lip nervously and there was a blush to her cheeks.

"He is, somehow," she admitted softly.

Olivia glanced out the window toward the drive. The earl's carriage had been parked there for nearly ten minutes, waiting for Violet to be ferried to his estate somewhere outside of town.

"Are you questioning the prudence of this arrangement?" she asked, torn between wanting to support her friend and just wanting Violet to go so that Mal could come.

Violet laughed, though the sound was filled with tension. "No more than I question any other decision I've made in the last few years."

"Then I suppose there is nothing more to do than ride away in his carriage," Olivia encouraged. "I'm certain you will be your usual self once you see him and remember what you are doing this for."

Violet's smile fell. "Yes. I must always remember that." She kissed Olivia on the cheek. "If all goes well, I may not see you until morning. Enjoy your night, my dear."

Olivia followed her into the foyer and stood in the doorway as she scurried toward the vehicle. "Good night!"

To her relief, Violet merely nodded and then stepped into the beautiful carriage, waving out the window before the vehicle pulled away. Olivia sighed and shut the door, but she had not gone more than two steps across the foyer when there was a knock behind her.

She pivoted as one of the servants moved to answer. "No need, I'll answer," she said, waving her away.

She pulled the door open and there on the stoop was Mal. He smiled at her and the action made his intimidating figure far less daunting.

"Great God, I thought she'd never leave," he said as he stepped inside, pushed the door shut and immediately gathered Olivia into his arms for a passionate kiss.

She melted against him, offering no resistance as he cupped her hip and drew her against him, letting her feel the evidence of his desire as their tongues tangled. Against her will, she moaned with need and wrapped her arms around his neck, lifting to her tiptoes to offer more of her mouth to him.

He took it all, stroking his tongue over hers, sucking until her knees went weak, taking and mimicking the act of sex until she couldn't see or feel anything but him.

Finally, he pulled away, his breath short and his eyes filled with intent.

"Your room," he grunted—an order, not a question.

She nodded, took his hand and all but dragged him up the short staircase to the living quarters above. Violet had taken the larger master chamber, but her own chamber was certainly serviceable and had a bed large enough for what she wanted to do at present.

She threw open the door and they stepped inside. Mal paused and looked around at the plain room and its drab colors.

"It isn't like you at all," he murmured.

She started at his observation, but shrugged. "It isn't my home. My room in my home is much more reflective of who I am."

"I would like to see that," he said, catching her eye.

She kicked the door shut. "Not tonight."

He laughed as he cupped her face and drew her in for another kiss. This time he moved more slowly, as if the fact they were alone in a bedroom made him less desperate, less needy. But the desire was there. She could feel it in the press of his tongue, the heat of his body, the hard ridge of his cock that nudged her thigh as he urged her back a few steps toward the bed.

The room was quiet other than the occasional crackle of the fire as he drew back a fraction and began to unfasten her gown. Although the long line of buttons was along the length of her spine, his deft fingers moved swiftly and he met her stare as each one popped free. She forced herself to hold his gaze, unwavering until her dress drooped around her neck and he slowly drew it down and around her hips. She shimmied it loose and stepped free, kicking it aside to stand before him in her undergarments.

She had always liked fancy underthings. In her vocation, they sometimes made more impact than a gown. Now he stared at her nearly sheer, pink chemise that just barely touched the top of her thighs where her stockings stopped, and she arched her back slightly in pride. In this, at least, she had utter confidence.

"You are beautiful," he murmured, stealing a hand out to cup her shoulder and allowing his fingers to play along her upper arm.

She shivered at the heat of his hands but refocused quickly.

"I am also at a disadvantage," she whispered, shoving the coat that he had never bothered to remove downstairs from his shoulders. He smiled as she did the same with the jacket beneath.

He wasn't wearing a cravat, and she let her fingers slide up his chest to touch the triangle of skin that was revealed by his far-too-casual attire.

"I want to see the rest," she said, meeting his eyes as he had done to her and slowly unfastening his shirt. As more and more flesh was revealed, she stepped closer and slid her hand inside the space she had created.

He sucked in a breath as her palm stroked over the hard muscles there, her fingertips playing briefly with one flat, hard nipple.

"You are in dangerous territory," he warned, looming over her but making her anything but afraid.

"I hope so," she said and opened his shirt fully. She tugged the ends from his trousers and lifted up on her tiptoes to shove it away. Then she stepped back and stared.

He was...spectacular, unlike any man she had ever seen in a state of undress. There was nothing soft or pale or weak about him. His muscles were formed like a statue of a god from Rome. She wanted to touch him, to lick him, to claim him and be claimed by him. Just looking at him like this, her body was already soaked and ready, her thighs clenched and her knees shook with anticipation of what he would do with that body in a few short moments.

"Do you feel less disadvantaged now?" he asked, but his voice had changed. It was rougher now, darker with desire.

"Not quite," she said and let her fingertips drag down that glorious chest to the waist of his trousers. He chuckled as she slid her fingertips beneath and then began to open the fly of the pants.

Wordlessly, he toed his boots off and as the pants fell around his ankles, he kicked everything away and stood before her utterly naked, his cock at full attention.

She stepped back to admire all she had revealed and could scarcely breathe. If his upper body was a sight to behold, the rest of him was equally magnificent. Muscled calves and thighs sheltered his sex. His very large, very hard sex, probably nearly twice as big as any other man she had been with.

"Malcolm," she whispered, unable to keep herself from reaching out to trace a finger around the head of him.

He growled out a breath and caught the wrist of her exploring hand, pushing her away.

"Not so fast," he muttered on short breaths. "It is I at a disadvantage now."

He grasped the edge of her chemise and tugged it up and over her head, throwing the scrap of fabric away to slide under her bed where she would probably never find it again.

"There, we are even now," he said, staring at her only in her stockings and heeled slippers.

"These don't count?" she laughed as she touched her silken-clad leg slowly.

He grunted again but managed to say, "They do, but I want them on while I'm inside of you."

Her smile faded, replaced with a burning desire she hadn't experienced in years. She wanted this man. Desperately, completely...and she wanted him *now*.

Moving toward him, she molded her naked body to his and kissed him. He swore against her lips and then thrust her back to fall upon the bed together. She opened her legs, gripping them around him as he pinned her to the coverlet.

"I want to go slowly," he grunted against her neck as he suckled a path down the slope of her throat.

She shook her head. "Slowly later," she gasped, clenching her fingers against his bare back as he kissed her collarbone.

He ignored her, at least for a moment, and his mouth continued its hot trail lower, lower, until he hesitated at her right breast. She arched the moment he sucked her beaded nipple between his lips and licked her.

She couldn't breathe, couldn't see, as starbursts of pure pleasure seemed to come at her from every place, every nerve ending. He sucked hard, bordering on pain but eliciting pleasure, then moved to the opposite breast to repeat the action.

She burned beneath him, her sex wet, pulsing, making demands as she flexed. She wanted him inside of her.

"Please," she begged between peppering kisses along his shoulder. "Please, please."

He straightened to look down at her and she could only imagine what he saw in her wild face, with her hair half-down around her shoulders and pillow. Normally she could hide, pretend, be calm and cool with a man. Not now.

"You beg?" he chuckled.

She nodded without hesitation and for a moment he seemed to consider denying her demand. But then he reached between them, positioning his cock at her entrance.

"Very well," he whispered, his voice breaking. "But only because I've been dreaming of this claiming since the moment you appeared in the entrance to that alleyway. But later, I will go slowly."

She might have replied, but before she could, he drove forward and filled her. His cock was thick, and her wet, weeping body stretched deliciously to accept him. She arched at the claiming, crying out against his arm as roaring pleasure shook her.

She had always had to fight for release in her previous relationships, using fantasy and self-stimulation to bring herself to orgasm in the arms of her lovers. This was different. Already her body quaked, her clitoris tingling, her inner walls pulsing as they did before the explosion of orgasm.

And he hadn't even moved yet.

"Look at me," he whispered.

She hadn't realized she wasn't, but her head was turned into his arm, eyes squeezed shut. Slowly, she peeked at him from the corner of her eye.

"Wh-why?" she panted, scarcely able to speak when her body was so far out of control.

"I want to see you," he said, putting a finger beneath her chin and turning her face fully toward his. "I want to see every moment."

He kept his finger there for the first thrust, holding her steady, forcing her to watch him and to be watched in return. He groaned as he slid back and forward, but he didn't shut his eyes or turn away.

Olivia forced herself to do the same, even as aching, mind-altering pleasure gripped her. He was magic with his hips, swiveling as he drove into her, hitting every spot she normally only found for herself. And the pleasure she almost always had to reach for rushed at her in a blind fury, taking over as she screamed out an orgasm that shook the walls, rocked the bed and took her over the edge toward a loss of all reason.

Through it all, she forced herself to hold his gaze as he held hers. It was amazing, for she felt his stare all the way through her, felt him connected to her not just with his body, but with something deeper.

Finally, the rippling echoes of her orgasm faded and she gasped out a breath she hadn't even recognized she'd been holding. As he continued to move within her, his thrusts becoming erratic as his face strained with pleasure, she reached up to touch his cheeks. She drew him down and sucked his tongue into her mouth, swallowing his moan of pleasure, so lost in sensation that he barely reined in control long enough to withdraw from her slick body and spend his seed away from them.

With a groan, he flopped down next to her, dragging her close to press a few kisses along her neck. They lay like that for a short time before Olivia rolled toward him, allowing herself the pleasure of touching his angular face as she stared at him.

"So 'ow—" She cut herself off in horror. She had just allowed her accent to slip and she darted her gaze toward Malcolm before she corrected herself. "*How* did you come to be lurking just outside my door when Violet arrived?"

He laughed and gave no indication that he had been aware of what she'd said. "I wasn't lurking." She arched a brow and he shrugged. "I might have been lurking just a bit," he admitted. "I actually rode over in the carriage Windbury sent for her. I popped out when we arrived and discreetly…"

"Lurked in my garden?" she finished for him when he hesitated.

"You should be complimented," he said with a wide grin. "It only goes to show you how much I wanted to be here that I would be willing to crouch behind a prickly rosebush to get to you."

The words, teasing as they were, warmed her heart and she blushed despite herself.

"I'm glad you came."

"So am I," he said softly, pressing a few kisses along her shoulder that served to light her flame once again. How could she want him so swiftly and so powerfully? "I needed that."

"So did I," she admitted, her breath catching on the renewed desire. "I admit, it has been a very long time since I did anything that was only for me."

He leaned on one elbow, watching her intently for what seemed like forever, even though it was less than a minute. Then he pushed to his knees and caught her hips, flipping her on her back a second time. He slid her closer and then parted her legs gently.

"I would greatly like to give you something just for you," he said, voice rough and filled with promise as he began to kiss a trail down her body.

She arched as he licked and sucked her flesh, teasing her nipples with his fingers and tongue, tasting her belly and finally settling between her thighs where he paused just to look at her pink sex, still slick from their previous joining.

He parted her flesh with his thumbs and then dropped his mouth to her, stroking one long, languid lick along her length. She arched immediately, moaning out her breath as pleasure ricocheted from his tongue.

He repeated the action, licking over and over, but without ever giving the nub of her clitoris the attention it needed for her to find release. Normally, Olivia might have simply touched herself, but his mouth was so talented, his strokes so sure, that she relaxed, closed her eyes and surrendered to his ministrations.

Once she had done so, she was amazed by how swiftly her pleasure built. With his gentle probing tongue, he had her near the edge of release within a few moments and there he held her, one hand on her hip, his tongue working furiously as she gasped and sighed in pleasure.

He seemed to sense when she had reached her limit, when she needed release as much as she needed breath. With a low chuckle, he removed his hand from her hip and instead pressed two fingers into her pussy, pumping them slowly as he pressed his mouth to her aching, tingling clitoris.

Her eyes flew open at the sudden overwhelming pleasure that stole her voice, stole her breath, stole her reason and had her gripping at the coverlet in wild release. Her body left her control and she allowed it, enjoying the crashing, pulsing, beautiful release his mouth created. The pleasure he drew out for what seemed like eternity.

Finally, she collapsed, her body weak as the tremors faded and her clouded vision cleared. She found him watching her, a slight smile on his shining lips.

"I take it back, that was not just for you," he said. "I highly enjoyed it myself."

"I can see that," she said, reaching out to cup the hard cock between his legs.

He muttered something beneath his breath, then covered her again, filling her and making her lose track of everything, anything, but him.

Chapter Four

If Liam had noticed Malcolm's absence the night before, he made no mention of it when Mal strolled into the dining room the next morning. He didn't even say anything about the fact that his friend was wearing the same clothing as he had been the prior day. He merely watched as Mal poured himself a strong cup of coffee and took a place beside him.

"And how was your night?" Mal asked, deflecting any potential questions.

Liam laughed. "I think you know the answer."

Mal held back his own smile. He did, but only because he had seen Violet return home about the same time he was leaving Olivia's bed. It had been a merry game of switching places to escape the townhome undetected. Not that Violet would have judged Olivia's night of passion, nor would Liam.

But it was satisfying to have a secret, something just for them that had nothing to do with their friends.

"I invited Violet to come here, to stay with me and continue this..." Liam hesitated, "...well, this affair, I suppose you would call it, for a while."

Mal's thoughts faded, replaced by a lurching realization. If Violet took Liam's offer, that would mean Olivia would likely come here as well.

And even though they had made no promises to see each other again, the very idea gave him more than a little pleasure. They could continue what had started as a brief interlude. Only...would increased time together make it something more?

"Is that a good idea?" he murmured, more to himself than to Liam.

But Liam met his eyes in surprise. "I would think you would approve. You are the one always badgering me to move forward with my life."

Mal shoved aside his thoughts of Olivia for the moment and returned to his normal state as Liam's friend, his protector. It caused more regret than he had expected it to do.

"Is that what you're doing?" he pressed.

He couldn't help the worry. After all, Liam had been steeped in the past for so long...almost always to his detriment.

"I want her," Liam said softly. "I've not wanted something in so long..."

He trailed off and Mal didn't respond. He understood the desire he saw in Liam's eyes, the unexpected effect of a woman who had seemed to appear from nowhere and now infected his every thought, feeling and physical need.

"Do you want me to look into her character, her past?" he asked, just as quiet.

Liam swallowed hard. "No. It's only an affair, after all. It should be short-lived and easy to forget."

But as his friend picked up his paper and returned his attention to the news, Mal couldn't help but wonder if that was true. Either for his friend or himself.

Olivia had pretended she'd been asleep when Violet returned, rubbing her eyes and playing the role of lazy courtesan. Now she felt like a fraud as she stood beside her friend's tub, listening to her talk about her night with Lord Windbury, while Olivia acted as lady's maid and helped Violet undress.

"He wants me to stay with him," Violet said.

Olivia's fingers faltered on the last button of her friend's gown, but she managed to slip it free as her mind raced. Go to Windbury's estate? Where Mal lived?

"Really?" she asked, hoping to seem calm, and failing.

Violet shoved out of her gown and caught up the robe that was draped over the chair beside her fire. Before she could respond, her maid Rachel opened the chamber door and smiled.

"Good afternoon, miss. They're bringing the water now."

Olivia could hardly contain herself as servants filled the tub and Violet gave directions about laundering her gown. It seemed they would never be alone again, she would never hear more about Violet's plans, or even if she would be included in Violet's exodus to Windbury's home.

Finally, Olivia touched Violet's arm and met Rachel's eyes. "I'll help her."

Rachel said a few more quiet things to Violet that Olivia ignored, then the servant slipped from the room.

The moment they were alone, Olivia turned on Violet. "You are trying to drive me mad! What did you say when Windbury asked you to stay with him?"

Violet didn't respond, but removed her robe and stepped into the tub. It took all Olivia's control not to throttle her dearest friend, for it seemed Violet was purposefully making her wait just to torture her.

"Violet!" Olivia repeated with a forced laugh as she dragged a chair up next to the tub.

"I told him I would consider the request," Violet finally replied.

Olivia leaned back, eyes wide at the answer. It was as unexpected as it was disappointing that Violet hadn't immediately acquiesced.

"Consider it? I thought that was your whole purpose in coming here."

Violet grabbed the soap and scrubbed a thick lather onto her hands.

"It is," she admitted. "But I need him to *want* me, to pursue me."

Relief flooded Olivia's mind and this time her laugh was much lighter. "Ah, I see. A merry chase, even if it is only pretended on your part. You *are* cold."

She saw Violet flinch and immediately regretted the statement, even though there was some truth to it. After all, Violet was lying to Liam.

Just as Olivia was lying to Mal.

"Does he want to be your protector?" Olivia pressed, hoping Violet would forgive her accusation.

Violet shook her head. "No. It is as has always been rumored about him. He doesn't want a woman to keep."

"And yet he asks you to stay with him throughout the duration of your stay here." Olivia arched a brow. "I have always heard a woman could only expect a night or two in his company."

Violet shrugged. "I suppose, as you say, I have manipulated him into wanting more."

Olivia bent her head. Was that what she had done with Mal? Their night together certainly hadn't felt like a manipulation. Just a surrender of two people who rarely gave in to their own desires, thanks to their duties and professions.

Violet shifted and looked at her evenly. "I was going to tell him that I am in town with a friend and ask if you could join us at his estate."

Olivia only just kept from jumping to her feet in joy. "Me?" she said, as if this suggestion were not something she had been hoping for since Violet's revelation of the arrangement Liam wanted to make.

"You can keep his guard or friend, or whatever that man is, busy." Violet waved Mal off like he wasn't important except as an obstacle, and Olivia frowned.

"Malcolm?" she said, stressing his name so that Violet would acknowledge he had one at all.

Violet examined her closely. "Malcolm. I didn't see him last night or this morning, but I think if I stay there he might take an interest in my intentions. That could prove difficult for me."

Olivia swallowed. So Violet hadn't guessed the reason for Mal's absence. She would leave it at that, at least for now, but she still had to let Violet know she was more than willing to "distract" Malcolm Graham.

Probably too willing.

"Malcolm," she said on a sigh, her tone far lighter than her thoughts. "He was awfully handsome. And quite a good kisser. I wouldn't mind distracting him."

Violet smiled. "Then I shall write Lord Windbury this afternoon and tell him I will accept his offer, as long as you may accompany me. I'm certain he will say yes, since I will make it clear you won't be any interference to our...*connection.*"

"Excellent," Olivia said, rising to her feet to clap her hands. "Then I will have my maid begin packing right away. And so it begins!"

With a squeeze of her friend's shoulder, Olivia scurried from the room and down the narrow hallway to her own. Once inside, she spun around the room, her arms around herself in a joyful hug.

She should not want this connection so much with a man who was all but a stranger, and yet she did want him. Somehow, in a very short time, everything had changed.

And she only hoped that her appearance at Windbury's estate would be as pleasing for him as it was for her.

Olivia had always steered clear of the highest bred of men. She had lived in fear that they would see through her façade the easiest and reveal her for what she truly was. So as the carriage stopped in the wide circular drive at Lord Windbury's Bath estate and she stepped down to look up and up at the magnificent house, she let out her breath in a low whistle.

"Lor'," she murmured and immediately tensed. Her Cockney accent was something she'd fought for years to suppress and, here it was, coming to the surface when she needed to tamp it down most.

"Yes," Violet whispered with a laugh. Her friend had never fully understood how painful her accent and poor upbringing was to her. "And Liam behaves as if this is a snug little cottage."

Olivia regained some semblance of composure and rolled her eyes. "Men with money are so often utterly ridiculous."

Violet might have answered her, she might have sung "God Save the King", for all Olivia knew. Her attention was suddenly dragged, almost physically, to the tall, broad-shouldered man who was coming around the house from the direction of the stables. Malcolm.

But he wasn't looking at her. He was staring at Violet and his concern was something he couldn't fully mask. Olivia hesitated. If he questioned Violet's motives, he might doubt her own at some point.

And then she would have to lie to him outright, rather than by simple omission. The first felt so much worse than the second.

"Miss Milford," he said as he reached them. "I apologize, I would have been here to greet you the moment you arrived, but I was called to deal with an estate issue."

Violet smiled, all enviable confidence as usual when she took his hand and shook it.

"You were here not a moment after our arrival," she said with a wave of dismissal for his apology. "You must be Mr. Graham."

"I am."

He nodded and released her hand. He was so businesslike, and still he hadn't looked at Olivia at all. Would he be unhappy once he noticed her?

"Your items follow behind, do they?" he continued. "You had no trouble with the move?"

"No trouble at all," Violet reassured him. "Thank you for arranging for the multiple vehicles to ferry both us and our items."

His lips thinned ever so slightly. "I was following Windbury's directives."

Olivia saw the tiny twitch of Violet's lips. She recognized Mal's hesitation when it came to her as well. And she dealt with it by motioning over her shoulder and becoming the first to acknowledge Olivia's presence.

"I believe you have met my friend, Olivia Cranfield?"

As Olivia held her breath, Mal swung his gaze to her. She could only pray he wouldn't pretend he didn't know her or look at her with disregard or disappointment. Everything seemed to slow, until his expression shifted to one of happiness and unmistakable desire.

"Mal," Olivia whispered, nearly sagging with relief as she took a step toward him involuntarily.

Mal caught her hand and lifted it to his lips. "Miss Olivia Cranfield. It's been too long."

"It's been less than a week," Olivia laughed, shooting a look at Violet, who had no idea of their meeting in secret. She swatted him playfully. "But I do agree."

As expected, Violet stepped away from them, leaving Olivia to what her friend thought was a duty, but was nothing more than an immense pleasure.

"Violet doesn't know about us," Olivia whispered.

He smiled. "Are you embarrassed by me, Miss Cranfield?"

"No," she said, shaking her head swiftly. "I just like having you as mine."

He drew back and she realized what she had said. Stuttering, she tried to correct her overstatement.

"M-my secret," she said. "I like having you as my secret."

"Hmm," he said, his voice rippling low in her belly and making her thighs clench.

He might have elaborated, but suddenly Violet was coming toward them. At her side was a tall, handsome man with a scar that stretched across his face. Olivia started, for she hadn't even realized they'd been joined by a fourth member of their party.

"Liam, may I present to you my dearest friend, Miss Olivia Cranfield," Violet said, motioning to her. "Olivia, the Earl of Windbury."

Olivia shook away all her stunned and desire-filled reactions and stepped forward, offering Liam a hand. "Good afternoon, my lord. I'm so pleased to meet you. Thank you so much for including me in your invitation to Violet. I would have been gutted had we not been able to spend our planned holiday together."

She might have been laying it on a bit thick, but if Liam had any hesitations about her being here, she had to put them to rest.

"We are happy to have you join us," Liam said, casting a quick glance at Malcolm, rather than at her. "Some of us more than others."

Out of nervousness, Olivia laughed, but she didn't like that Malcolm scowled at his friend's observation.

Liam couldn't have cared less. He already had his attention back on Violet, and there was no mistaking just how much the earl wanted her friend. What was shocking was that Violet couldn't seem to hide how much she wanted the man in return.

"Mal, why don't you have Miss Cranfield shown to her chamber?" Liam asked, his gaze on Violet.

"With great pleasure," Mal said as he offered Olivia an arm. "Shall we?"

Olivia hesitated. The moment she took Mal's arm, everything would change again. But she did it, and she could only hope that whatever happened next was something she could manage, because she presently felt decidedly out of her element.

Chapter Five

Mal led Olivia up a very wide, very fancy staircase to an equally beautiful hallway that led to no-doubt ridiculously well-appointed chambers. Her heart pounded nearly out of her chest as she tried to control herself, remember herself and not make any mistakes in front of Mal, especially since she wasn't yet certain how he felt about her being here.

But as if he had read her mind, he smiled at her. "I'm so glad you came with Violet," he said softly, "I have been thinking of you since we last met."

"You have?"

He smiled as his answer and Olivia realized in that moment that he did truly *like* her. In her world, that wasn't always true or even wanted. And yet, here it was, clear on his face. More to the point, she *liked* that he liked her.

She was less keen on the fact that he seemed so very loyal. She'd been witness to that fact outside when he met Violet. Obviously, in his mind, his duty was to protect his friend.

And if he ever found out Violet's true reason for being here, if he ever uncovered that she was a spy, he would be angry.

But perhaps that would never come to be. Violet seemed truly attracted to Lord Windbury, beyond any duty she was sworn to uphold. If their affair was brief and purely physical then there could be no harm to come of that.

"You are very quiet," he said, stopping in the hallway to look at her.

She shook her head. She didn't often indulge in spiraling thoughts when in her role with a man. How it had happened in this moment was a mystery.

"I am simply thinking of how very pretty the earl's home is," she lied. "I don't think I've ever seen a finer estate."

"Then I'm sure you'll like your room."

He opened the door closest to him and motioned for her to enter. She did so and caught her breath. It was a lovely chamber, done in tasteful, muted grays and bright whites. The furniture was dark cherry.

It was elegant enough to have welcomed a queen or a duchess.

Immediately, she stepped back into the hall. "Certainly I don't need something so large," she said, anxiety rising in her chest.

His brow wrinkled at her refusal of the room. "If you don't like it—"

She cut him off by spinning on him. "Oh no, it isn't that I'm ungrateful. It's beautiful. But..." She hesitated and heat flooded her cheeks. "Malcolm, you understand I am a courtesan, don't you?"

He nodded slowly. "Yes. Our first conversation made that clear."

She held up her hands and motioned to the room. The reminder *had* to make him see.

"And?" he said when it was clear she wouldn't speak.

She huffed out her breath. So he would force her to speak her humiliation. "This room is for someone above my station, Mal. If I stay here..."

She trailed off and her blush grew even hotter.

Slowly Malcolm reached out, took her hand and guided her into the room. "If you stay here, nothing will happen except that you will have a good time." His gaze stole to the bed. "A very, very good time, I hope. A room is a room, Olivia. It has no station."

"Of course it does," she whispered.

He tilted his head and leaned in closer, close enough that his breath stirred against her lips and suddenly the issue of the chamber felt far less important.

"This one doesn't," he said, then touched his lips to hers.

She was shocked by how gentle his touch was. She had certainly expected—and hoped—to be kissed, but she had assumed it would be like before: heated, claiming. This was...this was comfort. And no man had ever offered her that before.

She drew back in surprise and Mal stepped away. For a moment only silence hung between them, then he took her hand again and drew her closer.

"Stay in this room, Olivia. Because it's pretty and the bed is comfortable. Stay because my chamber is just down the hall. Please."

She found herself nodding. "Of course."

He grinned, the expression lighting up his face and making him impossibly more handsome. She expected him to kiss her again, to tug her into that bed and show her how apparently comfortable it truly was.

But instead he slipped her hand into the crook of his elbow and said, "Since your things have not yet arrived, may I show you the grounds?"

She blinked. The tension between them crackled and yet he was offering her something beyond passion.

"Very well," she said, casting a quick glance at the bed.

He smiled. "Oh, don't worry, Olivia. You and I will share that bed soon enough."

And with that sinful promise hanging in the air between them, he led her down the hallway.

Although their walk around the grounds had been nothing but pleasant, Mal still felt the tension coursing through Olivia. It had never occurred to him that she wasn't utterly comfortable in her place in this world. But now he could see that she was troubled by the fact she didn't entirely "fit" in the world of earls and dukes and country estates.

And though he had been born into a gentleman's home, he didn't exactly feel he fit either. Yet another fact that bound him to her.

"What do you think of the earl?" he asked.

She jolted at the question and her discomfort was clear on her face. "I only met him for a moment—it would be difficult to make a judgment only from that."

"But you've heard stories about him," Mal said, looking at her from the corner of his eye. "Everyone has."

Olivia bent her head. "Yes."

Mal tensed. People always thought they knew Liam because they knew about the scandalous war that had been long fought between his family and the house of the Duke of Rothcastle. They talked about the carriage accident that had maimed Liam and killed Rothcastle's sister. They whispered about the marriage that had ultimately formed between Rothcastle and *Liam's* sister.

It all boiled Mal's blood, because sometimes people took *pleasure* in the vicious gossip about a series of events that had been nothing but hell for his friend.

"The vultures," she continued quietly, "label your friend as a fallen angel, broken by the death of his lover, hardened by a war, hiding like a beast. But I would wager there is more to it than that."

Mal tilted his head. "You sum it up perfectly."

"Sometimes one has a better view of the truth when looking from the outside in," Olivia said with a shrug.

They were almost back to the house now, so Mal steered them into the rose garden near the back of the estate. He motioned to a narrow bench that sat under the shade of a juniper tree and they sat close together, her knees brushing his. It was an innocent enough touch, but it still made his body hot.

"I imagine you are right," Mal said. "People are always clearer from a safe distance."

"And in my profession, I must study the true character of those I meet, in order to guess if…" She trailed off. "I'm sorry, that is inappropriate. I'm certain you don't want to hear about the details of my profession."

He hesitated. "Perhaps not the sexual conquests of your past, but I imagine you were going to say you have to be a quick study of those around you to determine threats, as well as good matches."

Her eyes went wide. "Yes. That's exactly right."

He smiled at her shock. "It isn't only courtesans who employ those methods. I am Liam's friend, but I am also his estate manager. I must also make quick judgments about those around us, to decide if their motives about the earl and his money are true or not."

She shifted slightly. "And have you made a determination about Violet."

Mal pinched his lips together. Normally he might have, but he had been so totally consumed by thoughts of Olivia since they met. Not that he would tell her that.

"Your friend is difficult to read," he admitted. "But I know Liam wants her."

She leaned closer. "And what about me?" she whispered. "What do you see when you look at me?"

What she asked for could very well reveal more than he wished for her to see. And yet he still found himself answering, "I don't think about what anyone else wants or feels or thinks when I look at you. I only think of myself. I am utterly selfish, and I like that."

A small smile tilted her lips slightly and she reached up to cup the back of his neck and draw him to her. Before she kissed him, she whispered, "I like it too."

Their lips met and almost immediately the kiss stoked a fire deep in his loins that made his cock harden and his body scream at him about need and want and *now*.

He rose to his feet, dragging her with him. "Come."

She laughed as she was dragged up a back stair and offered no resistance when he tugged her into her room. Olivia's maid was hunched over a portmanteau and straightened up with a start as they stumbled into her presence.

Mal tensed, ready for Olivia to show that same shame she had earlier. Instead, she smiled at the girl and nodded for the door.

"Belle," she said quietly.

The girl needed no other direction and immediately left the room with only a knowing smile as she closed the door behind her. Olivia faced him with a clear expression of desire, but not a hint of embarrassment. Her confidence made his cock swell all the more.

"Take off your clothes," he ordered.

She arched a brow, but immediately began unfastening her dress.

"You too," she said, her voice full of laughter despite the demand.

It quickly turned into a race to nudity. Olivia kept her gaze locked on him as they both tugged free buttons and loosened ties. He could hardly breathe as she shoved from her gown, her chemise, her slippers, her stockings, and finally stood in front of him utterly naked.

Of course, by this time he was the same and she worried her lip with her teeth as she looked at him.

"I don't know how you don't have women lining up to bed you by the dozen," she growled as she reached out to press a hand to his chest.

He hissed out pleasure at the heat of her touch and barely kept himself from flipping her onto the bed and fucking her without any seduction beforehand.

"Or do you?" she asked, brown eyes lifting to snare his.

He could hardly breathe and certainly couldn't stop his hands from covering her breasts. As he began to massage lightly, he grunted, "Have women lined up for my pleasure?" he asked. She nodded with a throaty moan. "No. Not recently, at any rate."

"What has made recently so different?" she gasped, her head lolling back as he pinched her nipples. Her legs were beginning to shake. He wanted to make them go out from under her.

"Busy," he grunted and covered her mouth with his so they would both stop talking, stop analyzing. He just wanted to *feel* her. Beneath him, around him.

She didn't resist; in fact, she only broke the kiss to start a hot, wet path with her mouth down his body. Her knees hit the carpet and she looked up the length of his body, stroking her hand down his chest before she cupped his cock and slowly took him into her mouth.

He had been fantasizing about making her knees buckle, but now it was his legs that threatened to go out from under him as she sucked him deep into her throat. And it wasn't just the fact that she knew exactly how to suck or that she swirled her tongue around his girth until he thought he might lose consciousness, but it was that she watched him. With every stroke of her mouth and tongue, her dark eyes held his, daring him to lose control, daring him to come at her bidding.

He plunged his hands into her hair as he let pleasure be his guide. Hairpins scattered on the floor around her, but she didn't stop the magic she was performing with her mouth. He felt his balls tightening, the rush of his seed imminent, and that was the moment he forced himself to pull free of her tempting, torturous lips.

She yelped in protest. A sound that turned to a moan as he spun her around to lean facedown on the bed, lifted her hips and speared her wet sex in one long thrust. She gripped the coverlet with her fists as she let out a low cry. With a grin, he drew back and began to grind into her, rotating his hips in smooth circles as he reached around her body to flick at her nipples with his forefingers.

"Touch yourself," he ordered, his breath short when every thrust made his already edgy body move ever closer to explosion.

She whimpered, but did as he decreed, sliding a hand between her legs and stroking herself as he took her. Their rhythms merged and he squeezed his eyes shut as her body tensed and released around him, welcoming him in, letting him go, tightening so that he felt hot, sharp pleasure, releasing so that he didn't come too soon.

She was a master, made for sex, sin. Made for him. And he took full advantage of that as his hips jerked faster. Suddenly her sheath tensed and she let out a keening wail as her body twitched with release. She tugged at him, urging him to let loose his seed and he could no longer deny what she did to him.

With a bark of pleasure, he pulled from her body and milked his own release with a hand. Then he collapsed over her, pinning her to the bed as he scattered kisses along her neck and shoulders.

She caught his hand and held it against the coverlet near her face as her breath returned to normal. Finally, he rolled from her body and let her turn on her back to face him. She was smiling, no hint of shame on her face, no whisper of regret. There was only lazy, sensual pleasure there.

"Mmm," she said as she touched his cheek with the tips of her fingers. "I'm certainly glad I joined Violet if this is to be my welcome. Are all your other guests treated in such a manner?"

He laughed. "Not quite. Although we haven't had many guests as of late, so perhaps this should become the standard of the household."

She swatted his arm playfully. "Then I wouldn't be special. How tragic."

His laughter faded as he stared down into her face. "I think it would be impossible for you not to be special."

Her expression changed, softening with surprise. Then she cupped the back of his head. "How long until we have to meet Violet and the earl for supper?"

"Eight o'clock," he said as his lips lowered.

"Just enough time, then," she said, then drew him to her for a deep kiss filled with even more passionate promise than before.

And as he surrendered, randy and ready as a green lad, he couldn't help but wonder what spell this remarkable woman had woven over him. And if he would ever be free again.

Chapter Six

Olivia sighed with pleasure as the servant set yet another beautiful dish before her. Their supper had been magnificent thus far, at least in flavor and appearance.

The company, on the other hand, was another story. Since the earl and Violet had joined her and Malcolm in the dining room almost an hour ago, Liam's state of mind had been clear. If the way he jabbed at his food was any indication, he was frustrated and angry. Meanwhile, Violet held her face very still and hardly seemed to notice the meal before them.

It was clear the two had had some kind of quarrel. Normally, Olivia wouldn't involve herself in such things, but she knew how much this meant to Violet.

Olivia swallowed hard and smiled in the hopes she could lighten the mood and help her friend in some small way.

"You do have a splendid cook, my lord," she said as she took a bite and hummed out pleasure at the explosion of flavor on her tongue. "I envy you these delicious meals every single day and night."

Liam looked up to answer, eyes narrowed, but if he had an answer for her, he didn't speak it because Malcolm leaned closer to her. She tensed at his invasion of her space and at the memories the scent of his skin put into her mind.

"Wait until you taste dessert, pet," he murmured, his eyes meeting hers with a message that could not be ignored. He wanted her and, God help her, but she wanted him just as desperately.

And right here at the table, utterly inappropriately, they were showing their desires. It was unlike anything she had ever experienced in her life.

"How long have you worked for Liam?" Violet asked.

Olivia jolted at the sound her friend's voice. Violet's brow was arched and she did not look as though she approved of the obvious connection Olivia had formed so swiftly with Mal. Olivia's cheeks flooded with heat, so she returned her gaze to her plate.

Mal straightened up as well, the spell between them temporarily broken.

"Windbury and I have been friends since..." he shook his head and cast a quick glance toward Liam, "...school, I suppose. I began managing his estates when—"

He cut himself off and Olivia jerked her gaze to him. There was a certain hesitation to his tone...a sadness that drew her as close as her physical attraction did. What had he gone through in the tumultuous years since the accident that had scarred Windbury and killed the sister of the current Duke of Rothcastle? What had he seen while the rest of the world whispered about the state of the earl?

She reached a shaking hand out to squeeze Malcolm's arm, needing to touch him, to comfort him as she pondered those questions.

"Violet and I have also been friends for an age," she said softly, then looked at her friend. "Haven't we?"

Violet cleared her throat and glanced at Liam. "We have," she responded. "I think it is lucky that both I, and Lord Windbury, have had such good friends."

"Foolish as they may be," Liam grumbled.

Olivia's nostrils flared. Was the arrogant earl speaking of her or of Malcolm, a man who had stood by him no matter what? Either way, she refused to rise to his disgruntled bait.

"And now we've all met thanks to those friendships," she said, keeping her attention on Mal. "We're lucky indeed."

Malcolm hesitated and Olivia saw his eyes flicker toward Liam. Then he slowly let them turn back to her. Only her.

"Very lucky," he agreed, and her body tensed at the focused stare Mal gifted her.

The moment was broken, though, when Liam pushed his chair back. Mal stared at him as the earl clenched his napkin and stared at the group. Then he threw his napkin across his plate and left the room without so much as a glance behind him.

Olivia stared as Liam disappeared from the room. Was this what Malcolm had endured for the past two years? Was *this* the man he called friend?

She leaned back in her chair, hoping to appear nonchalant. "His ill humor is impressive. I didn't mean to bother him with my silly chatter."

Mal shook his head, staring at the door where his friend had departed. Olivia watched him. He was worried about Liam—the lines of concern were deep in his handsome face.

"I apologize, ladies," Malcolm finally managed. "My friend has been a little...*rough* since his accident. And he doesn't keep company often, probably because his emotions can overtake him when he isn't expecting it. I think the reality of being around others remains troublesome to him."

Olivia covered Mal's hand with her own, hoping again to offer him comfort. "He was hard on you."

He shrugged, but his frown deepened. "Sometimes he lashes out. I can ignore it most times, though we do occasionally have words if he takes things too far. I have been through the worst with him and seen him when I thought he might—"

Malcolm cut himself off and his face twisted with pain and worry and deep sadness. He took a breath before he continued, "I understand Windbury's motives for lashing out. Though I admit, he can be harsh."

Violet tilted her head. "And yet you stay with him."

Olivia jolted. She'd been so focused on Mal she'd almost forgotten Violet was there. Her friend was drinking everything in, using the intimate moment between Olivia and Malcolm to gather information for her own quest. Olivia wasn't certain she liked that thought.

Mal looked at Violet and shook his head. "He needs me."

He said the words without any kind of judgment or regret, and Olivia's heart swelled. This was a man who would sacrifice, who *had* sacrificed, everything he wanted or had for someone he cared for.

She shifted at the thought of how Mal would feel if he knew she had come here as an accessory to a betrayal of that someone.

Violet pushed her plate away and folded her hands on the table before her. "I would like to follow him, talk to him," she said, looking at Mal.

He drew back and his expression was very hard to read as he said slowly, "I warn you, he will likely be inhospitable."

Violet swallowed. "Yes. But if his anger comes from pain, then he may need company, even if he refuses to acknowledge that fact to any of us. He may desire a friend, if you don't mind my offering myself in that position instead of you."

"Is that what you want to be to him? A friend?" Mal asked, tone carefully neutral.

Olivia turned her face. Violet would lie now, pretend. And Olivia was torn between understanding her friend's motives and hating that Mal was caught in the middle of them.

"If he would allow it," Violet whispered.

Mal was quiet for a long moment, pondering her request, it seemed. Then he nodded.

"Actually, Miss Milford, I think what you offer may be what he needs more than anything I can provide. If you want to follow him, I would assume his office is where he will lick his wounds. It generally is."

Violet got to her feet slowly. "Good evening, you two. If I don't see you again, I hope you enjoy your dessert."

As Violet turned, Olivia reached out and caught her hand. Now that Violet would truly go into the den of what seemed to be an ill-tempered bear, Olivia couldn't help but fear the consequences, her own hesitations and guilt be damned.

"Are you certain?" she asked softly.

Violet hesitated, but then she gave a weak smile. "Of course. Good night."

Her friend slipped away, leaving Olivia alone with Malcolm. But the tension in the room between them was no longer physical and fun. It was rippled with their worries, shared and yet different.

"I don't want to offend," Olivia said softly. "But he wouldn't...he wouldn't hurt her, would he?"

Mal stared at her in surprise. "Liam? No, no, of course not. He is not an abuser of women, I promise you. I wouldn't stand for that."

Relief flooded Olivia's entire being and she relaxed against the chair. "I'm sorry, I must ask, you know. Women of our station..."

She trailed off and Mal nodded. "I imagine you have seen and gone through a great deal."

"Not often," Olivia said.

He tilted his head. "But sometimes."

She swallowed. Somehow, in her defense of Violet, she had opened a door to her past she hadn't wanted to unlock. Now she felt a little foolish as this handsome man stared at her expectantly, giving her some kind of permission to confess her past.

"Once," she admitted. "Very early in my time as a courtesan."

His jaw tightened. "Who?"

She shook her head. "I won't give you a name."

His eyebrows lifted. "Why?"

"Because right now you look as though you might ride to London and murder him," she said with a small smile. "And while I appreciate your wanting to be my hero, I don't want you transported for the trouble."

"It would be worth it," he said through clenched teeth.

She shook her head. "He truly would not be."

She didn't add that *she* wasn't worth it either, at least not out loud. It was the truth, but he would feel compelled to argue the fact and that would lead to no good conversation the rest of the night.

He was quiet for a while, then he leaned forward, folding his hands on the table, his attention focused on her entirely. "You said this bastard hurt you early in your career. What made you become a courtesan?"

Olivia tensed. Her past was something she protected judiciously. Even Violet didn't know her whole story.

"It is a boring tale, I assure you," she said with a dismissive wave of her hand.

He arched a brow. "Would you like me to send Runners to investigate you instead?"

Her eyes widened. "You wouldn't do that."

"If I wanted to know something badly enough, I would," he said with a shrug that belied the importance of the topic. "And I find myself *wanting* to know the woman behind the mask you wear. I think I'd rather know from your lips than from the lips of a man with bad breath, a gut and no teeth."

Olivia drew back. "What kind of Runners are you employing?"

"Apparently disgusting ones." He laughed. "Please tell me. I promise you it will remain between us."

She stared at him. It was the *please* he had added that stopped her in her tracks. Very few men ever used that word with her. And here he was, waiting patiently, truly seeming to want to know her origins. For the first time in her life, she wanted to tell the story. To be true, real, with another person.

But it was a terrible risk.

"How do I know you won't use whatever I tell you against me?" she whispered, holding his gaze evenly. "Or against my friend?"

He leaned back. "Right now, I don't give a damn about Violet Milford," he said. "Unless you tell me she has somehow forced you to do something you didn't want to do."

"Of course not," Olivia said with a shake of her head. "In fact, I'm the one who brought Violet into this world, not the other way around."

His eyes widened with surprise, an emotion she wasn't entirely certain she wanted to see. Most people saw her as glib and in control. If he thought her so passive, would he respect her?

"Then how did you become a courtesan yourself, if not led here by a friend like Violet?" he pressed.

She cleared her throat. "I was born to a very low family," she admitted, heat filling her cheeks. "Very low, Malcolm."

He did not move or show any hint of his reaction.

"I was not educated, I was barely cared for at all, for my mother lived in a bottle and my father preferred the slap of his belt to conversation with his children. I had to get away, run away, or I knew I would end up no better."

He flinched. "That must have been painful for you."

She shrugged. "I knew no better; I had no comparison point. I suppose now, having seen people who love their children..." She trailed off, thinking of Violet and the son she adored but was forced to keep as a secret from the world. "But at the time, my circumstances caused me no pain, only fear that I would be caught and punished if I failed in my escape."

"When did you leave?" he asked, his fingers stroking hers on the tabletop, a soothing, simple gesture that meant a great deal.

"I was seventeen," she admitted. "I slipped away with a pocket full of money I stole and no plans. And I staggered, quite luckily, into a hell where I met my first protector."

Mal's jaw tightened. "The one who hurt you?"

"No. Quite the opposite," she reassured him.

His face remained tense. "Was he titled?"

"No, but a gentleman," she said. "Lower quality, but high enough that he was far above my station. And yet, he didn't care. In fact, he seemed to see me as a project. He told a maid to teach me to read and let me have books. And he told me to rid myself of my accent so that I wouldn't be seen as low and stupid."

Mal was still staring at her, his expression totally unreadable. "I cannot imagine, Olivia, that you have ever been either low or stupid, no matter how young or inexperienced or uneducated you were."

She stared at him. She had been with a handful of men over the seven years she had been a courtesan. None had ever said anything like that to her. None had really ever seen anything about her beyond her body.

"Yur kind t'say so, guv," she said softly, allowing her hateful accent to come through fully. She had never revealed it on purpose before and now it sounded like something better left in the gutter. "Raised as you was."

His lips tightened. "A gentleman like them, those who turned you away."

She nodded slightly and returned her accent to the one she had been using for years. "You must see that my past forces me to hide my true self in every way. I cannot speak as I spoke when I was a girl. I cannot act as I did. I can't even let someone know what street I was born on in London, for fear they will toss me out because I'm too far beneath them even to warm their beds." She shook her head. "I am always pretending, Malcolm."

He leaned closer. "You don't have to pretend with me."

She smiled. He thought that was true, but it wasn't. "No?"

He cupped her chin. "No."

Then he kissed her, sweeping away her fears, her lies, her past, and replacing it all with the warm and wonderful sensation of *him*. He was hers in that moment and she drank him in, tasting his tongue, arching toward him artlessly. She wanted him and that was not pretended, which would have to be enough.

She stood up, grabbing his arm to urge him to join her. When he did, she lifted to her tiptoes to continue kissing him. She was out of control, her body aching to be touched, filled, in a way no other man had ever inspired.

"I want you," she admitted between kisses.

He drew back to stare at her. "Now?"

She nodded, drawing him back toward the wall. He didn't need much coaxing and soon he pinned her there, pressing his delicious weight against her, making her shake as she rubbed her hips against his and felt his cock harden with her attention.

"You are a minx," he grunted on a laugh as he began to lift her skirts. His hands went under the silk and he cupped her between the legs, pressing his palm against her sex and slipping a finger into her slit.

"Oh God," she moaned, pressing her head back against the wall as he began to stroke inside of her. "That isn't going to be enough."

He chuckled and withdrew from her entirely, and she gasped in disappointment. But when she looked at him, he was unfastening his trousers, allowing that thick, beautiful cock free from the confines of fabric.

"Will this satisfy, demanding miss?" he teased as he grasped her hips, lifting her up. She wrapped her legs around his back and forced a hand between them to guide him to her entrance.

He stroked into her hard and she cried out.

"Yes, I think that will do the trick," she gasped, clinging to him as he began to move inside of her.

His thrusts were hard and steady, pinning her to the wall and giving her no room to return his movements with ones of her own. She was helpless to him, completely at his mercy and that fact excited her far more than it should have.

Her body reacted as he kissed her, fucked her, and slowly the dam of pleasure built in her loins, rising, rising until she felt the strain of near release in every vein, every nerve, ever part of her being.

At that very moment, he broke the kiss, stared into her eyes and rotated his hips slowly.

She dug her fingers into his shoulders, bucking wildly as pleasure so intense that it bordered on pain rocked her body. The orgasm was unlike any she had ever known, lifting her high and going on and on until she couldn't breathe, couldn't see, couldn't experience anything but pleasure overtaking her, ruling her.

He grunted as he thrust through her crisis and suddenly he pulled from her, leaving her quivering sheath, quaking as he spent into his hand away from her. He panted as he set her back on the floor and pressed a warm kiss to her forehead.

"You certainly inspire a man to do amazing things," he said as he stepped away and rebuttoned his trousers.

She laughed while smoothing her skirts back over her still-twitching sex. "I will take that as a compliment, sir."

He moved forward swiftly and touched her chin. Lifting her face, he forced her to look at him.

"It *is* one, Olivia," he whispered. "I admire your strength, I admire *you*, and I don't want you to ever believe otherwise."

She stared at him for what seemed like an eternity and then she nodded as she prayed her eyes wouldn't fill with tears at his sincere declaration.

"Thank you," she whispered.

He released her finally and the intensity of his stare faded. "Now I would like to take you upstairs and be further inspired. Will you accompany me?"

He offered his arm and she laughed as she took it. But even as they went up for more untold pleasures, Olivia felt a niggling concern deep within her. Malcolm Graham was unlike anyone she had ever met. And she could not be so foolish as to mistake his infatuation with her body as anything deeper.

Nor could she allow herself to feel deeper feelings for him. That could only end in heartache.

Chapter Seven

It had been three days since Olivia's arrival at Liam's estate. Three days, and yet Malcolm still couldn't help but stare at her in wonder when they were together and crave touching her whenever they were apart.

Only, at the moment, they were anything but parted. He lay across her bed, stroking his fingers along her naked hip as she smiled down at him.

"You have a very serious look about you, Mr. Graham," she teased, reaching out to press the tip of her finger to his nose. "What solemn thoughts have you so dour?"

He propped himself up on his elbow and did his best to clear his mind.

"I was only thinking that we have been cloistered in this room for a very long time. And I fear I may not be a very good host to you."

Her face lit up with one of her astonishingly beautiful smiles. "You could not say I have been bored here, Malcolm, sequestered in this room or not. But I wouldn't object to an outing. What do you have in mind?"

He thought for a moment. He didn't want to share her with the world, nor did he want to stray too far from this bed. Which left him with few options.

"There is a lake on the property," he said. "We could have a picnic lunch there."

She sat up and smiled. "That sounds wonderful. And why don't we see if Violet and the earl would want to join us?"

Mal squeezed his eyes shut. Liam. He hadn't exactly been thinking about his friend in the past three days. He hadn't been doing his *job* at all, in truth. Not that the earl had complained. His friend seemed to be as caught up in his own affair as Malcolm was with Olivia.

If Mal was on his game, he probably would have investigated Violet further, despite Liam's rejection of that action, but...

"Mal?" Olivia tilted her head. "You are faaaarrr away, my dear. Come back."

He grinned at her teasing and nodded. "Of course. How soon can you be dressed and ready?"

She flopped back against the pillows with a mock sigh. "Oh God, leaving this room does require clothing, doesn't it?" She threw her hand over her eyes as if this were the worst news ever given to anyone. Mal couldn't help but laugh louder.

"Especially if we're inviting other people on our outing, yes," he confirmed.

She peeked over her arm at him. "Give me an hour. I will fly through my preparations."

He pushed to his feet and stepped into his trousers. As he slung his wrinkled shirt over his shoulders, he leaned down to kiss her. "An hour, then."

He moved to the door and rang the bell for her servant as he passed into the hall, but the moment he was alone, his smile fell. Something was happening to him since he'd met Olivia Cranfield. And with every moment he spent with her, he was forced to face it more and more.

Olivia took a long breath of fresh air as she slipped a hand into Malcolm's and allowed him to lead her away from the house toward the rolling hills.

Behind them, Liam and Violet followed, and Olivia felt their stares on her back with every step. Perhaps in the past, she might have removed her hand from Mal's out of propriety. Now she didn't care. She was with this man, this remarkable man, and she refused to do anything but enjoy it to the fullest.

"This is a beautiful place," she sighed.

Mal looked down at her with a broad smile. "Not as lovely as my companion."

Warmth filled her cheeks, but Olivia refused to show how much his words had moved her. Instead, she rested her head against his shoulder as they continued up the path. "I'm glad I came with Violet," she said softly.

He looked ahead of them. "So am I."

They walked in comfortable silence for a while as Olivia took in the surroundings. She had been raised in London and lived there her entire life, so the freshness of the country, the greenness of it, made her heart hurt it was so lovely. She would certainly keep these memories precious in the future, both of this place and of the man she had found here.

"This is it," Malcolm said, motioning to a pretty little hill overlooking a gorgeous, clear blue lake.

Servants had gone ahead of them to prepare, so there was a thick blanket spread out on the grass with various picnic items across it. Olivia released Malcolm's hand and moved toward it.

"Perfection," she breathed as she turned to face him. "Mal, you were right, this is divine."

He smiled and together they began to spread the food out for everyone's consumption. But even as they began to eat together, Olivia felt Liam and Violet watching them. Her friend was all but oozing confusion at how quickly Olivia had grown close to Mal. And who could blame her? But there was something about the man that made her trust him.

The more troubling reaction was Liam's. The earl alternated between staring at Mal and glaring at her. His scarred face was dark with emotions, first and foremost of which seemed to be anger.

And if Mal's best friend despised her, how could Mal continue an affiliation with her?

Not that they had ever spoken of a future. Not that she *wanted* a future with any man.

She blushed as she pushed those thoughts away.

This wasn't why she was here. Violet had brought her to be of assistance. Not just to distract Malcolm, but to aid Violet with her plans for Liam. And perhaps if she did that, it would help her remember her place in the world.

"Violet," she said, smiling at her friend, "didn't you have plans in London at the end of the month?"

Violet jolted. They had never spoken of such a thing and Olivia could see that her question had thrown her friend. That in itself was proof that Violet was struggling, for normally the other woman was more than capable of adapting to any conversation and turning it to her advantage.

"I—" Violet began, voice shaking. "Did I?"

Olivia drew back. Violet wouldn't make this easy. "I thought you had something drawing you back. Certainly we cannot hide away in the country forever." She tossed Mal a smile. "No matter how much we would like to do so."

He smiled in return, but there was suddenly distance to his stare.

She cleared her throat and focused her attention on Liam. "Will *you* ever return to London, my lord?"

The earl blinked and finally looked at her. "You are asking me?"

Olivia frowned. Did he ignore her out of distraction or because he didn't think her worthy of listening to? Did she even want to know the answer?

"Yes, Lord Windbury," she said, trying to keep her tone light. "We were talking about our return to the city in a fortnight or so. And I wondered if we might expect to see you and Malcolm there at some point in the future?"

She smiled at him, but the earl didn't return the expression. Instead, he stared at her as if she had sprouted a second head that was now bobbing up and down on her shoulder.

"I don't know," Liam finally said slowly. "I haven't put much thought into where I will go after our time in Bath is finished. But I don't care for London. I swore to myself I wouldn't return there again."

Olivia drew back, surprised he would reveal so much. It was well known that the earl didn't speak about the past that had scarred him and driven him from his home. Normally she would leave the poor man alone with his memories, but this was an opening Violet could desperately need. So she continued.

"I suppose I can appreciate that vow. After all, there is little to bring you back to London. You have cut ties with your sister since her marriage, haven't you?"

Beside her, Violet sucked in her breath in surprise and Mal physically jolted. And despite how uncomfortable she was, Olivia held her stare on Liam, waiting for his answer.

"I do not speak about such things." Liam sounded as though he were choking on the words.

Olivia hesitated. How she wanted to stop. To leave it be, as would be polite. But she found herself speaking again. "Of course, after what you went through—"

With a grunt, Liam pushed to his feet and turned away from them all. He stood on the edge of the blanket, hands clenched at his sides.

Olivia froze, but Violet moved, rising to her feet and moving toward Liam. Gently she touched his elbow and he looked at her.

"Why don't we walk around the lake?" she asked softly. "I think we could both use the exercise."

Liam stared at her a moment, then he jerked out a nod and the two of them walked away.

Olivia watched them go in shock. She hadn't expected Liam to spill his every secret, but he responded to her like she wasn't even a person.

"He thinks low of me," she whispered, refusing to look at Mal.

Malcolm touched her hand. "He is simply very private. And...broken, which I'm sure you know from gossip. Truly, you cannot take his moods personally. I've known him for almost two decades and he still cuts me off just as he did to you."

Her embarrassment faded as she looked at Mal. There was a pinched, pained expression on his face as he watched their friends disappear from view.

"Were you always in his service?" she asked.

Mal shook his head slowly and lay back on the blanket with his hands propped under his head. As he motioned her to join him, she rested her head on his shoulder, spreading her hand against his chest as an act of comfort.

"I was not as elevated as he in status, but we ended up at the same school. It may be hard to imagine, but at the time I was a very slight boy."

She sat up slightly to stare at him, all perfectly formed muscle and sinew. "No!"

He nodded. "Indeed. Some of the more popular boys saw me as a target. Liam was their leader."

Her lips parted. "And he attacked you?"

Mal smiled. "No. He stepped in and made it clear that I was to be his friend and if anyone else wanted to remain so, they would straighten up." His smile faded slightly. "He was different then, charismatic and made to lead. Everyone wanted to be his mate and somehow *I* was chosen."

Olivia stared at him in wonder. It was hard to picture this strong, virile man at her side as a weak and frightened boy.

Mal continued, "He took me in at school, but also at home. My father was not kind, often he was violent."

She flinched. *That* she did understand. "I'm sorry."

He shrugged, but she saw the tension on his face that showed her how much he cared, even if he dismissed the past. "It was a long time ago. But Liam made certain I was invited to every Christmas, every summer holiday with his family, in order to separate me from my father. He made what would have been a living hell into some of the best years of my life."

Olivia sighed. He had confided some painful facts to her, ones that explained perfectly why Malcolm would stand by Liam, despite the earl's prickly disposition. They were bound as best friends.

And Liam despised her.

She sat up and turned her face so he wouldn't see how much that fact affected her, even as she tried to gather her emotions. But her eyes stung with tears and the familiar press of humiliation at not being quite good enough began to make her chest ache.

Mal sat up too.

"What is it? Olivia?" He tilted his head, trying to see her face, and when she couldn't stop a tear from sliding from her eye, he caught her arms and turned her toward him.

"Why do you cry?" he demanded, smoothing the tear away with a thumb.

She shook her head. "I'm being stupid, so foolish," she croaked out.

"That doesn't answer the question," Mal insisted. "Tell me."

She looked down at the blanket. "He thinks so little of me. It's clear by the way he treats me. And I'm not saying I don't deserve that disregard, but, Malcolm, you care for him. His opinion means something to you—"

He cut her off by pressing two fingers to her lips. "You foolish girl," he said with a smile. "Haven't I made it clear over the past week that I am captivated by you? For the first time in years, I don't give a damn what Liam or anyone else thinks. I want you, I *care* for you. And if my friend doesn't like it, then..." he trailed off, "...then I suppose he can find someone else to run his estates and calm his moods."

Olivia's eyes went wide at this brash statement. "You cannot mean that you would abandon a friendship of such importance, not for a whore."

His jaw tightened. "I would thank you not to refer to yourself that way. Not in front of me." He leaned closer. "And I would grieve the loss of my friendship if it came to that, but not enough to turn away from you."

He leaned closer and pressed his lips to hers. Immediately, she wrapped her arms around his neck and dragged herself closer, losing herself in him, in his sweet words and even sweeter kiss.

He pulled back with a chuckle. "Too much of that and I'll be forced to strip you naked and have you right here and now."

She arched a brow, her body leading her with its incessant needs. "How long will it take for Liam and Violet to walk around the lake?"

He pondered that a moment, then began to unbutton her gown. "Long enough."

She laughed, then began to help him, stripping him out of his shirt, lifting her hips to facilitate the removal of her gown. Soon their clothing was all discarded and he pulled her over him, his mouth moving over hers as she straddled his erection and slowly eased herself over him in slick welcoming. He turned his face into her shoulder with a garbled moan, his fingers digging into her arms, his hips lifting to spear her fully.

She smiled, loving how she affected him, loving how he affected her too. Then she began to ride him, hard and fast, driving her hips over him, stroking her clitoris at the base of his cock with every thrust.

Her pleasure began to build and her hip movements grew erratic as impending release stole her rational thoughts. Mal chuckled beneath her and suddenly he sat up, his arms folding around her back, clutching her close as he lifted his hips up into her.

She clenched her legs around his back and met him stroke for stroke, her head dipped back as pleasure began to mob her, overtake her. The orgasm was powerful, swift and all consuming, and she cried out Mal's name into the wind as her body clenched his, milking him with her release.

He cursed as he flipped her onto her back. Her mind spinning with pleasure, she managed to let her hands slide down and grab his muscular backside as he began to drive into her in earnest.

The tendons in his neck tightened, his face twisting in a mask of pleasure as he grunted out release and poured his seed deep into her body. She clung to him, taking it all as he cupped her face and kissed her deeply, passionately.

Now they were bound in a way they hadn't been before. And as she clung to him, panting, her body still flexing around him, she knew that nothing in her life could ever be the same.

Chapter Eight

Olivia paced the parlor, her mind tangled by memories of her passionate joining with Malcolm earlier in the day. Even now, just thinking of it made her body ache and her heart swell with emotions that frightened her.

There was one person she longed to talk to about her confusing feelings—her best friend. But Violet and Liam had never returned to the picnic spot, leaving Olivia and Malcolm to return to the house together and reluctantly part ways when Mal had some estate business to take care of.

Olivia sighed as she left the parlor. She would find Violet if she could, for she truly needed pragmatic counsel in this matter in order to return to reality.

As she moved up the hallway, she encountered a maid dusting and approached the girl.

"Excuse me, have you seen Miss Violet?" she asked.

The girl bobbed out a nod. "Yes, miss. She's in the library."

The girl indicated which door down the hallway and Olivia headed that way, drawing calming breaths as she walked so that her emotions wouldn't be clear on her face the moment Violet looked at her.

When Olivia entered the library, she found Violet sitting in a comfortable chair by the window, scribbling on a piece of paper. At Olivia's appearance, her friend frowned, folded the sheet and tucked it away. She didn't stand, but merely stared and seemed to be waiting for Olivia to explain herself.

Olivia shook her head. "Where did you and Liam go? Why didn't you return?"

Violet pursed her lips and anxiety gripped Olivia. She had displeased Violet, apparently.

"Before we discuss that, I want to talk about something else." Violet arched a brow. "*Why* did you try to talk to Liam about his past?"

Olivia stared at her. Here she had been trying to help her friend, and now Violet was upset with her?

"Isn't that what you're here for? To wheedle the facts about those things out of him and report back?"

Violet shot to her feet and rushed around her to close the library door. "Mind your tone, Olivia, you could ruin everything!"

Olivia folded her arms, refusing to feel guilty over something that had been done out of a desire to be of assistance. Especially since her friend seemed to need it.

"What *everything*, Violet? We've been in Bath for over a week. Have you even tried to pry anything out of him?"

"Not exactly. I told you, it's part of my plan." Violet turned her back so Olivia couldn't see her expression.

Olivia stared at her in surprise. Here she had been fearful about her own feelings, and it seemed Violet was no more clear or calm about her own.

"Yes, I do recall the plan, but it only works if you begin to obtain information from your target," she pointed out as gently as she could.

Violet shook her head. "He isn't my target—you make it sound as though I'm attacking him."

"No, you aren't. Though you should be." Olivia sighed. "I'm sorry you feel I interfered by asking Windbury a few questions, but I was trying to help you. Though I judge by your upset with me that you didn't attempt to walk through the door I created by bringing up tender subjects."

Violet sat back down hard in the chair she had vacated. She rubbed a hand over her face. "No," she admitted softly, "I didn't. I suppose I could have, I think he might have told me something had I pushed. But...I couldn't."

Again, Olivia thought of Malcolm and her tangled feelings. She took a seat beside Violet. "Why?"

"Because I have been increasingly questioning what I'm doing here, Olivia. This man has been through so much and though his sister means well, what she and her husband have asked of me is a terrible violation. The guilt of that..." she cut herself off with a gasp of breath, "...it eats at me."

"You are a good person, Violet. You always have been." She thought of Malcolm and the fact that he didn't know of her true motives in being here, any more than Liam knew Violet's. "You are much better than I. But you cannot forget your goals, my dear. You have more to think of than just yourself."

Violet dipped her head. "I know. I *know* that and I know that what I'm working for, *whom* I'm working for, it's worth this. But I can't focus on the future too hard, Olivia. I don't want to be disappointed if it doesn't work out."

Olivia was shocked when a single tear rolled down Violet's cheek. Her friend never cried, or at least she hadn't in a great many years.

"It will," Olivia said, squeezing her hand. Violet needed encouragement and she would give it, no matter her own situation. "If you do this."

"I know you're right."

Olivia smiled gently and shifted the topic of conversation in order to lift the tension in the room. "Now where *did* you and Liam go today?"

Violet lifted her eyebrows. "Oh, you have questions about that? I'm surprised, considering what you and Malcolm were doing while Liam and I took our walk."

Olivia's jaw dropped at Violet's implication. She couldn't possibly mean that the pair had seen her with Malcolm on the blanket, sharing an utterly tender, but ultimately very sexual moment.

"I—we—you—" she stammered, her blush nearly setting her on fire.

"Oh yes, we came back earlier than perhaps you thought we would and we saw you," Violet confirmed with a shake of her head and a half smile. "We saw *all* of you, actually."

Olivia squeezed her eyes shut. So it was out and in the most humiliating way. But she *had* wanted to talk to Violet about this.

"We may have gotten a wee bit carried away," she said slowly. "I was truly sorry I upset Liam and Mal decided to...comfort me."

"You did seem *comforted*," Violet teased. "If comforted is a euphemism for something else."

Olivia covered her face. "I am embarrassed. I'm sure Lord Windbury dislikes me more than ever."

Violet shifted slightly. "I wouldn't say that," she said. "But tell me about you and Malcolm."

Olivia pondered all the things she could say, should say, to hide her heart. But in the end, she couldn't be false, not about this. Not now. She lowered her hands and smiled.

"He's—he is—I—" Olivia stammered, the words so hard to find.

Violet drew back, her eyes widening as Olivia's inability to express herself made her heart clear to anyone with eyes or ears.

"You care for him?" Her friend said the statement with such incredulity, as if she hadn't thought Olivia capable. And perhaps she hadn't been until the moment she met Mal.

Olivia nodded slowly. "I do, Violet. I truly do."

The words had been said out loud and Olivia's heart swelled. She did care for him. More than cared for him.

"I can see that," Violet whispered when the silence between them had hung long and heavy. "Does he feel something for you in return?"

Olivia paused, thinking of all Mal had said and done since her arrival. His tenderness, his acceptance of her past, his revelations of his own—it meant something. She knew it did.

"It is hard to say, for men are so difficult to read when it comes to matters of the heart," she said softly. "But I have reason to hope he does care for me."

Violet's brow wrinkled. "What about the future? Will he become your protector?"

Olivia dropped her chin. And this was where her experience, or in this case, lack thereof, made her hesitate. She had never cared for someone, nor wished for them to care for her. What in the world *did* happen between a woman like her and a man like him?

"Perhaps that is all I should expect, considering my past."

"But you want more." Violet said it as a statement, not a question.

"I do," Olivia whispered.

Violet reached for Olivia. "Then I wish for nothing less than you deserve, happiness and joy...and love."

"Do you think that is possible?" Olivia asked, hardly breathing as she awaited the answer.

Violet nodded. "I...I do, Olivia. And you have earned it—that is the truth."

Olivia could hardly breathe. Violet would never be anything less than honest with her, she knew that to be true if nothing else in this world. The fact that her friend could hold out any hope for her future made Olivia believe even more that it could be true.

But as she hugged her friend, there was still a niggling concern that kept her from a perfect happiness. And that was the fact that Malcolm knew nothing of the deception which had brought her here. Nor did she know how he would react to it.

Malcolm was angry as he stormed down the long hallway toward the office where he knew Liam was working. He hadn't been angry for a very long time.

Actually, that wasn't true. He *had* been angry, but he had stuffed it down, swallowed it, forgotten it, forgiven it, all to protect his friend. Only right now he had someone else in mind to protect and she was beginning to trump everything else in his life.

He threw the door open, letting it bang against the back wall, then slammed it shut behind him.

Liam's head jerked up from his ledger, but Malcolm refused to allow him to speak, to argue or to make this moment about him. Instead, he folded his arms.

"Do you know that you made Olivia cry?" he managed to ease out past tightly clenched teeth.

Liam took a moment to close the ledger before him and then spoke. "How did I do that?"

"Getting up and stomping off like a child does that sometimes," Malcolm snapped. "And you have been cold to her since her arrival."

"She attempted to intrude upon—" Liam began.

But Malcolm didn't want to hear it. He slammed his hand down on the desk to shut his friend up. "She attempted to connect with you, as people sometimes do. You *do* remember how human beings treat each other, don't you?"

Liam pressed his lips together and Malcolm could see he was fighting his reactions. But this was Liam, and Liam didn't recall the finer points of self-control anymore.

"Horseshit," his friend snapped. "She wasn't worrying over me as a friend and you know it. She was poking at a wound, hoping to see if it would bleed."

"She isn't like that," Mal snarled, his face heating at this new slur.

Liam barked out an ugly laugh. "How would *you* know? You've been fucking her for a week—you know nothing but her body."

A veil of red rage settled before Mal's vision and the emotions that had been simmering now bubbled to an almost out-of-control level as he grasped Liam and shook him.

"Shut up, Windbury," he shouted. "You're talking about the woman I love."

Liam wrestled free and stumbled back, staring at his friend in utter disbelief. Disbelief Mal felt himself. Until he'd uttered those words he would not have admitted such a depth of feeling. But it was true, all true. He loved Olivia. Despite their short acquaintance, despite the obstacles, he loved her.

"Love her?" Liam repeated in surprise. "What the hell are you talking about?"

"I love her," he repeated and now the words didn't sound as foreign or outrageous. They were just...true. "And I want to marry her."

Liam went as tense as a piece of steel before he muttered, "You idiot."

Mal's eyes narrowed at this response to his confession. "You would prefer that I follow you around my whole life, trying to keep you from walking over a cliff or putting a bullet through your ear?"

Liam's eyes widened, but Mal didn't stop. This showdown had been a long time coming and in reality, it had nothing to do with Olivia or love or anything except what Mal had been protecting Liam from for years.

"Oh yes, I know your dark thoughts," he continued. "I've seen them on your face when no one else was looking. And I have watched you, guarded you from yourself because I care for you, you pompous ass. Because I know you will allow no one else to intervene on your behalf. I don't regret any sacrifices I've made to be your friend and your confidante. But I do not agree to live in your misery forever, Liam."

"My *misery*," Liam repeated and his voice was choked with indignation. "I never asked you to."

"No, but you tend to drag everyone else into it with you." Malcolm flinched at the truth of his words, a truth he had denied to himself, but now came crystal clear. "I have done my best to help you, to carry you through your suffering, but there comes a point when *you* must stand up and decide to live again. But you won't. You utterly refuse to do anything except stand with one foot in the grave, waiting to die alone. Well, that is your choice, my friend. But I think you are a god-awful fool to let the past destroy your future. And for what?"

Liam clenched his fists. "Have a care, Malcolm."

He ignored his friend. "For what? Guilt? Or is it fear that stops you from moving on? I have no idea, but I do know that you dishonor Matilda's memory every time you lock away those who would love you. Every time you think of taking your own life, you murder her all over again."

Liam swung without warning and Malcolm had no chance to duck as the fist hit his face at full force. Mal staggered backward, hitting a chair so hard that the wood splintered and flew in all directions as he hit the floor.

For what felt like an eternity, he sat there, surrounded by shattered furniture, staring up at the broken face of his utterly damaged friend. All he felt then was pity. Pity for Liam's loss, pity for his refusal to see a future. Slowly, Mal got up, checking his jaw and recognizing it wasn't broken.

"Feel better?" he asked, eyes narrowed.

Liam still had his fists raised. But his eyes were so empty.

"You won't fight?" Liam barked.

Malcolm sighed. "You haven't fought for two years—why should I? Haven't fought for anything worthwhile, anyway. I just hope you remember how before you lose everything and anything of value in your life."

Malcolm turned, perfectly aware that his friend could attack him, hurt him, despite his old injuries. And trusting that even in the depths of his anger and frustration Liam wouldn't do it.

But he still felt like utter shit as he left his best friend standing alone in his office, his knuckles bruised and their friendship damaged.

Chapter Nine

Olivia looked up from the book in her hand as the knock sounded at her door.

"Yes?" she called out.

As she rose to her feet, the book fell away. Her visitor was Malcolm, and his eye was swollen with a bruise while his face was long and drawn with emotion.

"What happened?" she breathed as she rushed to him, ushering him inside and shutting the door. She pulled him down to look at his eye. It was bruised purple and puffed from what looked to be a very hard blow.

"We fought," he said, his voice flat and pained.

She took a long step back as horror hit her at the meaning of his words.

"You and Liam?" she whispered, her shaking hands clenched at her sides.

He swallowed. "Yes," he bit out. "I couldn't allow him to behave so callously, to hurt you and—"

She shook her head, raising her hands to interrupt him. "Because of me? Because of today?"

He met her gaze. "Yes."

"No," she whispered. "No no no." She paced away from him, trying to wake up from this nightmare, trying to make this go away. "You shouldn't have done that!" she said, more to herself than to him.

He caught her arm and turned her around with one smooth motion. "He has behaved like this for years, he needed a setting down."

"But not over me," she said, pulling at her arm, though he wouldn't release it. "Surely you must see that I'm not worth losing a friendship that means so much to you."

His eyes narrowed and for a moment she thought he might agree and cast her aside. That would be a reasonable reaction, although it would break her heart. Still, she steeled herself for his rejection.

But it didn't come. Instead, he gently cupped her face.

"You are more than worth it," he whispered. "Can't you see that? Olivia, since your arrival, I have said and done things I never could have imagined. I have given you my body and my soul, I have trusted you with those things. I *trust* you."

Now she did pull her arm away and stagger even farther back. He trusted her, though she was a liar, though her motives weren't pure, though she was in league with a woman who would spy on his closest friend. She had kept those facts to herself to protect Violet, but now she knew what she had to do.

She had to tell him.

"Malcolm," she whispered. "You must know—"

He shook his head. "No, *you* must know. Olivia, I love you."

Her words fell silent on her lips as she stared at him. Once again, she wondered if this were a dream, but this time it wasn't a nightmare. This man, this glorious, handsome, wonderful man was staring at her, not blinking or hesitating or lying...telling her he *loved* her.

Her, with all her faults and her damaged past.

He reached for her, pulling her close, and she melted against him with no hesitance, no fear, just the love she felt in return. Love she didn't speak because he kissed her, pouring all his passion and emotion into her.

She drank it in, relaxing against him, allowing her mind to clear, to forget confessions. She clung to him, tightening her arms around him and opening herself to him with her body and her heart.

His kiss grew more passionate as they held each other, the driving of his tongue beginning to become more intense, more insistent.

They didn't stop kissing as they moved toward her bed, unfastening buttons and hooks slowly, only parting when they were forced to do so in order to remove an article of clothing. Finally she lay back across her pillows, staring up at him in all his naked, beautiful glory. Her heart ached with desire and love, her body shook with need.

She reached for him, drawing him down, opening her legs, and he slid into her gently as he whispered "I love you" once again.

He began to move slowly, so slowly she thought she would go mad as her desire mounted. She lifted her hips to meet him, hoping to force him to speed his thrusts, but he only smiled down at her.

"No rush," he murmured, circling his hips once again in slow torture.

She huffed out her breath. No rush for him, but her clitoris was tingling, her sex aching, and every glorious time he drove into her, she felt herself inching toward release at a snail's pace. A very pleasurable one, but still...he just might kill her at this rate.

But just as she was about to mention her frustration or even try to take control of the encounter, he cupped her cheek with one hand. Her eyes met his and locked there, and suddenly nothing else mattered. She was one with this man, lost in him, and she forgot everything else as he held her gaze and continued his gentle, constant drive to her pleasure.

Her orgasm was so sudden it took her off guard and she arched beneath him, gasping for breath, trying to keep her gaze on his, clinging to him as he brought her to completion.

He smiled at her. "See, no rush."

She laughed even as tears flooded her eyes at the magic of this connection, of her feelings. She drew him down, kissing him as his thrusts grew faster and harder, his control fading now that her release had been found. He groaned into her mouth and his seed moved within her before he collapsed across her body and held her tight.

She kissed his shoulders, his neck, and rolled into the crook of his body as he moved onto his back. She spread her hands out across his chest and looked at her pale skin against his. They were different and yet matched. She could be happy with him, but not unless she swallowed her fears.

"Mal?" she whispered, not daring to look at him.

"Hmm?" he grunted, his voice heavy with sleep.

Now she did look up at him. His eyes were shut, his breathing steady.

"Nothing," she murmured, leaning up to kiss him gently. "Sleep. You deserve it."

He muttered something unintelligible and cuddled her closer, but even as she settled into his arms, her unease made her stomach turn.

Lying to a stranger or even a bed partner was one thing—lying to a man who loved you...well, that was something else.

So she would have to find a way to remedy that, and soon. And she could only pray whatever words she found would be ones he would understand and accept or else she could lose him forever.

Malcolm frowned as he walked downstairs into the servant area of the house to his small office. He had so many other places he'd rather be. Well, one, at any rate. But he had a few things to tend to and, in truth, he was still sorting out his feelings. Now that he could admit, both to himself and to her, that he had fallen in love with Olivia, he had some decisions to make.

He opened the door and stopped dead, for Liam was already there. His friend pivoted to face him. Liam looked slightly sick as his gaze fell upon Mal's blackened eye.

"What do you want?" Mal growled, refusing to feel sorry for Liam.

He expected his attitude to bring out the worst in the earl, but, instead, his friend's shoulders rolled forward in defeat.

"I came here to tell you I'm sorry for my reaction to our conversation yesterday," Liam said softly.

"Are you now?" Mal asked, almost uncertain with how to proceed.

Liam pursed his lips. "Yes. I am. More than you will ever know. I'm especially sorry I punched you, which was entirely uncalled for."

"It was."

Mal kept his arms folded, but his anger was beginning to fade, for he had never received an apology from Liam before.

Liam shifted, as discomforted by this show of emotion as Mal was.

"You are my best friend," he said softly. "In truth, my only friend. I recognize the value of that, even though I rarely show it and probably less often express it. And I owe you a great deal more than I offered when we last met. I hope you'll accept my apology."

Mal stared at him, disbelief his first reaction to the words coming from Liam's mouth. His friend truly meant them too, that was clear from the hangdog expression on his face and the drooping body language he currently possessed.

"I would only *just* call it a punch," Mal said with a smile meant to lighten the mood. "It hardly hurt."

Liam listed his eyes and grinned, but there was no mistaking the relief on his face. "I blackened your eye, didn't I?"

Mal shrugged as he motioned for Liam to sit across from him at the desk. "Ladies always like a man with battle scars."

"Olivia tended to you, then?" Liam teased as he took a seat.

Mal thought of their night together, of the confession he had made, of the sweetness of making love to her, and he smiled. "Indeed she did."

"So perhaps you should thank me."

Mal shrugged. "I'll keep that in mind, though I certainly hope we don't go around coming to blows regularly just to impress the women into comforting us."

Liam shook his head. "Amen to that."

"How are you, other than suffering from racking guilt that obviously brought you down to my lair this early in the day?" Mal asked as he fidgeted things on his desk.

He had been so wrapped up in Olivia that he had been neglecting his usual duties of watching over Liam. Now he wondered what was truly happening with him and Violet.

"I'm well, especially now that we have resolved our differences," Liam said. "But I do need to talk to you about something."

"Yes?"

His friend hesitated before he blurted out, "I-I am going to offer to become Violet's protector."

Slowly, Mal lifted his gaze to Liam's face. It would do no good to reveal his shock at this declaration, so he fought to keep a neutral expression, but inside he was reeling. After the death of Liam's love, Matilda, Mal had often wondered if his friend would ever care for anyone, including himself, again. To want to keep a woman was an astonishing step for the earl.

"Her protector," he repeated slowly.

Liam nodded, but beneath the surety, Mal sensed a hesitation. Not one about keeping Violet, but something else. And he understood it. The situation was...complicated.

"Will it be enough?" he asked, meaning the question both for himself and for Liam.

Liam pushed up from the seat and paced across the room. He was tense as he stopped in front of the fire, refusing to look at Malcolm.

"It is all I can give her," he finally said softly. "I have nothing else—the rest was buried with Matilda."

Mal flinched out of pity, and for the first time he understood a fraction of Liam's pain. He couldn't imagine losing Olivia now that he loved her, let alone witnessing her violent death in an accident. The very thought turned his stomach.

"I know you well enough that I doubt this confession doesn't have a motive. What do you need me to do?" he asked.

"I haven't had a mistress in years," Liam said with a shake of his head. "And even though I trust Violet, I still have things I want to know, to be certain of..."

Mal nodded, understanding what Liam was loath to say. "Would you like a cursory investigation, some basic background?"

Once again, Liam's face filled with relief that he wouldn't have to say those words out loud. "Exactly. How soon could you complete something like that, being in Bath?"

"If I send a missive to the solicitor this moment, I could have it reach London before tonight," Mal said, glancing at the clock on the mantel. "With a day or two for investigation and a return message, I would say it would be no more than three to four days before you'd have the answers you'd like."

Liam nodded. "Yes, that is perfect. I can wait."

"Then I'll compose something and send it immediately." Malcolm reached into his desk and drew out a few heavy sheets of paper to write the note without delay.

"Excellent," Liam said, backing toward the door. "I'll see you at breakfast."

Mal nodded as he began to scribble and Liam left the room to allow him his privacy. He had done this before for his friend—looked into the background of others—even before the accident. It wasn't a pleasant task, but in this case he rather relished it. Liam might not be willing or able to admit it, but he seemed to care for Violet Milford more than he said.

And if that was true, it could very well free Malcolm up to pursue a very different kind of life than he lived now. One with Olivia.

A life he very much wanted.

He folded the letter and carefully addressed it. As he stared at the paper before him, he shook his head.

"Once this duty is resolved, once I know the truth about Violet, I will ask Olivia to marry me," he said, wanting to hear the words out loud, even if he only said them to himself.

They rang so true and sweet that he couldn't help but smile as he said them. It was the perfect plan. And in a few days, there would be nothing standing in his way.

Chapter Ten

Olivia smiled at her maid, Belle, as the girl finished the last touches on her hair. "Thank you, my dear. That will be all."

If her companion thought it odd to be dismissed, she didn't show it and only smiled as she slipped from the room. Probably she thought Malcolm would soon be joining her mistress, and it wasn't a terrible assumption. After all, he had been coming to her room, or drawing her to his, every day and night since her arrival.

And the past four days since he confessed his love for her had only been more intense. She had felt the change in him. He was lighter when he was with her, he talked to her more and more about the family he was distant from and the life he had led since he began assisting Liam. She had done the same, telling him secrets she'd never thought she'd reveal to another soul.

They had gone on walks and played cards and of course made love until she was weak from him. It would have been the perfect time together except for one thing—her cowardice.

She'd had so many opportunities to tell Malcolm about the reasons she'd come here, but she hadn't. Either he had distracted her or she hadn't wanted to spoil yet another lovely day together.

Now she stared herself in the reflection and her frown deepened. She had spent a lifetime pretending who and what she was, but with Mal she could be real, she could be herself. And she didn't want to lie to him, not even for Violet.

"Perhaps that is what makes me hesitate," she said to her mirror image. "Violet would be in a spot if I just spouted off the truth to Mal. But if she knows I *need* to do so, if she understands that I love this man and lying kills me, then at least I'll have given her time to prepare and perhaps even tell Liam the truth on her own terms."

She nodded, for that seemed like the best solution, the one most fair to all parties involved. She stood and smoothed her dress one last time before she headed downstairs. She could hear voices in the dining room and took a moment to catch her breath before she walked inside to face her friend and, if all went well, create a future for herself.

Malcolm sat in the carriage as it rolled back down the long road from Bath to Liam's estate. He had been reluctant to take the vehicle to town rather than his horse, but Liam had muttered at him about official business and insisted. Now he was glad for his friend's foresight. There was no way he could safely ride a horse, not with his eyes burning and his entire body shaking.

He stared at the notes clenched in his fist. They were wrinkled because he was crushing them, and he swore before he started smoothing them against his legs.

He didn't have to read them to know what they said. The summary his investigator had given him in Bath still rang in his ears.

"Miss Violet Milford, a whore," Stevenson, the investigator, had begun, "had a meeting with Lord Windbury's sister before she came to Bath. Judging from a sum of money deposited in her accounts and a variety of letters that have come from Miss Milford to a mysterious solicitor since her arrival...I have every reason to believe she is working in league with the Duke and Duchess of Rothcastle, perhaps to spy on Lord Windbury or to influence him in some way."

Stevenson had kept talking, droning on and on, but Mal hadn't heard him anymore. He'd just stared at the reports, the steps of the investigation, looking for something, anything that would prove this was all a misunderstanding. Or at least exonerate Olivia of any knowledge of her friend's deeds.

Mal clenched his fists against the carriage seat.

"There is nothing that can make Olivia innocent of involvement," he snapped at himself.

She and Violet lived together in London, he had found out. He already knew they were close, thick as thieves. And she had been meant as his distraction outside the baths in town. She'd told him so herself. At the time, he'd thought it charming, seductive.

Now he knew the game the women were playing, and everything he thought and felt was shattered.

The carriage came to a stop outside the estate and one of the footmen came around to open the door for him, but Malcolm didn't move. He simply sat in the carriage, staring out the door and up at the house.

He didn't want to go in. He didn't want to destroy Liam with this news. More to the point, he didn't want to see Olivia. Because once he did, this charade would be over and she would be gone forever, leaving him with only memories of what had turned out to be a most foolish love for her.

"Sir?" the footman said when he continued to remain in the vehicle.

Mal shook his head. Ah yes. His duty.

"I'm sorry," he managed to say as he climbed from the carriage. "Woolgathering."

The servant tilted his head. "Are you well? Can I...can I get something for you, sir?"

Mal looked at the house another moment, then back to the boy. "Yes," he said and turned toward the driver. "Nichols," he said, finding comfort in his role of estate manager, "do not put the horses or the carriage away, merely take them around to the side of the estate and wait. Miss Milford and Miss Cranfield will be leaving us today. And they will need a swift return to Bath."

The driver blinked in surprise, but nodded. "Yes, sir. Of course, sir."

Mal began to move toward the house, but the little footman was at his heels like a barking terrier. "Have the ladies begun packing? Where shall they go? I haven't heard anything about this from his lordship, Mr. Graham."

Mal stopped on the top step, his hand hovering above the front door handle. He shook his head.

"His lordship doesn't know," he said softly. Then he glared at the boy. "Just do as I say."

He didn't wait for further insubordination, but entered the house and slammed the door behind him. Simms rushed into the foyer from some unknown place and took Mal's coat.

"Where is Lord Windbury?" Mal asked, hardly able to look at anything but the proof in his hands. He folded it into the inside pocket of his jacket.

"His lordship is in the dining room with Miss Milford," Simms said.

"Thank you," Mal replied, shooting the butler a quick glance. Liam would become a bear again when the truth came out and Violet was gone. How Simms would hate that, but he would have to endure it.

Just as they would *all* have to endure this betrayal.

Mal walked down the hall, each step making his anger all the more real, all the more focused. Violet had used Liam. She had pretended to care for him when all the while it was a lie. Violet had *known* about his friend's pain and it had meant nothing to her except a blood payment from Liam's worst enemy.

The damage she would do...Mal could hardly stand it.

He stopped outside the dining room door. It was slightly ajar and he could hear Liam talking inside.

"Violet," Liam said, his tone sharp, "what are you keeping from me?"

She didn't answer and Mal shook his head. The little bitch was probably trying to formulate a new lie.

"Liam," she began, her voice shaking. He could hear her false tears, a fresh manipulation.

With a growl, he threw open the dining room door and strode through.

"I overheard you in the hallway, Liam, asking the young woman what she was keeping from you," Malcolm said, trying hard to control the anger in his voice, though he'd failed. "I believe I can answer that since she will not, or at least not with honesty, since that is not in her nature."

Liam scowled at Malcolm's slur. "What do you mean?"

Violet stepped forward, her hands raised as if in surrender or pleading for her life. He ignored it.

"Your lovely paramour came here at the behest of Ava and Rothcastle." Mal softened his tone as he looked at Liam, the friend he would break after he had been broken so many times. "*You* have been sleeping with a spy."

Violet turned away with a sob that actually seemed real, despite the fact that Malcolm knew she was a liar.

"What are you talking about?" Liam asked. He sounded hollow.

"I'm sorry, Liam," Mal said softly, hating that he had to do this to Liam. "The report from London was very clear."

"Report?" Violet repeated and turned toward Liam. "You had someone looking into me?"

Mal glared at her, despising that she actually sounded offended at that fact.

"And for good fucking reason, don't you think?" He pivoted toward Liam. "She was hired by your sister and her husband a few weeks ago."

Violet sucked in a breath, but before she could respond to Mal's charge with more lies, Olivia entered the parlor, smiling broadly. Malcolm forgot everything else except for her and her part in this. It was no longer a betrayal that harmed his best friend. It was a betrayal of him and the love he felt for Olivia.

Love she had never stated she returned and now he knew why.

"Violet?" she murmured, looking between the three of them as the mood in the room became clear to her. "What—"

Mal clenched his fists at his sides. So she turned to *Violet* first, her coconspirator.

"Did you know?" he hissed. "Did you know why she was here?"

Olivia jerked her gaze to Violet and for a moment the women held stares. Then Violet jerked out a single nod.

Mal's stomach turned at this silent, anticlimactic verification of the truth he had already guessed.

"Of course you knew. You two are so bonded together you would probably stab me through the heart if she told you it would help." He shook his head in disgust and tried to push the pain away with his rage. "So you were the distraction not just the first time we met, but all along. How hard did you laugh, Olivia?"

"Malcolm," Olivia sobbed and, like Violet had, she sounded truly pained. They were both wonderful actresses.

She reached for him, but he couldn't bear her touch in this moment. He jerked away and exited the room without a backward glance or another word. But as he rushed down the hall alone, his vision blurred by intense emotion and his broken heart throbbing, he wanted nothing more than to grab Olivia and make her take back all she'd done.

But that wasn't possible. Nothing between them would ever be possible again.

Chapter Eleven

As Malcolm stormed from the room, his hatred of her stamped on every line of his handsome face, Olivia's legs gave out from under her and she sank onto the settee.

This was the nightmare she had feared most in the past few days. The nightmare she could have avoided if she had only been honest with the man she loved. He might have been angry, but at least he would have known the truth from her own lips, not some investigator's, who had likely twisted all she'd done in the worst possible light.

Although, at present, there didn't seem to be a positive light. She shuddered, her stomach turning and her eyes filling with tears she blinked away. She didn't deserve them.

She glanced toward Violet and Liam. They were arguing, but nothing they said made any sense to her. Their words had no meaning in the face of what she had just lost due to her own stupidity.

"Please leave," Liam finally said, his words piercing Olivia's fog.

"Liam," Violet gasped and there was true pain in her voice.

"Just go," he repeated.

Violet only stared at him for a moment.

"Did I not make myself clear?" he sneered.

She shook her head. "No, my lord. You are very clear. I'm sorry. I'm so very sorry."

Violet moved to the settee and caught Olivia's elbow to draw her to her feet. As she wrapped an arm around Olivia's waist, she whispered, "Come, Olivia. Come away."

Olivia was too weak to resist; she simply let Violet take her into the foyer. Simms stood there with the front door open, his expression hard.

So they were to be put out. It was fair, Olivia supposed, but painful. She glanced at Violet and when she saw her friend's lip quivering, she managed to straighten up and find some dignity as they linked arms and walked together out of the house, down the path and into the carriage.

Only when the door had been shut and locked behind them and the carriage began to move toward Bath did Violet slump down in her seat, shaking, even though she didn't cry.

Olivia, on the other hand, merely leaned her head against the cold glass of the window and watched as the estate disappeared from view. She had lost everything. And the emptiness that accompanied that thought was almost too much to bear.

Olivia sat at her window, staring out into the gathering dark of the evening. In the hallway, she heard the bustling of servants and the banging of trunks and bags being brought in.

So Liam and Malcolm had sent Belle and Rachel home with Violet and Olivia's things. She could imagine just how cruel a duty that had been for their loyal maids, but when Belle knocked at her door, Olivia ignored her until the girl stopped tapping and went away.

She wasn't ready to face anyone just yet. Her mind was too full of other thoughts.

She had never expected much from her life. Her difficult childhood had taught her that nothing would be given to her easily. After she became a courtesan, a mistress, she had known she was only a commodity, another thing rich men collected because they were bored or thought they needed something pretty on their arm while they clawed their way up the ladder of society.

She had been passive through it all, never asking for more than she was given, never arguing when a relationship was ended and a settlement made for her troubles. A ruckus would only be unpleasant. So she didn't fight.

Still, the circumstances with Malcolm had been so very different. Yes, she had come to him under false pretenses and, yes, she had lied about that, sometimes by mere omission and sometimes more directly. She understood perfectly why he would hate her and never wish to see her again.

Her habit told her to accept that fact. To let him go.

But now there was something different stirring inside of her. Something she had never felt before, something filled with power she had never felt before.

She loved this man. She knew that as surely as she knew she was alive and breathing. And for the first time in her life, she wasn't willing to stay quiet, to accept the inevitable, to lie down and let life happen to her.

She wanted to fight for him, for *them*. And even more terrifying was that she believed, in some small, niggling part of her, she could win that fight. He loved her, didn't he? He'd said he loved her, he'd shown her he loved her, so if she could overcome his anger, there was no reason why he wouldn't forgive her.

"At the very least, I must try," she whispered.

There was another tap on her door, and Olivia pursed her lips. She was going to ignore it, but then she heard Violet's voice, tired and pained, in the hallway.

"Olivia, darling, it's me. Let me in, won't you?"

With a sigh, Olivia crossed to the door and allowed her friend entry before she returned to her perch at the window. Violet closed the door behind her and stared.

"Olivia, have you been sitting there all this time?" she asked as she dragged a chair over and sat across from her friend.

"I have," Olivia replied, unable to say anything else, if only because she was so focused on her own thoughts. On the decision that was forming in her mind that had nothing to do with Violet.

"It was an ugly scene," her friend said softly.

Olivia flinched and to her horror, a tear escaped to roll down her cheeks.

"Very," she choked out.

Violet gasped and caught Olivia's hand. Olivia saw her friend's guilt, her pain, and it broke Olivia's heart. This was as difficult for Violet as it was for her.

"We knew it could happen," Violet whispered.

Olivia looked at her evenly. "I *never* knew any of this would happen."

Certainly, falling in love hadn't been on her list of potential outcomes when she accepted Violet's offer to come to Bath.

Violet rose to her feet, all seriousness and business, as if that would make the pain go away for them both.

"Tomorrow we'll go back to London," she said. "I will collect my ill-gotten gains and then that will be all. I'm sure eventually we will forget this...we'll forget."

Olivia doubted that Violet believed her own words. Certainly, she didn't look convinced. But she wouldn't be able to stop Violet. She knew that perfectly well.

She glanced up at her friend and said words that surprised even herself, "I'm not going back to London."

Violet jerked her gaze toward Olivia. "I—what do you mean? Of course you'll come with me!"

She shook her head. "No."

Violet dropped down to her knees in front of her friend and caught both her hands. "Oh, Olivia, please don't be angry. I'm so sorry I involved you in this; I didn't mean to bring you grief. You are my best friend and my sister. Please don't hate me—I couldn't bear it if you hated me too."

Olivia drew back in horror at Violet's assumptions. Gently, she touched her face.

"Dearest, my reasons for not going have nothing to do with you. I'm not angry with you in the slightest."

Violet's head came down and her breathing slowed with relief, but when she looked back up, there were tears in her eyes. Ones Violet blinked away. Olivia wished she could do the same to the ones in hers.

"Then...then why won't you return with me?" Violet asked.

"Because of my feelings for him," she admitted.

Violet stood slowly. "For Malcolm."

Olivia nodded. She drew a deep breath before she said, "I am in love with him, Violet."

She expected Violet to express surprise at this statement, for Olivia had spent a lot of time cultivating an outward appearance of frivolity and emotional detachment. Even her earlier admission to Violet that she cared for Malcolm couldn't have been fully believed by her friend.

Instead, Violet nodded. "Of course you are."

Olivia sighed in relief that she wouldn't have to defend her feelings. "And *because* I love him, I have no choice but to stay and try to fix this wedge between us. Even if it takes a great deal of time, I must try."

Violet paced away and was quiet for almost a full minute.

"If you love the man, you should fight for him," she finally said without looking at Olivia.

Olivia heard the pain in Violet's voice and got to her feet. "And what about *you*?"

"What about me?"

Olivia tried to meet her eyes, but Violet refused to do it. "I think it is evident you care deeply for Liam. I wager you may love him too."

Violet's face crumpled before she could turn to the window and ball her fist against the glass.

"You are mistaken," she said.

Olivia understood the hesitance of her friend. After all, it had been Olivia's long-ago training that told Violet never to allow feelings with a lover. It was dangerous.

As their current situation certainly proved.

"Am I?" she whispered.

Slowly, Violet turned and looked at her friend.

"Even if I did harbor some kind of tender feelings for Liam, he despises me now. And with good reason." Her voice broke and she sucked in a harsh breath.

"Oh, Violet."

Olivia moved to comfort her, but Violet stepped away and Olivia allowed it. It was better to have a little distance since their paths would diverge, at least for a while. A fact that broke Olivia's heart. Until Mal, Violet had been the person she'd let closest.

"It doesn't matter," Violet said. "I did what I did in order to be with my son. And as soon as I can finish this dreadful business with the Rothcastles, I can go to him. It will be worth it. It has to be worth it."

Olivia nodded in understanding. "You go back tomorrow?"

"In the morning," Violet said.

Olivia dipped her chin. She would be alone once Violet was gone. And she would have to battle alone for Malcolm's forgiveness and for her own happiness.

And even though that thought terrified her, she lifted her chin in readiness. She could do this.

She had to.

Malcolm was angry. In truth he had been angry for the past twenty-four hours, since his final encounter with Olivia, but now he was even angrier as he stomped down the hall and burst into the breakfast room without bothering to knock.

As he slammed the door behind himself, Liam turned from the picture window where he had been staring out at the beautiful morning outside.

"Malcolm," he said.

"She left," Malcolm announced as he slammed a plate onto the sideboard and shoveled food onto the dish. He wasn't even hungry.

"*She*?" Liam repeated. "Not *they*?"

Mal's fork clattered against the sideboard as his heart swelled with pain.

"Which she?" Liam asked when Mal didn't respond to him immediately.

Mal flinched, damn his wayward thoughts about a woman he didn't even want to acknowledge. He refocused.

"*Violet*," he clarified. "Gone early this morning, back to London. Olivia remains in the home that was let by Rothcastle."

Liam let out a long sigh. "Why do you track their movements?" he asked. "I don't want to know."

Mal clenched his fists at his sides and through clenched teeth he admitted a very painful truth. "*I* want to fucking know."

He swept up his plate and sat down at the table. Immediately he pushed the unwanted food aside and clenched a fist in front of him. Liam was staring at him. Just *staring*.

"Why?" Liam asked.

Mal felt the heat go out of him, replaced by something far sharper and more painful. For the first time, he fully understood why Liam was always so disgruntled. It did protect one from the pain.

"I told you I loved Olivia a few days ago," he said. "In the heat of an angry moment."

"Was that a lie?" Liam asked softly.

He rubbed his face. "It was never a lie. It was just utterly stupid. I do love her."

Liam didn't look surprised. Just filled with pity.

"And how is that utterly stupid?" his friend asked.

Mal shook his head. "Come, Liam, she was as much a part of this deception as Violet was. She came here to keep me from developing suspicions about her friend. I was just a pawn in their game."

Liam seemed to ponder that for a moment. "Let me ask you a question."

Mal shrugged.

"Would you lie for me?" his friend asked.

Mal jerked his gaze up. "What?"

"If I asked you to lie, would you?"

Malcolm hardly had to consider the question. "Yes."

"In fact, you have lied for me in the past, haven't you?" Liam lifted his eyebrows.

Malcolm understood his question, but rolled his eyes. "Yes, but that is different."

"Probably not to those you lied to." Liam shook his head. "If Violet ever told me the truth, and I think there were times when she did, then the bond she and Olivia share is powerful, *very* powerful."

"And so that means I should forgive?" Mal said slowly, not wanting to give in to this line of logic when everything in him screamed that he had been betrayed and made a fool.

"What you do is up to you," Liam said. "But the fact that Olivia didn't go back to London with Violet says a great deal to me about where she stands."

Mal bit out a bitter laugh. "Perhaps she thinks she can get something from me."

Liam shook his head. "Weren't you the one who told me if I wanted to die miserable and alone, that was my prerogative, but that you didn't approve? Seems you might wish to follow your own advice."

Mal rolled his eyes. "Says the man who has been in hiding for years."

"Well, do as I say, not as I do." Liam gave a thin smile. "At least go talk to the girl, Mal. At least let her explain. Unlike Violet, she didn't orchestrate this mess. And she *stayed*. As I said, that has to mean something."

"I'll consider it," Mal said, but the thought of doing so brought him a flood of confusing emotions. Part of him never wanted to face Olivia again.

But part of him—most of him, nearly all of him—needed to do just as his friend said. Whether to get her out of his system or to keep her there forever was something that remained to be seen.

Chapter Twelve

Olivia looked around the small bedroom in the home she had let in Bath just that very morning and sighed.

"It will do," she said, more to herself than to Belle, who was hanging her things in the small wardrobe.

Her maid looked at her. "May I ask why we didn't simply stay in the other home? Miss Violet said the Rothcastles had let it for the entire month."

Olivia couldn't blame Belle for the question. After all, her servant now had a tiny room in a drafty hall below stairs.

"I'm sorry the accommodations aren't as lavish as they were," she said. "But I am determined that Malcolm see I am not taking any further part in Violet's scheme. Staying at the home the Rothcastles let would undermine that vision."

Belle lifted her eyebrows slightly but continued her unpacking. "The boy you sent said he delivered your note to Mr. Graham."

Olivia stiffened. Her early morning hours had been spent saying goodbye to Violet and arranging for her new accommodations, but she'd also written the first in what she assumed would be a long series of letters to Malcolm, asking him to see her so she could explain and including the new address where he could call on her.

"Thank you," she said. "At least it was accepted; I suppose that is all I can expect from the first note. I shall write him again this afternoon."

Her maid had seen her through all her protectors and normally didn't raise a brow at her behavior, but now she straightened up. "So soon?"

Olivia hesitated. In truth she was uncertain about her plan to contact Malcolm twice a day until he agreed to see her, but she had to do something.

"Nothing ventured..." she murmured, but she could hardly believe her own words. There might be nothing left to gain.

Before the conversation could go further, there was a knock on the chamber door. Belle opened it to reveal their new housekeeper, Mrs. Jenkins. The older woman was a jolly, friendly sort.

"Good afternoon, Miss, there is a gentleman to see you."

Olivia gasped, exchanging a brief glance with her maid before she whispered, "His name?"

"Mr. Graham, he said it was," the housekeeper said. "Malcolm Graham."

Malcolm wiped his suddenly sweaty palms on his trouser front and leaned uncomfortably against the narrow mantel. The parlor was small and he felt giant in it. Out of place.

And wasn't he? He shouldn't even be here.

The door opened and he turned, catching his breath as Olivia took a step inside and slowly shut the door behind her. God, she was lovelier than he had allowed himself to remember. Her blonde locks were wispy around her pale face and her dark eyes locked on him.

"Malcolm," she whispered, "I'm so glad you've come."

He nodded, staring at her still, unable to tear his eyes away. He had come here with the intention of ranting, railing, demanding answers, but now that he was here, now that he saw her, all that seemed to fade away. He only wanted one thing now. One thing that had nothing to do with her explanations, with his future.

"I wanted to tell you—" she began.

He interrupted her by crossing the room in three long steps and caught her in his arms. His mouth was on hers, hard and insistent.

She stood frozen for a moment, but then she melted against him, her arms coming around his back, her fingers clenching hard through his clothes. She made a low moan in the back of her throat and he lost all reason.

He tugged at her gown, loosening buttons, popping a few off completely, but he didn't care. She didn't seem to care either, for she never broke their kiss and she joined him in the frenzy of clothing removal. When her dress was around her ankles, he cupped her backside and picked her up, carrying her across the room and pressing her hard to the wall next to the fire.

She had been working at removing his shirt, but he ignored that and went straight for his trouser buttons. His cock already strained at the fabric and had been since the moment she walked into the room, so it was difficult to get the hooks loose. When he did, his erection bobbed free and he breathed a sigh of relief at the end of constriction.

But relief turned to pleasure as she reached down to cup his hardness, stroking him a few times.

"Malcolm," she whispered.

He silenced her with another kiss, opening her legs, stroking her sex and finding it wet, then positioning himself at her entrance. He glided forward into her tight body and turned his face away from hers with a heavy moan of deepest pleasure. He wanted her with a power that took his breath away.

He braced one hand on the wall behind her and held her backside against him with the other and stroked into her. She made a gasping, keening sound and her body fluttered around him.

He smiled at her responsiveness and then began to take her in earnest. He didn't slow down, he didn't offer her respite, he didn't do anything except drive toward mutual orgasm with as much speed and pleasure as he could manage. He circled his hips, he lifted her with his thrusts and, finally, with a cry that filled the air, she moaned in pleasure. Her body rocked out of control against him, her legs shaking, her breath broken.

Her body milked him with her orgasm and he felt his seed move. Gently, he set her aside and spent away from her.

As he wiped his hand on a handkerchief, he looked at her. She had smoothed her chemise over her body and was watching him with a frown.

"Did I hurt you?" he asked softly.

She shook her head. "There was no physical pain."

He flinched, for that left the question open for other kinds of pain. Of course, he felt those too. And hadn't she been the one to cause it?

He tugged his trousers back up around his hips and buttoned his half-open shirt. As he fixed himself, she continued to watch him. Finally, she drew a short breath.

"Did you come here to talk to me?" she asked. "To hear me out?"

He faced her, straightening his shoulders, hardening his expression. But he couldn't fully harden his heart. When he looked at her, he felt both a huge swell of love and a stab of betrayal and pain. At the moment, the pain was strong, almost as powerful as the love.

He turned away. "I don't know why I came here," he admitted.

Olivia couldn't help the sharp intake of air at his answer to her question. She just wished she didn't have to feel the anguish that accompanied it. She had been so hopeful when Mal showed up at her door. She had dared to believe that he had come here to hear her out.

Instead, it seemed he had only come here to fuck her. Was that a pleasure or a punishment?

She carefully gathered her composure and whispered, "Mal, I want to tell you my side of the story."

She had hardly gotten the words out that he began to shake his head in the negative.

"Not yet, not yet," he muttered as he made for the door.

She took a few steps after him. "You say 'not yet'—does that mean you'll come back?"

He paused at the door and looked at her briefly. She couldn't stop her lip from trembling or the tears that kept stinging her eyes. But she could lift her chin and straighten her shoulders and show him some tiny bit of strength.

"Yes," he finally admitted in a rough and broken voice. "I'll come back tomorrow night."

She nearly buckled with relief. She could see his emotion and that meant he still cared for her. He was hurt, but what they had wasn't entirely broken. Still she pushed him, challenged him. Because she loved him and she wasn't about to give up so easily.

"When you return, will it only be to bed me?"

He shrugged. "I don't know. Will you turn me away?"

She met his stare, holding it until she sensed his discomfort. "I would never turn you away, Malcolm Graham. Even if I have to wait a year or ten years. I'll be here, waiting for you to hear me. And some day you *will* hear me. Only then will we be able to decide where we go from here."

He swallowed hard and hesitated for a very long moment. Then he said, "I'll see you tomorrow night, Olivia."

And he left her standing alone and half-naked, with only a flickering ember of hope to keep her warm.

"Your sister has arrived in Bath," Malcolm said without preamble as he stepped into the doorway to Liam's office.

Liam kept his eyes on the ledger before him, but there was no doubting his tension when he said, "It has been nearly three days since Violet left. I'm surprised it took Ava this long. I assume she will knock on my door before the afternoon is over."

"Violet is with her," Malcolm said, watching his friend carefully.

Liam had said very little about the women who had crushed them both less than half a week before. But he saw the pain around his friend's eyes as surely as he felt the same around his own heart. The difference was, he knew where Olivia was. Against his better judgment, he could see her whenever he liked.

"Why?" Liam finally asked.

Malcolm shrugged. "My spies do not go so far, Windbury."

Liam arched a brow. "No? Not even Olivia Cranfield?"

Malcolm jerked in surprise. His visits to Olivia over the past three days had been done quietly and Liam was so lost he hadn't known his friend was aware. But now Liam nodded before he continued speaking.

"Yes, I had speculated you've been seeing her, sneaking out at night to meet with her."

Malcolm entered the room now and slowly took a place at the desk across from Liam.

"Do you judge that as a betrayal?" he asked softly.

Liam was quiet for a moment, then he shook his head. "I told you myself to go to her, to hear her."

Mal stiffened. He hadn't exactly been doing that. He had made love to Olivia, but he always stopped her from telling him her motives in what she'd done. It was unfair and he knew that, even as he did it.

Liam continued, "I believe my misery has extended to everyone else in my life, especially you, for far too long, my friend. If you care for her, if you love her as you told me you did...then love her. Be with her. You have my blessing if you require it."

Mal tensed. He did care for Olivia. He did love her. And the days since her betrayal hadn't lessened that feeling. He feared nothing ever would.

And if he was bound to love her for the rest of his life, didn't he owe it to her to finally let her speak?

"I don't need your approval, actually, but I appreciate it nonetheless, as well as your graciousness regarding the situation."

"I suppose I'm making up for lost time in the grace department," Liam said with a humorless chuckle. "Olivia must have explanations that soothe you, for you were so very angry with her just a few days ago for her part in Violet's deception."

Mal nodded. "I was. But I also understand the sacrifices one makes for a friend one loves like a sibling."

The two men met gazes and Liam nodded, taking his friend's meaning completely. "You probably understand that better than most, I would wager."

Mal smiled. He *did* understand that, for he had spent a great many years protecting Liam from himself. But it seemed that time was coming to an end. His friend looked healthier and more equipped to face his past than ever. His lack of resistance to his sister's arrival proved that.

So it was time for Malcolm to create his own life. And as they continued talking, all he could think about was going to Olivia, not just to take the body she offered, but to truly resolve the barriers that had been erected between them. And he could only hope that they weren't so high that they were insurmountable.

Chapter Thirteen

Olivia rushed through the streets of Bath, her heart racing. It had only been fifteen minutes since her maid delivered the news, but it felt like every step took an eternity. Finally, she rapped on the familiar door of the townhome the Rothcastles had let for Violet just a few weeks ago and waited with very little patience for a servant to answer.

It was one of the many maids who did so.

"Hello, Miss Olivia," she said with a welcoming smile.

"I have heard Miss Violet has returned— Is that true?" she asked.

The girl took in her disheveled appearance and her panting breaths and ushered her into the foyer, out of the cutting spring breeze.

"Yes, miss," the girl said. "They arrived just this morning and—"

"Will you tell her I'm here?"

The servant nodded slowly. "Yes, of course. Will you wait in the parlor?"

Olivia nodded, but instead of doing so, she followed the girl up the stairs and down the hall. The girl began to announce her, but Olivia couldn't stand it any longer.

She stepped toward the servant and the poor maid moved aside, knowing when she had been beaten, and allowed Olivia to pass into Violet's chamber.

"Olivia!" her friend cried and the two women embraced as the maid shut the door behind them.

Without speaking, they moved to the window seat and perched there together.

"Why didn't you tell me you were coming back?" Olivia asked.

Violet shook her head. "I didn't know where you were. When we arrived and we were told you'd left this residence, I didn't have a thought of where to write. I didn't dare send a message to Liam's home, even if you were there."

Olivia dropped her chin to cover the pain that accompanied that very wrong assumption. "No, I'm not there. I let a smaller place almost as soon as you departed. I didn't want Malcolm to see me staying here, in case he thought I was still under the direction of the Rothcastles. Of you."

"Of course," Violet said with a shake of her head. "And has he decided that is true? Will he see you?"

Olivia nodded. "Yes. He comes to me every night."

"Excellent!" Violet clapped her hands together. "Then my actions didn't permanently damage his regard for you. I feared I had destroyed your chance for happiness."

Olivia cleared her throat and heat flooded her cheeks as she admitted, "He comes to me, but he is changed. I feel him holding back. And when I try to explain myself, when I try to tell him my heart, he only distracts me in the most pleasurable ways. And then leaves me before the night is over."

It was amazing the relief that accompanied such a humiliating admission. But she hadn't been able to talk to anyone else about it. Belle was kind, of course, and discreet, but the fact that she was a servant kept a wall between them. With Violet she could be completely truthful.

Of course, at the moment Violet looked very guilty as her smile faded. "He wouldn't come if he didn't feel something for you. He is conflicted."

"Yes, I'm certain that is true. But what side of the conflict he will come out on is another story entirely," Olivia said, thinking of how passionately and tenderly he had made love to her the past three nights. But also how quickly he had left her, denying her the ability to connect with him on anything but a physical level. It was like they were stuck and couldn't break free of the lies that had separated them.

Violet caught her hand. "I never meant to catch you up in my difficulties. Not after the true friend you've been to me."

"I was happy to be caught up," Olivia said with a true smile. "If I hadn't, I wouldn't have even met Malcolm. And I cannot live with that idea, even if he never comes back to me again."

And as she said the words, she knew how true they were. She loved him. And she wouldn't trade that for the world, for it was a beautiful thing.

"I doubt he'll *never* come back," Violet reassured her friend.

Olivia felt her strength returning just because she could finally talk about her ordeal. And that strength translated to a new devotion to regaining his love.

"Yes, I intend to simply break him down. Wear him out until he can do nothing *but* love me back."

Violet laughed, but there was a flicker of darker emotion in her friend.

"Does he tell you anything of Liam?" she asked softly.

Olivia shook her head slowly. "No. That subject is off limits between us, I'm afraid. But the fact that they have remained in Bath, rather than departing to avoid Lord and Lady Rothcastle's arrival certainly says something, doesn't it?"

Violet pressed her lips together. "You are right," she finally said. "Before, Liam would have done anything to escape the confrontation Ava has brought down upon him."

"So you see," Olivia said, squeezing her hand in the hopes she could comfort Violet, since she assumed her friend had also been removed from confidantes since her departure, "you saved him."

"I wouldn't go that far." Violet got to her feet and smoothed her dress, watching out the window toward that long, lonely road that led to Liam's estate. "And even if I did, he will hate me for it for the rest of his days. The disdain on his face a few days ago told me that better than any words he could ever speak."

"I'm sorry," Olivia whispered, and it was true, for she felt exactly what her friend did. "You have been hurt and I wish I could repair your heart."

"You can't. That is the way of broken hearts. They only heal with time and distance." Violet hesitated, and then she added, "I'm leaving."

Olivia jolted. "Leaving?"

"Yes. I believe there is a stage leaving for Hertford in a short time. I could make arrangements there for transport to Romwell."

Olivia shook her head in shock. "But what of the duke and duchess? Did they not make some arrangement with you?"

Violet nodded. "They did. But I will break it. They'll understand, I think. And it isn't as if I had much to do here at any rate."

Olivia fully comprehended her friend's desire to run, but she couldn't believe she would do it without even attempting to repair the damage between her and the man she so obviously loved.

"Don't you want to see Liam again?"

Violet stiffened at the inquiry. "Of course I do. I want to see him so much that I ache whenever I think of it. But he doesn't want to see me. And if I forced that issue, I would only find ruin and deeper heartache. It is time for me to forget this folly. To go to my son and live the simple life I was meant to have."

"And there is nothing I can say to dissuade you?" Olivia asked, searching her friend's face.

In a way, Violet was taking the same road out as Malcolm had been trying to do. By avoiding the pain, they each thought they could conquer it.

But she was certain that wasn't true.

"No," Violet answered softly. "I never should have returned to Bath in the first place. I let my heart lead me when it was time to put my head in charge. I must remedy that now."

Olivia wanted to say more, but at that moment a flash of movement from the road outside her window caught her eye. There was a man riding hard up the road toward the house. A man she recognized, even from a distance.

"Malcolm," Olivia gasped, pressing her hand to the glass, Violet's decisions forgotten.

"Has he ever come to you in the middle of the afternoon?" Violet asked softly as they watched him turn toward the small home Olivia had let.

Olivia could hardly breathe to answer the question. "N-No. Not since the first day."

"Then it seems you might have worn him down far faster than you thought."

Olivia's heart leapt at the thought and she shot a quick glance toward Violet. She wanted to run to him, but she couldn't when her friend remained in pain.

Violet laughed. "Go. Write to me in Romwell in a few days and let me know all the news."

Olivia briefly embraced her. "I wish you would stay."

"I can't," Violet insisted as she turned Olivia toward the door and gently pushed her. "Now go!"

Olivia didn't have to be asked again. She hustled from the room, thinking of nothing but Malcolm. She could only hope this unexpected appearance meant he was willing to listen to her.

But even if he wasn't, she had made her own decision. She wasn't going to let him hide from her, from love, anymore. Today they would resolve this, one way or another.

"As I have already told you, sir," Olivia's maid, Belle, said, her arms folded as she glared at him. "Miss Olivia left the house and I have no idea when she will return."

Mal shifted but did not remove himself from the parlor he had claimed upon his arrival.

"And as I have already told *you*," he retorted, "I will wait."

The maid rolled her eyes and shot a look at the footman who had been called to handle him once it was clear he wouldn't leave. The man was not nearly his size or strength and he looked rather nervous.

"I will sit here quietly," Mal said, changing his tone to a friendlier one as he settled into the chair in front of the unlit fire. "I will not require refreshment or entertainment. And I will not cause any trouble."

"No more than you already have," the maid muttered.

Mal wasn't entirely certain if the girl was talking about the ruckus his intrusion had caused today or the trouble caused for her mistress since Olivia had arrived in Bath, but he had no chance to ask her to clarify, for at that moment, Olivia herself shouldered through the servants and stared at him.

He scrambled to his feet. "Olivia."

She didn't reveal any emotions on her face, but she also did not look away from him as she said, "Belle, Yeardley, you may leave. I will see Mr. Graham."

The servants seemed just as happy to let her handle Malcolm and left the room. She stood in the doorway for a long moment before she stepped inside and closed the door behind them to grant them privacy.

"Olivia—" he began.

To his surprise, she held up a hand to silence him.

"No, Malcolm. You have said and done quite enough. *I* would like to say something now."

He raised his eyebrows but didn't stop her as she paced across the room to the window, where she faced him, wringing her hands in front of her.

"I realize that my coming here under a false pretense, that my knowledge of Violet's plans for Liam and my keeping that knowledge to myself, even after you confessed your feelings for me...those were all very wrong actions."

He opened his mouth, but she shook her head. "Please! Allow me this."

He pressed his lips together and let her speak.

"But you must understand that Violet has been my best friend, my sister, for a very long time. I trained her to be a courtesan, but she shared in her financial success with me, as well as her support and kindness. I love her as my family, *more* than my family. And I knew that if she succeeded in her plans with Liam she would obtain a freedom from our lifestyle that she has craved for many years."

She shook her head and her gaze was far away. "When I came here, Mal, I never expected to be anything but the distraction Violet needed. But you are...*you* and you are frustratingly impossible not to fall in love with."

Mal straightened up at that admission. She had never said anything like it to him, even before her secrets were revealed and he was confessing his heart every moment he was with her.

"You love me," he repeated.

She nodded as she met his stare. "I love you. I was as shocked by that fact as anyone, trust me. But it is true. And I did want to tell you the truth about Violet. I started to so many times, but I feared your reaction, that I would destroy that beautiful gift of love you kept giving me. I also feared I would hurt my friend. So I was cowardly and kept finding reasons to hide the truth. But I would have told you, Malcolm."

He stared at her, trying to determine if she was telling the truth. She had such wide, clear eyes as she kept her stare locked with his.

"When?" he choked out.

"That day you confronted Violet and me," she admitted with a sad shake of her head. "I was coming to the breakfast room to tell Violet that I wouldn't keep her secret any longer. And then I would have told you. But by then you already knew, everything was already ruined."

He swallowed at that assessment. "Damaged," he whispered. "But I don't know about ruined."

Her eyes went wide. "I hope that's true. Damage can be repaired. Are you saying what we felt, what we built, can be repaired?"

She waited for his answer, not pushing, not forcing, not even asking again as he struggled with the words to say.

"Like you, I have forged a strong bond, stronger than the one I hold with my blood brothers, with Liam. I was so wrapped up in protecting him that what you did in league with Violet felt like a double betrayal."

She winced and began to turn away, but he moved to her, catching her arm and keeping her in place.

"But I understand your motives, Olivia. And I believe you that you would have told me the truth," he whispered.

She reached up with her free hand, trembling fingers cupping his cheek. "And do you believe that I love you, Malcolm?"

He couldn't help the wide smile that broke across his face at that question.

"I do," he admitted. "I believe you and those words are so sweet that I can scarcely believe I am hearing them, especially after the abominable way I've treated you over the past few days."

She shook her head. "I understood your anger. And I knew that if you still came to me, still *wanted* me, that at some point I would have the chance to prove myself to you."

"And you did, quite forcefully, today." He chuckled.

She laughed in return. "Well, I was tired of waiting for your forgiveness, I decided to demand it." Her smile fell a fraction. "But beyond your forgiveness, I must know something else."

He tilted his head, drawing her closer, into his arms. "What is that?"

300

"Could *you* ever love *me* again? Even though I broke faith with you?" She said the words so softly, but there was so much fear and hope on her face, in the way she trembled in his arms.

He cupped her cheek. "I never stopped loving you, Olivia. Anger cannot change that. Nothing could. I love you and I will always love you, even when each of us makes mistakes, even when you frustrate me, even when I am hunched and wrinkled. I will love you until my last breath. Which is why I must ask you now..."

He hesitated and her eyes went wide.

"Will you marry me?"

She stared at him for a moment, her mouth open in shock, her dark eyes dilated wide. He saw her hesitation and it made his stomach drop.

"That isn't what women of my station do," she whispered. "You are a gentleman's son, Malcolm. If you marry me—"

He shook his head. "Then nothing in the world will change except my happiness will increase a thousandfold."

She shook her head, so he continued before she could come up with more excuses. "I may have been born a gentleman's son, but I haven't lived a gentleman's life for a long time. Even if I had, I have learned through close observation that love is not something to be taken lightly."

"You could lose something, everything," she whispered, her voice shaking. "People could find out what I am, what I was."

"Perhaps," he conceded. "But I already know what you are, what you were and what I hope you will be. Why would I give a damn what anyone else thought?"

"Mal, I don't want to hurt you," she said, her eyes locked with his. She had been giving him reasons why he shouldn't marry her, but he could see now that she was searching to find one to accept.

"Then don't refuse me." He smiled as he bent his head to kiss her gently. "Accept my proposal and be my wife."

She worried her lip a moment, but finally she nodded. "Yes. If you think you can accept the potential consequences, then yes!"

Tears flooded her eyes as she wrapped her arms around his neck and hugged him with all the considerable strength in her far-smaller body. He laughed as he drank in her warmth and her love, filled with the knowledge that he would have this, have her, for the rest of his days.

He pulled back.

"We have so much to do, so much to plan," he said. "But I can hire a carriage within the hour and we can be to Gretna Green before the week is out."

She stared at him. "Gretna Green! You mean to marry me right away?"

He lifted her chin. "As soon as I can have you be mine, yes."

She was laughing as he kissed her and she laughed until he stole her breath, possessed her body and claimed her as his bride and his love for all time.

About the Author

Jess Michaels is the award-winning author of over forty romances, erotic romances and urban fantasy novels. She lives in Arizona with her fantastic husband and two adorable cats. When not writing about sexy gentlemen and wicked ladies, she can be found doing geeky things like playing video games and performing aunt duties to two nephews. You can find her online at www.authorjessmichaels.com, on Facebook (Jess Michaels) and on Twitter @jessmichaelsbks.

It's all about the story...

Romance

HORROR

www.samhainpublishing.com